LOVE OF AN UNKNOWN SOLDIER

by

**John
Howlett**

Love Of An Unknown Soldier is the first volume in the Harry Cardwell
Series.
A Long Road Home, ***When War Came Again*** and ***First Snow of Winter***
will be published in 2012.

Cover: *Christmas 1916: an Australian Observation Post near Fleurbaix,
on the Somme front* - painting by William Barnes Wollen (1857-1936)

The incidents described in these pages are the memories of their war told to me fifty years ago by Harry Davison (of the Royal Naval Division), Ted Banister (of the ASC) and 'Hof' Hall (of the Royal Warwickshires). This book is dedicated to them and to the anonymous author of 'Love of an Unknown Soldier - Found in a dug-out' - published by the Bodley Head in 1918. The letters in that book suggested this story

Chapter One

'Spanish Farm' the officers called it, remembering perhaps a group of gipsy dancers who'd lived there in the spring and early summer of 1915. The men simply referred to it as 'Station Inn', the end of shank's pony on their long road home, a place of refuge where cattle-trucks waited, *hommes 40, chevaux 8*, to trundle them onwards towards the Channel ports. Unless of course, like Harry, you were on your way back into the line.

The war was already three winters old this evening of his return, Harry's worn battledress covered in a shaggy overgarment that made him look more like an arctic explorer than a warrior, hands protected by rough mittens, the bolt and barrel of his rifle wrapped in oiled cloth. He could hear a dozen cheerful voices as he led his travel companions through the door into the fug of warm smoke, an aged Estaminet whose inhabitants were making small fortunes from the watered beer and wine they sold to soldiers too tired to visit the women in the barn across the street.

Whistles had been blowing by the railhead when they'd clambered from the train, voices shouting: "Off the road! Take cover!" - from what? From an enemy airplane? It was another Flanders twilight, the occasional distant shell or spent bullet marking that swift passage towards night: stand-to in the trenches up ahead of them; teatime back home.

The voices and faces at the bar that turned briefly to look at them were happy leave drafts from the Manchesters, the Buffs and the Seaforths, drinking in two's and three's as they waited to be called to the train. Harry and his companions, moving in the opposite direction, were regarded more in dread or superstition than pity. After all, the leave detail would, like Harry, be on their own way back in but a few days' time.

The piano was playing in the 'Officers Only' room across the bar, a head of wild wavy hair Harry recognised - Lieutenant Ordish's lazy eyes through a mirror recognising him in turn: Lance-Corporal Harry Cardwell, 3rd Section, 4 Platoon, one of the old-young, not yet two and twenty but his youth already well worn with fear and privation.

The three men travelling with him were nearer thirty than twenty, crisp in their new uniforms but apprehensive as they watched the young Lance-Corporal for any clue that might reveal the mysteries of this 'great adventure' that awaited them. So far so good, one of them was thinking as he carried four beers for them from the bar: his boots and uniform were still clean; his pipe was ready to smoke; the room was warm. If the strange twangs and thumps outside were to continue, they might spend the whole evening in here. Not that the other two had much to say for themselves. They'd looked ill all through their tough ten days training at the 'Bullring', and not much brighter when the silent Lance-Corporal picked them up at Base Camp. This young bugger with his fur garment and single stripe hadn't smiled at anything or anyone; wouldn't even talk, except a grunt and nod to indicate which way they should go. Hope to God I'm not in his Section, Benson thought, then hearing the safety-valve blow on the steam engine outside, remembered from somewhere far away the smell and feel of shovelling damp coal on the waterfront, the wail of hooter as the swing-bridge prepared to open - and suddenly wished he was back home.

"Gather round!" - even that someone's voice boomed across the room like a foghorn on the Tyne. "There's pretty girls in here," it boomed a second time, a Seaforth Sergeant opening a tin in front of him. "Tuppence a picture! Penny for a letter!"

Benson planted the four beers and sat down next to the Lance-Corporal, a nod from the younger man acknowledging the drink as he picked it up in both his mittened hands. "Reckon we'll be staying in here, Corporal?" Benson asked him.

"Twenty minutes if we're lucky." Harry was watching the loud

Sergeant at the bar, already deciding he didn't much like him.

"Is it a long way yet?" It was one of the subdued newboys, coughing in the smoke as he spoke.

"Four hours."

"HOURS?!"

"Wouldn't be sitting in here next to a steam train and a railway if it wasn't," said Harry. "They'd be shelling buggery out of us."

"'Your beauty and your elegance,'" boomed the Liverpool Sergeant. "'Your soft voice and softer smile! The flush of your skin' - Hello!" with a laugh: "Letters for your sweethearts written by a poet and a gentleman! One penny each! She'll think she's died and gone to heaven!"

Lieutenant Ordish was also watching the Sergeant through the mirror above the piano, that booming, vibrating voice unsympathetic to his music. But then Ordish had himself swallowed a glass or two too many, wrong notes now creeping into the Schubert, the clean, young 'schoolboy' subaltern behind him glancing round at one of his more obvious errors. 'Schoolboy' Nyren was the only other occupant of the Officers-Only room, carefully sipping his beer, nervous, excited and, like most other men as they first approached the realities of warfare, desperately afraid of being afraid. Through the mirror Ordish watched the Schoolboy blush when the Flemish barmaid's come-hither body brushed against him as she wiped his table.

"'Breasts!'" boomed the Sergeant. "Breasts unbuttoned! Breasts touched! Breasts naked!" Other conversations died away. "Tuppence at least for this letter! Listen!" He was reading now with exaggerated dramatic effect: "'Your eyes watch me as I hold you in this hell and strip your clothes away and bury myself in the soft, wet warmth of you - and hear you whisper my name.' Whisper?! I should think the poor bloody girl's screaming by now!"

Harry's quiet voice cut across the laughter: "That's a private letter."

"What the bloody hell does it matter? The man's dead whoever he was!" The Sergeant was passing round the photographs, addressing one of his own men: "Come on, Sankey. It's worth tuppence to anyone. You don't read these kind of things in books!" The Sergeant glared around the room, even through the bar at Ordish.

6

"Who's raising me? She's a bonny lass, for fuck's sake!"

"Bloody nurse, that's all she is." This Sankey was looking at one of the photographs. "Up to her elbows in blood all day. No wonder she's wet and warm!"

" 'I peel you naked every night and feel my own body hard and ready.' " The Sergeant was reading again. "'Never, never, never have I felt such longing and such need.'"

Harry spoke again his quiet voice carrying: "Let him alone."

"Go fuck with yourself," laughed the Sergeant. "I want my beer money when I get home!"

Harry rested his rifle against the table and stood up, Benson and the other two newboys watching him in disbelief and some apprehension. The Sergeant was bloody huge. If there was a fight, would they be expected to join in on the Corporal's side?

Harry walked down the room through the leave detail. He collected each photograph from their hands, returned them to the biscuit tin, then looked the Sergeant in the eye: "Private property. That's someone's life in there." As Harry pushed the lid back on the tin, the Sergeant grabbed his wrist. It seemed to the others a most unequal contest, Harry's hand and wrist half the Sergeant's size. Instead the Sergeant found a wrist he could not move, a wrist that forced his hand away, twisting his own arm slowly back until it seemed the bone must snap.

The Sergeant let go, not quite drunk enough to use his fists and risk bringing the redcaps across the road. He lowered his voice: "You're on a charge, Lance-Jack. Unless you want to make me an offer."

"A shilling for the lot." Harry laid the coin on the bar, picked up the tin and turned away. And in that moment, with the Sergeant still contemplating murder, the whistles blew outside, the "All Clear" called, the train across the street already ready to move. The leave detail scrambled for the door, even the Sergeant without a backward glance.

Harry and his new boys were less hurried. There was nothing to invite eager spirits along that long dark road outside.

Never, never, never have I felt such longing and such need. The silence sinks like music on my heart. Do you remember your Coleridge, my soft love? The Mariner is always with me - 'Like one, that on a lonesome road Doth walk in fear and dread' -

*

Their road this twilight had drawn what little was left of the day into one long line of reflected grey towards the horizon, damp, cold and forbidding. Benson watched the steady, slighty stooped pace of Harry's walk in front of him and thought maybe this Lance-Corporal wasn't such a bad sort after all. He'd faced down the bullying Sergeant without a hesitation or second thought and returned as silent as before to their table. All three of them had been watching the tin in his hand, hoping they'd get to look at the pictures themselves. But Harry had pushed the tin into his kit-bag, finished his beer and stood up to go. And like nervous children they'd had to follow.

There'd been a brief flurry of activity outside after the all clear, a line of horse wagons, a pair of chuntering motor lorries, all moving in the wrong direction for them. It didn't seem to be a road much used by vehicles. Too many shattered trees and shell holes perhaps. "Hell-fire Corner," Harry would mutter later at one of the cross-roads, though so far the evening had been quiet. Marching with the Company they might even have been singing. Tonight the five men walked in silence, only the metal sound of their boots on the pockmarked road, the young subaltern's lighter sounding shoes to the rear, each and every man wondering to himself if he'd ever come marching back again.

'Schoolboy' Nyren wasn't too sure about the protocol of officers walking with the men. Bound for the same unit, he'd decided to follow Harry and the recruits ten yards behind them, though ever a little closer as the evening darkened and he feared to lose his way. He was carrying a shiny new valise with pressed clothes, penknife, a set of pencils, binoculars, a spare watch, letter-paper for writing home. It hadn't been much different from setting out for another term at school. Though now he was wondering how long his uniform would stay clean, how long before he'd be as patched and worn as the other officer at the piano in the Inn. He could still hear Schubert faraway behind them, the Lieutenant clearly in no hurry to renew his acquaintance with the war. It had all been quite confusing in there, the first time in his young life that a woman had deliberately touched him with her breasts, the barmaid winking as she'd leaned across him. How hotly he had blushed, as also when he'd heard anatomy and sex read out loud from that someone's private letters. The Lance-Corporal had been right about it being wrong. Not that letters to girls had never been scrutinized by friends at school for signs of 'passion'.

He saw sudden wild flashes in the sky not so far ahead and wondered if a storm would break before they could reach cover. Then his heart and whole body jumped as the sound reached them, vibrating from the ground and through his ears. Shells? Mortars? What could they be? Ours or theirs? How far away? Should he be afraid? One of the other newcomers ahead of him had laughed, without much conviction. The Lance-Corporal, the 'old soldier', just plodded on in his rough sheepskin and mittens. No doubt they'd learn from him when it was necessary to take evasive action.

The 'Schoolboy' glanced back at the road behind them and shivered. A tall shadow like a ghost seemed to follow them half a mile behind, appearing and disappearing as the moon came and went through the clouds.

This Flanders landscape hadn't changed since Harry had first seen it, a year after the early fighting when the German guns had been nearer to create this bleak wasteland of splintered trees, flattened village and broken road. Yet to Harry it now began to feel like coming home, the single dread the fear that in his absence someone in his Section had been killed.

Real home no longer had been home, tired father and anxious mother proud of his stripe but having to endure his exhausted silence, neither of them able to imagine from where he'd come and where, suddenly, irrationally, he longed to return. For their sake he'd blamed it on the journey. The trains had been slow, the Channel crossing disrupted by the weather, three days travelling that became nearly four by the time he'd walked home fifteen miles up the valley. He helped his father repair stone hemmels, tramped across the hill with letters for Frank's family, met his brother off the cart from school on Saturday, saw the other neighbours at Sunday Chapel. He couldn't have been further from the war if he'd tried, yet still had lived with it inside his head hour by hour, through each detail of its dirty and fearful monotony.

"Not much of a way to have to be, I expect," his father had suggested out on the moor. But Harry had just shrugged, leaving the implied question unanswered. Four more yards of dry stone wall they'd built without another word between them, though, as always when they worked together, harmony was there with the odd look, nod and gesture as they humped the slabs of rock.

Mother instead had wanted to be reassured that soldiers were given water to wash with and two hot meals a day. Harry hadn't liked to tell her the only warmth on most days up the front that winter had been the tot of rum after stand-to. Or the odd brew-up if anyone found water that was something less than frozen solid and someone else had scrounged the matches or the flint to start a fire.

The evening before he left, father took him out to listen to the hundred rooks in the wood by the river far below them. "Us'll be lambing in the snow this year. Have to shoot some of they buggers. Scottish ram blew over the border in a gale. Serviced all my ewes two months early. See what happens when you wear a kilt!" Harry had laughed and felt his father's hand briefly on his shoulder. First time Da had touched him since he'd been a little lad.

*

They smelt Divisional Transport Lines from half a mile away back down the road, coal and wood smoke from a shell-ruined farm, familiar to Harry but like a foreign country to the others: kitchen fires, laundry fires, mess-room stoves, all forbidden in the daylight when the smoke could be spotted by German artillery observers. Officers and NCO's were crouched in small, scooped-out rooms beneath the shattered buildings, lists and pro forma under hurricane lamps where the Schoolboy had to introduce himself to an elderly Sergeant Major: "Second Lieutenant Nyren, sir. 'B' Company Royal Border Rifles."

"Corporal Cardwell!" the Sergeant Major yelled out at the darkness, "one of your officers!" - and in a lower tone added to the 'Schoolboy': "You don't 'sir' me, sir."

Harry Cardwell was down the line of fires looking for the blacksmith where he'd left his trenching tool for repair on his way out on leave. "Fuckin' arms of fuckin' steel you have," the smithy grumbled as he retrieved the tool from behind a stack of wiring spirals. "You break this one, I'll put you up for regimental boxing."

'B' Company's Transport Officer had also heard the Sergeant Major's yell, peering through the smoke as Harry emerged - another young subaltern not many months out of sixth form, 'Bunny' by nickname and smiling a weary "Hello Harry", before quickly reassuring him that all his mates were 'chipper'. No casualties. "I've a ration party," Bunny said. I'll take you up the line myself."

The 'Schoolboy' was waiting for them: "Second Lieutenant Nyren," he murmured, holding out his hand to Bunny.

"The Tonbridge Nyrens?" asked Bunny with his tired smile. And at Schoolboy's nod: "I once played cricket with your brother."

And so they continue, six of them now, rejoining that black and moonlit road, the ration party ahead of them, Bunny passing on cryptic, hard-earned wisdoms to his younger brother-officer, the one year difference between them enough to have turned Bunny, like Harry, into an ageless veteran.

"Machine gun," declares Bunny at a sudden, lazy, buzzing whip-whip-whip above their heads. "Spent bullets. Wouldn't even break your skin."

"Waste of money," says Nyren with a nervous laugh.

Harry's novices ahead of them strain their ears for every word of advice.

"Germans have fixed guns on most roads near the front and Jerry's not a bad shot. When they start banging away you don't want to be caught out in the open." And as they approach the next shell-blasted hamlet, Bunny's voice warns all four of the new arrivals: "You have now reached the outer limits of the known world. From here on, my friends, be dragons. Say your prayers"

Well might Nyren shiver, for behind them along that long dark road the shadow, the ghost, the spectral figure is following them once again in and out of the moonlight - Lieutenant Ordish, the piano-player from the Inn.

"Hello Sam," grins Bunny at Ordish over his shoulder. "Back already?"

"Welcome to the war", Ordish mutters to them all as they leave the now ominously pitted road to descend into another, subterranean universe of communication and support trenches, half-buried duckboards between unstable walls of clay where the horizon is suddenly restricted to the uneven sandbag parapet and barbed-wire entanglements against the moon.

"Enter and discover your new world," Ordish murmurs again. "Let us teach you how to live or die, north and east along the Menin Road."

Who was it in the Bible who described an abomination of desolation? He had been here. Talk to me, my love.

*

A half hour of mud and muttered cursing later and they were stumbling down the trench signposted 'Regent Street', a facetious 'Goodbye Piccadilly' whistled by a pair in the ration party ahead of them. Bunny hadn't said where the Company was positioned but Harry knew if the guide turned into 'Haymarket' they were destined for the front line. At least that meant no wiring parties out in no man's land for the next few nights. "Lucky it's so quiet," Bunny muttered behind him. "There was a bit of a strafe last night. Jerry must have thought YOU were back already."

But no sooner had he spoken, an express train came hurtling towards them, at first a whisper then a sudden roar, the Flying Scotsman through the night. And this time, with or without Harry's example, the new boys crouched and covered their heads in terror, the sound above them so full of fury. The shell landed 30 yards beyond them, a brief, savage flame of heat and percussion that, for those who'd never felt it before, seemed to batter their very brains against their skulls. Shrapnel whined above them; a cloud of mud rained down, not quite reaching them. They heard the forlorn, faraway cry a few moments later - "Stretcher-bearers!"

"Reserve trench," said Bunny. "The DLI's." Their neighbours at home from Durham.

"Jerry must have heard us." And yes, thought Harry as the ration party turned left, it **is** the 'Haymarket'.

The newcomers didn't even realize they'd reached the front line when they finally arrived. All Benson could see were rolled-up gas-cape bundles on a mud shelf to one side, one of which turned out to be a man, swearing an almighty growled "Bastard angels!" as Benson tripped on the end of a duckboard and cannoned into him.

"Sorry, mate," Benson said and, picking himself up, saw another soldier ahead and above him standing on that mud shelf, leaning on the parapet, helmeted head in silhouette, rifle into his shoulder, staring out into the night. Fuck me, we're bloody here, thought Benson: that bloke's looking into no man's land; he's watching for the enemy.

This was Number 1 Platoon, the Company dugout round the next sand-bagged traverse, Captain Prideaux climbing the steps to be greeted by his new officer: "Second Lieutenant Nyren, Captain."

Harry was next in file along the trench: "AND three newboys, sir."

"Nice to have you back, Lance-Corporal. Newboys to the Sergeant Major. You might have to wake him up." And as Harry led his new boys past, Captain Prideaux looked into their eyes with what he hoped was a kindly smile. "No saluting in the trench, soldier," he said as Benson raised right hand towards his helmet.

Prideaux turned back through the sack curtain to lead Nyren down mud steps into the fug of the cramped dugout, one arm reaching a bottle from the shelf, the other arm gesturing at a pair of wire-netting bunks: "Pick your bed, Lieutenant." He poured two tots into mugs as someone in their sleep snorted a sharp grunt behind him. Nyren didn't like to tell the Captain he'd never tasted whisky before.

Sergeant-Major Trussal had been tasting the rum instead, head back, mouth open and snoring in his tarpaulin covered lean-to. And none too pleased to be woken; nor too impressed to be looking up at the apprehensive faces of three bewildered recruits. Harry beat a quick retreat forwards round the next traverse; and had to pass two more sandbagged zig-zags before he found the officer on watch - Lieutenant 'Uncle' Sinclair tonight, trying to light his pipe in the lee of a bay: "Hello Harry! Enjoy yourself back home?" Everyone in the Company knew poor Uncle had been waiting months for a leave, his wife expecting their number four somewhere short of Cumberland along the Hadrian's Wall.
"Three rookies with the Sergeant-Major, sir. New officer bloke with the Captain."
"What's he look like?"
"Like a schoolboy, sir."
And Harry plodded on, unwilling to witness anymore of Uncle's frantic waste of matches.
Another five traverses and he was nearly home: 4 Platoon, last in the line, as always Company anchor, Sergeant Banister asleep under his ground-sheet, fag-end still in his mouth; Barnes on watch in One Section; Tottie Bell in Two; Corporal Scotty in Three: "Well blow me, Marra', did you ever take your time!" Harry checked Reggie and Frank rolled up on the firestep like corpses in their capes; then climbed up next to Scotty, unwrapping the rags from his rifle barrel and bolt: "Everyone alright, then?"
"Dead men walking."
"Nobby?"
"On the scrounge."
"Where?"
A nod from Scotty at the darkness round the next abandoned-looking traverse. "The Buffs. Our dixie got blown to buggery last night." Another nod from Scotty at debris in a sap behind them: "Fucking

minnies from Last Post to Reveille. We thought Jerry was coming over for breakfast. We bin rebuilding the parapets most of the bloody day." Scotty looked about ready to drop.

Harry crouched to light a cigarette: "Get some kip. I been sleeping for a week." He felt round inside his kit-bag. "Letter from your missus somewhere in here. She left it at the station."   Only then, pulling out the biscuit tin and wondering what the hell it was, did Harry remember the Sergeant at the Estaminet. Sod knows what he was going to do with a tin of letters and photographs. He straightened up and stuck the fag in Scotty's mouth. "Anyone out front?"

"Craig and Lars with the Lewis gun in the fire-bay. Fast bloody asleep I should think."   They both faced forward as the moon emerged behind them, thin spirals of barbed-wire, shadow and silence. Scotty's finger pointed out the gap in the wire marked on their side by a pair of short white posts: "Password 'Craster' " he told Harry.   " 'Sandwich' for the Buffs." Scotty drew deep and long a couple of times then handed back the cigarette. Less than a moment later down he went, flat-out, full-length on the firestep, rolled in his cape and fast asleep.

Staring alone out into the darkness of no man's land, Harry had come home.

Chapter 2

"Not the best of guests," laughed the Virgin Mary, sluicing a bucketful of deeply coloured water out of the train over the ballast into the night. "They seem to have left us just about every possible liquid or solid the human body can produce, delivered from every conceivable orifice the body ever knew or did not know it could possess."

Annie watched weary from her hands and knees, scrub, scrub, scrub on metal floors, amazed as always how this most infuriating of women could, in an apparently spontaneous conceit of words, neutralize a filthy, god-forsaken day. And still go home and pray.

But not tonight it seems: "Sleep on board, girls. It's far too late to fuss around with mealtimes and parade."

That dreaded word 'parade', heard by Annie for the first time two years ago, two days out from New York when, in fear of German torpedoes, they'd been gathered on deck for lifeboat drill. War had seemed much simpler then, danger exorcized by precaution, fear by fun, the only irritant a nightly obstacle race to find forbidden ways to Patrick's bed, war having thus far failed to incorporate matrimony within its various organisations. Shy, lovely Patrick whose body she remembered from those nights but whose face she could only recall twisted and screaming in the flames.

Another sluice or three and the cleaning of the train was deemed sufficient. The Virgin Mary smiled again: "Tonight we enjoy the first known paradise of women on earth" - (their Train Commander, the only man still among them, had been abandoned sometime after midday, pushed out onto a grass embankment, too drunk to issue orders or even move of his own accord). Mother of Christ and Stentor

16

called her final orders in an echo down the aisles and corridors: "Dress in the morning!"

They each carried one change of uniform internal and external, only to be used for parade at reveille. But the internal ones Annie decided she would have to change tonight. Blood was still wet through to her skin, all the way from her breasts down to her ankles.

Chapter 3

Who now can possibly remember that earlier, seemingly sunlit war when, all novices together, we first arrived from England marching and singing down the tree-lined roads of Picardy towards a battle we as yet knew nothing about? A time, not much more than a year ago, when birds still sang in hedgerows, when officers and men still had faith, when this generation of young men still remained more or less intact. Yes of course, we all needed to believe. We had our men to care for. They trusted us. A whole Company from our town of the finest fellows you could ever wish to see. We had encouraged them, we had to some extent even paid for them to come - who from his lathe, who from his shop, who from his office, who from his mansion.

And was it not then that I first met you? A rather dishevelled and disorganised officer begging a lift on your train because he'd left his Company orders back at base camp! To be greeted by the freshest voice and smile that I had ever seen.

And how your smile does strengthen me. How many times is it possible to think of someone each day? One thousand four hundred and forty? Once for every minute of the day, asleep or awake. The eyes of my American Angel haunt me as I saw them in the horse carriage that evening when you drove away.

There followed a pair of lines in which Harry could only decipher the word 'love' repeated three or four times. He felt he was intruding. Perhaps it was just as well that, apart from the pages read out by the Sergeant at the inn, this was the only sheet in the tin he could even begin to make sense of. He pushed it back with the others and took out one of the photographs. The half smile and eyes that looked at him were indeed extraordinary and made him suddenly shiver. Unless it was the midnight chill.

He looked up. Banister had given him a half hour relief, knowing that he had in turn relieved Scotty. It wouldn't be fair to leave the old man up on the wall too long. Harry slipped the photograph into his pocket and closed the tin. None of the letters were signed; no address at the top; no envelope; no clue to reveal an identity - except that maybe he was a Captain or a Major in charge of a Company and that she was an American and that the two of them had met on a train somewhere in the vicinity of what the newspapers back home liked to call the Western Front.

Harry turned down the Sergeant's lantern and clambered back through the tarpaulin into the trench, the tin restored to his pack. Perhaps he could hand it in to the officers as lost property; leave it up to them to decide what to do with it.

"Can't sleep, can you," grinned Banister as Harry rejoined him on the firestep. "Always takes a couple of days and nights after leave - getting used to it again." Sergeant Banister knew the game from years ago, out in the Sudan as an 18 year old when Prideaux had been his subaltern; then six years playing football with the army all around the Empire before coming home to sign up as reserve centre-half for Newcastle United. A senior NCO and Territorial, Banister had been recalled a month before the war had even begun.

"You know, no one back home has the first idea what it's like out here."

"How could they?"

"Bloody newspapers don't print anything real."

"They never do." Banister smiled, remembering the corner shop at home where his brother cut out and kept the local football reports to send him.

Harry mistook the smile for a yawn and nudged him: "Go on, Sergeant. I'm wide awake. You push off back to kip."

"Who's the new officer bloke?" asked Banister as he stepped back down into the trench.

"2nd Lieutenant Nyren. Another schoolboy." Harry looked down at his Sergeant. "He won't last long."

Whisky round his brain; the snoring of two fellow officers; tobacco and a strangely sweet decaying fug; something rustling in the corner the Schoolboy dare not even think about; his own ears straining for other sounds outside; his head further confused by the information rattled off at him by a no-nonsense Platoon Sergeant: nothing much had conspired to send young Nyren to sleep. One of those snoring officers was up and pulling on boots when 'Schoolboy' finally rolled out of his wire bunk wondering where on earth he was meant to clean his teeth and have a pee.

"Raven", the other man said, with a yawn, sticking out a hand, head of thick black hair still bent over his boots.

"Second Lieutenant Nyren, sir." They were speaking in undertones, not to wake the others.

"Don't have to sir me, old son. We're all Seconds in here. Except for Ordish and the Captain." Nyren remembered this Raven's voice from somewhere in the middle of the night, grumbling when the duty officer had blundered in searching for tobacco. The black head of hair straightened up from his boots: "Had time to look around?"

"I saw my Platoon Sergeant. Most of the men were asleep."

"Better come with me then. Be stand-to in twenty minutes."

Nyren followed him up the steps into what was left of the darkness. At least out here the air was fresher with the breeze. And more dangerous. No sooner they'd turned along the trench, Nyren heard, felt almost, a sudden hiss and zip above his head as though a snake had spat at him from up on the parapet.

"Sniper," said Raven. "Saw the blink of light when we walked out through the curtain."

Nyren decided to keep his head well down, doubled-up as he followed Raven round the next zig-zag. Judging by the smell from a sap they passed, he'd also now discovered the whereabouts of the nearest latrine.

It was only seeing suddenly his Platoon Sergeant standing up to attention that Nyren realized he'd reached his own command, not without a sudden panic: was it Sergeant Prentice or Sergeant Percival? Dear God, it would not do to address such a precise man by the wrong name. As a Platoon Commander, Nyren now had sixty such names to learn. Raven resolved the panic with a curt nod and "Percival" as he passed, Nyren sure that Raven had used the name deliberately to help him. Nyren contented himself with a "Good morning, Sergeant!"

"You won't have much work to do with him around," muttered Raven. "You'll find Percival'll run your show himself. But then most of our Sergeants do. I mean, what the fuck do we know about soldiering?"

Harry, when he heard the duckboards creak and squelch, guessed it would be Raven - come to pull the Lewis gun back in before the dawn. Quite proud of 4 Platoon Lewis gun was Raven. They always won the prize when there was a Company or Battalion competition; thus their now long-standing 'privilege', anchoring the right wing of the Company line. Some privilege! They'd even amalgamated two sections to double up the gun team, Harry standing Corporal for the 'machine-gun', Scotty for the others.

Raven nodded at him: "Nice to see you back. Call them in, Harry."

"Sir."

Schoolboy Nyren was watching a few feet behind Raven, recognising the rough-clad Lance-Corporal from their journey the previous evening; remembering also that strange scene at the Inn, the soldier's purchase of that tin of letters and photographs and, yes, the barmaid rubbing her breasts against him. Nyren blushed even here, as though someone might overhear his thoughts.

He watched Harry shrink himself below the parapet and hold up a wood box to his face. Periscope, Nyren remembered from his lessons. And sure enough, as soon as Harry whistled a call and they'd heard it answered, the whole sky exploded into white light, a quite blinding light that seemed slowly to float back down towards the ground. Parachute flare, thought Nyren from another of his lessons.

Raven turned his head towards him with his gruff undertone: "You get caught out in the open with one of those, you stand so still you're made of stone. Snipers can't see unless you move. So they say."

A loud zipping and hissing arrived along the top of the sandbags, the distant, lazy, lethal yackety-yak sound Nyren would come to recognise as a German machine gun. Raven turned back past him down the trench the way they'd come. Mission accomplished, wondered Nyren? He was still watching Harry who glanced round and offered him the periscope, one firm hand on Nyren's head as he clambered onto the firestep to keep him well below the parapet. Nyren pressed the bottom of the wood box to his eyes, but could see nothing except blackness. "Be another flare in a moment, sir, if you keep looking." Harry was holding his arm to keep the periscope still, the slim, sheepskin soldier like a steel post beside him, making him feel quite safe. Nyren remembered how that slight wrist had turned away the Sergeant's giant hand and arm at the bar the previous evening.

Sure enough there was a second flare, a moon exploding over landscape Nyren could not understand, a chaos of barbed-wire, shell-holes and craters large and small, upstanding shapes that might once have been trees or even houses, and through and around it all a total emptiness, suddenly foreshortened into darkest shadow as the flare sank to earth. Nyren closed his eyes and told himself it was one of those cardboard tubes you hold up to the light and shake around to make strange coloured patterns - except out there there was no colour. A kaleidoscope. Harry was looking at him as he handed back the wooden box. "Thank you, Corporal."

Harry checked through the periscope again, two helmets now bobbing along under the wire in the shallow sap that ran out to the fire trench, the Lewis gun returning. Nyren could see Raven waiting for his men at the barbed wire 'gate' where the sap reached the trench.

"Mission accomplished then," said Nyren's voice beside Harry. And after a silence: "I'm afraid all this is quite a new experience for me, Corporal."

Harry watched the schoolboy step back down and walk away to rejoin Raven. Poor, bonny lad with all that apprehension in his young blue eyes. Fuck them for sending children, Harry thought, forgetting he'd been just that age when he had first come out.

The commotion of the returning Lewis gun began to wake the others, Frank the first to climb up on the fire-step beside Harry, one hand on his arm as he whistled back at the starling in the bushes out in front of them: "Everything alright back home, then?"

Harry nodded.

"Did you bring a letter?"

Harry nodded again. He could hear Reggie below them, blowing and sucking at his harmonica as he unrolled himself from his cape, echoing a distant sound, a bugle far away: Reveille back at the transport lines, warning those crazy cooks and blacksmiths to put their fires out.

"Stand-to," called quiet voices Platoon to Platoon, Company to Company, Belgian to British, British to French, 450 miles all the way from the North Sea to Switzerland, zig-zag to zig-zag down the line, every soldier one by one peeling the oiled rags from their rifles to join the others at the parapet and defend the break of yet another day.

*

Prideaux, Trussal and Colledge, the Medical Officer, faced each other, old campaigners across the table, whisky bottle and hurricane lamp between them, the dugout cleared of other bodies, officers and batmen dispersed to their Platoons for signal practice and kit inspections. Company CO and Company Sergeant-Major were taking their weekly 'review' of all the Company names, Officers, NCO's and Men, the MO's sick list adding an extra dimension. The meeting, as always, had been called for mid-afternoon, before anyone had started serious drinking; though by evening all three of them intended to be well advanced along that road.

Prideaux had observed the practice of 'review' as a young subaltern before the war at both Company and Battalion levels under a Captain and Colonel he much admired. In the then heat and dust of the Sudan the participation of a Medical Officer had also been recognised as useful and given the conditions of trench warfare in France and Flanders, Prideaux usually insisted on his presence.

Morale, they agreed this morning, was fair though nine casualties in the last month had left gaps that four newcomers had not quite filled. America's entry into the war seemed to have cheered everyone, though they'd been warned it would be ages before their soldiers actually arrived. Section by Section Sergeant-Major Trussal now read out 'B' Company's names: a couple of men recommended for a stripe; another for a second stripe; a half-dozen malingerers on fatigues; a young soldier in 3 Platoon who hadn't uttered a word for ten days; three pale waifs from 2 Platoon on regular sick parade and suspected of extracting and swallowing gunpowder from bullets to aggravate their condition; four men with trench foot; and one Corporal with a chest infection who should be sent on sick leave. The ordinary leave roster was updated for Battalion and comments on the officers asked from the Sergeant-Major.

"Even with Lieutenant Stevens absent, sir, 2 Platoon's still a problem."

"How about swapping Sergeants - have Percival lick them into shape?"

"Maybe in a week or two. Our new officer needs Percival for the moment, sir. He's nothing but a wee bonny lad."

"Mix 2 up with 4 Platoon?"

"4 Platoon's our best soldiers, sir. If we're ever in trouble, we need them as a unit."

Captain Prideaux poured their first mugs of whisky. "Sergeant-Major, I bow to your experience and wisdom." He looked up at Colledge. "The Boer war, Jack. All I had was Egypt and Sudan. And back into civvy street of course."

The Sergeant-Major raised his mug: "You'd be a Colonel otherwise, sir."

Colledge folded his medical list away. "Anyone heard about Harry Cardwell's dirty postcards?"

Prideaux raised his eyebrows: "Doesn't sound like Cardwell."

"It's a story in the transport lines. He had a fight with a Sergeant on his way back in from leave. Over a tin box of pictures and purple prose?"

The Sergeant-Major laughed: "I'd rather take my chance with lady luck and face Jerry's guns than pick a fight with Harry!"

"Why not put HIM up for another stripe or two?"

"Wouldn't damn well take it, would he, sir. He only went Lance-Jack to keep his bloody Lewis gun."

The tin box lay forgotten in Harry's pack for another 48 hours until the Company swapped with the Durhams and moved back into the reserve trench. An easy, silent move. They'd done it twice already. Nothing that roused even a mortar or a minnie from Jerry. Apart from their fixed machine guns, they'd been quiet now for two days. The newcomers were beginning to think life was almost safe.

"Lance-Corporal!" someone called. It was Ordish, lying bang out in the open on a slab of dried mud reading a book under a splintered hazel, upwind of the latrine and Harry peaceful in the middle of a pee, only his helmet visible. "There's regulation angles for your headgear."

"Sir." Harry finished his pee and clambered gingerly out on top, cramming the helmet back onto the front of his head.

"It's alright. Jerry sniper can't see us here. And their artillery use my little nut tree for range and bracketing."

"Maybe we ought to cut it down, sir. I mean we don't want to make things too easy for them, do we?"

Ordish reached in his pocket and pulled out a coin. "Bet that was your last shilling the other evening."

"Shilling, sir?"

"Your scouse Sergeant in the Estaminet. Should have been my call." Ordish handed the shilling to Harry.

Harry handed it back: "Big bugger with no brains, sir. Best left to the likes of me."

"If he'd known our Harry Cardwell, he certainly wouldn't have picked a fight with you."

"Not much of a fight, sir."

"It could have been." Ordish yawned hugely: "What happened to the little tin box?"

"In my pack, sir. I thought of handing it in."

"Lost and found?"

Harry nodded. "Except there's no names inside. Well, no surnames."

"Have you read the letters?"

"Far as I can. It's bloody odd writing, sir."

"Want to show them to me? There must be some clue somewhere as to who he is. Or who she is. Your decision, Harry. The box is still yours if you won't take my shilling."

Harry took the photograph from his pocket and showed it to Ordish: "There's a name on the back you can't read."

Ordish turned it over and deciphered the scrawl on the back: "Annie, I think. Annie in Amiens. May 16th, 1916." He looked again at the woman's face. "Quite a girl, it must be said."

"In two of the photographs she's dressed as a nurse. Seems they met on what he calls her train."

"Ambulance train?" Ordish looked up at Harry with one of his rare smiles. "If you can't find him, perhaps we should find her."

Harry grinned back. Surely it was a joke.

Over their heads the wind began to blow rain in from the North Sea; down in the trench voices were shouting for roll-call.

The officers' dugout in the reserve line was more spacious than their front line home. In a sense it had to be to allow room for all the paperwork laid out on the table in front of Captain Prideaux: "Pro forma and bloody nonsense," he was muttering; then out loud as he turned the next sheet over. "Leave papers." Everyone looked up. Prideaux pushed them over to Raven. "For you, John. You're a day late already." Raven, halfway down a bottle of whisky and sneezing with a roar, watched Uncle Sinclair turn away in bitter disappointment. Poor Uncle was still without news of his expected child.

On an impulse, out of his fever and whisky haze, 'bloody-minded' John Raven pushed the papers over to Uncle: "Do a swap? I'm not that damn keen on going back with a four by two stuffed up my nose. Wouldn't even be able to taste my food." Raven looked over at Prideaux. "Change the names, can't we? You write a note and Uncle gets it endorsed at Division?"

"I've a wiring party tonight," Uncle warned.

Raven shrugged: "I'll take it out myself."

Ten minutes later, happy, embarrassed, bubbling in disbelief, Uncle shook Raven's hand for the umpteenth time and stumbled up the steps with his bag out into the rain on his long journey home. Raven picked up the order sheet for the wiring party and penciled in Sergeant Percival's name.

Benson watched the Lance-Corporal in the light of the Sergeant's lantern, trying to copy each move he made: the padding he placed inside his shoulders; the dark cloth wound around his puttees; a khaki handkerchief over the buckle of his belt; burnt cork smeared on his face; thick gauntlets pulled over his mittens. It was the first time he'd seen Harry since the evening of their arrival, and felt strangely reassured that the tough young Lance-Jack would be just one place ahead of him in the wire party. 'Party' had sounded quite fun until the reality of it became clear. Some party out in no man's land and apparently the furtherest line of wire to repair.

"The blooding of the innocents," Sergeant Percival called the motley group that assembled by Trussal's dugout. And indeed all four newcomers were there, Schoolboy Nyren up front with the Sergeant and five others, the other two newboys in the middle, Harry and Lieutenant Raven at the rear, Benson in their sandwich.

"Take a run at it, sir?" Percival asked Raven and didn't even wait for an answer. Clearly Sergeant Percival had already decided how it would be done. "Your group stops on position and anchors all the one ends," he told Harry. "My group will roll them out."

"Five fucking reels," muttered someone. "We'll be there all night."

"If a flare goes up, you freeze," said Raven to the newcomers and single-file they set off down the communication trench, a pause at a stores dump to pick up rolls of wire, spirals and wire-cutters, Harry shouldering wire, Benson the corkscrew pickets. Harry pulled one of them out and stuck it in the ground: "Twist them in," he said, demonstrating; "That way they make less noise." Harry looked him in the eye: Benson seemed calm enough but it was never too sure with rookies on their first time out. Harry pulled a piece of sticky tape off his wrist and stuck it over the safety catch on Benson's rifle.

"Going to be pointing up my arse, that is."

They crouched along a sap under the first line of wire into a fire-bay, then one by one in single file climbed up and out into the dark, confused mystery of no man's land, Sergeant Percival leading them. Knowing him, thought Harry, he's been on the periscope all day memorizing every stone and lump of mud. Light rain was still falling, a slime on top of the hardened clay and difficult to balance with the load on your shoulders. Harry felt apprehension tighten the back of his scalp from ear to ear. The pitchest black seemed like daylight out here; it always felt like the whole damn world must be able to see you. Benson would be alright until the first flare went up and he saw how vulnerable they really were.

Percival was waiting at his pre-ordained spot through the gap in the second line of wire. The third line had been blown to buggery by shelling. Jerry knows damn well we'll be out to mend it, thought Harry. He'll have a fixed machine gun or sniper ready trained and ranged, set up for the kill. "Twist in a quick three and hit the ground," he whispered in Benson's ear as he slipped the spirals off his shoulder.

Benson looked round. He and Harry were the only two left on their feet, the others lying flat, Raven with the look-outs, Percival and the Schoolboy waiting with their men to move with the wire. Harry held the first picket upright, Benson twisting it into the ground; then in quick succession the second and the third. And down they went a full two seconds before they heard a flare go up. Benson was face to face with Harry on the ground, Harry reaching a hand to indicate he should cover his eyes against the glare. "Next two one by one," he whispered in his ear. Bloody Percival had already hooked up the first three reels of wire the moment the spirals went in. Harry hoped someone had remembered to grease the rolls to keep them silent.

It was Schoolboy Nyren who was waiting for the last two reels, eyes wide, excited and not yet afraid. Harry pushed the Second Lieutenant's head down further to the ground. Sure enough a sniper fired before the next flare had even shown. When the second flare died, Schoolboy grabbed his two reels, one to each of his men, and disappeared into the darkness after Percival. So far so good, thought

Benson, though the unrolling wire seemed to be making one hell of a din.

It seemed only minutes later the Lance-Corporal was whispering in his ear again: "Sergeant Percival leads back; you and Lieutenant Raven at the rear. I'll take the Schoolboy."

The sniper fired again, at random into the pitch darkness, though the crack of the bullet was near enough to make most of them flinch. Percival was driving spare pickets through the new wire to give it more rigidity, working his way back to their exit point, one eye on the two new boys with him.

"So far so good," Benson was still thinking as he saw Raven loom up out of the darkness. Then the third flare went up turning no man's land white again like a snowscape. "Quite still everyone," murmured Raven. But it was Raven himself, suppressing his head cold all night, who doubled up suddenly with a sneeze. Benson couldn't help grinning as he watched him, catching Raven as the officer seemed to sag, straightening up from his aaa-ttish-ooo, his cap falling off. There wasn't a mark visible on the Lieutenant until blood ran out of his thick black hair to mask his face. The sniper's next bullet cut through the bulging front flap of Benson's tunic. Benson dropped Raven and bolted for the gap in the wire, followed by the other two novices, Percival's whispered curses following them. The flare faded to the ground and into darkness.

From the sound the bullet made, Harry guessed someone had been hit in the head. But he was faced the other way, watching the Schoolboy take the wrong turning in that moment of fear and get himself caught up on the wire. Harry dragged him bodily out with one hand, tearing the officer's uniform, pushing him in the right direction as grenades were thrown and a mortar fired from the German trenches.

Harry reached the parapet and safety of their own fire-bay, only to have Percival grab his arm: "We're going back for him" - the Lieutenant he meant.   And into the darkness and the bullets they returned, Harry crawling on his belly, Percival crouched and running, ignoring the danger, yelling back at Harry - "What are you frightened of?!   On your fucking feet!" - not the first time Harry had been the victim of Percival's dangerous contempt for anyone who fell short of his own manic courage. They each grabbed one arm and dragged the lifeless John Raven over the rough ground back to the line.

As they pulled the body into the fire-bay, so the heavens opened, Schoolboy Nyren slumped stupefied with Benson and the other rookies on the duckboard at the back of the bay - all staring at the small burnt hole in Raven's forehead and all watching the rain wash Raven's blood and brains from the smashed open bone at the back of his skull and from the sleeve of Harry's uniform.

Chapter 4

She often wondered where the bodies ended up. All they had room for on the train were canvas bags, the whole process like a ritual of housekeeping, two of them to each bag, two to the body, the red identification disc cut from around the man's neck and handed to Virgin Mary, the sewn up body-sacks off-loaded usually at night when the nurses had gone home to their billets. Annie had seen on the edge of town whole fields of simple wooden crosses where she presumed dead soldiers had been buried. But the numbers were so vast, France might run out of fields before this war was over.

There wasn't a woman on the train who didn't fear (or had not grieved) for some man in the war: Virgin Mary with her ever-diminishing list of brothers, Annie who had lost her husband, two younger girls whose fathers were officers in combat, and the troubled Viv who in her own private grief no longer knew where emotionally she was.

Annie was already in bed that night when Viv came in from a game of cards downstairs, a glance exchanged while Viv undressed, Annie watching her through the very minimal ablutions advisable when the water in the jug was so damn cold. Viv was a younger girl with a country town background somewhere in the south of England, in awe of her American room-mate who had come from what she supposed to be a very sophisticated background in Boston. As usual she sat on the edge of Annie's bed, a look at the book Annie was reading and waiting for the American girl to take her hand. She looked again at the spine of Annie's Henry James.

"You must miss your university life with all us stupid girls around you."

"My father's a shopkeeper, Viv. I just happened to be good at school."

Oh dear, how often had they had this conversation?

Annie took her hand and Viv whispered: "Can I come inside and keep you warm?"

Viv had been in love with a soldier and lost him five months ago on the Somme. Children grow up quickly in such circumstance but still remain abandoned and afraid.

Chapter 5

It seemed in the end to have rained forever, relentless as it filled the bottom of the trenches and softened the mud walls of the parapets. The whole Company, officers and men, had passed most of a week digging, pumping and shoring up the collapsing structure of their subterranean world. Whether in reserve or front line, the quagmire became more important even than the minnies, the mortars or the bullets. Not that they or any other offensive weapon diminished in activity. The Germans were well aware what was going on in the British lines and determined to increase their misery. It was Jerry after all, with his thirty foot advantage in ground altitude, who was releasing thousands of gallons each hour through what was left of the flatland dykes into the enemy front line.

After the trauma of no man's land (that oh so predictive 'blooding of the innocents'), the claustrophobic misery of trenches under the rain, the digging half buried in mud, the sleeping cold and wet, there seemed left nothing for the rookies to look forward each day except the tot of rum that was always too little, too late to warm them up. The three of them, distributed between the platoons, hadn't yet had time to discover the essential solace that was friendship and the sharing of misery.

They learnt instead how easy it was to disturb the dead within the parapets and remind oneself of a likely fate. Benson, drooping with tiredness and cold one late afternoon, was pulling away a half-collapsed A-frame from the crumbling parados they were repairing when a partly uniformed skeleton slid with the mud into his arms making him shout out loud in alarm. "Stand him upright" his older neighbour laughed. "His bones'll help keep t' mud in place."

Little wonder, thought Benson, that their trench rats were so large and sleek.

He lay awake that next night listening to and sometimes feeling their scuttling feet and hoped their pink snouts and white teeth could tell the difference between flesh that was quick and flesh that was dead. After being told next morning (again by his older neighbour) that these front-line rats had often been known to gnaw the ears and nostrils of sleeping men, Benson vowed never to sleep again without a hood around his head, his hands buried deep inside his battledress.

Unknown to Benson, he and his two fellow-rookies had been the object of inquiry and savage disagreement in those days following the wire party. Sergeant Percival made several visits to the officers' dugout, trying unsuccessfully to persuade Captain Prideaux to have the three new boys put on a charge of first desertion, then cowardice and finally disobeying orders. As the surviving officer from that party, Schoolboy Nyren was expected to make judgement but knew he was as guilty as the others of panic and disorientation and would have probably ended up dead himself had the Lance-Corporal not pulled him off the wire. In the end, as they moved back into the front line, Prideaux tore up Percival's paperwork and told the Sergeant to drop the whole issue.

In front line or reserve, the Company officers displayed each day a grimmer and more bloody-minded disposition as though John Raven had bequeathed them all a little of his dour, humourless spirit. Half drowned by the rain, both dugouts flooded, they'd even run out of whisky, reduced to scrounging tots of rum from the Company Sergeant Major. Subdued by Raven's death, they dreaded Uncle's return and the inevitability that he would blame himself for what had happened. Though actually Prideaux quietly - eventually not so quietly - blamed himself. He should never have let Raven out in no man's land coughing and sneezing as he had been. "Funny," he said to Ordish wading up and down the flooded trench one evening stand-to: "last summer the Company lost 160 men in just ten minutes at

White City, three out of five officers in our dugout. Yet now one isolated death almost feels worse. We must be getting soft."

Only Bunny's arrival from the transport lines (complete it has to be said with whisky) cheered them with his irrepressible smile. He'd been summoned to take Raven's place as 4 Platoon Commander, Harry glad to see the senior 'schoolboy' back in charge of them. The combination of Sergeant Banister and subaltern Bunny had always worked well, even in the slaughter-house of 'White City', Banister doing most of the soldiering, Bunny rousing their spirits and prepared to make the correct decision at the right time - on that occasion the order to retreat. He was also a lot more concerned than Raven had ever been about the comfort of the men. It was noticeable the very first day of his return how miraculously from somewhere they were able to collect three urns of hot water (brought in through the Buffs in the trench on their right to avoid pilfering by the other Border Platoons). Bunny had become quite the expert in his manipulation of that mysterious and all-important world of reciprocal favours behind the lines.

Uncle returned the day before they were to be pulled back into a rest area, joyful at the successful arrival of a second daughter, laden with smoked salmon, stilton and malt whisky, most of it intended for Raven - "Where is the gloomy old bugger?" And yes, his pain, his guilt, his sheer sorrow yelled out loud - "Christ Jesus, NO!" - when Captain Prideaux had to tell him. Prideaux wouldn't let him unpack, sending Uncle back to pick up a horse at the transport lines and sort their billets wherever the rest area was destined to be. Finding and fixing billets and comforts for a Company in 12 hours would take up all his time and thoughts and the further away Uncle was from the front line in his present mood, the better his chances of survival as a father.

Ordish walked him back as far as Division, distracting Uncle with the story of Harry's tiff with the burly Sergeant at the estaminet and the tin of letters and photographs that had ended up in Harry's kitbag. Uncle was suitably intrigued, insistent as they parted that Ordish encourage Harry to find this 'American Angel' on her hospital train.

Unfortunately that tail-end of their conversation was joined by 'Rowdy' Stevens, himself just arrived at Division on his way back to the Company from a signals course near Amiens. Four and five years older than Bunny and Nyren he was in many ways more of a schoolboy than they were, rumbustious, immature, full of ill-conceived practical jokes. Ordish told him as little as possible about Harry's 'treasure', returning their conversation to the practical in's and out's of Steven's 2 Platoon that Ordish had been caretaking in his absence - the worst of the four platoons with no one in it, including Stevens, from those halcyon 'family' days before the Somme. Predictably Stevens had been quite unmoved to hear of Raven's death, much more responsive to the news that the Company were on their way back next evening to a rest area well away from shells and bullets. "Bloody bon!" he laughed. "Wine, women and song!" Ordish thought by the expression on Uncle's face that Stevens might well find himself with the least salubrious billet in whichever farm or village they were destined to occupy.

They moved out after stand-to, handing over a reasonably repaired trench to the Fusiliers, the usual muttered banter - "soldier on old chum" - as they squeezed past one another along the duckboards, section by section, platoon by platoon along the line. Over a tot of whisky Prideaux gave the Fusilier Captain a sketched map of the no man's land in front of them with a warning about the sniper with his fixed point on the gap in the wire; and wished him well with the drainage. They'd managed to lower the level of the water on the dugout floor to a last quarter inch, that final covering always the most impossible to drain.

Then, with a shake of hands Prideaux was up the steps and out into a rain that had actually ceased to fall.

Harry, as ever, was the 'tail', last man out of the line with Sergeant Banister ahead of him. They'd been tail-talismen for the whole Company ever since the retreat at 'White City' where the two of them with Frank had been sole survivors from a pair of rear-guard Lewis guns in a shellhole holding off a German counter-attack while the remnants of the Company withdrew.

In the end, on that July day the previous year, they'd waited for the twilight, man-handling both guns back across the pitted and body-strewn field of grass and flowers that had been their line of advance earlier in a misty morning. The thin, scratching wails of sound all around them that evening had not been children playing or even screech-owls in that terrible darkness, but men slowly dying, abandoned and alone. And Harry and Banister had had to leave them there, imagining, who knows, that stretcher-bearers would eventually be allowed to find those of the young men who were still crying out for their mothers?

Only at midnight had the German guns fallen silent, a dozen Indian and Portuguese stretcher teams venturing back into that desolation. When a flare eventually went up, the whole British line could see three German officers standing, spaced along their own parapet, hands on hips as though to indicate that, while they were still standing there, German guns would stay silent and allow the stretcher-bearers to complete their grim work.

*

.....I remember last summer, willow trees and swallows along the banks of the Somme - a drive with you in a carriage to Amiens cathedral, a holding of hands, a dinner in a smart restaurant - and a farewell that anticipated the battle to come. Our brief afternoon and evening was, I believe, June 25th. Perhaps the 26th. I know we could hear the barrage from anywhere we were - the Cathedral, the restaurant, the 'train station' as you like to call it. Where else did we go? I know where I had wanted to go but never dared to ask. A lingering look at the small hotel on that piazza set me off instead on some foolish reminiscence of Tuscany. And that desperately meant desire to one day take you there. Live there with you. Laugh there with you. Paint and write and think! 'Poets, warriors, idlers all'. And still that barrage of guns would not leave us alone (they wrote to tell me they could even hear it in London!).

Then a week or so later came the July dawn when that barrage did at last stop and when, consequently, the whistles finally shrilled for us. The glorious moment we had all been waiting for. "For King

George and for England!" No, we did not really shout such things!
We simply climbed out of our trenches in full kit and, with orders
not to run, walked, a whole army of us, across long uphill summer
fields to die by the tens of thousands in the early morning sun. My
dear, my sweet, my American Angel, I still do not understand what
went wrong.

Ordish looked up from the page he was reading out in his low faint Geordie.

Harry nodded: "Same bloody show."

"Same bloody day."

They were lying in the sunshine, propped on their elbows under an apple tree, the entire Company sprawled around them across a hillside fast asleep, only Reggie awake beside them blowing softly into his harmonica.

They'd marched all night, full pack out of the trenches, out of Flanders south east into France, the officers taking turns on their two surviving horses, exhausted men sleeping on their feet, the weaker brethren having to surrender their rifles to subaltern or Sergeant, then reclaim them at the next five minute rest.

Uncle had been waiting for them at dawn, hearing their marching when they were still two miles away. Their destination was a small village, untouched by war but populated entirely by old men, women and children - most of whom had stood at windows or crept out into the cold early morning to watch the marching men arrive, still curious after three years of war, still grateful it seemed that British soldiers had come to fight for them. When they'd seen them along the village street each man had straightened in his march, shoulders back even after 30 miles. Harry, Reggie and Frank instead, pulling the Lewis gun cart, gave rides to the children who came running alongside them.

Uncle had done well: he and Ordish billeted with the village priest and a piano in his front room; Bunny and Nyren sharing the home of a buxom farmer's wife with a frail and pretty daughter who bobbed a curtsy at both of them, causing the Schoolboy to hotly blush once more; Prideaux in what might just be described as the village manor house; and, yes, rowdy Stevens a half mile away from all of them in a room over the railway station where the trains would hopefully rumble all night long!

The men had haybarns and cleaned-out stables scattered through the village, one or two to each platoon. Ordish even promised hot baths for everyone over the next two days, courtesy of a crippled steam engine on the railway siding and a former North Eastern fireman from the Northumberland Fusiliers stationed nearby.

Captain Prideaux had paraded the Company in mid-morning for a roll-call then fell them out on the hillside to take off their boots and socks and sleep under the apple-trees in the unaccustomed sun.

You cannot imagine what it feels like to watch your own men die. Though of course you can imagine, since every day you are caring for so many of the horribly injured and mutilated and having to watch them end their life in agony. How do you have the strength to keep yourself going? I fear my own strength in that respect is failing. Do I still believe what we are told to do? It is my duty to believe - and to make all the others believe. But those of us who came out of that awful day alive know that something was very wrong about it all. We sometimes look at one another and without saying anything think treason or mutiny.

My men seemed to fall over in that field of flowers like figurines you knock down with balls in a funfair. I thought at first they were falling out of clumsiness or fear - not timidity, you understand, for all my boys were anything but cowards - but then I heard some of them cry out so terribly that I knew they had been hit. And when I looked back for the others, well, most of them had also fallen in awful, grotesque attitudes of pain and despair.

I now know why I was not afraid. Our long and beautiful field had never been badly shelled and was not, for some reason, even shelled that morning. And it was shells I most feared - the shrapnel that can tear such fearful wounds into human flesh and bones. That morning our men were all falling from the machine guns yet I don't believe I could even hear them. Only the bullets as they hummed around like a swarm of bees. In the end I was begging for one myself, walking slowly in a straight line waiting for my head to explode. Yes, I saw that happen to my Sergeant-Major two paces in front of me. It was as though someone had hurled a bowl of eggs against a wall.

Where was I finally hit? Well, in the end my arm, my shoulder and my hand, left not right. I hold this letter paper with what looks like a fat bandaged stump, but is in fact a quite healthy five-fingered hand that should be ready to return to duty in two weeks time.

My wife came to see me yesterday, as ever loving, vivacious, proud of her husband. But unlike you she now has no idea from where I come - nor ever will. There is no real contact anymore.

Shall I see you again? You know I would never leave her and so have no right to call upon your time - yet I need you more than wine and water. The healing of your eyes. The calming of your voice. How your husband must have loved you. Shall you touch my damaged hand and let five fingers play across your body?

Oh dear no. Time now to put these pages aside and write you the more measured words you would expect from an officer and gentleman.

Ordish looked up again at Harry: "So there you have it, Corporal! He never signed his name because he never ever sent the damn letters!"

"Little wonder if he was married."

"Even if we found his name, these are not letters we could send back to his wife."

Harry lay on his back staring up through the branches of the trees, buds well swollen on the twigs, a bullfinch in the crown of the tree stripping them, flakes of his silent massacre floating down over them. Harry remembered the apple trees in the garden back home. They'd have had the catapults out for a bastard bullfinch there, though here his orange-crimson breast seemed more a hopeful sign that some normal natural life might yet survive the war. "She also is a married woman."

"Was, Harry." Ordish read again from the page: "How your husband must have loved you."

"Killed in the war?"

"An American?"

"IF he was American."

Ordish rolled over, looking down at Harry, their eyes meeting. "Wouldn't do any harm to find her."

"Fat chance, sir."

Their low voices were interrupted by a sudden explosion of verbal abuse on the far side of the orchard - an immaculate, over-dressed, overfed staff-officer on a horse, spluttering and swelling with rage, wanting to know why an entire Company, officers and men, are sleeping with filthy uniforms and naked feet in the middle of the day.

"He," muttered Ordish, "who has never himself been within ten miles of the front line."

They watched Captain Prideaux drag himself to his own naked feet and walk slowly down to the road, every ear in the Company now listening as Prideaux appeared very deliberately to salute the horse and not the man: "Myself, my officers and my men, Major, have been in the front line for ten weeks with little sleep and without relief. Last night they marched 30 miles through no fault of their own. I respectfully claim, sir, their right to a day of rest while they wait for baths and clean clothes."

The swelling of that outraged chest threatened to burst the Major from inside his colourful uniform: "This afternoon, Captain, I should like to see your planned organisation of route marches and football."

Prideaux saluted: "Sir"; and watched the buttocks of the Major recede, bounce-bounce at a trot, every inch as wide and round as the horse's own rump.

Harry was smiling now at Ordish. "I think our Captain in the letters would have stood up just the same, sir, for his men."

"Lance-Corporal, I'm sure you're right." Another rare Ordish smile: "All the more reason to find his lover."

Ordish stood up to go, Harry watching him amble away through the trees, one hand reached down at Bunny to raise him also to his feet. Five minutes later the two subalterns were leading opposing teams from their two Platoons, playing football with an empty pack stuffed with dirty socks.

*

Uncle had hardly slept since leaving home three days ago and was now held even further from sleep, reliving every reported circumstance of Raven's death, its reality as present on him as though he himself was wearing that thick black mop of Raven's blood-soaked hair. Ordish's Schubert on the piano in the priest's sitting room sounded like a requiem for the dead man's sneeze in no man's land.

Uncle had been writing lists, the billets, food and fuel requisitioned in the village, invoices for the Quartermaster. He walked with them up the quiet street, as quiet as his home in Haydon Bridge, as quiet as Hadrian's Wall on a similar primrose spring evening under a similar primrose sky. One thing he knew he could not do - tell his Marion of what had happened to the man she'd blessed for letting her husband come home.

Uncle knocked on the 'manor house' door, hoping he'd be able to leave the bumph for Prideaux without conversation. But the Captain opened the door himself, leading Uncle in to introduce him to the elderly Madame, forgetting that Uncle himself had found the billet and negotiated with the lady the evening before. Madame smiled and Prideaux laughed at his mistake. "You did well, Uncle. We'll all of us have a fine rest here. Madame even reads me Lamartine."

Not that Uncle's heavy silence escaped his Company Commander as the lists and invoices were laid out on the table. Prideaux steered him into the twilight garden and spoke quite sternly: "Mea culpa, Lieutenant. I was the one who let John out there in his unsafe condition. My guilt is very clear and weighs a great deal more heavy than your regret. I'd rather not be also made to feel responsible for your gloom." He pulled a handful of francs from his pocket: "I am invited to dine with Madame tonight. I'm asking you to take the other officers for a drink. I'm told there is an Estaminet somewhere near the station." And when Uncle shook his head: "I'm giving you an order, Sinclair. This evening you drink. And tonight you sleep."

You couldn't really call it an Estaminet. Nor even a bar or a pub. But the village, descended upon at regular intervals by exhausted units of soldiers out of the front line, had improvised a beer and wine hall in the basement chamber of a former abattoir, defunct since the invading German army in the Franco-Prussian war had used the building as a barracks and a prison nearly fifty years ago. Legitimate entertainment of the troops was only a secondary consideration, the local and reasonable priority the containment of drinking soldiers in one location that could be effectively controlled by their own officers and NCO's, or *in extremis* by redcaps called in from the local Division. And since the building stood that half mile out of the village beside the railway, there was always hope the walk home would sober up the worse of the afflicted.

That long sleep in the sun had softened all their brains. Relying on whoever had the money to buy, they most of them sank into a comatose cheerfulness, officers and other ranks only minimally segregated, the buzz of chatter feeding rumour like a line of mercury.

'Schoolboy' Nyren was quickly tongue-loosened, revealing to brother-officers what exactly HAD happened between Harry and the burly Sergeant in the estaminet by the railhead. Everyone had half heard the story, the three rookies bringing with them the outline of exaggerated confrontation that now threatened to become another legend: Harry with his wrist of steel who all but broke that Sergeant's arm. But then there weren't many of the older hands in the Company who hadn't suffered the 'Cheviot Sting' in earlier long-ago days when impresario Nobby would lay the odds against Harry for an evening of arm-wrestling, Frank and Reggie his accomplices. In those days Harry had done it for a laugh. Beer money for all his 'marra's'. He'd been used to spending long summer days in his short adult life playing similar sport around the sheep fairs both sides of the Border - wrestling, fell-running, shearing and sheep-carrying, even bareback racing on the local nags. In another age he might well have been a prize-fighter.

By the end of that night, with great exaggeration, in many different resonances and greatly differing interpretations, everyone was more or less gossiping that same story - about which, at the officers' end of the slaughterhouse, Second Lieutenant Stevens now considered himself to be the informed expert. After all, he'd heard Ordish and Uncle discuss it in the closest of detail. "The tin box," Stevens declared, "belonged to an officer and is not the soldier's rightful property. It should be confiscated forthwith." Steven's braying voice carried to more of the cavernous room than perhaps he had intended - most especially to Reggie on his way back from what passed as the abattoir toilet.

Uncle walked back that night drunk enough to guarantee sleep, arm in arm with Ordish and both of them meandering from verge to verge.

"We could all be dead tomorrow - that's the thing," said Uncle, louder than he'd intended. "And when we go, all our memory goes with us. Obliterated. Everything we've ever done. As though we'd never lived."

"Others will remember, old chap. You have a wife and children who will remember." Ordish lost Uncle's arm for a moment, swaying dangerously near the ditch. "There's even one or two who might remember me."

" 'Like pilgrims to th'appointed place we tend' ", recited Uncle, grabbing for Ordish's hand. " 'The world's an inn, and death the journey's end.' "

Ordish was giggling. "Then we, my friend, have made a covenant with death, and with hell are we at agreement." And hand in hand they both came safely home to bed.

*

Harry had always treated Stevens for what he was: an inexperienced officer without either the necessary humility of ignorance or the urge to improve his knowledge - without even the ability to communicate in a natural way with his 'inferiors'. Their few encounters had been at best a syllable or two short of insolence or insult. For Stevens, Harry became 'that obnoxious, insubordinate, arrogant little Lance-Jack' who needed taking down a peg or two. All such enemies are dangerous when they have the rank to enforce their prejudice.

As Duty Officer next morning, Stevens marched into the Four Platoon barn for a kit inspection with Sergeant Percival at his side - oh yes, he had chosen his non-com with malice aforethought. Stevens knew that Harry had been dispatched that morning with Bunny to ride the two surviving Company horses in search of a blacksmith. They wouldn't be back until the afternoon. The only price Stevens would have to pay for prying was the graft of continuing the kit inspection through all the other platoons. As pretext for a Company inspection he'd chosen one of the more inane communications from Division concerning 'the danger of pacifist literature or enemy propaganda being spread among the troops'.

Officer and Sergeant moved from soldier to soldier through the Platoon, pockets and packs emptied, the disapproving Banister watching their search. When finally they came to Harry's belongings, Stevens himself upturned the pack. But all he could find was one photograph loose between a pad of paper, Annie in Amiens written on the back. "Where did this come from?" he asked Frank. "Wasn't there a tin of photographs and letters?"

"He must have thrown it away," Frank replied. The other soldiers grinned.

"Stolen property - property of an officer." Stevens held up the photograph. "This is confiscated, you can tell him." And in irritation at the others: "The rest of you get smartened up. You heard the Major yesterday, Sergeant Banister. The Company does not intend to lose face at Division. And you can wipe that smile, Lowburn!" snarled the Sergeant. It was Frank who'd smiled again with a wink at Reggie - Reggie who'd guessed the possible motive for the kit inspection (Reggie who'd heard Stevens' bray at the abattoir the previous evening); and Reggie who, in Harry's absence, had whipped the tin box from his friend's pack to stuff it deep under the straw before Stevens and Percival had even entered the barn.

Returning with his Lieutenant on the newly shod horses, Harry accepted the loss of the photograph with a resigned shrug. Not so

Bunny, furious that Stevens had imposed a kit inspection on the Platoon in his absence.

At the evening meeting with Prideaux at the 'manor house', Bunny challenged Stevens about the confiscated photograph, a heated exchange between the two of them about the continued insubordination of Lance-Corporal Cardwell, about the protocol of kit inspections and Stevens' barely justified excuse of that Divisional pro forma.

In the end it was Ordish who intervened: "If this tin box IS the property of an officer missing or dead, I can assure you, having read some of the letters, it would not be appropriate to have them or the photographs sent back to his family - even if we DID know his identity."

"An adulterer?" asked Stevens in tone of disgust, the word and his expression sounding almost comical to the others. "In which case they and the photographs should be destroyed."

Prideaux seemed to remember from some long-ago conversation that Stevens' father was a Methodist minister near Morpeth. "Give that thing to me," Prideaux said to Stevens and took possession of the photograph to bring the argument to a close.

Instead he distributed more bumph to them about various courses on offer to officers and men. "I can't afford to let any of YOU go," he told them. "But put the men up for something. They deserve a rest. Maximum of two from each Platoon."

Once Stevens had stomped off to his distant billet, Prideaux poured whiskies for the others and handed the confiscated photograph to Bunny. "A very beautiful woman," he commented. "Sort it out, Bunny. Tell Lance-Corporal Cardwell to hide the damn things - or burn them."

Afterwards walking into the village together, Ordish quietly suggested to Bunny that Harry Cardwell might be nominated for the gunnery course.

"Harry knows his gun stuff backwards."

"Only on the Lewis."

"Well they ain't ever going to give us anything better than that."

"He'll pick up new tips."

Bunny glanced sideways at him: "What conspiracy are YOU hatching, Sam? Is this those damn letters again?"

"Gunnery's outside Pérignon."

Bunny shook his head: "You don't mean gunnery. What YOU mean is the big base hospital there!" He shook his head in disapproval: "Agent provocateur!"

"We'll see if our Harry tries to find his American Angel. We can lay odds with Uncle - without telling Stevens."

Chapter 6

The train had been pulled off onto a siding for two hours, wounded and dying men considered less important than the truck-loads of upright shells now passing them on banging axles in the opposite direction. There were men who would now die because of this delay and Virgin Mary was not best pleased. In fact she was hopping mad, berating their new, and equally useless, Train Commander. Not that there was very much he could have done about it.

They had to let ten supply trains through before they were allowed to continue, far too late for one of Annie's charges whose face now screamed in silence at every tiny movement of the iron bunk. Annie wished he would scream out loud, and told him so. There was so much suppressed tension in his body from unbearable pain - and morphine today rationed, only available for the likely living. One of the medics had been pilfering from the store. Half of Pérignon, it seemed, had acquired the habit. All Annie could do with her Johnny McCann who'd lost his balls, his bladder and his bowels, was wipe his brow and hold his damp young hand.

"I'm sorry, Miss, to be such trouble," he kept whispering. And at the very end in the moment before he died:

"Don't tell them, Miss, please don't tell them."

"Don't tell them what, Johnny?"

"Don't tell them, Miss, it was like this."

That evening in their tiny billet Annie asked Viv to help her write a letter to this Johnny's mother, in an English that wouldn't sound too strange. She knew she would not sleep if she did not communicate her admiration for the courage of that young boy.

Virgin Mary had prohibited such correspondence - not from hardness of heart but from sheer practicality: "Once you start to do it," she'd warned them, "you'll never stop." All that was officially permitted was to help the filling-in of pre-printed cards if casualties wished to send news home of their 'wounded but well' condition.

Even with Viv stretched out against her, Annie still did not sleep, seeing before her all night long the blackened crimson flesh and white bone against the green gangrene cavity where Johnny's penis, scrotum and backside had been.

Chapter 7

Harry arrived by train in Pérignon down the same track used by Annie's hospital train, squatting in one of the now empty trucks that had been carrying the shells. Shanks's mare, cart, lorry, cart again and train had been his grand tour today - destination a tiny bedroom in a labourer's cottage on the outskirts of town with orders to report for his gunnery course next morning at the range one mile away.

It was certainly strange to be on his own again so soon after leave. Strictly speaking it should have been Frank or Reggie given the chance for time away from the line. He'd said as much to Bunny: "Whatever they learn they'll bring back to the gun crews." But no. Harry was Lewis gun Lance-Corporal; Harry was the one who had to go. So what was the real reason? He reckoned Ordish and the Lieutenant's infatuation with 'Annie' in the photographs. WOULD Harry try and find the girl?

He knew he would - no point buggerin' about wondering if; much better bugger about trying to decide how to do it.

"The railhead", Ordish had suggested. "Show the photographs where the hospital trains come in." So that first evening Harry explored the town to find the different rail yards - one for the troops, one for the hospital, one for general stores and one, closely guarded, for shells and ammunition. How carefully, how tidily the war seemed organised at this distance, and all to end up in the dirty and deadly confusion of that front line.

Twice he was challenged this first evening by the Red-caps to establish he was neither a deserter nor absentee. He certainly looked different from most of the town toffs. The streets were full of clean uniforms, some French among them, all presumably engaged in Staff and clerical jobs, their expressions relaxed, their laughter hale and hearty and none of them with anything approaching the worn look of Harry's young face and clothes. The shops were all well-stocked, but most of them designated for 'Officers And Civilians Only'. Harry wondered where on earth he'd be able to buy something to bring back for Frank and Reggie.

Of nurses there were few, and those few all in the company of officers. Harry saw a pair of them wearing that same style of uniform as 'Annie' in the photographs, but it would be inconceivable to approach them with those gold crown poodlefakers at their side.

Harry found himself an Estaminet for some egg and chips and a glass of beer. Then walked back to his billet to make full use of the unaccustomed bed and sheets.

In fact next evening and the following Annie was nowhere near the town, the train engine broken down and blocking the single-line track, supply trains built up behind them making a rescue near impossible. Nor were there any engines up the line in front of them to tow them out. It would take engineers from the Service Corps the best part of two days to rebuild the cracked cylinder and piston. Just as well they'd been on their way up empty, though Annie and Virgin Mary wondered how the wounded men they were meant to have picked up would cope instead with the 20 mile rough ride in the motorised ambulances.

The Train Commander chose to catch up on his sleep (back at base in Pérignon he was said to be very nocturnally active) while Virgin Mary decided instead that this was the opportunity for a major spring-clean. Buckets of water were carried from the nearby river, heated to boiling over trackside fires, and the entire insides of the carriages sterilised, floors, walls, roofs, windows, folding bunks, toilets, operating room, even the doors and doorhandles - and the Train Commander's hutch.

From his course each late afternoon and evening, released from endless stripping-down, reassembling and firing of Colt, Lewis, Maxim and Vickers, Harry pursued his search, from railhead to hospital with the photographs of Anna in his hand, the tin box of letters in his knapsack.

The manner of the search was awkward, embarrassing even - the accosting of people, the "excuse me but can I ask you...." Who was interested in those dark streets to peer at photographs? "There are 200 bloody nurses in this town," one exasperated medic told him. And everyone naturally assumed he was pursuing an infatuation with this nurse and thus were less inclined to help. Besides, he was getting into the town far too late in the day. By the time they were released from the gunnery course, by the time he'd walked home for the statutory meal at his billet, it was well into the evening, the hospital trains already emptied, the nurses all back in camp or barracks. Yet Harry wasn't going to risk skipping even one afternoon of the course. Once he'd beaten everyone on the Lewis gun, it had become a point of honour to complete the course with high marks and respect.

On the third evening of his search Harry further handicapped himself. He couldn't quite remember afterwards exactly how the fight had started - an exchange of insults down one of the narrow cobbled backstreets, though he was sure the other man had been the first to raise his fist - or more accurately his cosh. And, after all, he was a one stripe Lance-Jack just like Harry; in terms of rank they had been equal.

"Geordie piss-pot!" the man had snarled. For the lack of public toilets, Harry had been pumping ship against the wall.

"I'm not fuckin' Geordie, ignorant pig!" 'Pig', yes, had been a deliberate retaliatory insult - but at least with some factual basis. Like so many in this town, the man was overfed and very rotund.

"Pig?!" The plump crimson cheeks under the red cap were apoplectic.

"Where d'you get your food from, fat man? Why not send some of it up the line?"

Harry seemed to recall that was the moment when the redcap drew his cosh, red rag to a bull. Harry held the wrist with the cosh and hit the policeman hard under the ribs. One blow was all it took, the man collapsing like a jelly pudding, gasping for breath. Harry turned and walked away. Should have hit him in the balls, he afterwards thought, though by the time the winded man got up and called for help, Harry was a good two streets away and looking to every passer-by as innocent as a child. Where, he wondered, had the second redcap been? They always walked in pairs. A question he answered for himself next evening when he ventured back into that same cobbled alley. The two houses at the end of the narrow street were discreet brothels. Maybe the fat man's mate had had his trousers down when he'd heard his Lance-Jack call for help.

How many times has it been said to Harry: "Don't make enemies"? Now for the remaining two evenings Harry had to creep around town with eyes at the back of his head for the redcaps. They'd all be looking for the 'Geordie'.

By the end of the week he was as far as ever from even beginning to find that 'American Angel', staring at her pictures each night by the candle in the tiny bedroom, wondering why the expressions on her face caused him such turmoil. He'd never felt quite that way about girlfriends back home - Peggy in the next valley, Mary in the market town where the railway ended. He believed he'd been in love with both of them: with Mary (still at school) when he was sixteen, walking 15 miles down the valley one Saturday each month to sit together by the river; and at seventeen with Peggy, who'd followed him round the sheep-fairs one summer, 'holding his coat' and cheering him on - and coaxing away his virginity one mid-summer evening in the bracken above Kirk Yetholm. Harry smiled at the candle. They'd decided to walk home over the high border instead of taking the cart round the mountain - and later, somewhere under Russell's Cairn on Windy Gyle, had watched a hundred sheep stampede through the heather towards the rising moon. Full moon under which they'd again made love a second and a third time before reaching home. Bonny lass, Peggy, unafraid of anything. But, quite rightly, she wasn't going to wait for a soldier maybe never to return.

In the end discovery was more or less an accident, marking targets at the butts that last afternoon on the range. His neighbour asked, for the sake of saying something: "Where the hell do YOU disappear every evening?"

Sitting smoking, waiting for the next line of guns to fire, Harry told him. And even showed him two photographs of the girl. What was there to lose in terms of face? They'd all be returning to their units next morning.

The neighbour laughed: "She was one of the nurses on the train that took me out the line."

"How long ago?"

"Now. Coming down for the course. They were half-empty. We were allowed to bum a ride."

"From where?"

"This side of Arras."

So with that one evening left and skipping his billet meal, Harry ran for the rail yard where the hospital train had arrived to discharge its load of human suffering. And there, in flesh and blood, before he'd even shown a photograph, he saw the American girl, tired and drawn, but real and still unbelievably beautiful..........

...Annie, weary and dirty, was 'marched' in formation with the other nurses by their battleaxe Virgin Mary out of the railhead, down a small-town street to their assembly point in a school yard. Harry was watching and following as the nurses dispersed, hurrying to their various lodgings adjacent to the school. It was their weekly evening out, that compromise agreed for the American and Canadian girls. English nurses and VAD's were usually forbidden male company but the hospital trains out of Pérignon were run by mixed units and the rules consequently more relaxed.

Harry was still watching later, wondering how he would approach her, when Annie and Viv emerged, cleaned and dressed up, to be met with another nurse by three well-fed Staff Officers. Harry followed them at a distance, inconspicuous in the crowded streets, until at one point he had to cross over to avoid a pair of Red-caps. When Harry looked back for his group of nurses and officers, they had disappeared. Which doorway or other street had they turned into? He watched the redcaps out of sight before swiftly retracing his steps. How could he lose her now, having just found her and with his time fast running out? He felt the tin box in his pack. All he had to do was hand it to her.

The nurses had been taken to a smart 'officers only' restaurant, Annie glad that the rather close attentions of one of the officers were being chaperoned by her friends. It was the third time he'd asked her out, his company, his conversation pleasant enough - but she certainly didn't wish for anything more intimate. There was something about these 'château wallahs' that seemed to detach them from any reality about the war. She'd invited one of them once to join them on the train and ride with the wounded and the dying. The invitation had been laughingly turned down: "That would NOT be appropriate."

Annie noticed the thin young face of a soldier out in the street, peering in at them through the misted glass, and felt instant guilt about the plate of fillet, truffle and foie gras the waiter had laid in front of her. Her escort laughed: "I think I spy the poor man at our gate". But when she looked again, the face had disappeared.

Annie saw the same haunting young face on their way back, a Lance-Corporal leaning up against a wall holding something in his hand, watching her as they passed. It seemed almost as though he would move away from the wall to confront her, but in that moment their escorts swung them aside across the street. There was a shyness about the young man, a reticence, that made him seem very vulnerable. She tried to look back but her escort was talking again, on and on about horses and the hunting they had managed last weekend in the Forest of Compiègne. "No season in wartime," he laughed. "No rules or regs."

Annie glimpsed the face again, behind them, shadowing them on their escorted way back to their lodgings. But he was spotted also by their escorts who gave chase, 'tallyho'ing as though they were hunting again, and in so doing attracting the attention of a pair of redcaps. None of them, redcaps or officers, were any match for the pace of the lean and now angry young soldier.

Annie saw Harry a fourth time that evening: "Your handsome soldier's waiting for you outside," Viv laughed. He was standing in the street below as she closed their curtains for the night, Annie at Viv's shoulder to take a look.

Next day in a cold dawn the nurses reassembled in the school yard to march back up the street to the railhead. Where finally in the confusion of medics and a milling-about Battalion of the West Yorkshires, Harry approached Annie to abruptly push the tin box of letters and photographs into her hands - only to be hustled away by Virgin Mary. "If your name's Annie, Miss, then this belongs to you -" was all he managed to say; yet he felt a strange recognition, an exhilaration when their eyes met. It was as though for that brief moment he knew everything about her. Of course, in some ways he **did** know her from those letters, the expression in her eyes, the 'swan-like' neck now covered in her uniform ruff. He even knew the 'Virgin Mary' nick-name of that battleaxe Sister who'd pushed him so forcibly away.

It hadn't been enough what he had told her. Perhaps he should explain how the tin box had come into his possession; how no one knew whether the officer who'd written the letters was alive or dead. Perhaps he should have tried to warn her of the passion in those letters. She might not want to read such things.

The Battalion of West Yorkshires clambered on board the train with the nurses that morning, the Train Commander insisting they climb up on each carriage roof to cover the red cross markings - an act of honesty which the nurses hated since the lack of marking made them a prime target for any cruising enemy airplane. Annie was sitting with the tin box on her knee in a cordoned-off section of the train, the metal bunks in seating mode, the nurses like animals in a cage stared at obsessively by the soldiers crowded into the other section of the coach, shoulder to shoulder with their packs and rifles. Annie had no idea what the tin box contained and opened it with some apprehension. Then recognised the writing in those thin sheets of letters and remembered her Gentleman Officer who'd four or five times taken her out during the months before last summer's battle. She remembered him on their first arranged meeting, in the cathedral at Amiens, looking at a group of soldiers in long greatcoats silhouetted in a shaft of sunlight down the nave, trying in his low voice to express to her the love he felt for the men under his command. She remembered him then taking her gloved hand to his lips.

Tucked away in one corner, she began to read, and was amazed. Of course she'd known his feelings for her. They were clear in his eyes and with every movement he made. But the open loving in his written words made her feel a guilt, a sharp regret - and an anger. She might have returned some of that warmth if he'd only had the courage to ask. Courage? Or folly. Or desperation. He'd written on one page (where she could read his writing) 'it would take more bravery for me to kiss you on the mouth than face another wall of bullets'. He'd described himself as trying always to be honourable and, of course, he loved his wife and children and looked upon another love as being a betrayal of everyone. Yet in the middle of war when a shell or bullet can finish you from one moment to the next, such considerations were at times irrelevant.

Annie had been deeply married herself and devastated by the death of her husband. But knew how soon afterwards in the midst of all this destruction and desolation, she might have welcomed someone else's arms around her.

The train was clanking to a halt, the shoulder-to-shoulder soldiers taking a last lingering look at soft feminine faces, then jumping from the carriage to form up and march away. An orderly walked along the carriage roofs to uncover the red cross markings; and Annie stowed away the tin box as the wire beds were folded down and the wounded carried on board. She remembered the young soldier's haunting face as she'd first seen him the night before, peering through the misted-up window of the restaurant.

Due to return to his unit that same evening, Harry had not hurried back to the barrack at the range, clear in his mind that he would miss his transport and invent some mishap to have his warrant endorsed by the benign instructor who seemed to look on Harry as his star pupil. But the instructor had also gone by the time he did get back, leaving only the glowing report for Harry to take back to his Company Commander. Not much of a safeguard if he was challenged by redcaps in the town.

Had Harry persuaded himself that those other things needed to be told to the girl for her peace of mind? Or did he, for his own sake, need to see her again?

Back at the railhead in the evening Annie looked around for the face of that young soldier in the crowd of medics and stretchers but he was not there.

She saw him instead an hour later from her bedroom window as she was washing. He was standing against the wall across the street as on the previous night.   She slipped downstairs, unlocking a forbidden door onto the street, the tin box in her hand.   "How did you find them?" she asked. "How did you find me?"

Harry seemed to have lost his voice, staring at her.

Her questions tumbled on: "Did you know him? Did he ask you to give them to me? Is he dead?"

"I don't know. The box was - well it was found. We don't know who he is. You were the only person we could think of finding."

She pressed the box into his hands.   "The letters are not mine. He never sent them."

"You mean I shouldn't have given them to you?"

"I don't know. I really don't know."

"I looked for you and brought them to you - because you knew him." A silence. Harry went on: "That's maybe all that's left of him. They shouldn't be thrown away."

"I only knew him for a few months."

"A lifetime for him, it sounds like." Harry corrected himself. "I mean I know I shouldn't have read them. I was looking for his name."

She touched his hand. "You were kind to find me."

"Perhaps it hurts you to see the letters."

"I didn't really know him. I liked him but I did not know him." She looked round as a bell sounded faintly somewhere in the building. "We have dinner." And as Harry stared at her eyes, hypnotized: "Last night," she said, "we were allowed out. One evening a week. In the company of officers."

Harry handed her back the tin box: "I brought them to you. I wouldn't know what to do with them now."

"Who are you?"

"Just a soldier."

Harry looked round at the sound of footsteps somewhere in the darkness. She looked round with him: "Did you come alone?" Harry nodded. "Are you allowed to be here?"

"No."

Annie drew him inside the door and closed it, the two of them having to stand very close to see anything in the pitch dark. She touched his face as though he were one of her wounded patients: "You are very young. And very tired. Tell me your name."

"Harry. Harry Cardwell. Lance-Corporal Harry Cardwell. You are Annie."

"Annabel Donovan"

"From America?"

She nodded.

"I never heard an American voice before. Is Donovan your husband's name?"

"He was a doctor. He was killed."

Harry nodded. "I'm sorry. I'm very sorry."

"We volunteered as a medical unit. Our ambulance was hit by a shell. I lived. He died."

"That's terrible. I mean to volunteer like that and come so far for someone's else's war. That's not fair."

"Nothing of this war is fair to anyone." She was looking at his eyes that hid nothing of what he was thinking or feeling - and with a sudden premonition thought how awful it would be to find him on one of their metal bunks, damaged in any way. She wanted to reach out a hand and touch wood and did so, reaching beyond him to the door. "Are you stationed in the town?"

"I have to return to my unit. I'm a day late already."

"Because of me?"

"I felt I had to see you. To explain."

"And now you'll be in trouble."

Harry looked beyond her at what seem in the darkness to be endless bundles of canvas sacks stacked against the wall. "Missus, this whole world is full of trouble much more worse than mine."

The bell deep inside the building rang again, Annie turning her head as she heard it: "I have to go."

Harry opened the tin box in her hand; extracted the photographs on top of the letters; slipped them into his battledress pocket. "Can I write to you?"

Annie took both his hands briefly; then pushed him out and locked the door.

END OF PART ONE

PART TWO

Chapter 8

Harry and Frank had been friends since they'd held hands together at the infant school in a tin hut down the valley, a three mile walk there and back for the little Harry, a two and a half mile walk for the even littler Frank. He'd always been tiny, so small that at 12 years old his father had once lost him in the snow, digging out sheep after a blizzard. With the wind blowing drifts over their footprints the father hadn't known where to begin a search and in the end they'd all been out looking, Harry's family summoned by Frank's older sister calling, shouting from the top of the hill. Harry could remember even at that age a sense of panic that Frank might die. As now on his return, crawling on hands and knees through the rows of Four Platoon's sleeping soldiers: Sergeant Banister winking at him, Nobby, Corporal Scotty, Reggie, but no Frank.

"Where is he?" he asked Reggie's wide open staring eyes.

"Blighty."

Harry stared back: "Wounded?!"

"He got a short leave." Reggie's gap teeth grinned: "Did y'e find her now?"

Harry crept under the gas cape next to him: "Go back to sleep!"

"I see it in your eyes, you horny bugger!" And under the cape Reggie blew two lines of 'Rose of Picardy' into his harmonica which didn't much help Harry's attempt at a silent and unchallenged return.

"How long's Frank been gone?" he whispered and pulled from a pocket one of the slabs of chocolate he'd brought back for them both.

"Day after you fucked off." The gap teeth grinned again: "Tell us about her!"

"Go to bloody sleep."

The Company was marching on, south towards 'Ocean Villas' and a 'quiet' sector on the northern edge of what 6 months ago had been the anvil of the Somme. The two day march through spring countryside lifted the men, the roadside banks full of scent and flowers, birds around them that had learned to sing again, as indeed had the Company itself, ringing the changes between *When this Blasted War is Over*, *The Old Barbed Wire* and *Far, far from Ypres*. Even Harry forgot the punishment hanging over him, though truth be told and Stevens told it often, punishment ran off Harry like water off a duck.

He'd caught up with the Company already on the march, slipping into that first night barn, as he thought, canny enough to avoid detection, the wink from Sergeant Banister suggesting his 24 hour delay in reporting back might be overlooked. Reggie had covered for his kit; Corporal Scotty hadn't even noticed. But oh no, it was 2nd Lieutenant Stevens on duty that night, and bugger me if he didn't breeze in to check the roll upon the midnight hour and ask for Harry's warrant.

"Day and a half late. You're on a charge, Lance-Jack. See if we can't lose you your dog's leg."

A charge he **would** be on, Harry reckoned, but unlikely to lose his stripe. Not yet.

He watched Steven's tight arse strut away and smiled to himself at his own panic over Frank. Frank was indestructible. Even in the snow. In the end it'd been Harry to remember Frank's scrawny thorn tree by the waterfall where he used to watch the dippers wade and mimic their 'zit-zit-zit' call or the 'clink-clink' of their warning. It was a good twenty paces off the track but he'd always make the detour whenever they were passing. And sure enough little Frank had fallen through the overhanging snow above the waterfall, down into the river. Well, more beck than river. Even at 12 years old Frank would never have drowned in it - though he might have died of cold.

"And why in bloody goodness didn't you shout?" the frightened and exasperated father had asked.

"Because I knew Harry'd find me."

First time a girl had kissed him that day: Frank's sister, full on his mouth, bending down from her great height. In contrast to her brother, Kate was even at that age ten foot tall and Harry her hero - for a day or two. Usually she and her parents blamed him for any of the scrapes he and Frank landed in.

They probably blamed him even now for having talked Frank into the war. Though neither of them had needed any talking. It was as easy as saying: "Well, we're going, aren't we," or, "shepherds be buggered;" and Harry couldn't remember which of them had been the first to say either. Next night and day they'd walked the thirty-five miles into Alnwick to sign on.

'K-Ones' they'd been, along with all the others in the original Battalion - Kitcheners first 100,000 volunteers, most of them now dead, the Border Rifles 'B' Company with maybe only forty left out of their original 250.

And the 'blasted Somme' was still the Somme - white mud around your boots like glue, battledress glowing in the dark with chalk and the German Howitzers still picking on selected areas of the enemy line. 'Quiet' their sector was meant to be, yet five men were posted as casualties before they were two days back in the line, three of them from Schoolboy's Platoon. Schoolboy wrote home: 'I lost my Runner'. It sounded less horrific than the real picture he might have described - the sound and smoke of a mortar in the next sap, the cry for 'stretcher-bearers', the pounding of Percival's angry face along the trench while Schoolboy remained frozen to the wall. Two down and one to go. For the impatient Percival sent Guy, the Platoon Runner, over the back wall to hurry up the stretcher-bearers and a German sniper picked him off from 600 yards away with a bullet in his lungs. He choked to death, the Schoolboy holding his hand for the ten minutes it took him to die. 'Quiet' it was not.

"You know our trouble, Corporal?" Ordish muttered somewhere near Harry's ear in the darkness: "Your bloody Lewis gun heroics. Division thinks we're a good fighting unit. So they stick us in anywhere they want to plug a gap. More than two miles of line we're covering. Jerry could send schoolgirls over and walk right through us." They were lying in a shell-hole 100 yards out in front of their line, the Germans another 400 yards ahead of them. "We're A.S. sodding P."

"Sir?"

"Advanced Suicide Post. Means everyone sleeps easy behind us because they'll hear us being killed. Bloody good mind to sleep myself." Which of course he wouldn't. Anyone who'd known him long enough knew Ordish had a strange affection and respect for no man's land. Something to do with the silence and the isolation. Harry guessed he'd volunteered for lookout patrol, coming to check the Lance-Jack wasn't asleep at his post. Harry'd had no choice. A week in the forward saps was the night duty imposed as part of his field punishment. Midnight to Reveille out in front; midday to Last Post turd-walloping on the sanitary fatigue.

Ordish muttered into another silence: "You're not going to bloody well tell me, are you."

"Sir?"

"Did you find our American Angel?"

"Yes sir."

"And?"

"I gave her the letters."

"And?"

"And - she held my hand - " Harry turned and winked at him: " - sir."

"Does she look like her pictures?"

"I'd say so."

"And talk like an American?"

"I'd never heard an American before."

"Does she remember her gentleman officer?"

"Yes sir."

"They were lovers?"

"No sir."

"And her husband?"

"Their ambulance was shelled."

A silence. "And?"

"And I'd like to write to her."

"That's more like it, Lance-Corporal."

"Not sure I'd write well enough for her to read."

"I've seen your letters home. You write well enough."

"I meant more the language, sir."

"Music and poetry, Harry?"

"Something to tell her what I feel."

Ordish looked at him in the darkness: "My soldier is smitten."

"Sir?"

"Shouldn't ever take notice of what I say." Ordish slid down to crawl away. "Don't go to sleep. I'll see you in the morning," came his whisper. "If Mr Stevens will allow."

Bugger Mr Stevens, thought Harry, eyes following the gliding flight of a barn owl almost at touching distance in front of him. Huge, slow-flapping wings. Even the wild hunter had learned to keep extra silent out here in no man's land.

It was afternoon a few days later before he saw Ordish again, leading a duckboard patrol of Officer and Sergeant trying to tie together the scattered sections along the front line, some scheme dreamed up by Prideaux - 'reciprocal contact' - that could insure regular ten minute visual acknowledgement up and down the two mile wide Company exposure. Officer and Sergeant, looking up at a high-flying shell, literally fell upon Harry at his latrine duties, the bucket of slops emptying itself over Ordish's trousers and Percival's boots. Any officer other than Ordish would have had him on another lengthy charge, as would Percival on his own. Instead, turd-walloping was postponed while Harry found clean water to wash the offended articles. And if I heat the water, thought Harry, I'll steal another few minutes away from these stinking latrines.

Ordish and Sergeant Percival returned from their patrol along the trench to find warm water AND soap AND a canteen of sweet tea. Even Percival had to laugh at Harry's ingenuity - and it usually took Charlie Chaplin to make Percival even smile.

"Dismissed, Sergeant," Ordish said to Percival when the trousers and boots were cleaned and the tea had been drunk. "Lance-Corporal Cardwell's going to show me where he takes this bloody mess."

Ordish even carried one of the shit-buckets himself, following Harry into an old and disused communication trench where the previous inhabitants had dug a new sump down into the side of the parapet. Being the Somme and not the Salient, the dirty liquid and solid bubbled briefly and slipped slowly away into some subterranean chalk gallery. Perhaps a future generation would one day find the soldiers' sewers and wonder at the life they had led. Or so thought Ordish. Harry simply tipped lime from another bucket over the hole and stood up to light a fag. He'd guessed Ordish wanted to talk.

"Write your letter and give it to me," Ordish said. "No one'll read it."
"Not even you, sir?"
"I'll run my eye down it for forbidden military information. That's all."
Like fuck, thought Harry. You'll run your eye down to see the language I'm using. "Perhaps YOU can write some words for me, sir."
"I can't do that, Harry. She wouldn't know who she was talking to. Be as bad as the gentleman-officer who never sent his real letters."
"I couldn't put things down like he did."
"Just write natural. Tell her whatever you want."
"Perhaps I shouldn't write at all."
"Why?"
"Different class of lady to where I come from, sir."
"Class be buggered!"
"Coming from America, she wouldn't hardly understand. I mean what I am. Where I fit in."
"Coming from America, I dare say she doesn't care."

Harry gave Ordish the letter that same evening. He'd been turning words over and over in his mind for days as though he was standing in front of her and talking to her face. But writing words always made them seem more dangerous - make one mistake and it'll be read over and over, examined like exercise books at school or the letters he used to write for his father to the market auctioneers and merchants.
It may not please you that I write this to you. I wish to apologise for the way I gave you the letters without asking if you wished to see them.........

Whatever it was, it was no poem, he thought, and doubtless Ordish would laugh. But the words roughly said what he wanted them to say. And she would do with it what she pleased.

Though later that night he kept trying to remember each syllable and regretting everything he'd written. It was his last night in the forward sap, his punishment tomorrow at an end. He'd almost miss these long dark nights in the middle of nowhere where a man was really alone, until a Sergeant or an officer came to check he was not sleeping. Tonight it was the Schoolboy, announcing his arrival as he failed to find the shallow sap and made a bollocks of crawling through the wire, jingle-jangle like a whole fucking Platoon out on patrol. And sure enough, within two minutes, the How's were on the rampage, shell after shell all around them, bracketing the middle part of no man's land, one of them flinging up a wall of mud to half cover Nyren on the edge of the crater. He fought his way out of the mess, arms and legs flailing as though he was drowning, trembling like a rabbit with a ferret at its throat. Harry reached a hand to him: "You hurt, sir?"

"I'm sorry. I wasn't expecting it." There was something in the voice close to breaking point and Harry slid lower in the hole, sitting up to take the boy in his arms and, with the pretence of looking for damage, hold him, head against his chest. Nyren clung to his shoulders: "Don't know what came over me."

Harry rubbed the back of his head, the boy's hair matted with that white mud: "We're all frightened, sir. It's nothing to feel strange about."

The young Lieutenant still clung to him and Harry let him cling. He could feel the boy's every muscle in spasm as another shell showered them again. "I don't mind the bullets, you know. It's just the noise of these damn things. You never know when they're coming."

"Wear a tin hat, sir, you'll feel better. Most officers do out here at night."

Harry slid back up to the horizon but kept an arm around the boy, and felt his body press against him. And when the shelling stopped Harry used his hankerchief to wipe some of the white slime off Nyren's face. The boy didn't take his eyes away from him. Truth be told,

Harry was wiping him just to keep the lad's face held in his hands and make sure he was calmed down. "You don't have to worry, you know. We all think you're a good officer, sir."

Ten minutes later as he prepared to return, the 'Schoolboy' whispered his reply: "I feel safe with you, Lance-Corporal. It's the strangest feeling. I know I haven't been out here long but I think you're the finest soldier I've ever known."

Chapter 9

The Virgin Mary had lost another brother, the third in two years: one at Ypres in 1915, one on the Somme last year, and now the youngest sibling buried four days ago in a dugout south of La Bassé. A telegram arrived in the morning before they marched to the train, though no one knew till lunchtime what it contained.

"I now have only two brothers left," she told Annie as they brewed a midday tea. Then showed her the telegram. Because of Annie's own experience in desperate loss, the battle-axe had never minded telling her anything though, as always, she kept her private grief well hidden.

```
Deeply regret death of Ronnie killed with two
fellow-officers    after    shellburst    on    dugout
stop My greatest sympathy Captain Raynor
```

Virgin Mary wondered how long the War Office telegram would take to reach her parents. Should she try to warn them first? Maybe telegraph the neighbours? Annie told her not to. In terms of how the news was broken the element of chance was much the same and there is never a good time to hear that another of your children has been killed. Annie stood at the door of the train commander's hutch holding it shut while Virgin Mary knelt inside to pray.

That same afternoon, in a freak spring blizzard, they evacuated a whole trainload of Canadians ferried down to them on ambulances from their 'victory' on Vimy Ridge. But the push around Arras, cheerfully promised by these casualties, ended up in seven long days of desperate trainloads, once more the wounded and the dying victims of the usual reluctance to acknowledge another stalemate until yet another ten or fifteen thousand casualties were chalked up on the blackboards.   Annie and her companions worked almost without sleep that week, shuttling to and fro night and day from clearing stations to base hospitals, knowing that many of the badly wounded were being carried straight onto the ferries with minimal medical attention. At least she knew her young English soldier was nowhere near Arras.

She'd found herself sifting through the post each morning and evening, something she had never ever done. Her mail was regular and predictable: one letter every two weeks or so from her family in Boston - a sheet from her mother, half a sheet from her father, the other half sheet from her brother; once a month family friends in Ireland sending parcels of food and, like her mother, entreating her to go back home; maybe the occasional note from a Staff Officer who'd taken her out. And of course, until two months ago, a letter every ten days from the Gentleman-Officer who'd also written the other letters she'd now been given by that young soldier whose eyes she still could see watching her in the darkness.

There wasn't a single day she didn't recall his face and his voice - usually when the stretchers were carried on board and she'd have to walk the whole train (with Virgin Mary or a surgeon if there was one on board) to assess each wounded soldier. Perhaps that was the reason for her preoccupation, a fear that if something happened to him, she'd have no way of ever knowing. For who would tell her?

She'd even sketched his face, several times before it satisfied her memory. Why? Perhaps there was something about him that reminded Annie of her husband, the sunken cheeks, the eyes that watched everything and missed nothing and that always spoke his thoughts and feelings.

Viv found the drawings one evening, without too much surprise. Annie was always sketching - trees and river banks whenever the train stopped, the faces or limbs of wounded men she remembered, buildings in the town, the debris in the rail yards.

But then Viv recognised the soldier: "The face in the window while we were eating? The soldier in the street?" So Annie had to tell her - that was how she and Viv shared together: nothing volunteered, but if a direct question was asked, they kept no secrets from one another. Viv didn't know the soldier had returned the evening after to stand again in the street outside - or that Annie had gone down to talk with him.

"How did he speak?"

"I have no idea. His voice was clear, his words like a sing-song."

Annie knew what Viv really meant: was it an educated voice; was it a correct voice? The English seemed inordinately concerned about such things, as though the future of their entire world depended upon good syntax.

Did Annie expect her soldier to write? He'd asked if he may and she'd said neither yes nor no. He seemed to be a man who'd never say anything he did not intend to do. But she wondered if he'd taken note of her unit number (written on the main door of the school building and in the rail yard - had he seen it?); she wondered if he even remembered her name.

And then one morning there it was, an envelope with her name and unit and his name and unit, written in a clear and simple hand, the letter inside short and direct:

It may not please you that I write this to you. I wish to apologise for the way I gave you the letters without asking if you wished to see them.

I did not believe the photographs. I did not believe that anyone could be so beautiful. Now having seen you I do believe and that is why I had to keep them. Perhaps I should hide that feeling. I shall hide all my others. You were very kind to come down into the street and meet me again that evening.

We are in the line not far from you. At night I'm out in front and alone and think often of the building where you sleep.

Everything was said in those few lines and nothing was said. Just like the gentleman-officer in the letters he **had** sent; and, yes, just like her own Patrick. Why do men feel so much more vulnerable? As in the act of love they are also more vulnerable, if they are really men and not just animals.

She replied that same day, trying to make both her writing and her words as clear as his and even more direct:

It pleases me that you write and give me the chance to address this to you – not from the building where I sleep but on board the train as we travel to the clearing stations to collect more of your unfortunate companions. I must tell you it would be very painful for me to ever hear that you had been hurt or wounded in any way – and I beg you to take care of yourself.

I seemed to know you from the first moment I saw you – you were looking through the window of the restaurant where I was eating with those dreadful officers. I should not say that about them, should I? But then I'm sure they are not in danger and will not die. I think you remind me of my husband (again I should not say that). Your eyes and your expressions are so much the same. Yes, it does please me that you have written and give me the chance to say these things to you. But it does not please me that you hide your feelings. We are two strangers who meet in hell. We know nothing about each other; we come from different worlds and have no mutual friends – except the dead Captain and his letters. Why should we hide anything from one another? I want to know who you are. I want you to know who I am.

I came from Boston in New England with my husband as volunteers in a Harvard Medical Unit and since his death have found it impossible to return – as though I would be deserting him. I do not even know if I wish to go home. It would feel so unreal. Perhaps I need to find out why this war is being fought and why he had to die. Which might seem to you a little selfish since so many others have also died and continue to do so. It amazes all of us how even in a 'quiet' time our train still seems to fill each day with the wounded, many of them, even at the cost of terrible wounds, only too relieved to be out of it all, at least for a while. Having experienced it once myself, I cannot imagine what it must be like to live each day with fear. I remember each particular of the moment when our ambulance was shelled at Loos - every shock and sensation and sound and smell - the smell in particular of my husband's burning flesh. Which I have never told to anyone. My husband's name was Patrick and he was quiet like you.

Were you ever wounded? Do your calm eyes ever show fear? Does that low voice ever cry aloud?

Chapter 10

Stevens picked the nurse's letter out instinctively like a dirty belt or buckle on a parade-ground, the Red Cross frank on the nurse's envelope held between his fingers with an expression of outrage and distaste. The adulteress had been found, no doubt the box of letters returned to her, and she was now writing to a common soldier? It took the physical intervention of Uncle to prevent Stevens from tearing open the envelope and reading the contents. The letter in question spilled under the table, Stevens reminded there was as yet no censorship of incoming mail.

Schoolboy watched Steven's rage in disbelief. It had seemed to arrive from nowhere and without reason, directed at the one soldier in the Company whom Schoolboy most admired. What business could it be of the 2nd Lieutenant to question who was writing to a Lance-Corporal in someone else's Platoon. Schoolboy rescued the letter from the floor, wiping it clean and restoring it to the 4 Platoon pouch while Uncle fended off Steven's verbals.

"How can we be expected to maintain discipline and sense of purpose if the whims of one soldier are to be so abjectly indulged? Clearly he has searched out this woman - not only an adulteress but a lady neither of his class or language."

"God help you if Ordish comes in and hears this tosh," said Uncle.

"He's another who should know better. Encouraging all this informality. All of you. You should thank your stars you're not in a more traditional regiment where such matters would be better taken care of."

"You should thank YOUR lucky stars," said Uncle, "that the men in your Platoon can't hear this nonsense and laugh you all the way forward to Berlin or backwards to Paris, wherever it is we end up going."

Schoolboy, mouth opened, tried unsuccessfully to decide how he should intervene. Bunny, more circumspect, let Uncle take the flak. At least Uncle was still more or less smiling and Bunny knew nothing of the history of these letters. Besides, ganging up two or three to one in the dugout was always best avoided. Quarrels escalated in such confined quarters and Captain Prideaux had already opened one warning eye from his bunk. Bunny bundled the 4 Platoon pouch into his batman's hands down the kitchen passage, a nod to signify immediate distribution. The batmen had their own service exit back up into the trench. The letter would be long gone before Stevens had calmed down enough to look for it again.

'Dippy' was Bunny's batman, short and wire-thin as all batmen needed to be in the cramped quarters of their work and sleep. Delivering the mail was an afternoon out in the fresh air; a walk in the sun; a nodding re-acquaintance with faces otherwise forgotten along the Company line. And handing out letters always made you popular. In combat Dippy was a Lewis gun reserve and knew Harry and his mates from long ago, another veteran of that terrible withdrawal from White City.

Harry was asleep when he found them, Frank and Reggie round a brew-up, a mug of sweetened tea Dippy's reward for playing postman. "We're on our way out in two days' time," he told them. "Into reserve down near Suzanne. Have a bath, Get some sleep. Make a change."

Frank laughed: "With your cushy job, you wouldn't know the difference."

They all turned round as Harry rolled off the ledge and out of his cape to join them. "Dippy's a shipyard man," he said. "Reserved occupation. He needn't even be out here."

Reggie pocketed his mouth-organ. "None of us need be if we hadn't been bloody fools. I was down the mines. Could have stayed there forever."

"They're looking for miners up north again. For the tunnelling. You and Scrace should volunteer."

"Not me, pal. There's underground and under the ground. I only go digging where the rock is good and hard."

Harry flicked through the envelopes in Dippy's pouch: "Letter from your missus, Reggie. She can't hardly keep her hands off you!"

Harry had already seen the Red Cross frank on the nurse's envelope, his voice threatening to dry in his throat. Everyone now was crowding round, all of Sections 2 and 3, as though Dippy's box of letters smelt of bacon butties. Everyone in the Company would soon enough know that 'American Annie' had written back to the Lance-Jack.

Harry secreted the letter, unopened in his tunic next to two field dressings and their safety-pins. He didn't yet feel ready to read her words, knowing every man's eyes would be watching him, his every reaction scrutinized. Even Frank was smiling at him in a peculiar way, with an envy and curiosity that friendship could not hide. Harry rolled himself back into his cape and closed his eyes. He was on duty that night and could well pretend to sleep.

Ordish heard about the letter from Uncle that same evening, both of them on duckboard patrol after stand-to, half a mile out and back to the south-east, another half mile out and back to the north-west, covering the extremities of the Company line on this their second six day tour. They'd twice swapped front and reserve with the London Scottish who'd been equally appalled at the vulnerability of their long thin line. Prideaux and their Captain had composed a joint communication to Division requesting a third Company to split line and reserve - only to be informed they should increase night activity if they were afraid of attack. Trench raids would confirm the low calibre of the troops they were facing. But London Scottish and the Borders agreed among themselves that trench raids would only encourage retaliation. Better for each Platoon to push a fortified listening position out in front of the line, the advanced suicide posts as Ordish had christened them. And thus also the evening perambulation, the swapping-over duty officers taking the names of whichever soldiers were to spend their night in no man's land.

"The American nurse has written back to Harry," Uncle volunteered halfway through their walk as though it were their own shared secret. Ordish turned in surprise: "So soon?"

"What did we say were the odds?" And when Ordish didn't respond: "A drink next time we're out of the line?"

Ordish wondered what she might have written, what she had said and whether Harry would ever tell him - or if he'd ever dare to ask. It was certainly a more interesting prospect than the slow ticking clock of a letter he'd received from his mother. As always she spoke of his younger brother, dead at Gallipoli. For her the Western Front barely existed; hardly counted as the war.

Uncle was still on about Harry's letter: "Stevens damn near took my head off when I told him to leave it alone."

"What did he want to do?"

"I don't know. Confiscate it; burn it; read it? Schoolboy and Bunny were on my side, I'm sure of that." They'd stopped on the north-west edge of their tenure, Ordish nodding round the corner at the Norfolks in the next sap. Uncle was lighting his infernal pipe, accumulating enough used matches to make a bonfire. Ordish watched him in irritation. Why should everyone else have taken possession of this *amour* between his soldier and the nurse? Uncle knew next to nothing about it beyond the little Ordish had told him. Only Ordish had read those original letters and seen all the photographs. In a sense Harry had brought them to him. Now the whole damn Company dugout was joining in. Don't they have anything better to occupy their minds?

"Did you ever find out," Ordish asked, "if Raven had anyone back home you could write to?" He was malicious to ask the question. It would plunge Uncle back into darkest introspection and Ordish knew full well that both he and Prideaux had written to a sister and a father. Benson, hunched on the firestep inside his cape, heard him ask the question and was watching them both, officers still to him a race apart. Shifted now to plug the gaps in 2 Platoon, he'd come up against the bullying Percival who always liked to knock new boys around until they were sufficiently 'disciplined'. Benson had been five days on fatigues, wishing he'd volunteered for the artillery when given the chance back home. Ordish nodded at him, remembering him from the estaminet by the railhead. His nod made Benson feel a little better.

"Good night, Sergeant," Uncle muttered at Percival, whose close critical eyes observed him coldly head to toe in the half-light. To Percival, Uncle was the very epitome of a 'temporary officer', the ultimate amateur gentleman, good-natured, bumbling, potentially lethal.

Uncle and Ordish walked back in silence, past the Company dugout and into the opposite sector. It was another twenty minutes and full darkness before they came to 4 Platoon on the south-east anchor, Harry Cardwell and his pals on the very end. Lance-Corporal Harry watched them arrive and said nothing. He hadn't yet opened the envelope. And Ordish didn't feel it right to ask.

Back in the dugout, still in silence, Ordish poured a tin cup full of whisky and opened a book to avoid anyone else's conversation. Someone thankfully had sent Stevens on the evening ration party; Schoolboy was next on watch and resting; Bunny, last night's duty officer, was already fast asleep; and Prideaux conspicuously reading and not engaging. The evening died in silence, Uncle writing home.

*

It pleases me that you write and give me the chance to address this to you - Harry read Annie's letter under his cape by the light of a candle twenty minutes before he was due out into the 'ASP' position with Frank, their Lewis gun now a fixture out in no man's land, part of Prideaux's early warning system.

We are two strangers who meet in hell. Why should we hide anything from one another? I want to know who you are. I want you to know who I am. How many times would he read those words and all the others over the next few days, looking, hunting for any emotion he might have missed? *My husband's name was Patrick and he was quiet like you?* *Were you ever wounded? Do your calm eyes ever show fear? Does that low voice ever cry aloud?* He couldn't even believe what she was saying so straight and open. Like the way she'd looked at him in the darkness that evening inside the door off the street. The way Peggy had looked at him once on a crowded afternoon, as though they already both were naked and alone.

Shall I call you Harry, and will you call me Annie? Is there someone at home who waits for you? I really do want to know everything about you whether it is good or bad.

I send you every best wish and the touch of my hands

What on earth could he say to her in return? What would she wish to read; what might she expect? He didn't want to frighten her into silence. Yet did not want her to doubt that he cared. The absolute truth would sound too serious or morbid - that only the violent death of a friend had come anywhere near the extreme of emotion she made him feel. Perhaps birth itself if he could remember it: that strained bursting out into the light he remembered from his brother's arrival on the kitchen floor (the bedrooms had been too cold, a drift of snow all down the valley and the midwife nowhere near them; his brother's birth had been registered three weeks later, by which time no one could recall whether he'd appeared before or after midnight, his birthday always celebrated on both the days). Maybe he'd tell her that story one day - though how could she possibly imagine the life they'd lived, the life they still lived, so far from other people. He imagined her childhood in the crowded streets of a crowded city, full of electric light, conversation and laughter.

Out in the ASP Frank had taken first kip, but it was far too dark to read again. Harry let her words envelop him. He already knew them in his head as clearly as the Lord's Prayer and knew also he'd be able to repeat each and every one of them on his deathbed - if bed it ever was allowed to be and not the cold mud he now lay on, his breath like cigarette smoke out over the even colder barrel of the gun. For the first time since he and Frank had walked together down the valley to sign on, he really did not want to die. And that made him feel the sudden chill of fear.

The arrival of the duty officer, the Schoolboy, this time silent in his approach, had Harry spinning round, safety catch off his rifle and finger on the trigger.

The Schoolboy grinned and whispered: "Caught **you** this time!"

"Sir."

"Getting better at moving around, aren't I?"

"Very good, sir."

Schoolboy moved up next to him on the lip of the sap, pulling something from his pocket and handing it to Harry: "Came from home this morning."

A bar of chocolate. The Schoolboy grinned: "Will you teach me the Lewis gun one day, Corporal?"

Had Schoolboy been out to the other ASP's or had he deliberately chosen Harry? Making up for losing his nerve last time they'd been out together? Their ASP had been modified with that night's shell damage, white stone and mud pushed up into a parapet. Schoolboy seemed to have taken a good grip in the intervening ten days. "I like being on watch," he said. "I like being alone. It concentrates the mind."

It certainly concentrated Harry's mind once the young Lieutenant had returned to the trench. On a moonless night out here you could only listen; and when the wind blew even hearing was impossible. And who knows, one of Jerry's high-flying planes might have spotted the Lewis gun during the day, a patrol sent out now to bomb and bayonet them out. Harry forced his eyes beyond the darkness from left to right in front and behind until anxiety forced him to shake Frank awake and share the watch, Frank surprised at his sudden funk.

"Think they're coming over tonight?" he whispered.

"We'd know bugger all about if they did. Not until too late." Harry could imagine the figures looming at them from a yard or two, thrusting down with their bayonets, he or Frank managing one long squeeze of the Lewis trigger to warn the others before the steel or bullet did for them.

They both of them stayed awake now into the dawn and listened when the wind died down to a newly arrived nightingale wandering from bush to bush somewhere in front of the German line. Frank hadn't known nightingales at home and spent the rest of the watch trying to imitate that waterfall of sound.

Thinking what to write, Harry didn't sleep all next day, fiddling with routine things, his shirt off with Frank and Reggie when the sun was shining, holding lit candles to the seams to fry the lice, warming water over those same candles for their shaving, looking up at Bunny when he passed thinking the officer's trousers might be Ordish. Yes, he did need to know his words would not be read out loud round the Company dugout. So he had to find his melancholy friend in something of a hurry, for the words he wanted to use were already burning through his head. He wanted them sped on their way, into her hand one late evening as she clambered tired from her train.

Harry wrote the letter after stand-to that evening and kept it in his pocket until Sergeant Banister sent him with a kit inspection report to the Company dugout. Where sure enough Ordish eventually followed him back out into the twilight. Harry didn't know what he was going to tell him; he could hardly ask the favour yet say nothing about her letter.

"What did she tell you?" asked the officer.

"Better read it yourself, sir, if you'll let mine go through." And Harry passed Ordish both the letters, unaware of Stevens' poke-nose through the sack curtain of the dugout watching them.

Ordish handed her letter back to Harry. "No need for that, Lance-Corporal. Wouldn't be my business, would it."

"If you're involved, sir, you're involved. You read it then you'll know what mine is all about."

"You're drawing me into conspiracy, Harry."

"I wouldn't know what that was, sir." He pushed Annie's letter into Ordish's pocket. Ordish, still holding Harry's letter, sealed it into the envelope without even a glance and, returning into the dugout still observed by Stevens, dropped it in the mail pouch.

Later that night, with the oil lamp burned out and everyone asleep,

Stevens used a match to find Harry's envelope in the mail pouch on the dugout table. The match burned out as Stevens heard Ordish stir on his wire-netting bunk. In the now total darkness Stevens found what he believed to be his own jacket hanging on the hook, undid the buttoned pocket and slipped the envelope inside. The letter was uncensored; he would read it himself next day and, if necessary, destroy it.

'We are two strangers who meet in hell' you write. 'Why should we hide anything from one another?' If I am to believe you then your words make me more free than I have ever been with anyone. A girl called Peggy taught me how to love and yet I never felt for her even a tenth part of what I feel for you. I told her that I loved her - I did love her - so what do I tell you? What is love multiplied by ten? You make me dream of things that make me for the first time frightened of this war.

I give myself to you in every way you might wish and keep inside me your face, your heart, your soul, your mind and your body.

Nothing in my life has ever been so clear nor will ever be again.

Harry imagined his words along every mile of their intended journey, carried in the mail pouch by the ration party in the morning, transported by horse and cart to Division, by motor-lorry to Base; then back to Pérignon in the nurse's unit sack. Two days? Maybe three? Mail was usually given priority. Even that winter in the month-long snow and ice when rations never came, letters and packets had always arrived, a parcel of food from home often the only half-decent supplies they managed to get their hands on.

'B' Company was packing once again, 'full kit', for a move in two days' time. All the extra gear off-loaded not even a month ago, squirreled away into disused saps, was distributed once more between the various disciplines of men - the bombers with their grenades, the snipers with their doctored ammunition, the Stokes mortar with their colour-coded shells, the Lewis guns with their spares and endless heavy cartridge pans, the batmen with their secret supplies of tinned food, Company HQ with its kitbags full of pro forma, the riflemen with their reinforced trenching tools, the spare fuel, the spare dixies, the whisky and the rum - anything they didn't want to leave to the next inhabitants, anything they might need in a new home not so well prepared. Reserve down near Suzanne, Dippy had said though no one quite believed they'd be going back to rest.

Stevens had no chance to read that letter until the afternoon, sitting on a latrine behind his 2 Platoon, a comfortable half-mile away from Ordish. But when he put his hand into his buttoned pocket, there was nothing there. What had the pocket felt like in the dark last night? Stevens, scared that Ordish might open his eyes, had just pushed the letter in and buttoned it shut again. What could it mean? That Ordish had seen him, replaced the envelope in the mail pouch, and yet said nothing? Stevens could hardly challenge him for stealing back the letter. Would Ordish plot revenge?

An hour later he scrutinised him in the dugout - but Ordish was as quiet and undemonstrative as he always was, deep away into his dreams without a second glance for Stevens.

Ordish had another letter on his mind, read like Stevens' unread letter, squatting on his Platoon thunder-bucket, the words now chasing through his mind. Just as well he liked Harry Cardwell and resisted envy. Most men would have bargained limbs for the words the American nurse had written to him. And he knew he should not have read them, however firmly Harry had plunged the letter into his pocket. How would he reply to such an open declaration? It was as though she'd said, 'Here am I. Come into my life'. How had Harry replied? What on earth could he have said? And how on earth would he ever meet her again?

Ordish had only experienced a more distant perception of courtship, untouchable girls at tea parties when he'd been at the Grammar School, a fiancée on a pedestal when he'd finished university, desired yes, but above all respected and expressing her own feelings in coded language. He'd had a lover but on a very different level, a shop-girl who'd once smiled back at his smile and agreed to meet him after church one Sunday morning. She'd taught him what there was to learn about desire on bicycle rides into the country but he thought, he hoped, she'd known as he had known that he would never marry her. Maybe she had also turned to nursing. Perhaps, if he survived the war, he **would** go back and marry her.

Not unreasonably his fiancée had abandoned him for a 'sounder man'.

Ordish on duckboard patrol that evening returned the letter to Harry but found himself unable to say a single word to him even with the younger man's eyes seeming to ask so many questions. How they looked at him, probed him, entered him. And how, Ordish imagined, they must have looked at the American girl - to read her very soul, to trigger her heart.

Chapter 11

The train was thankfully back to a single run each day, most nights back sleeping in their quarters and the Virgin Mary allowing them two evenings out this week in the company of men. Annie had noticed how she softened each time a brother died, as though what little ordinary life was left inside this war should be allowed to breathe. There were three available invitations, each of which Annie rejected. Was it the catastrophe of April that made her unwilling to join staff-officers at a dinner table - the memory of all those wounded men from Arras? Or did her young boy soldier watch her with his eyes and take away the charm of other men?

Instead Annie asked, insisted in the end, that Virgin Mary dine with her on the birthday money she'd received from home. The old battleaxe was quite astonished and naturally reluctant, fearing pity and a sacrifice on Annie's part. So Annie told her: "I shared my birthday with my husband, just one day apart. We'll drink a bottle of good wine in memory of him and of your brothers."

And out they went arm in arm together, astonishing everyone: the other nurses dressing for their 'escorts'; the 'escorts' gathering outside; above all the waiters and clientele in the restaurant who'd clearly never seen two women come alone through their velvet-draped door to order a bottle of vintage Taittinger and a Gevry Chambertin. How the two women smiled at one another at such a raising of eyebrows and ill-concealed stares.

"The second paradise of women on earth?" Annie ventured in a stage-whisper.

Virgin Mary laughed hugely from deep inside her considerable body, all male stares sliding hastily away as she declared out loud. "At least after this war they'll no longer be able to deny us the vote."

But for both women it was the past that needed to be exorcised that evening: Annie's husband and Mary's brothers, parents, childhoods and upbringings; Mary from a well-heeled Manchester suburb, Annie from well-heeled Boston. Even so, within the rigid demarcations of English social layers, Virgin Mary firmly decided they could in no way be considered equals: Annie's father the owner of a store (trade); Mary the daughter of a doctor (profession). Which careful distinctions provoked disbelief from Annie and another bellow of laughter from Mary. "Don't worry," she said. "My father is a socialist and has nothing to do with caste. I believe within himself he is also a pacifist. Which must make it even harder to accept the manner of the dying of his sons."

"Your brother was very young," said Annie.

"They were certainly too young to die, every one of them."

Her brothers had been accountants and solicitors, grey, dreary and safe in their jobs, all too ready to answer the call to arms the very first day of war. Only the good sense of their father had prevented them all enlisting together in one of the local battalions, using his not inconsiderable influence to make sure each and every one was destined to a separate regiment - Cheshire's, Lancs, Artists, Queen Victoria's and the Welsh. Not that separation had stopped them dying. But at least they hadn't had to witness one another's deaths.

As Annie had witnessed, participated in her own husband's death. "We never thought we'd be in danger," she said when asked by Mary. "Uncomfortable yes, but not within the reach of guns."

"And yet within the reach of guns and bombs you've stayed."

"By choice. Though the odds are really very long."

"You and I came together because our train had been shelled. Our train and your ambulance. Nothing's ever quite safe if you're as close to the line as we sometimes go."

Annie smiled: "Do you remember how they fussed about putting all our different uniforms together?!"

"I think if we pushed the lines of discipline and command we'd still find we're the only autonomous unit on the Western Front."

"You send your reports somewhere."

"To base. And from base we receive our rations, our medical supplies, our movement orders. But if we chose to disobey, I'm sure no one would know by whom we should be punished."

Annie watched her: "You're very good with the girls - us girls, I should say. Some of them are still so very young."

"In their heads they'll be old as their grandmothers by the time they go home."

It was as the waiter served their main course that Mary asked a question she'd been wondering for days: "Will you be wanting to leave us now that America is in the war?"

"It hadn't even crossed my mind," Annie replied. "I have no desire to transfer to a unit new to what we've been living through for these two damned years. I believe their innocence would drive me mad." It really had not crossed her mind. She was surprised the Virgin Mary had brought it up.

"I'm sure you could find placement as a Matron. I'd be happy to write a reference to that effect."

Annie shook her head: "Until this war ends - **if** it ever ends - I am at home where I am."

"You don't miss your real home? You don't feel cut off, being so far away?"

"From my family, yes. And one or two friends. But then if I met them now it would be difficult to communicate. They wouldn't understand where I had been."

"I always thought in India, I'm three weeks away from everyone. Even writing a letter. So a reply to anything is nearly two months away. By which time you'd forgotten what you asked anyway."

"Unless you send a telegram."

"How long do your letters take?"

"Depends what boats are leaving. Ten days or two weeks."

"I wouldn't like to lose you," said Mary after a silence. "You learned from your husband and in some ways you're as good as any surgeon." She smiled: "Though of course I would not tell them." And a mouthful later: "It's important on the train to have someone who's not afraid to use the knife. You've saved a lot of lives."

Annie looked away: "And lost as many."

Mary touched her hand across the table. "Even without your knife, I think your manner and your smile bring many men back from the edge."

"All of us, not just me."

They both became aware of Viv across the room with her trill of laughter, one of three nurses at a table of Staff-officers, Mary watching her now in the mirror.

"Can she look after herself with those men? You're usually with her."

"She knows how far to go without inviting trouble."

"Do you?"

"I'm not sure I want to anymore."

"Know how far to go - or how to avoid trouble?" And without waiting for a response Mary with a smile went on: "When I was engaged I was always looking for 'trouble'! Unfortunately he was far too serious. Or maybe otherwise involved." And at Annie's expression of dumb surprise: "He was in India. We were both in India. Both at the same hospital. He had some trouble with a younger man and they sent him home. He disappeared from the ship before they reached Suez."

"I'm sorry."

"For what? I don't think we were cut out for one another at all."

"And you never knew what happened to him?"

"I expect he's living with Arab boys somewhere in North Africa. Isn't that what they do?" Mary looked up at Annie. "I don't blame him in any way. They get sent to those awful schools at the age of seven and end up like Catholic priests, understanding nothing of how the world goes round." She laughed her huge laugh again. "Now I've shocked you."

"Oh, I'm no Catholic. No nothing really."

"I understood religion in India. All of them. They seemed more relevant."

"You stayed on there?"

"Until the outbreak of war."

"And your brothers - did they go to those awful schools?"

Mary shook her head: "My mother's Irish. She wouldn't have any of us sent away from home."

"So you **are** Catholic?"

"Not that you'd notice." Mary looked up: "And your parents?"

"Irish," Annie replied. "A long time ago." She watched the waiter clear their plates. "Talking with you is very easy."

"Out of school, you mean."

Annie smiled: "You frighten us all at times."

"Only when things need to be done."

"You're very strong."

"All of us are strong if we chose to be."

But she wasn't strong an hour later, Mary for the first time crying softly for her dead brothers when she was alone that night.

Viv was not yet back and Annie with the room and her bed to herself. She hoped Viv's escort might have reawakened the younger girl's emotions. Annie herself couldn't hope to fill the gap of that dead fiancé.

As for her own soldier, she now knew she ached to read his words - to discover where her own provocation might have pushed him. His eyes that night seemed to find her whole body in the darkness.

But his words did not arrive. For two entire weeks she thought that she had frightened him away and the more she believed she had, the more often his face came through the darkness at night to visit her.

Chapter 12

Harry had been anticipating her reply for ten days. Maybe even twelve. Did he think of her 1440 times as the Gentleman-Officer had confessed in his letter, once for every minute of both day and night? I never asked her his name, Harry thought. And nor did Ordish ask me if I'd asked. The next letter I write, if there is another letter, I shall ask her - even if the Gentleman-Officer would surely not approve of this common soldier, common man, involving his emotions with someone so 'exceptional', so 'aristocratic'. But Harry now knew exactly how that Officer had felt. 'I need you more than wine or water', he had written. "More than the blood that pumps to my head and hands and feet", Harry might have added. He didn't even dare to look at her hidden photographs in case her smile had changed; didn't dare to re-read her words for fear he'd misinterpreted them. What if the words in his letter were now causing shock or even merriment? Perhaps, mocking, she will have shared his letter with her friends. Perhaps her own letter had been a joke, and now his reply read out loud to disbelieving laughter. His words had been so ill-considered, written down as they occurred to him, unexamined. Given the chance, would he have rewritten them?
It was just as well he didn't know the letter was still there with them in the trench. No one knew, not even 2nd Lieutenant Stevens. The night Stevens had taken the letter from the mail pouch, his coat had been hanging next to Uncle's on the hook. It was into Uncle's pocket the letter had been pushed, and inside Uncle's buttoned pocket the letter still remained, undiscovered, unsuspected. Stevens convinced himself that Ordish had 're-stolen' the envelope and restored it to the mail pouch - though he couldn't for the life of him understand why Ordish had kept silent. As for Uncle, he was never one to know what

was or was not inside his pockets, apart from his pipe, his tobacco and his matches. The letter seemed destined to stay where it was for the duration of the war.

The movement order had been postponed, the Royal Border Rifles to remain in occupation of their extended line, this time in partnership with the Highland Light ('a dirty lot' Sergeant-Major Trussal claimed, though no one else found any evidence of his calumny). The listening posts (Ordish's ASP's) had been strengthened, three men and a Lewis gun in front of each Platoon night and day, an Officer and two Sergeants on duty at any one time down the line. They were raided twice that week, the ASP's on both occasions failing to give early warning. A flurry of grenades was all they heard, quick shooting in the darkness, and each time one unfortunate soldier dragged away as a prisoner (one of them the more silent of the three newcomers who'd arrived with Schoolboy and Harry all those weeks ago). The snatching of men by night unsettled everyone as did the uncertainty of what those prisoners might reveal under interrogation. The raiding parties themselves must have realized how thinly the line was held, three men at most to each traverse. The grenades and shooting had wounded five more, a total now of ten casualties in their short time on this 'quiet' sector, three of them Lewis gunners. Company Commander and Sergeant-Major evened up the numbers as best they could, the Cheviot trio divided under protest as Frank was drafted into 2 Platoon to 'fill-up' on their gun, Benson swapped with him to learn his Lewis drill from Harry and Reggie.
Spring seemed far away again, the wandering nightingale no longer heard, a damp chill mizzle restricting their field of vision and increasing misery. The tot of rum was marginally increased as a medicinal precaution, the daily foot-parade enforced, each man required to strip boots and socks in front of their officer and rub in the whale oil Colledge had prescribed.

Benson thought the Lance-Jack and Reggie might have shunned him as Frank's unwanted replacement; and perhaps for a couple of days there was a coolness from them both. But one morning Benson started singing what he called 'Geordie Hinny' set to something like the Blaydon Races and had Reggie blowing into his harmonica all one day long trying to find the tune, till the Germans themselves were shouting out, begging him to stop.   That day Benson became their marra' and began for the first time to understand what kept men sane in this cold, wet hell. Your pals looked after you: they knew what you needed night and morning; knew when you wanted to laugh or when you needed quiet; knew how you took your tea; how much beer or wine you could drink before falling down, how short your fuse and when to extinguish it.

Benson entered the hierarchy of Three Section 4 Platoon and became number six of the Lewis gun five: Harry, Reggie, Nobby plus the absent Frank and Bunny's usually absent batman, Dippy. And even Dippy had to do his stint in the ASP's whenever Bunny was on watch, two daylights with Harry and Benson, one night with Reggie and Nobby when the Germans had to listen to their chatter and laughter from dusk till dawn, undeterred by machine gun, uninterrupted even by a half hour 'hate' of minenwerfer.

Nobby and Dippy were friends from long ago, from the day they'd first joined up, both of them 'prowlers' given to exploring beyond their territory, scroungers-in-chief, often enough for the whole Platoon whenever, behind the lines, they could get their hands on a pig, a sheep or a bullock. Nobby was an apprentice butcher's boy from Alnwick whose parents were in service at the castle. On his two leaves home he'd been allowed back into the Percy mansion and given one of the attic rooms in which to sleep - and both times came back with a kit-bag full of warm clothes and blankets (in addition to a side of sheep). Yes, Nobby and Dippy had always been the foragers, Dippy bagged by Bunny for the officers' dugout (what a pair **they** made scrounging behind the lines!), Nobby making himself too obnoxious to be poached and remaining provider for Harry's enlarged Lewis gun team.

The rest of Section 3 was Corporal Scottie with the other riflemen, solid, unafraid and now very unimpressed with the conduct of the war. They made up what was virtually Section 4-attached. All of them, except now Benson, had been there from the very beginning.

Even at White City they'd survived, most of them wounded but alive. No wonder the whole bloody Battalion resented them.

And as a result Frank was having a less than congenial time in 2 Platoon. By nature shy, he wasn't going to impose himself as a master of Lewis gun technique and Sergeant Percival had always considered 4 Platoon's Lewis gun an over-rated team and suspected Harry's pals of currying favour. So Frank was shouted from pillar to post, stuck out in the ASP six hours at a time giving instruction on the gun and thus attracting the constant attention of German guns and trench mortars. Luckily 2 Platoon's ASP was well down in a dip and Jerry couldn't sight the minenwerfer with any accuracy. Only two of them landed in the sap and Frank was an old hand at listening to those flying oil-drums, facing them to pick up their trajectory, clearing the sap with a yell if he judged them too close. Even so they lost four men out there, two to snipers, two to bombs - and for every death Sergeant Percival seemed to blame Frank. "Won't earn your stripe getting men killed," he'd mutter each time a dead or dying man was dragged back into the trench. Until Frank in the end said: "Bugger the stripe - I'm only doing the best I can."
"Don't take any notice of that bastard," one of the 2 Platoon Corporals told him. "Head down, knuckle under, soldier on." But Sergeant Percival's insidious moral pressure took its toll and Frank withdrew a little further inside himself. He'd even given up whistling his birdsong, which had become another cause of Percival's ridicule.

The officers' dugout in line and in reserve had stayed silent for all two weeks, Ordish avoiding Uncle, Stevens avoiding Ordish, Prideaux buried deep into his translation of Lamartine, no jollity even from Bunny, who had the massive squitters from drinking dirty water. No, Nearly-Ocean-Villas was not a happy place, already a graveyard from last year's battle, their route in and out of the front line lined with make-shift wooden crosses from last summer's fields of killing. And their short occupancy there still had one more death to deal them.
They were moving back into the reserve line one night, swapping

with the HLI's, a delicate handover in the comparative isolation of those ASP's, manhandling one Lewis gun in and the other out. As duty officer, Uncle was left in the line to wait the withdrawal of the four Lewis guns. They ended up going out in numbers line astern, Uncle in the middle, Frank with 2 Platoon Lewis gun ahead of him, 3 Platoon behind him, Harry, Reggie and Benson bringing up the rear. Some noise had been inevitable, provoking a bloody stupid yell from Sergeant Percival. The change-over was duly noticed by Jerry and their first shell arrived with brief and sudden sound and fury, the flash not far in front of Harry, one zig-zag, one traverse away. He knew Frank was somewhere up there ahead of him and felt that dread cold fear when the call passed back down the line for "stretcher-bearers".

There were muttered oaths as in the darkness the file of soldiers had to clamber up with their kit along the parapet to bypass the wreckage where the shell had landed - and where two bodies now blocked the trench. One of them was Uncle, sitting there in a stupor, his hands groping over the smashed duckboards and through the mud. "I've lost my bloody pipe," he kept saying over and over again - poor Uncle who'd also lost both his legs, torn off at the knees and visible suddenly in the light of a match as Harry leant down to stick a cigarette in Uncle's mouth. The other body was Uncle's batman, Simon, his eyes wide open, no visible wound on him but dead beyond question, killed by the blast.

Harry unbuttoned Uncle's jacket pockets for his field dressings, though little good they'd do on such huge wounds. The jagged stumps were pumping blood into the mud, Harry shouting for a pull-through from someone's rifle. Reggie knelt with him on Uncle's other side, both of them tying pull-through cords tight around Uncle's thighs as tourniquets. They stayed with him till the stretcher-bearers came and helped lash him to the wood and canvas. Harry found and restored Uncle's pipe to his top pocket, making Uncle smile.

"Where are you from, Harry?" he asked.

"Coquetdale, sir."

"We live in Haydon Bridge. Will you go and visit them when this damn war is over?"

"You'll be back there long before me, sir."

Uncle smiled again but his eyes were slowly closing and though he kept on breathing for another three hours, they never opened again.

Harry wasn't to know his fingers had twice actually touched the letter, mud and blood on the envelope now, the jacket pocket left unbuttoned and threatening to spill its contents.

Colledge was waiting for the stretcher at the Regimental Aid Post, one look sufficient to know that Uncle didn't stand a chance. But he had another five wounded from the other shells and it was Captain Prideaux hours later who arrived to empty Uncle's pockets - and in so doing find the letter. He cleaned the envelope and posted it on; Captain Prideaux who'd now sit up all night and write home to Uncle's wife and children, returning to them Uncle's wallet, photographs, pocket-book and pipe.

Chapter 13

I was giving up my hope of your reply when your letter arrived with the open, challenging gaze of your eyes in every word. Your message is as clear and unambiguous as the church bell that rings the quarter hours across the road from my room (I write late at night, Viv fast asleep in my bed dreaming like a cat dreams with small movements of her hands and feet). How is it you live so powerfully beside me, your young body imagined though I've done nothing more in reality than touch your hand and face. What kept your letter so long on its journey – twenty endless days?

Used to always dating his father's letters Harry had written the day of that distant April evening above the letter. Annie now looked round at the letter with his penciled words. It was lying on the pillow next to Viv, where earlier the English girl had asked to read it - and then wept for the memories of her own young man whose face and heart and soul and mind and body never had been found.

I fear for your safety all the time, each day's broken men and boys on the train a reminder of bullet and shell. Where are you now in this very moment? Are you asleep in the dark? Are you out of the line? Do you know, do you feel that I am writing to you? You also will be waiting – will have been waiting for many days. Are you afraid that I have turned away from you? I could not bear you to even think it possible.

You say that I have made you afraid of the war for the first time. If that helps to keep you alive it is no bad thing (not that I believe you've never been afraid – it isn't possible to see so many people maimed and dead without feeling terror – is it?). But I think I know what you mean and thank you for saying it. You are no longer hiding! And nor shall I. What little has passed between us has taken possession of my conscious and my unconscious. You live with me all the time; I talk with you endlessly, explaining my life, what I have done previously, what I am doing and thinking now, the present and past, but never the future which is out of reach, forbidden. Perhaps we should stay like this, talking with distance between us for I now fear the moment you will see me as I really am with all my many imperfections. I could not bear to be anything less than your vision of me – and I know that I am not. Our Gentleman-Officer also made of me a person I could never hope to be – perhaps also my husband with whom I certainly did not have the time to quarrel, disagree or even disappoint – though I could already begin to understand where we might damage one another. We were only six months married and to what little time we did have together we could only cling like suddenly shipwrecked sailors to wreckage in a storm. When we first arrived in France the regulations would not even let us walk arm in arm, let alone share the same bed!

'I am a shepherd in the hills', you write, 'and that is the only life I could ever understand'. Yet for three years now you have been living a life infinitely more complex than anyone from any walk of life could ever begin to understand. Including the old soldiers themselves.

One newspaper writes 'the world is changing and will never be the same again'. If that is really so, then you, your friends, myself, even the Virgin Mary herself, we ARE that change. There is no way of life, no suffering, no despair to which we could not now adapt – if we do not break or are not broken. Which means what I wonder? That we are perfectly qualified to stay at war for ever!?

Talking of Mary, we had an evening out together and talked like never before. She has lost a brother, another brother, the third of five, and softens with her sadness. She's quite a wise old bird and I almost told her about you. But there are limits to even an old bird's wisdom.

I want this letter in the post tomorrow and my eyes are closing. Wherever you are I think of you and beg you to avoid danger. Write to me soon. If it's not too awful tell me what you hear and what you smell and what you see.

Harry would read the letter far removed from danger. They were out of the line at last, sent to the rear from reserve four days after Uncle's death, marching into a warm spring morning away from the sound of guns.

They'd buried Uncle and Simon a mile behind the line on the edge of a splintered wood one late afternoon, all the officers and a squad from each platoon in attendance with a bugler from Division. It wasn't often they had the chance to honour their own dead and when they were able it was considered important to observe the strictest formality, the long dying notes of the Last Post bowing each man's head to hide his tears for the dead present, the dead past and the inevitable future dead.

Sergeant-Major Trussal was absent on a course at Division and Percival at his own insistence appointed acting CSM for the move out of line, ignoring Sergeant Banister's longer standing in the Regiment. But then Banister had had his 6 years playing football back in civvie street which according to Percival lost him his seniority. Not that anyone was counting. Banister was far happier marching alongside his own Platoon, without the responsibility of map-reading or governing the hourly rest. But it did mean that Percival was able to purloin the Lewis gun cart for his own chosen few - and wasn't having any of the weaker brethren dumping their packs and rifles on the wheels.

Bunny had reclaimed Frank for 4 Platoon, to rejoin Harry, Nobby and Reggie, the four of them once again marching, column of four, with their rifles in the ranks. "Quite like the old days," said Harry, "if these buggers'd only let us sing."

Which once the other side of Albert they were allowed to do. "No music?" Prideaux asked from his horse as they left behind the gilded Virgin hanging in her wire cradle from the cathedral tower and the shell-smashed houses of the town. And Percival had to loosen his heavy hand and march the men 'at ease', Reggie the first to bring out his harmonica and play them into their personalised hymn, 'The Church's One Foundation':

We are Fred Karno's army,
The ragtime infantry
We cannot fight, we cannot shoot,
What fucking use are we!
And when we get to Berlin,
The Kaiser he will say,
"Hoch, hoch! Mein Gott,
What a bloody fine lot
Are the ragtime infantry!"

15 miles south-east and a dozen songs later they found the Somme river near a village called Suzanne and marched into a field of tents beside a mill singing their usual puzzlement to the tune of 'Auld Lang Syne':

We're here
Because
We're here
Because
We're here
Because we're here.....

*

It seemed at first that they were there to rest and nothing more - a day in hot bath tubs, an issue of clean uniforms, a detailed medical inspection, two proper cooked meals, four more horses brought in for any officer or Sergeant who wished to ride, a gift of footballs and cricket gear from the Colonel, boxing and athletics organised for the Saturday, a full-dress church parade for Sunday.

By Thursday the whole Battalion had gathered and sporting events took on real edge, a gang of 'volunteers' with borrowed scythes mowing a couple of hay-fields for a makeshift cricket and football pitch, Company to play Company on a points system like league football and county cricket back home: suicidal stuff with everyone looking for a 'blighty', a broken bone to send them safely home.

"Any half-arse, half-fuck injuries," yelled Sergeant Percival at halftime, "will be considered as self-inflicted wounds!" And he turned and yelled the words again into the adjoining field where the cricket had just started, the Battalion Chaplain wincing at the Sergeant's choice of words.

The cricket teams were somewhat incomplete and agreement made for nine-a-side. Not everyone had played before. Villagers in the border hills weren't exactly used to the game, Harry among them. It was a girl's game to him, like rounders or pat-ball in a school playground - though the thwack of a hard ball sounded dangerous enough. An old French farmer, still gathering what he could of the cut grass, had never seen anything quite so strange and later in the day brought a crowd out from the village to sit on a grass bank and watch - until one of them was hit by that very hard ball, well and truly thwacked by the Chaplain, the French spectators retreating rapidly to the cover of the trees. This war, the elderly local priest decided, really was a very strange affair.

On parade at the end of the afternoon names were taken for a cross-country race next day, uphill from the river where a point-to-point course for the horses had been marked for the weekend: "Officers and men!" Percival was shouting. Bunny and Schoolboy stepped forward to set the example, followed by two dozen of the men, Frank and Harry the last to emerge from the ranks, sauntering out to a cheer. That evening in the tents some serious money now changed hands, most of it on Harry, most of it from 'B' Company, most of that from 4 Platoon.

"The money's all on Coquetdale, Lance-Corporal," Sergeant Banister told him. "If I was you I'd loosen up those legs tonight." Sure enough, in the twilight later that evening Harry stripped down to his underpants and ran barefoot up the river bank to cough and spit the tar out from his lungs - only to meet Schoolboy running in the opposite direction equally half naked. They stopped facing one another in the moonlight with a grin. The Lieutenant looked so fresh and young Harry had a strange desire to put his arms around him once again. But instead shook the hand that Schoolboy offered before they both ran on. "I'll be catching you tomorrow, sir," Harry shouted back at him.

Next afternoon was sultry warm when they gathered by the river bank, football shirts, socks and shorts handed out from some unwarlike part of Battalion stores. The starter's gun, a 303, had the wildfowl and the swallows up in clouds along the river, the runners off in a pack eyeing one another. Frank, as agreed with Harry, led the way at speed for the first flat mile to tire some of the other legs, Harry waiting for the hill to increase his pace. As he accelerated away from the others up a chalk slope into trees, he remembered not only his own fells from home but the woods from last year's battle, the ones he'd seen, the ones he'd thankfully only heard about - Thiepval, Delville, Trones, Gommecourt, Mametz, High Wood and their own sparse thickets in front of White City and the valley towards Beaumont Hamel or round the Hawthorn Crater where the mine had been exploded. It seemed an age away from the birdsong on this gentle afternoon, in reality a year, two months and barely half a dozen miles away.

Harry glanced back: only Schoolboy had kept up his pace, ten yards behind him as they entered the second wood, Harry slowing down to join him under the haze of 'beech flush', green sunshine through the transparent young leaves that made both men think of the added blue mist of bluebells in the woods back home. Harry looked round at Schoolboy and grinned: "We'll be 1st and 2nd for 'B' Company, sir, if you can keep it up!"

"You're not even out of bloody breath!" Schoolboy gasped, grasping Harry's hand to scramble up a bank. Ahead of them the Colonel himself was sitting on his horse upright and magnificent on top of the hill at the outer marker, a Sergeant standing to one side writing down the names they shouted to him as they passed.

"Jolly good!" the Colonel barked. "See if you can't beat me back to the finish!"

"Not damn likely," muttered Harry as he heard the Colonel wheel his horse away first into a trot then a canter round the further side of the hill. But Harry increased his pace all the same, not to be disgraced - and nearly did reach the river first, Schoolboy watching Harry's long strides flow down the slope, 30, 40 finally 50 yards ahead of him, Schoolboy making 2nd just in time to see and hear the Colonel lean from his horse and shake Harry by the hand: "We'll have you in the next Olympic games, Cardwell!"

Nobby, Dippy and Reggie were waving fists in the air, Sergeant Banister and Scotty yelling their heads off - God knows how much they'd wagered and won. Harry had a grin and a wink for Schoolboy, rank forgotten in the flush of victory, both young men, hot and perspiring, racing each other again, now along the river bank to find a deeper pool, stripping off their clothes to dive naked into the water as a red sun disappeared behind the willows.

There was a barrel of beer for 'B' Company at roll-call that evening and an extra barrel bought by Captain Prideaux for 4 Platoon, 2nd Lieutenant Stevens and Sergeant Percival, scowling from their respective Platoons, bad losers both.

But this blessed lack of war could not last forever. One week later the playing fields were becoming classrooms, lines of innocuous white tape that took on sinister significance once it became clear that they denoted trenches. Maps were studied, measurements taken, the tapes rearranged. They were in effect laying out a full-scale plan of somewhere else, a battle-plan whose geographical whereabouts were confined for the moment to reference points 'Alpha', 'Beta', 'Gamma' and 'Delta'. Staff-Officers visited on horse-back and in motor-cars, prodding at their plan with walking-sticks, then watching with visiting American officers one morning as the entire Battalion attacked, 'over the top' from one line of white tape to another, the battle-plan unchallenged by enemy shell or machine-gun. No wonder the visitors, the Generals and their ADC's appeared so satisfied.

Their game became more elaborate, another dozen fields to be mown, flat ones nearer the river, this time with wire laid, a perfect trench dug, lined with sand-bags and pit-props and floored with dry clean duckboards. 'Over the top' was once again practiced and satisfactorily concluded, the 'enemy' wire having been miraculously 'destroyed', the 'enemy' guns silenced. No one even dirtied their boots.

The Battalion officers were taking bets as to the real whereabouts of 'Alpha', 'Beta', 'Gamma' and 'Delta', the choice of these flat water-meadows suggesting Flanders and the Ypres salient. It wasn't only Captain Prideaux who quietly guessed they were rehearsing for another 'show' later that summer.

The swaddies had more precise ideas as they dug out the positions day to day, lining up the tapes, planting different coloured, numbered flags for the American visitors to admire. One particular feature exercised their minds with especial fascination - a long thoroughfare that linked each one of the marked-out fields and was itself in most places boarded as 'unsuitable for wheeled vehicles'. "No buses or taxis," muttered Ordish. "I think we're going to Italy."

"But don't you see, sir, where we are," said Sergeant Banister. "We've walked down here often enough ourselves. Zillebeke Lake and Hooge? Sanctuary Wood up ahead of us?"

"Alpha, Beta, Gamma, Delta, Sergeant. Ours not to reason why. Someone has to go and help the Italians - or so they say." But all the same Ordish also stepped out between the tapes onto the 'thoroughfare' and looked ahead without enthusiasm at the next three fields.

Banister dropped his voice: "We can all read numbers, Lieutenant. We're marking out a line of attack, sir. Along the Menin Road."

"Then why are we putting on these shows for the Americans?"

"To help them. sir. To show them how it happens. To show them what we've learnt."

"Have we learnt anything, Sergeant?"

"I don't know, sir. But I do know the army is very different from even just one year ago. We know better how to survive."

Harry was standing beside them listening to the exchange, a shrug at him from Ordish as he turned away.

And later: "Do we, Harry?"

"Sir?"

"Know better how to survive?"

"If they leave us here, we do."

It was early evening by the river, Ordish sat on the bank with fishing tackle, Harry on a walk to read a letter.

Annie's letter had eventually found Harry in his tent that afternoon, handed from the mail pouch by Sergeant Banister, the envelope recognised by his pals but thankfully unseen by Stevens. Now Harry ached to read her words in private and instead was trapped by Ordish's melancholic musing.

"Italy would have been pleasant."

"They're fighting in the mountains there, sir. We're only used to hills."

"I went there as a student. Took the train to Venice, Florence and Rome. Fell in love with an Italian girl." He looked round at Harry. "Only, you understand from a distance. Like you with Annie."

"Sir."

"Has she written again?"

Harry tapped his pocket. "This evening, sir."

"Then I'll leave the two of you together, Lance-Corporal." Ordish called after him as Harry walked on along the bank: "If we were ever given local leave, I dare say you could take a train from Bray to Pérignon."

*

.......Wherever you are I think of you and beg you to avoid danger. Write to me soon. If it's not too awful tell me what you hear and what you smell and what you see.

The very moment I finish to read your words (for the first time for I shall read them a hundred times again) I have to reply, to tell you how they make me smile and bring my mind and body alive.

What do I hear and smell and see? I am sitting on a fallen willow by the river (the Somme - or is that a military secret? - yes, I'm not many miles away from you). I'm watching swallows, hundreds of them it seems, chasing and swooping as they feed. Later in the hawthorn round the camp there will be nightingales that drive everyone mad they are so loud and all through the night. I don't mind. I had never heard them before coming to France. I believe our hills at home are far too cold for them.

I can see Uncle's fishing line downstream and the splash and ripple it makes in the water - though poor Uncle will never use it again (he was killed by a shell *as we came out of the line). The fishing line's in the hands of another officer, Lieutenant Ordish who passes my letters to you without censor since there are others in the dugout who disapprove of a common soldier writing to someone like you. Fishing suits Lieutenant Ordish, though I don't believe he's ever done it before. He stares a lot and is sad and funny. And is also in love with the photographs of you. Do you mind? He has been to university (and travelling to Italy) - I think you would find him far more interesting than I could ever be.*

I suppose he and my own officer ('Bunny' everyone calls him) are the best of the bunch. And our Captain Prideaux who looks older and more tired with every passing month. They should send him home. And the youngest one of all, I suppose is not a bad egg - 'Schoolboy' we call him, for that is what he really is. We've been together out in front once or twice. Sometimes he's very frightened and I have to hold his hand or put my arms around him! Does that seem strange to you?

We have been 'resting' which means cutting fields of hay and digging trenches and laying out white tapes like a giant map. Lieutenant Ordish is hoping we will be sent to Italy which would put me in despair to be so far from you. But our Sergeant Banister believes the map of white tapes to be back in Flanders - where we will next attack? While we practice whatever it may be, we are also demonstrating war to your countrymen (officers only), our clean dry trench, battles without casualties, excitement without fear. Their men will find out for themselves soon enough - but I hope more wisely, less painfully than we had to. Do they come to reinforce us or the French I wonder? And will you be joining them?

Though I've never thought about it before, I imagine

that one day you will have to join them and go back home. Well, I shall not think about that. As you say, the future is forbidden.
My feelings for you grow stronger with every word you write.

Harry handed the letter to Ordish as he was packing up the fishing gear - and as before offered him Annie's two sheets to read. Ordish took Harry's written page and sealed it without a glance but shook his head at Annie's letter: "I'd love to read what she says - but it's none of my business, Harry. She certainly wouldn't want it herself."

Chapter 14

How to describe the feeling when I see your envelope – a warm and breathless shiver through my whole body – and it took only two days to arrive this time. If you are really so nearby, do I dare to hope that I might see you – standing one evening on the corner of the street below my window? To be able to know that you are out of the line is wonderful relief. How long can it last? Viv says the staff-officers drop hints of a big push later in the summer. And yes they also talk of how many men will have to go to Italy. If you go, I shall follow! I shall attach myself to your battalion and become a camp follower bringing you food and warmth!

Now you've spoken of them I too have seen the swallows, though I had to ask Viv what they were. Sometimes they seem to follow the train like sea gulls after a ship. I expect we attract the flies, however often we clean and wash the inside of the coaches – especially on the warm days we've been having. Sometimes the smell is overpowering for there is usually some poor man on board with gangrene or septicaemia. We have to scrub our hands against *infection so many times a day they are red raw cracked and hard. Not beautiful at all. Off duty we try to keep them rubbed with oil. Any sort of oil, even from the engine!*

Will you forgive my short letter? There is so little time these days. One of the other ambulance trains has been sent north and we've had to double our journeys, sometimes with two or three nights at a time on the train. They've put another carriage for us on the back, compartments (First Class!) where we are meant to sleep.

Wherever you are I think of you and beg you to avoid danger. Write to me immediately! And again tell me everything you hear and smell and see. That way I can live with you.

By the time Harry read those words the First Battalion Border Rifles had already progressed two more miles along the valley, laying out another tented camp and endless more fields of white tape, 'Alpha', 'Beta' and 'Gamma' in different configurations, colours and numbers. "It has a look of permanence about it," Bunny commented as they admired their handiwork one day. "And chaps, why not? One of history's wars out here in France lasted a hundred years. Why shouldn't this one be the same? Give us another fifty years we could have the finest army the world has ever seen."

"And the smallest," said Harry.

That last weekend on the river bank was 'B' Company's turn for a limited furlough, the officers swanning off to eat expensively in Amiens, the NCO's and men to Bray or Villers and Harry hitching a lift on an empty munitions train on its way back to Pérignon, Reggie and Frank with him, their 24 hour pass for the 'Lewis gun graduates' talked out of Prideaux by Ordish when no one else was listening. Quite what the 'Lewis gun graduates' were meant to do in Pérignon had not been specified. Presumably Reggie and Frank were sent along to make sure Harry did come back.

It all happened at the last minute, no chance at all of letting Annie know he might be on his way. The only opportunity to see her would be that same evening - **if** her train was in town, **if** they arrived in time. Harry watched the hours on every station clock they passed. Their empty munitions train was crawling, giving way to any other traffic. Sometimes through that long hot day it felt like they could get there quicker walking.

Harry had spruced himself up, all three of them had, with an early morning shave, their uniforms cleaned, their boots and buckles polished. Neither Frank nor Reggie had actually mentioned Annie. It was just assumed, as it had been by the long-suffering Prideaux, that she was the intended target of this cross-country marathon.

Pérignon loomed from a low haze of smoke in the sunshine, the church and town hall the only visible signs of a French town in the sprawl of canvas and tin roofs that made up the military encampments around it. Predictably the three soldiers were challenged the moment they clambered from their wagon, the sight of the redcaps reminding Harry that he was still a likely quarry for them here. But their passes were waved on without too much scrutiny, Harry following the rail tracks into the hospital rail yard. He picked out Annie's train with its mix of French and English carriages of different shapes and sizes that made it look from a distance like a child's homemade wooden toy. And yes, the train was parked and empty.

Harry walked almost at a run through the back streets of the town, his two companions barely keeping up with him.

When the moment came, Annie couldn't quite believe what she was seeing. Both she and Viv had often caught one another glancing down from the bedroom window at the corner of the street where first they'd seen the young soldier, but until this evening there had never ever been anyone there.

The nurses were early off the train that afternoon with an early meal served, ready to be back on duty for midnight and another run, this time from Pérignon to Boulogne with a train-load of stretcher-cases for Blighty, partial evacuation of the Pérignon Base hospital to allow building work for an ominous expansion. Annie left Viv still eating in the refectory and climbed the stairs to their room, wondering, with that news of the expansion, whether they wouldn't all still be here in 20 years' time. She glanced down from the window as she walked into the room.

Harry saw her in that moment from the street, her shadow first as the bedroom door opened, then her face in the window staring at them, her hands touching both her cheeks and her hair. Had she recognised him? Would she come down? Was she able to come down? She made no sign but turned quickly away.

"She's coming down," said Harry, Reggie and Frank like school kids as they waited, nudging each other and grinning. What on earth would she think of them - or they of her?

Harry had crossed the street to stand at the door as she opened it, every word he'd had in his head evaporating with the fear that she'd no longer see him now as she'd seen him before and that everything would have changed. But she smiled and took his hands to draw him into that doorway off the street and he smiled back. Was this the first time she'd seen those eyes smile, his whole expression changing as though a great coloured lamp had turned on inside his head? She kissed both eyes in turn to startle him.

He watched her look beyond him at Frank and Reggie staring at them from the other side. "We got given leave as a unit - well just the 24 hours."

She stepped out to close and lock the door behind her. "In town you will be challenged," she said. "Follow me the other way. There's a hotel where some of the doctors live and it's far too early for them to be around."

A hotel with a bar, she meant, and far enough from the middle of town not to be restricted - another improvisation of war, a farm that had been submerged by the spreading sprawl of huts and canvas barns, to then adapt itself as living quarters and avoid requisition, the farmer's wife becoming the Madame, letting rooms to the military surgeons and running an Estaminet in her kitchen for any passer-by. Not that she seemed too sure about the three soldiers who followed Annie inside. "They're patients," Annie said. "I promised I would buy them a beer." And the four of them sat politely at a table in Madame's parlour, Harry wondering if this had been a good idea.

"Frank and Reggie," he said by way of introductions.

She shook hands with them across the table: "Hello Frank - hello Reggie."

Reggie and Frank were wide-eyed and silent, staring as though they did not quite believe that she was there. They knew they should bunk off and leave the two of them alone, but Annie started talking with them, asking them questions, making them laugh as, no doubt, she made her wounded men laugh on the train.

"They give you an escort now, do they," she'd said to Harry. And turning to the others: "Needs looking after, does he?" Reggie and Frank were unusually lost for words. "It's not a church parade," she said. "We **are** allowed to smile."

Reggie laughed. "Not often we sit with a lady, Miss."

"Lady be buggered! I'm a nurse."

The look on their faces, all three of them, was music hall, their mouths wide open, chins down to their collars. Recovering first, Harry looked round at his two marra's and burst out laughing.

"If I ever get wounded," declared Frank, "I want to be sent to you!"

"I don't want any of you to get wounded," she replied. "The rate we're going, there'll be no young men left in the world."

Madame placed a jug of beer and four mugs on the table, Frank and Reggie again astonished as Annie filled all four mugs.

"She's used to me and beer," laughed Annie. "We come here sometimes when our matron looks the other way and the Madame sits us in here where we won't offend the good doctors. Some of them are very pompous." Then, looking at Frank and Reggie: "Do you live close to Harry at home?"

Frank put up his hand as though he was at school. "Next valley," he said. "Over the hill."

"Frank's also a shepherd," said Harry. "Reggie's from under the ground. He's a coal-miner."

"Maybe you'll take me back there one day and show me all these places." Annie was still looking at Frank and Reggie.

"Aye," Reggie replied, "blurry right we will, pet!"

Annie laughed, Harry watching her in surprise. That was the first time she had ever allowed herself to mention the future. She took one of Frank's proffered cigarettes and watched in fascination as Frank rolled the flint on his wick lighter and blew it into life. Frank looked up at her: "Only way to get anything burning when it's blows in the trench."

"Stay with us you"ll learn something new every day," said Reggie, finishing his beer and standing up. "Frank and I are going to look round town." He nodded his head at Annie: " Nice to meet you, Miss"; and at Harry: "See you back at the railway."

Frank had to move with him, caught short with a long swallow of his beer and his cigarette half lit, a wide self-conscious grin for Annie as he followed Reggie out through the door.

Annie and Harry watched them go, neither of them sure how to start again on their own.

"I didn't believe you'd be able to come."

"Won't be so easy anymore. We've had all of three weeks out."

"What happens next?"

"To the 'Bullring' for training they say. Then back in the line, I reckon, wherever it is, for whatever it is."

"They're building up Base Hospital here. And asked us to come under Corps and not Division."

"Asked!?"

"We're an amalgamation. No one knows quite who we belong to - some of us being funded volunteers. But it's as bad as being told, isn't it. And it means they can send us anywhere they like."

"Take you off your train?"

"I think that's what it's all about. We're a good unit - maybe a bit wasted on the train."

"So, if they send you to Italy, I'll have to come following you."

Annie smiled: "And be arrested as a deserter?" She watched him. "You had my letter then?"

"I can never believe that you're saying those things. I mean, I **do** believe but I can't believe you're saying them to me."

"Neither can I with your letters."

"I can't write things like you can write them."

" 'I give myself to you in every way you might wish and keep inside me your face, your heart, your soul, your mind and your body. Nothing in my life has ever been so clear nor will ever be again.' "

 Annie recited his words almost in a whisper, smiling at him.

"First time someone's talked my own words back to me."

"I'm sure it won't be the last. No one's ever written to me like that before."

"Your Gentleman-Officer."

"But he didn't in the end, did he - "

"What?"

"Write to me."

" 'We are two strangers who meet in hell' - "

"Less strangers now than then?" she asked. Harry nodded, Annie watching his eyes: "But?"

"There are so many other people in this war."

"You mean better than you?" Harry didn't answer. "Like your Lieutenant Ordish who's meant to be more interesting to me because he's funny and sad and he's been to Italy? I suppose he's more of a gentleman, is he?"

"Something like that."

From looking angry she suddenly exploded into laughter: "I was going to say 'you bloody English'! But all I am is what they call a New Englander over there. And I have to admit that bloody Boston's just as bad as bloody England - except over there it's more to do with money than with birth. We're all as good as one another, Harry Cardwell. It's who you are, not what you are. And I know who you are. The first time I ever saw you, I knew."

Harry was silent for a moment. "Just being able to think about you has changed my life."

"And mine."

"You know there's a way of thinking about things like time and place and numbers, that become a pattern in the head. All of that is different now. All blown away. It's like I'm lost, completely lost - and only you can ever find me. Like Frank, when he was a kid he got lost once in the snow. Fell through a hole. But he didn't shout out or call for help because he said he knew that I would find him."

"You want to call for help?"

"No point, is there. There isn't no one else can hear."

Another silence - but not one that any longer worried them.

"Harry."

"What?"

"Nothing. I just like to say your name. My name's Annie. Say my name."

"Annie. Annabel Donovan."

She smiled. "Harry Cardwell. You wrote to me 'What is love multiplied by ten? You make me dream of things that make me for the first time frightened of this war'. If I knew how to say it I would say the same to you. And if that was a way of saying that you loved me, then whatever I'm saying to you now is a way of saying that I love you."

They were silent as Madame came back in to clear the jug and the other two mugs away. Harry cleared his throat: "I'm back on the train tonight."

"So are we." She covered his hand on the table, her fingers between his fingers: "I mean everything I say."

"So do I."

"And everything I write."

"So do I."

Annie looked at her watch: "I don't want to say goodbye. I can't do that. I'm just going to stand up and go. And I shall be waiting every day for your next letter."

Harry stood up with her, but did not move as she walked away.

*

Frank and Reggie had been stopped again, a whole scrum of red-caps this time, scrutinizing their faces and their passes.

"How many of youse Geordies in town today?" the podgy carrot Lance-Jack asked.

"Wouldn't know," said Reggie, cautious suddenly at the casual aggression in the other man's voice.

"There were three of you before, we were told."

"Wouldn't know how many we were."

"Long way to come on a one day pass."

"Sent here weren't we."

"Why?"

"'I expect the others had business."

"One of them a Lance-Corporal, was he?"

"I wouldn't know."

"Fucking everything you wouldn't know, would you."

Another of them joined in, addressing Frank: "Want to tell us where you've been?"

"Drinking."

"Drinking where?"

"I don't know the town."

"Drinking anywhere we were allowed," said Reggie. "Which isn't much seeing how the whole damn town's made over for Officers."

"Where you leaving from?"

"Transport lines."

"For where?"

"Bray."

Reggie watched them swagger off. "Looking for Harry, aren't they," he muttered to Frank.

"Why?"

"Said he had a fight with one of them, didn't he."

"That was bloody weeks ago."

Reggie spat on the ground: "Like fucking elephants, these red ruby reds. They never forget anyone." He spat again: "Split up. You get to the railway. I'll go back for Harry."

But Harry was already on his way, deliberately unobtrusive round the edge of town to avoid the police. He reached the rail yard unchallenged and unharmed.

The Quarter Master at the yard told him there was a ramassage train for Bray leaving sometime before midnight - and pointed it out to him across the tracks, a couple of carriages, a fuel tank, half a dozen coal wagons and a line of cattle-trucks already loading up with horses. Harry sat himself down out of sight to wait, Annie in his eyes, her face and body, his mind still racing over every word they'd said to one another.

When he saw the redcaps and the look on their faces, Frank knew he'd walked himself into trouble. Lost in the narrow streets, Frank reckoned he must have wandered in a circle to come up against them so soon again. The fat carrot-head Lance-Corporal pushed him into an alley where no one could see them: "Decided where your Lance-Jack's hiding, Geordie?"

"Don't know who you mean. There's a dozen Lance-Jacks in our Company."

Carrot-head hit him suddenly with an elbow, hard under the ribs. "How about the one you were with before?"

"Don't know who you mean." Stay on your feet, Frank was thinking to himself, or they'll kick the shit out of me.

"I want his name and number," said carrot-head, "then you can walk away." When he failed to respond, another of them pushed him up against the wall:

"His name, Geordie."

Frank wondered who taught them how to do it - beating him in all the places that no one would ever see. He tensed his midriff, covered his balls and let them get on with it, their pickaxe handles on his thighs, his upper arms and shoulders, what felt like a bag of metal ball-bearings across his back around his kidneys and finally a heavy boot up between his legs to flatten his hands and everything they were meant to be protecting. And this time Frank couldn't help but fall, rolled up in a wave of pain that made him sure he'd never walk straight again. If they do that once more, he thought, I'll die from it. But when he looked round he was suddenly alone. The three redcaps had disappeared, afraid perhaps they'd already done too much.

Reggie saw another, smaller group of the ruby-reds, ducked away round a corner and started to run. "Ils sont partis," the Madame had told him at the hotel and he was heading back towards the rail yard the way Harry had brought them earlier on; but deviated now in case the red-caps were following him. He didn't want to lead them to their quarry.

A quarter mile further on he saw Frank. Frank was walking slowly, limping, one hand on the wall of the building beside him, almost dragging himself along.

"What's up, marra'?"

"They chased me and I fell. Feels like I've broken everything."

"They caught you?"

Frank shook his head, Reggie sitting him down doubled up on a low wall. "You sure they didn't catch you?"

"Just let me rest a while."

Harry had been watching for an hour, the two passenger carriages filled and only a couple of half-loaded supply wagons that still had room for them. There was already an engine on the front of the train and everyone waiting for the French signalman to wave his green flag. I'll have to go back into town and find them, Harry was thinking. They're only here because of me. The green flag was already waving when they finally did appear, Harry yelling to show them where to come, the two of them running, Harry's hands outstretched to drag them on board the truck a moment before the train jerked into motion.

"Bloody hell!" said Harry. "Good damn thing you two don't have stripes." And having seen the way Frank was moving: "What's up with you?"

"The redcaps chased him," answered Reggie. "He fell over."

"Fell over or they caught him?"

"Fell over," said Frank firmly.

"They'd stopped us in town, looking for a Geordie Lance-Jack. I came back to warn you but you were gone."

Harry looked at Frank: "And then the bastards chased you again?"

Frank shrugged and kept quiet, however acute the pain in all his body. He knew if he told them what had really happened, Harry would be off the train and back into town to kill someone. Frank forced a grin out of his face instead: "She's a bonny lass your girl. I'm glad I seen her."

"I hope you'll see her again."

Reggie wagged his finger: "Too much bonny for you, young Harry."

"You mean she's a lady and I'm no gentleman."

"Know what she'd say if she heard you, marra? She'd say bugger that!"

Frank sat himself down against the back of the truck and held himself in the darkness. The pain he was feeling was another door silently closing in his mind, another brutality he couldn't understand.

*

She lay across the seat in her compartment later that night staring into darkness through the window, listening to Virgin Mary's slow and heavy snore through the thin partition, a guttural vibration that kept such perfect time with the swaying movement of the carriage as to seem to be the cause of it.

Annie remembered fellow-passengers snoring on her one and only train journey with Patrick, their honeymoon night of very experimental love-making in a very narrow sleeping berth almost directly behind the steam engine that was howling them swiftly south to Florida.

"For God's sake, we're qualified medical graduates," he'd whispered in her ear. "We're meant to know how to do this!" And she'd laughed and reminded him that only **he** was qualified and therefore only **he** knew how to do it.

Newspapers in the hotel next day had told them of the war in Europe and two months later they'd both signed up to go. Why had they volunteered so quickly? Because Patrick's Irish uncle had been killed in the first battle of the war? Because Annie couldn't face her final year of exams? Because two friends had volunteered and they thought it would be good experience? Or because they were both in something of a panic about being married and domestic, which didn't yet suit either of them?

What a different world that now all seemed - a way of life that even letters from home could no longer conjure up. The idea of returning to examinations seemed absurd - perhaps, even more simply, the idea of leaving Europe. They'd both of them walked mouths open and hand in hand to discover Paris together through the three short days they waited there for posting. The city seemed to both of them the place where all civilisation had been born - with Rome, Venice and Florence still waiting to be discovered, not now alas for Patrick.

In the end Annie had returned to Paris with the Gentleman-Officer, two days and a night (separate hotels), endless walking and a feast for her of experienced knowledge and erudition that seemed second nature to him. 'Our Gentleman-Officer'. Why couldn't she use his name? He'd been so secretive and so insistent upon her discretion. For what? But for the kissing of her gloved hand, nothing had happened between them, beyond a very pleasant and welcome friendship - which had all then changed with the delivery to her of the passionate and painful letters he had never sent; brought to her by a young soldier whose own face now haunted and possessed her.

Was it a betrayal of Patrick that her mind and body now chose to stop thinking about him and think instead of Harry Cardwell; even to imagine him lying along this seat with her and both of them on their way to Italy? Would he laugh like Patrick as they began to find their way around each other's bodies? She guessed he'd had experience of loving. He'd almost told her so. A shepherd probably knew more about it than a doctor. How his eyes had briefly burned all over her, in quick glances which he no doubt believed she would not notice.

And dreaming of such things Annie fell at last asleep - to wake an hour later with the screeching of the carriage wheels along rusty rails at Boulogne, the sound of gulls and the hooting of a ship, a sharp knock on the door and a call from Virgin Mary: all hands down on the quayside to help carry the stretchers on board the ferry.

Annie wondered if Harry and friends had also reached their destination - and silently wished them well.

Chapter 15

They marched into the 'Bullring' camp without song in their heart or spring in their step - or so wrote Bunny to his father a week later when they'd all been through the first workout under a relentless sun. Bunny could remember tortures like this at school - exercises to improve their rugby or merely imposed as a punishment. Obstacle courses they used to call them, and prefects with swagger sticks 'helped' the younger boys on their way round prodding their behinds. Here instead, and far more seriously, the bloodiest-minded Sergeant-Majors in the British Army had been put in charge - of everyone. And everyone, subalterns, Sergeants, Jacks and Lance-jacks, were fair game for the yelled ironies, the spat contempt, the endless repetition of drill, exercises, hand-to hand violence and weapon-training.

Bruised they all were after just one day, and Frank barely able to move. Bunny realized something was up and pushed him into sick-parade after the second day, when and where Colledge found the livid bruising on Frank's ribs and midriff front and back: "Who did this to you?" But Frank just grinned and stuck with his story of falling over - and after one day alone in the tent with a pill he was returned to the 'training' in the sand dunes.

They'd been through all of this two years ago when first they'd come to France as raw recruits but it had to be said most of their comrades were by now replacements or returnees from injury. The 'Bullring' was meant to restore them to fitness and discipline and, for the comparative newcomers, to hone the specialised skills that were needed for trench warfare - the wielding of a spade against the earth or a club against the head of an imaginary Hun; the hurling of grenades like children throwing stones; the rolling out of barbed-wire; and, cruellest of all exercises, 'attacking' that wire, rolls and rolls of the evil stuff eight yards deep with only the inadequate army-issue cutters to use against it while a machine gun fired live rounds a few inches above them to keep their heads down. Any Platoon that took more than eight minutes to cut and crawl their way through were sent back to start all over again. Accidents of course were bound to happen: the bullet that hit someone in the head; the grenade that didn't quite make the top of the dune you were throwing it over and rolled back towards you as the seconds counted down; or the men who simply collapsed from heat exhaustion or dehydration.

No one was spared, even Captain Prideaux participating, until he was withdrawn with Sergeant-Major Trussal for classroom and sand-table exercises at HQ. Only Sergeant Percival seemed to relish the whole experience, driving his Platoon onwards, upwards to win the accolades. How his men hated him and fantasized revenge!

'How much more of it?' Bunny scribbled in his diary on a day when two men died, one from Percival's own 2 Platoon and the other from the Norfolks. 'Do we really have to kill our men just practising for war?'

But someone somewhere must have had a finger on their pulse. When the yelling and the torment stopped, when final inspection and parade passed them out, Prideaux and Trussal found themselves at the head of a Company that really did march with song in their heart and spring in their step. Was it merely their release from hell - or also the shared experience of that hell? Like it or not, for good reason or bad, they were certainly now a motivated fighting force. "Show us the enemy!" they shouted on that last parade, once they'd heard, from sixty miles away, a truly massive bombardment open up in a thudding, distant wall of sound. "Ours or theirs?" everyone wondered.

Under the midsummer sun the Border Rifles marched in easy stages from France back into Flanders, east by north-east towards the salient and that thundering of guns, their evenings and nights in organised barns and farmhouses, Bimont, St Martin, Ecques, Sercus and over the border into Kemmel. A cooling breeze was blowing from the north, each village had its estaminet, and the marching was never more than 15 miles a day. Even Frank was singing when Reggie's music played.

"The bombardment is ours," Prideaux told them on the second evening, though by then no doubt Jerry was hurling back as good as he received. A week of bombardment could only mean one thing. Somewhere, sometime, someone would be climbing ladders to go over the top and attack the enemy trenches and the Border Rifles wanted to be there. Instead they were held in Kemmel, actually three miles short of Kemmel under canvas in a field, lying in the sun when they weren't required on parade.

It was on their third night there that the earthquake woke them at first light, the ground under Harry's palliasse shaking, a shockwave also on the eardrums one moment before the sound reached them. They realized the guns had fallen silent and discovered later in the day that that was the moment the mines had been detonated under the Messines ridge to bury the German front line. Simultaneously 80,000 men of the Second Army went over the top.

With the attack successful and Jerry on his back foot, surely now High Command would make the push through the rest of the salient while the weather was still warm and dry? But for whatever reason, the answer was no. The guns returned to normal and 'B' Company passed the rest of June in the woods and fields round Kemmel, playing once more with white tapes on the grass, 'Alpha', 'Beta', 'Gamma' and 'Delta' now finally decoded, as Sergeant Banister had correctly guessed, 'Hooge', 'Zouave' and 'Sanctuary' woods with what was left of the 'Menin Road'. It was like coming home again.

"Here we will attack," announced a Regimental Sergeant-Major, "protected by a 'creeping barrage' 50 yards in front of us. Here Jerry will fall back. Here we will consolidate." And, gung-ho still, they began to believe it. Within a week of the attack, they were told, the entire ridge round Ypres would be taken and command set up within a village called Passchaendaele.

They practiced every day, over the top on the tapes and timing themselves section by section, not to overtake their 'creeping barrage'. "Want to bet it creeps too slow and wipes us out," muttered the disbelieving Ordish. But even he at times expressed the impatience to 'get on with it and have a go'.

"It's now we should be going over," said Prideaux that same evening. "I never seen the Wiper trenches dry."

Instead they stayed where they were, only an occasional storm to interrupt the summer sun, Battalion energy diverted into a round of football games against the units parked nearby, teams from both Company and Platoons.

July came and they were moved a little nearer the line, camped in and around a farm outside Dikkebus, the jagged, shelled-out silhouette of Ypres now sharp on their horizon in the early morning before the daily heat haze closed them in.

"Anyone'd think they were waiting for the rain," grumbled Prideaux.

"Perhaps Messines was it for 1917," suggested Bunny. "The rains will start and Caesar will withdraw into winter quarters."

But they knew from the stockpile of shells all around them and the massing of the guns that something had to happen. As they also knew, and heaven help us hoped, that they would be a part of it. Sure enough Prideaux and Ordish were dispatched one day up to the front line to observe a section of no man's land that had been reserved for them.

*

Letters were taking longer in this increasingly crowded antechamber of the war, the exact whereabouts of each Battalion, village by village, farm by farm, field by field, straining the usual efficiency of the Army postal system. Annie had written in her first letter received at the Bullring:

I never thought to tell you how much I liked Frank and Reggie. You're very fond of one another but I shall try hard not to envy them – the fact they lie beside you every night, watch over you through the day, and equally receive your care and affection.

And Harry wrote back:

Then I must try not to envy Viv who seems to even sometimes share your bed. Frank and Reggie thought you grand - and that means grand wonderful not grand Grand!
The Germans have attacked with gas again, it didn't reach us, thank God - a new gas that comes from liquid looking like oil and burns if you touch it. Mustard gas, our MO tells us. So we've spent all day on gas drill, walking round like strange animals in our masks, suffocating in this heat. You must be careful if you ever have to treat for gas - the MO says just touching the victims has made many of the nurses ill.

We did have gas cases - I think from La Bassé - on our last train. How desperate the way that almost every young man who is wounded or dying ends up calling for his mother, even addressing us as though we WERE their mothers. God knows there is a comforting that sometimes we all need, like the schoolboy officer whose hand you held. I want you to hold MY hand.

In between they wrote of their more ordinary daily lives: summer thunder-storms; Virgin Mary's hayfever; Viv's sudden passion for 'an absolutely awful staff-officer'; Frank's apparent return to cheerfulness; Bunny, Sergeant Banister, Nobby and Reggie all away on leave, even, briefly, Captain Prideaux - until the day when Harry wrote:

Can you hear down south how the guns have started here again? Our Captain Prideaux says not long to go now - yet there are still no signs of us moving, or anyone around us.

Simultaneously Annie was writing:

They have taken us off the train, our bags all packed ready to move north, north and nearer you. We're going to be running a new Divisional Field Hospital. Can you believe we are departing on a London omnibus?!

On the very day she wrote those words, Ordish and Bunny were dispatched into Ypres to arrange billets for the Company with the Town Major. The Border Rifles were on their way back into war.

END OF PART TWO

PART THREE

Chapter 16

Bunny thought the Town Major had been far too near too many shells; Ordish merely considered him eccentric. In the manner of another Town Major in a town further south in France, he was carrying a furled umbrella, picking a way through the rubble across what had once been the main city square, beyond them a line of men leading laden horses on another pathway towards the ruined rampart that they called the Menin Gate.

"Extraordinary," the Major was saying. "Three years of shelling and the city still manages to hold its shape." Sure enough the jagged silhouette of the old Cloth Hall reared above them, a tribute to its medieval builders.

The Major led them into a long, vaulted cellar below the city rampart and marked with chalk on the walls the limits of their Company billet. "Every comfort guaranteed," he said. "But you'll have to carry your own water in from outside town." And jovially: "You'll be less cramped second time around. Don't suppose more than half of you'll be coming back."

Above them the shelling had resumed, explosions not so far away. As they returned outside into the daylight the Town Major unfurled his umbrella, raising it against the whistle of flying stone and shrapnel.

Approaching the gun batteries behind the town was to walk through continual rolling claps of thunder, every one of which could make you jump however used to them you were. By the time Bunny and Ordish reached their pre-arranged rendezvous for the Company, they were both deafened and now, with everyone else on the roads, threatened by the German counter-barrage searching out those heavy guns and transport, each crossroad particularly targeted, dead horses by the dozen on every verge. The Kruisstraat crossroad, Prideaux had pointed out on the map, not realising it was the German gunners' first choice target. A couple of heavies roared over their heads and ploughed into an adjoining field. The two subalterns hastened past in search of some less dangerous place to wait, a bridge over a dyke half a mile beyond where they could sit on the bank below the road as though it was a trench.

"Think we all should buy umbrellas, Bunny?"

"Bloody laugh, wasn't he!"

"They say he's been here since the war began." Ordish nodded up the dyke at a farmer loading stooks of cut grass onto a cart: "Like he has."

"Bit damn near the shelling for a farmer."

"He knows he'll get a price and a half for his hay when we need it in the winter for our horses."

Bunny unbuttoned his tunic. "How'll it be, Sam?"

"This next attack?"

Bunny nodded.

"Don't think we'll ever get it right."

"They must have learnt something."

"Put it this way - with or without umbrellas, if it starts to rain we can pack up and go home."

"What did you see when you went up the line?"

"Pip Beers."

"Pip what?!"

"Pill boxes. Back in depth. A dozen we must have counted. Jerry'll have a pair of machine-guns in every damn one."

"What did Prideaux say?"

"Just looked. And drew them on the map. You know him. He still wants to believe the château-wallahs know what they're doing."

"Don't we all." Bunny was taking off his boots and socks to dangle his feet in the water. "Did I ever tell you my old man's got a bank of fishing on the Tweed? You come up and rod some salmon with me when this lot's over."

Ordish laughed: "Come on, Bunny! You know I'll not be going home."

"Don't be bloody daft! You've been in from the beginning. If it had your name on, you'd have copped it long ago. Like our friend with the umbrella."

They were silent for a while, Ordish lying on his back staring at a dog-fight faraway in the sky, a German Pfalz and an SE 5. Over the rumble of wheels and staccato of hooves on the road above them, he could hear a thrush in the hawthorn and glanced again at Bunny: "This old man of yours - "

"Yes, I know. Bloody gentry."

"Does he live up there?"

"Only in the season."

"London aren't you?"

Bunny nodded.

"So how come you ended up with us?"

"I asked. Joined up with a chum of mine from school. He came from Hexham."

"Roberts."

Bunny nodded again. In that moment they both remembered Roberts at White City, decapitated so swift and clean by a piece of shell that his headless trunk and legs had gone on walking for two more paces, his heart still pumping a thick red fountain from his neck.

Ordish smiled. Not about Roberts. He could see on the horizon the Pfaltz smoking from the attentions of the English SE 5; and then, incongruously in the same line of sight, a double-decker London bus approaching in the traffic down the road.

Bunny had also seen it: "All aboard for Piccadilly!"

"They don't usually come this near the line. Too much of a tempting target." And sure enough the shell bursts seemed to creep towards the bus as it approached the bridge. The driver stopped right above them, climbing out to decipher a forest of Military road-signs. Bunny whistled in appreciation. The bus was full of nurses. Ordish sat up and looked round.

"Heuveland Farm," the driver asked.

Ordish shrugged: "We're new here ourselves," he said.

"Along the dyke," yelled an ASC Sergeant from a munitions limber. "You come too far."

Bunny had seen the nurses and was trying to pull on his shoes in a hurry. Ordish also stood up for a look at the women inside, most of them asleep. They seemed infinitely weary, as though they'd been in there for hours. He'd never be quite sure what he did see first - the girl's sleeping face against a window or the unit number on the side, a stuck-on piece of paper for the traffic-jacks to read as they passed by. Both were suddenly familiar. And both, Ordish realized, to do with their American Angel. And when her eyes opened briefly, blue-green eyes, her face **was** the Angel Annie herself, 'Annie in Amiens' on Harry's photograph, here in front of Ordish, half-asleep with her suitcase on her lap.

The driver had climbed back inside, the bus moving slowly back towards the track along the dyke, Ordish walking alongside it, keeping pace with the window where Annie was sitting. She opened her eyes again but wasn't looking at him. The bus pulled forward onto the track, grinding slowly away along the dyke.

Bunny joined him on the road, still pulling on his shoes, too late to see the nurses "Anyone nice?" he asked.

Ordish was so overcome by the face he had just seen, he didn't even pause to consider whether or not he should tell Bunny: "Harry's American girl - I saw Harry's girl."

"On that bus?!"

Ordish nodded.

"The one in that photograph?"

"She had to be her."

"Blimey!" Bunny wasn't going to be denied and set out after the bus, a shout over his shoulder as another shell winged overhead: "Sitting where?"

"At the back - with their baggage."

And a moment later as Bunny broke into a run: "Which side?"

"Right side."

Bunny was doing a 50-yard dash now, disappearing into the dust cloud kicked up by the omnibus. Both him and the bus seemed entirely oblivious of the screaming salvo of shells overhead. Ordish, dropping down onto the bank once more, was quite sure some evil-eyed observer on one of Jerry's distant hills had spotted the double-deck shape of the nurses' transport. The driver was wise not to stop and give the guns time to bracket, whatever the temptation must have been to bail out and dive into the ditch or dyke.

Ordish watched Bunny re-emerge from the dust cloud walking back towards him - then suddenly, like Ordish before him, dropping to one side for cover as a shell come howling out of clear blue sky. Ordish stood up. It seemed the shell had hit the omnibus, so great the percussion and the burst of fragments. But when the smoke and dust cleared the omnibus was still there, in the distance now, chuntering onwards swaying on its thin wheels along the ruts. Instead the shell had taken out the Flemish farmer with his ox and cart, nothing much recognisable from any three of them. The price of dedication or of greed. Another death barely noticed by the passing traffic.

"She's just like the photograph," said Bunny with a grin as they resumed their places on the bank below the road. And after a few moments silence: "You wouldn't believe any of us could have a girl so beautiful."

"She's just a nurse, Bunny. Like you and I and Harry are just soldiers."

"Bloody socialist!" said Bunny with a laugh.

'B' Company were the first unit up the road that warm early evening, their singing heard from a half-mile away over the sound of traffic and the occasional screaming shell.

When this blasted war is over,
Oh how happy I shall be!
When I get my civvy clothes on,
No more soldiering for me.
No more church parades on Sunday,
No more asking for a pass,
I shall tell the Sergeant-Major
To stick his passes up his arse.

And as Ordish listened with a smile:

N.C.O.s will all be navvies,
Privates ride in motor cars;
N.C.O.s will smoke their Woodbines,
Privates puff their big cigars.
No more standing-to in trenches,
Only one more church-parade;
No more shivering on the firestep,
No more Tickler's marmalade.

Bunny and Ordish clambered up their bank to meet Prideaux at the head of the column, the front ranks beginning to see the jagged silhouette of the city in front of them. The two subalterns stayed at the head of the column to guide the Company to its billets, Bunny glancing round to see if Ordish intended to drop back for a word with Harry. But Ordish kept his station and his silence, 1 Platoon changing tune and lyrics as they began to approach the ruined city:

Far, far from Ypres I long to be,
Where German snipers can't snipe at me.
Damp is my dug-out,
Cold are my feet,
Waiting for whizz-bangs
To send me to sleep.......

*

The whistle and explosion of shells had seemed to follow them all along that endless, rutted dyke, the nurses crouched on the floor away from the glass of the windows. Annie found herself trembling. Most of them had had some experience of bombs or shelling on the train, but only Annie could actually recall what it felt like to be lifted up inside a vehicle and hurled 30 yards by the force of an explosion. The shell that killed the farmer had all but knocked them over, girls screaming for a while, Virgin Mary shouting at them from the upper deck for calm, the omnibus teetering as the driver turned his steering against the blast until finally a rut helped bounce them back onto all four wheels again.

By the time they reached their intended Heuveland Farm the shelling had been left behind and they were once more out of range - but all of them were white with the various terrors they had been through in their minds. A detachment of the Cyclist Corps were working on a drainage channel at the front of the farm and had witnessed the shelling from a distance, their lovely Sergeant now bringing out the rum jar to give, with Virgin Mary's nod of approval, all the girls a slug of 'dutch' and watch their faces regain colour.

Those cheerful Cyclists helped a sense of welcome to a very cheerless place. The intended hospital was grouped round an abandoned and semi-ruined manorial farm, tin huts and the barns in the yard for stores and three fields behind the farm full of tents. Most accommodation would be under canvas, only wards for officers indoors and rooms for the nurses in the attic. Four operating theatres were subdivided from the main downstairs room and half the yard outside tented as a reception area for ambulances from the Regimental Aid Posts. There was a grim realism about everything here, one of the barns filled with body sacks and wooden crosses, the further field beyond the tents designated for burials. The building itself stank of carbolic, the entire ground and first floors piled high with folded sheets and blankets, trestle beds for the tents still to be erected, stored in the tin huts outside.

"A lot of bloody hard work," said Virgin Mary in her Lancashire as they gathered on the stairs with the waiting Medical Corps Captain. And said the same again to the RAMC Colonel waiting in the office.

"How long before you're operational?" the Colonel asked.

The Captain looked at Virgin Mary.

"How long have we got?" she asked.

Annie and Viv climbed together to the top floor with their bags. The attic rooms were tiny, little cells for Flemish maids. "Can I share with you again?" asked Viv. Annie could hardly say she longed to be alone - there were some even smaller single rooms - but they chose their room together, Annie's bed under the eaves by the window, Viv's where the ceiling was higher beside the door. Viv proceeded to organise herself with the making of her bed and the hanging of her clothes, asking Annie if she was coming down to eat.

Downstairs the kitchen was already operational, looking after the Cyclist Corps and a couple of the nearer Artillery Batteries. But all Annie could do was sit huddled on her bed, listening to the guns too near, remembering Loos and the smell of burning flesh, thinking of the soldiers whose death-bags and crosses were waiting in the barn.

Viv cuddled up to her that night, their arms around each other, both of them for their different reasons whispering warmth to one another.

*

Inside the city Bunny didn't know quite what to do about Harry. Had Ordish said anything to him? Would Harry consider it an intrusion into his privacy if Bunny told him he had seen his girl? Would he be unsettled by her proximity? God knows, this Angel Annie had caused enough problems already in the Company. No one wanted absentees or aggravation on the eve of battle. For those very same reasons Ordish also had so far kept his silence.

Their cellar billet enforced a certain equality, only curtains to separate Officers from Men or Men from Sergeants. But all that proximity could lead to easier indiscretion.

Like Stevens overhearing Bunny tell Schoolboy, in the strictest confidence, about Annie on the omnibus. Bunny had only said it to cheer up the boy. More or less like all of them Schoolboy was deep in his own thoughts that night - and not improved by the echoes down the long brick vaults. The occasional roar of shell and thump of explosion seemed to threaten them so much more down here than in the countryside and open air. Ordish could have disabused them: they were far safer in this cellar that had already resisted three years shelling than in any part of the mortar-demented countrysides they'd been inhabiting for the past two years. But then Schoolboy, like all the 'newcomers', had his own particular fears about the unknown nature of 'attack'. Not that his fears were any less than the fears of those who already did know and knew too well.

Stevens was predictably troubled by what he had heard about Annie; not to say outraged. He decided to keep a careful eye not only on Harry but also the officer he considered to be equally guilty, Sam Ordish.

The Battalion, and no doubt a quarter million other men, spent the whole next day organising mills bombs and ammunition and storing the kit they would not be taking into battle. Everyone wrote their pre-printed eve-of-battle postcards home.

All that anticipation only to have zero hour postponed again. Whose fault this time? Some said the politicians in London who were afraid of another large-scale failed offensive; others claimed that the Quarter-Masters had decided the British army was running out of horses, far more difficult and expensive to replace than men; then there was the rumour from the redcaps outside reporting that the French had been delayed taking up position on the British left, up the canal towards Ostend.

Stevens saw Ordish move mid-afternoon, walking down the cellar to stop where Harry and his pals were playing cards. Ordish said something and then moved on, to the end of the cellar and out into the daylight. A few moments later Harry stood up and followed him. Stephens grabbed his cap, looking round. There was still a coming and going with ammunition and stores; no one seemed to have noticed either Ordish or Harry - nor Stevens as he shadowed them up the steps out into the daylight.

Harry could see Ordish ahead of him, disappearing into the labyrinth of rubbled side streets on the far side of the square. "We're going for a walk," Ordish had said back in the cellar, Harry wondering what this was all about. For a few moments he lost sight of him in that labyrinth, until Ordish grabbed him by the arm from what once had been a doorway: "Poke-nose is following us." And sure enough there was Stevens trying to look like part of the rubble fifty yards away. "He's lost sight of us. When he turns the corner, run!"

Harry hadn't imagined Ordish capable of such speed, the two of them laughing like schoolboys when they saw Stevens plunge in the wrong direction far behind them. They were racing each other now, not such a good idea as Harry turned a corner way ahead of Ordish and ran straight into a patrol of Military Police one of them grabbing his arm, another drawing a gun on him.

"Running away, are we?"

"On an urgent message."

"Where is the message?"

"Verbal message."

"Where's your pass?"

"I'm with my officer, Sergeant."

"And I'm with my grandmother, Lance-jack."

"Name and unit?" asked another of them. And thankfully at that moment Ordish appeared, no longer at a run, another grin when he saw where Harry's run had ended up.

"Lieutenant Ordish is my officer," said Harry.

"We're picking up medical supplies from a Field Hospital, Sergeant." The Sergeant saluted: "Very good, sir."

Harry's arms were released, one of them calling after him as he moved away: "Hey, Geordie! You ever been to Pérignon?"

Harry walked on without reply and thankfully the redcaps turned the other way.

"What's all that about?"

"Word must get around, sir. I had a barney with one of them down there."

"And he came off worse?"

"Something like that, sir." From the corner of his eye Harry saw Ordish smile. "What's all this walk about, sir?"

"I saw your young lady in a bus, Lance-Corporal. Thought it was about time you introduced us." Ordish grinned again. "Besides, if I'm stopping a bullet or a piece of shrapnel tomorrow I'd like to make sure the beds in this place are going to be comfortable."

Ordish led the way up one of the dykes away from the city, twenty minutes walking before they began to see the outline of the farm and the tents in the field behind. The two men were silent against the constant barrage from the gun batteries around them. When finally they left the artillery behind Harry couldn't help but ask: "Did you recognise her from the photograph, sir?"

"She's not a face you easily forget."

"Did she see you?"

Ordish shook his head: "She was sleeping. A couple of minutes later they were nearly shelled." Harry looked round. "About 20 yards away from them. Nearly knocked them over. They had a decent driver. He just kept going."

"That'll have shaken her up. She was shelled once before. When her husband was killed."

They walked in silence again, the farm building coming nearer. Ordish stopped to observe the layout. From this direction there was no obvious way in. "You think we'll have to pretend to be walking wounded to get inside?" He looked round at Harry. "You're wondering why I walked you all the way out here." Harry kept silent - but yes he was wondering and worried. He still believed Annie would find the handsome subaltern irresistible.

Ordish laughed as though Harry had spoken out loud. "I'm just curious, that's all. I've never heard an American voice before." And a few moments later: "Don't worry. I'll not get in your way."

It was Viv looking from a window who saw them entering the yard; and Viv who suddenly recognised the young soldier, the soldier from the street below their window in Pérignon. "Annie!" she called.

Annie and Viv were preparing the officers' wards on the ground floor, Virgin Mary in the office upstairs with the RAMC Captain, the other girls outside making up beds in the tents at the back.

"Annie?!" Annie appeared in the doorway behind Viv. Viv turned from the window: "It's him! He's here! He's with an officer!"

"Who? Who's here?" But Annie already knew.

"Your young soldier."

Who else could it be? There **was** no one else. Annie stooped to a mirror and straightened her cap and uniform. "Where's the battleaxe?"

"In the office."

Annie walked into the entrance lobby as Harry with the officer both entered the open door. Harry turned and saw her.

"Harry - ?" She briefly took his hand.

Harry gestured towards Ordish: "This is one of our officers - Lieutenant Ordish - "

"Sam Ordish."

"Annabel Donovan." She gestured at what she supposed to be her dishevelment. "We're trying to make order out of chaos, Lieutenant. Unsuccessfully so far."

Ordish peered into the ward behind Annie: "I came to see which bed you'll put me in tomorrow."

"You mustn't say such things!" cried Viv from inside the room - and also came out to shake their hands. "I'm Vivienne," she said. In the silence that followed it was difficult to know who was being chaperoned by whom: Harry by Ordish, or Annie by her roommate. "There's some hot tea made," said Viv to Ordish. Viv glanced up at the stairs as though fearing Virgin Mary would suddenly appear, then led Ordish into the empty kitchen.

Annie reached out for Harry's hand and took him back into the ward. "How did you find out where I was?"

"The Lieutenant saw you on the bus. He saw where you were coming. He saw you being shelled." Harry took her other hand. "You shouldn't have been so near the guns."

"The driver lost his way." Annie smiled and raised his hands to her mouth. "I can't believe you're here."

"It was luck. And the officer."

"Your Lieutenant Ordish who helps us with our letters?" She paused: "You're both in the attack tomorrow."

Harry nodded: "Been waiting all summer for it."

Annie looked at the empty beds all around them: "Like we are waiting now."

"I'll be alright. I always have been."

"I'm afraid for you. Aren't **you** frightened?"

"Everyone's frightened."

From the kitchen Ordish could see Harry and his girl through the shafts of sunlight in that room of empty beds. They seemed to him like fawns together in a forest glade, wondering at the feelings they've aroused in one another, and not quite sure what to do about them, a multitude of unresolved, unasked or unanswered questions still between them.

"You mustn't ever believe you're going to be wounded," Viv was saying in the kitchen and Ordish turned towards her. The mug of tea was sweet and strong.

"We'll be drinking rum with this tomorrow morning."

Viv asked him the same question: "Are you frightened?"

And Ordish gave the same reply: "Everyone's frightened. **You** were frightened yesterday. I saw the shell that nearly hit your bus."

"They had to give us rum when we arrived!" Viv looked round in sudden alarm at a sound upstairs: "Oh Lord! The battleaxe!" And there was Virgin Mary sweeping down the stairs. Viv saw Annie in the far room draw Harry out of sight. But the battleaxe was heading for kitchen.

"Oh Lord!" said Viv again. Matron Mary stopped short in the door, staring at the stranger.

Ordish saluted and bowed: "Forgive the intrusion, ma'am. I am a cousin of Miss Vivienne and called to say hello. She kindly offered me some tea." He bowed again and shook hands: "Lieutenant Ordish, Royal Border Rifles."

"Any relative is very welcome to our hospitality, Lieutenant." Virgin Mary nodded for Viv to pour another mug: "The Captain also wants his tea."

Ordish watched the battleaxe return upstairs with the Captain's tea and winked at Viv.

"You saved my life," she said.

"Court martial for talking to strange men?"

They both looked over to the far room. "Annie'll be letting him out of the side door," said Viv.

Their eyes wouldn't move from one another, Annie looking at his mouth. "I never stop thinking about you. You're with me all the time."

"I can't believe what you feel for me," Harry said. "I'm just a shepherd and a soldier. I'm a nobody. I'm not anyone."

She laughed and held his face: "You are for me." For the first time Harry had to look away from her eyes until she turned his face back towards her: "If you really want to know, you've become the most important person in my life." At the side door and out of sight from anyone she touched his mouth and kissed him for the first time on his lips.

Virgin Mary was watching from the upstairs office window as the Lieutenant walked away. Then noticed a second man join him along the tree-lined canal and recognised Harry as the boy at the railhead who'd thrust the tin box into Annie's hands. But Mary isn't in the mood to discipline or even question. One of her surviving brothers is also in the attack tomorrow - that one more 'final push' to end the war.

Harry wasn't conscious of how long they'd walked in silence, it seeming to him that Annie was still by his side. "I want to imagine you in years to come," she'd said. "The future is no longer forbidden."

"What did you tell her?" the Lieutenant eventually asked.

"That I am just a shepherd and a soldier, sir."

Ordish laughed: "Your fault you're just a soldier, Lance-Corporal. We've offered you three stripes often enough. You could have been an officer by now." And after another silence. "The way she looks at you, the way she writes to you, I don't believe any of that matters to her at all."

Harry glanced at Ordish. Had he walked all this way just to make it possible for the two of them to meet again? "I want to thank you, sir."

"My motives were purely selfish, Harry. She really is a most beautiful and extraordinary woman." Ordish swished his horse-hair cane at a cloud of flies and laughed again: "When the old battleaxe came downstairs, I had to pretend I was Vivienne's cousin. You'd better remember that if she ever asks you."

They heard a bugle far away across the fields, Last Post from another burial. Harry sniffed the air and sniffed again.

"And what does our shepherd smell this evening?"

"Rain, sir. It's going to rain tomorrow."

Chapter 17

'B' Company marched out at ten o'clock that evening through the Menin Gate, 80 to 100 pounds of rifle and equipment on each man's back: ammunition, grenades, gas mask, rations, entrenching tools, with shovels or pickaxes for the unlucky ones. Guides led them onwards from Hell Fire Corner while each man tried to remember their training on the tapes and memorise the features they were expecting from Prideaux's drawn map. They were scheduled to take up position by three o'clock. Zero hour was ten to four.

The guides lost their way twice in the darkness, Prideaux and Ordish unable to pick up any of their carefully listed points of reference. The five days German shelling since they'd been up here had obliterated everything, the whole horizon changed. If it's wiped out behind the line, thought Prideaux, what the hell's it going to be like in no man's land where both sides had been shelling? Eventually a runner sent back from the King's Royal found them and led them forward towards their correct positions. The King's were holding the sector of front line from which the Border Rifles would attack.

At half past two that morning they filed into communication trenches behind their attack position and, standing up or squatting down, waited - and waited and waited. Harry was down on his haunches, the butt of the Lewis gun between his feet, Frank, Reggie and Dippy above him leaning on their rifles, their heavy load of magazines for the moment jettisoned. Harry could see Frank's face in the darkness, eyes closed, a giant yawn obliterating his face. Little Frank had seemed alright these last few days, full of his birdsong and now opening his eyes for a smile and "Good luck, sir!" as Bunny squeezed past them down the trench with a whispered word for every one of them: "Don't leave your gun behind, Harry!" Sergeant Banister instead was crouched somewhere in the middle of the Platoon, each man's eyes on the dixie of tea he was trying to heat over a small fire of dry sack and broken duckboard.

In the next trench along Benson was thinking of home and the shipyards and wondering what kind of lunatic would ever sign up for a lifetime in the army. His bladder needed emptying but there was nowhere he could do it without spraying someone else. In no man's land, he thought: I'll have to pee in no man's land. In front of him Sergeant Percival was already halfway up the ladder on the parapet with his binoculars plotting a route through what few he could see of the obstacles in the darkness ahead.

At the head of his Platoon Stevens was realizing he'd be first man up one of their ladders. 1 Platoon was attacking with 4 out of the right hand communication trench, 2 with 3 from the other. Bunny came up to him with a pat on his arm: "You go left, we'll go right, and straighten into a line." Stevens nodded. "It's never as bad as you think it's going to be."

Ordish was also walking down his Platoon from Section to Section, speaking each man's name with a quiet word of encouragement. Sombre and ironic he might be but his men had always trusted him. I hope they don't blame me if this goes wrong, he was thinking.

Prideaux had camped in the King's Royal dugout, checking out his map with their Captain. The King's would be going over an hour after them to consolidate the first objective, a shoulder of rough and splintered woodland a hundred yards in front of them where Prideaux had marked one pillbox with a cross. "There's two in there," the other Captain said. "Both undamaged."

"If our barrage lifts too soon we'll be sitting ducks," said Prideaux.

"Rather you than us, sir," said one of the King's subalterns.

The Captain marked the second pillbox on Prideaux's map. "Hope you manage to get rid of those wasps nests before we come over."

Every man in the dugout looked up as they heard the heavy guns change tune. Their own shells were falling nearer to them now, the ground shuddering and vibrating, the explosions like a curtain in front of them. The creeping barrage had begun.

Banister poured out the tea, hot and sweet with a double tot of rum into every man's canteen as 4 Platoon filtered down the trench alongside 2. "2 with 4?! You're not blurry next to us," laughed Reggie at one of them.

"Turned the wrong fucking way, didn't we."

Harry was staring at the ground, the Lewis gun half-slung and balanced, oiled cloth round the breech.

In the 1 and 3 trench Benson like a dozen others was peeing where he stood, into the trench wall.

Schoolboy at the head of his Platoon stared at the ladders in front of him where Prideaux was climbing to stand just below the parapet. The Captain turned towards them: "Lets go and win the war, boys!"

With a look at his watch, Sergeant-Major Trussal on the ladder next to him waved his arm and 'B' Company went over the top, one by one in single silent file scrambling up the ladders and away into the darkness.

So far so good, Benson was thinking.

Six men led them out: Prideaux, Sergeant-Major Trussal, Stevens, Bunny, Ordish and Schoolboy. At Prideaux's previous insistence they moved watching over their shoulders, not to lose contact with their men - and as they moved waving themselves into a longer line. Behind the sound and fury of the creeping barrage the Germans hadn't yet realized the moment had come. Their heavies were shelling into no man's land in response to the creeping barrage but two blessed minutes passed before anyone heard a machine gun or the soft swish-zip of its bullets, Prideaux willing onwards and faster their own shell explosions that moved slowly in front of them onto the German positions. If they moved too slowly he knew they would be caught from the pillboxes.

Ordish was also watching the rough location of the pillboxes on his right, urging his men towards the small scrub bank he knew from his recce would give them cover. He also knew that any moment now the machine-guns would sense them there - and he knew, once that happened, their first objective would be suicidal.

At the last minute Bunny, God bless him, had pulled 4 Platoon Lewis gun to the front behind him, knowing it would take them longer to make ground. Frank led them up the ladder behind Bunny, one hand behind him to help Harry with the weight of the gun. And once out in the open the four of them grouped and ran together. The ground was dry but uneven and loose with hard clay lumps, shell-holes over-lapping one into the other, some of them still smoking. The time it took them to make twenty yards they'd all fallen more than once, the magazine cans in their canvas bags swinging like cow's udders round their legs.

Then Jerry finally woke up in his pill-box, the machine-guns starting their lazy, relentless rhythm and men began to fall from something worse than tripping over. Was it to be the Somme all over again?

Harry was running in a zig-zag crouch, though he was sure it was still too dark for the machine-gunners to actually see them. Get close enough to the pill-box, he was thinking, they'll be firing over us. Then we can bomb them out. Ahead of him Barnes disappeared in a shell-burst, no sign of him when the smoke cleared - until Harry saw his arms and legs scattered round the crater. Tottie Bell threw up his arms, spun round like a top by a bullet somewhere in his upper body. Harry looked over his shoulder: Frank and Reggie were still running, Dippy behind them, his short legs racing like a frightened beetle. He saw Carter fall, and Haynes and Lowrie. Whether the Germans could see them or not, the machine-guns were cutting them down. When do you go to ground? When is it allowed to take cover? When can you be a coward? If there are men and your own officers still running ahead of you, you have to stay on your feet and follow them. They're your kith and kin.

As Schoolboy himself was also thinking, trying to pretend he was running an 800 yards in the school sports, machine-gun bullets hissing, zipping all around him. Sergeant Percival was behind him, yelling furies at the men to keep them going, but each time Schoolboy looked back the line was ever thinner. Another shell burst knocked them all over, Schoolboy looking back again as Percival yelled them on, seizing one man by his collar to drag him up, only to separate the man's body at his waist.

Ahead of them Trussal called when Prideaux reached the bank: "If we don't take cover, sir, they're all going to cop it." And when he saw uncut wire above them on the shallow bank Prideaux dropped to his knees and waved them down, the ones in front under that bank, the others into the nearest shell-holes. From where, shell-hole to shell-hole they came, a few yards at a time, trying to cheat the machine-gunner and the shells that were still bracketing no man's land. At least those under the bank were too near the pillbox for the German shells to fall.

4 and 2 Platoons were almost directly under the trajectory, 1 and 3 Platoons more exposed on the open slope and taking the worse casualties, their line closing instinctively towards the right as soon as they were near enough to see the cover of the bank.

Benson was hit thirty yards short of the bank at its far end, two bullets from the same machine-gun before he fell to ground, luckily for him into a hole. The first bullet had smashed his hip, young Webster stopping in the shell-hole with him pulling out his field-dressing and clamping it on the wound - "a blighty, you lucky sod!" - a hand on his shoulder before he was off again and Benson all alone. Benson was now feeling another wetness around his back that had to be bleeding, his hand moving gingerly under his battledress and down inside his trousers - only to find the second bullet had merely drilled sideways through his water bottle, another problem for later, he realized when he finally discovered he could not move.

The survivors of 'B' Company kept arriving, re-grouping along the thirty yards of bank, Prideaux moving the Lewis guns to either end covering their flanks. They were safe here from the machine-guns and safe from the shells and too far from the German positions for grenades, but the strip of that safety was only two yards wide and one yard high. The bodies of the men who'd strayed beyond those limits were already rolling away back down the field. Prideaux looked round at Trussal: "If we stand up and move forward we'll all be dead in 30 seconds."

There were two more machine-guns firing from positions in between the two pillboxes, small humps of earth that looked like roofed dugouts. The whole 'wood' was a fortification, clearly undetected by patrols or from the air, equally clearly undamaged by their two week bombardment or the creeping barrage that had now outrun them. They could hear that curtain of shells, uselessly half a mile beyond them now.

"I imagine the cavalry are expecting to be in Berlin by tomorrow evening" - Ordish's dry voice under the wall of machine-gun bullets to make Prideaux frown and Bunny smile.

Banister was using a pull-through cord like a lasso to try and hook the wire beyond them. Time and again he threw until finally the pull-through weight caught on the wire and Banister was able to drag some of it back off the picket. His example was copied up and down the bank as they tried to dislodge the metre wide thicket of wire in front of them.

Even that innocent, playground exercise cost two men a pair of their fingers when their hands strayed too high.

For the moment their stretcher-bearers had no hope in hell of reaching any of them. What little morphine Colledge had been able to issue was divided between the officers 'at their own discretion'. They'd been programmed to be in combat for 12-15 hours; they expected to be out for more like 24. Field dressings, the odd hip-flask and a few shots of pain-killer weren't going to be much substitute for proper medical aid. For the moment, to conserve the morphine, smashed fingers and hands were given whisky and a dressing. There'd be far worse injuries than these to cope with, the whole field behind them already scattered with the maimed and dying and no way the medics and stretcher-bearers could yet reach them.

Benson, staring at the sky, saw the first signs of dawn and wondered how long it would be before someone came to help him. His world was for the moment confined to the uneven rim of the shell-hole and the sounds from other wounded men in pain and fear. "Mother," Benson whispered to himself.

Prideaux was looking for his Signals group, not that there was much hope of an intact telephone line so soon. They had no apparent contact with anyone on their left or right and no way to communicate with Division other than their four pigeons, too stunned by the sound of shell and bullet to even take to the wing when, one by one, attempts were made to release them with a message.

In fact the signals group was still stuck out in the middle of no man's land, reduced to two men trying to repair the wire laid out behind them, already cut by shells.

Prideaux looked back at their own front line as the light widened aware that the King's Royal zero hour was now, with château optimism, only minutes away. Surely they would see that there was nothing yet for them to consolidate. "I hope to God they'll have the sense to stay where they are."

Of course they did not, obeying instead the timetable as laid down. The Border Rifles watched in horror as the King's Royal appeared up the ladders and out into the now open twilight. Their extended line formed up in a straggling run - and almost as quickly began to disappear. The Gentleman-Officer's 'figurines you knock down with balls in a funfair', thought Harry.

But in those moments it took the attention of the machine-guns away from the Border Rifles, bullets no longer cutting into the top of the bank above their heads. Sergeant Percival was the first to up and charge, at the small hump of dugout 30 yards in front of him, a pair of thrown grenades to throw up dirt and confuse them. Harry, the second to move, crawled over the bank with the Lewis gun and ran for the matchstick cover of the shattered wood, Frank and Reggie behind him with their cow's udders swinging. Harry set up the gun, Frank the magazines, Reggie scraping with his entrenching tool to excavate out another few inches of cover. "Dig deep," muttered Harry. "Dig for coal, Reggie." It was Scottie and Dippy from under the bank who hurled them a pickaxe and a shovel.

The Lewis gun was slant-on to the slit apertures of the concrete bunker, the machine-guns unable to swing towards them. But they were being shot at from the second pillbox behind their left shoulders. The four men who'd charged with Percival were trying to crawl round the back of the pillbox to take it from the rear.

Harry kept up short bursts of fire at the slit windows, until the sun, rising directly behind the pillbox, blinded them for a few minutes - and made of them an even clearer target for the machine-guns behind. "Like a bloody searchlight on us," muttered Frank.

They were pinned down where they were for what seemed like hours, Prideaux wondering when he'd have to order the suicidal charge into the wood. Sergeant Percival and his four followers had also come under heavy fire, two of them wounded or dead, the others digging in.

Scottie was hit trying to throw Frank a bag of grenades from the bank, sliding back down, a small dark hole through his forehead when Bunny turned him over. Dippy knelt beside him, risking a bullet himself. He was crying. The two of them had been like brothers, lovers some of the older NCO's had sometimes said. "The bastard war," Dippy said simply. "This bastard, bastard war!"

And not long after, as though in sympathy, the sun and its warmth vanished from them behind a growing bank of cloud.

In all the confusion and danger around them the rain came at first unnoticed, that dampness on the wind Harry had smelt the previous afternoon spraying lightly from the sky.

"A shower," Reggie said. But Reggie was a coalminer and they'd been having showers all that long hot summer. Harry didn't even want to look up at the sky. It's not a mere shower you smell the day before - and sure enough ten minutes later the downpour started - as it seemed at the time, their second opportunity. The rain obscured everything for a few minutes, the rest of the Company up and over the bank into the 'wood' - and still losing ten men to the 'blind' machine-guns from the pillboxes. God, how they wanted those damn pip-beers and murder everyone inside.

In the end they had to charge those slit-windows as Harry kept up a stream of bullets, Frank and Reggie changing magazines.

"Watch our men!" yelled Bunny. "Watch our men!"

Three of them had reached the pillbox, standing up to one side of the slits, a cautious hand reached round to throw the grenades inside. Five grenades then in at the door at the back and finally it was all over - definitively so for the Germans inside. Their bayoneted bodies were dragged out, Company taking over the pillbox as HQ.

"We report and wait orders," said Prideaux and sent back two runners spaced well apart, posting three men on the back edge of the wood to watch if either one of them made the old front line. Neither man reached his destination. The other pillbox, targeted by 1 and 3 Platoons, was still very much alive.

"Dig in, lads," Bunny was telling 4 - their positions on the far side of the wood facing any German counter-attack. "We done it," he grinned at Harry. "We captured the buggering thing."

Did he mean the pillbox or the wood? The wood had been their first objective out of five, to be taken, according to the château, in the first half hour of the battle. Only now, 10 hours later, were they peering through the rain for objective number two, Bellewarde Farm, whose buildings had been long reduced to rubble.

Prideaux moved Stevens' 2 Platoon to join Ordish with 1 and 3, crawling forward inch by inch around the second pillbox until they were under the line of fire. But it still took them another hour and a dozen casualties before they were able to bomb their way inside. Like 2 and 4 they also dug in along the forward edge of the wood, hoping against hope that Prideaux wouldn't order the attack on that second objective.

"I'd like to think we're not the only ones who've stuck," Prideaux was saying to no one in particular. But he had no real thought of moving on. Only forty or so of the King's Royals had made it to the wood, certainly not enough to hold the position. Another pair of runners were sent back with a situation report and this time, without the pillbox to knock them over, they both floundered through.

For floundering it already was. The rain was raining as never before and onto smashed-up clay that would not drain, no man's land becoming a lake.

Benson, still unable to move, lay face up to the downpour wondering how long it would take the shell-hole to fill with water. He'd tried to chuck the water out with his helmet, knowing it was bloody silly. He couldn't throw it far enough to clear the edge and back it all came streaming down. Yet on and on he went. There was another wounded man five or ten yards from him who'd been calling for his mother all day long. Until at dusk Benson yelled out and asked his name. There was a long, even shocked silence as though the other man had believed himself to be entirely alone. "Who are you, marra'?" Benson yelled again.

"Pimlott," came the reply, somewhere between a shriek and a croak.

"How's your bloddy hole, Pimlott?"

Another silence before he replied again, his tone already different, voice strangled but back under control: "Fucking wet."

"Same here, marra'. I'll be breathing through a tube bloddy soon."

"You got a tube?"

"Don't be bloddy daft!"

"So what's your name?"

"Benson. Where you live, Pimlott?"

"Wooler."

"Wooler of the wool. Too many fucking sheep up there for my liking." He paused to breathe more air, something pressing down his ribs. "I'm just waterfront Geordie, common as muck."

"Muck is country. Waterfront is coal and grime."

"How'd you know that?"

"Bin there. Bin there for a job and run away."

"That's what I did. Coaling ships. Shovelling up after the grabs had dropped it all."

"I was on the railway."

"Should have bloddy well stayed there." Benson heard another croak as though the other man had tried to laugh:

"Think it's too late to change my mind?"

"Too bloddy late for both of us, marra'."

"Think anyone's going to come?"

"Bound to when it's dark but I'll be drowned by then."

"Get yourself out the fucking water. There's no machine guns anymore."

"Can't bloddy well move."

"You still got your rifle?"

"Want me to shoot myself?"

Another croaking laugh: "Stick the bugger in the ground so a man can see you."

But as he tried to move, Benson still had the impression that he could not breathe, pulling open the buttons on his battle-dress and shirt. Then discovered the cause: his mother's knitted wool vest he wore for good luck and after 6 hours in the water shrunk onto him like chain-mail. He moved his hands in the water around him and found his rifle; slipped off the bayonet and cut through the vest. Laborious movements all of them. Ten minutes or more from start to finish. It was nearly dark. Was Pimlott still alive?

"Marra'!"

"You still there?" The strangled voice was coming from a different direction.

Benson held up the rifle behind his head and stuck the barrel in the mud. Court Martial offence if Percival finds me, he thought.

"Now I see you!" came another croak. Then silence again, Benson having now to use his helmet to keep the water from his face. I really am going to fucking well drown, he began to think. Then the croak came from behind and over his head:

"Bloody hell, Benson, you trying to swim with that damn thing?!"

Benson looked up and back at the face above him on the lip of the crater, the strangest face he'd ever seen, one piece of steel embedded through the helmet, another through the cheek and out the other side, blood like a red mask wet from the rain all over him. No wonder the bugger couldn't talk. Not that it stopped his strange cramped croak:

"You tell anyone I was calling for my mam, I'll fucking kill you!"

And both men started to laugh as best they could. A slap on the face or the bottom would finish both of them the state they were in.

Pimlott reached down to grip both Benson's hands and made Benson think of Harry, for Pimlott's wrists and arms had a similar grip of steel. Benson's body came sucking out of the mud and water, cracked pelvis rotating every which way. His yelling roar of pain was heard by everyone: in the wood, inside the pillboxes, across no man's land, old and new. Even the Germans in their forward positions heard it with a cold shiver. For there but for the grace of God they all of them would go.

When total darkness came Trussal called in the Sergeants and took from them an approximate roll-call of survivors. Of the 237 men who'd started, 139 still remained on their feet. 25 were lying wounded with them in the wood; of them maybe 9 might still be able to walk and pull a trigger.

Listening to the Sergeants' low voices, Ordish's tired brain calculated 73 men dead or wounded in no man's land behind them. Would the stretcher-bearers get to them under darkness? No one could bear the sounds that the wounded were making, like a chorus of frogs and geese out on a marsh. They'd tried to help those nearest to the wood but the majority lay beyond and orders were to leave them to the medics. Some hope.

Ordish watched Banister in the guttering candlelight, patient and enduring, ever the quiet pragmatist improvising comfort out of misery. He'd collected water bottles from the dead and, old campaigner that he was, always carried tea and kindling in his pack. Crouched in one corner of the pillbox, face turned towards his flint, he was blowing up a fire. Patience rewarded, he brewed four German helmets full of tea.

Working a rota of men out front, 'B' Company spent the night inside both German pillboxes with the water running in like a stream and the uncomfortable knowledge that the doorways were pointing in the wrong direction, towards the enemy bullets and shells. And how they kept on shooting, the world around them full of flying lead and steel.

Ordish was wondering out loud to Bunny about the economics of it all - not just the mechanics of profit for those who produced the ordinance but the logic of expenditure. They already knew a horse was worth more than a man; maybe the time would come when a shell, or even ten bullets, would also out-value human life. And then of course the war would have to end. Ordish looked around for approval of his thesis but Bunny was already fast asleep - the blessed innocence of youth or sheer bloody exhaustion?

Ordish didn't like that wrong way facing door and returned with a dixie of Banister's tea to the equally exhausted soldiers of his Platoon on duty at the edge of the wood. And allowed each of them a long sip from his substantial hip-flask.

Banister instead carried tea to his Lewis gun team. Company anchor on the right, they could only rota one at a time, and take turns out in the rain to try and sleep. Harry looked up from under the tent of his cape and grinned at the warmth of the tea: "You're a pal, Sarn't." He handed back the dixie. "Are we pulling out or going forward?"

"Waiting for orders."

"Reckon we're winning?"

"Who the hell knows?"

They had no idea what was happening to their left or right. The war was now confined to their own tiny theatre, that shattered wood, the concrete bunker pillboxes, old no man's land behind and, God forbid, the objectives still in front of them.

An hour later the two runners found their way back from Division, Prideaux wishing now he'd never sent them. They brought written orders to 'attack at 9 am tomorrow, August 1st, behind the King's Royal and make with all possible speed the second and third objectives'.

Sergeants and subalterns were summoned; orders given; an attack line agreed - three trench segments of the former German front line on the edge of the wood. The one surviving officer of the King's Royal insisted that he and his men would lead over as per orders, forty of them from the centre trench.

Prideaux glanced at Ordish: none of it felt good and with every passing hour of downpour and every shell that fell the mud beyond them deepened, their prospects diminishing.

Chapter 18

The mud was almost as bad inside the hospital as out on the battlefield, the wounded in the afternoon coming in caked from head to foot, the orderlies who carried stretchers to the tents outside treading clay all over the floors when they returned. Virgin Mary's girls had been at it now for nearly twelve hours, the ambulances in never ending sequence from all sectors north-east, south-east of Ypres. They were bringing the bad ones here, those who wouldn't make it back home on the train and boat, those with missing limbs or limbs for amputation, head wounds or bad internal injuries, many of them close to death after the rough ride in the ambulances. As ever the probable survivors had grimly to be separated from the doomed.

It was the first time since Loos that Annie had worked, as it were, on the line. Most casualties on the train had already had some form of treatment, even if only a clean-up and a bandage. These men today were coming in with torn and filthy uniforms embedded in their wounds, wet mud caked so thick their clothes had to be sliced off them with scalpels or razor-blades. In these conditions Annie believed it could be dangerously premature to condemn a man to death from the mere look of him. And thus mistakes were made. Three times already the Surgeon had muttered angrily at Annie, "Why am I wasting my time on him?"

The fourth time he said it, she replied: "Because, sir, no one is dead until they've died." The Surgeon then had her dispatched upstairs to the 'mobile' officers' ward. Angry though she was, she was not sorry to leave that post of executioner.

The upstairs beds were nearly full, with the usual mixture of the lucid cheerful and the catatonic. At least up here Annie had time to ask whether there was anyone from 8th Division and if they knew what had happened to the Royal Border Rifles. But no one had. So far most of their casualties were from the 30th and the 24th, south of the Menin Road.

At midnight the Surgeon downstairs went off-duty and Annie was restored to her post assessing the stretcher-cases from the ambulances in the yard. At two o'clock she was sent to her bed in the attic. The doors had closed. For the moment no more wounded could be taken.

Chapter 19

Prideaux woke as though he was drowning, dreaming of the lanes around his father-in-law's home in East Sussex, his billet for the three short days of his leave. He was drowning in those narrow, overhung country roads between curved-out walls of white hawthorn blossom and jungle-growths of cow-parsley along the verges that left no roadway to walk upon. He wanted open spaces. He wanted horizons. He wanted bare hillsides of heather. He was shouting those desires to his wife across a crowded room. Then found his face in dirty water, the sound of guns outside and Sergeant-Major Trussal shaking him awake.

If anyone survives to tell the tale, thought Ordish, they'll write in the Regimental history that one hour before dawn the Germans counter-attacked Bellewarde Wood to retake their position.

Harry saw them first. The marginally increased rate of shelling had alerted him. There were just enough shells falling to mask the sounds of anything out in front of him. That made him nervous and when he saw shapes appearing out of the darkness and rain, he knew there were none of their own men out in front of them. No need for caution or passwords.

He pulled his trigger and yelled: "Jerries in front of you!" And traversed the gun to and fro across the width of that flooded field. But they kept coming on in waves out of the darkness, God knows how, for they were running at less than walking pace through that mud.

Harry's yell was repeated from man to man through the wood and into the pillboxes, what was left of 'B' Company dragging themselves out of slit trenches to face the enemy: nothing less than hand-to-hand savagery on what had been the edge of the wood amongst the splintered trees and ditches and under the eternal rain.

On both sides they were fighting for their lives, swinging their rifles like clubs or jabbing with their bayonets; losing their footing and falling, then rolling desperately aside from a downward thrust of bayonet; and yelling, everyone, officers and men, yelling out of sheer terror.

It was too damn close and too confused to use the Lewis gun anymore, so Harry grabbed a rifle and bayonet and charged for the nearest German, with a roar in the best 'Bullring' traditions. But this Jerry wasn't waiting for the bayonet, off like a startled rabbit before Harry could even see his face. Harry swung his rifle at the back of another German uniform and in that same moment saw Bunny discharge his revolver into another unseen German face. Reggie and Frank had pulled another of them to the ground, Craig running him through with a bayonet but then, unable to withdraw his blade in time, being run through in turn himself, Lars behind them, yelling, shooting the final German in the sandwich, rifle barrel up his arse.

Harry, still running, kicked another man's legs away, one foot on his neck, pushing his face into the mud as he stumbled on, this time Ordish behind him to plant a revolver between the German shoulder-blades and pull the trigger. German uniforms seemed fewer now, no longer moving towards them but turning away. The counter-attack, brief and savage, was over, Harry returning to his Lewis gun, picking off the survivors as they waded through the swamp and back into darkness, still at less than walking pace.

It'll be no better for us, Bunny was thinking. And in broad daylight with another barrage to stir the pudding. "We'll never make 20 yards in that mud," he muttered to Banister.

"We'll have to do our best, sir."

Lars hauled Craig into the pillbox and dressed his wound. "A blighty," Craig grinned. Ordish's Sergeant Baker had also been bayoneted in his side, Prideaux dragging him back inside the pillbox; Stevens' Sergeant Charlton was dead where the German counter-attack had penetrated to the near side of the wood.

"Thirty German casualties and a dozen of our own," reported Trussal. But at least they'd held their line. A retreat in these conditions didn't bear thinking about.

They re-grouped at first light under rain and shells, 2 and 3 Platoons in the centre trench with the survivors of the King's Royal, 4 with two Lewis guns to anchor the right, Prideaux with HQ Section and Ordish's 1 Platoon on the left, hoping to make contact with whoever was meant to be fighting on their flank.

Five of their surviving stretcher-bearers had joined them, having worked all night long out in yesterday's no man's land, Benson and Pimlott the last two wounded to be evacuated, the bearers up to their knees in mud taking more than an hour to reach the aid post.

The deluge still continued, all of them soaked through with mud and water. "Has it ever rained like this before in August?" wondered Bunny out loud. "Whose bloody side does God think he is on?"

At three minutes to nine the creeping barrage announced itself in a screaming of express-train shells, far too near their own position to be comfortable and, of course, a wake-up call to the Germans. Jerry's machine-guns started firing before the attack had even started, three or four of them firing blind for the falling shells of the barrage were raising a wall of suspended mud, water and steam.

Schoolboy and Stevens watched the King's Royal climb over the top from the central trench - and with their men saw every single one of them fall before they'd advanced ten yards.

So it was to be. The château-wallahs **had** learned nothing and Schoolboy with the Border Rifles was there to help keep their revised timetable.

One minute later on that timetable it was their turn. Stevens at the north end of the trench, pragmatic for the first time in his life, made no move to ready his men. He knew they would not follow him. Sergeant Percival at the south end left Schoolboy no alternative, yelling himself and those around him into 'up and over'. Schoolboy climbed onto the sandbags trying to encourage his own and Stevens' 2 Platoon to follow. He walked up and down the parapet above them, blue eyes facing them, his back to the German machine-guns, exhorting, cajoling: "Over the top for me, boys! Over the plonk! Over the lid! Over the bags! Over the top for me, boys!" Crouched and leaning against his stick, his arms were twitching as though invisible strings were pulling at them. He seemed to be shaking with fear until the soldiers below him saw blood start to run from out of his sleeves and over his hands. Schoolboy's words began to thicken and choke in his throat: "Over the plonk... over the top!" Finally, coughing blood and perforated like a colander, he tipped forward on top of his men back into the trench.

Now the others, having seen dying proof of the folly they'd been ordered to commit, were somehow moved or angered or shamed enough to follow his example - "Let's do it for him, lads!" muttered one of them and started to climb the sandbags, the others, including the reluctant Stevens, following into the gentle switch-and-hiss sound of machine-gun bullets cutting through the rain. Crouching, crawling, yelling, they disappeared into the gloom of today's new bloodstained no man's land.

On the left their creeping barrage was still far too near them and Ordish could see one or two of the guns dropping short. Yet Prideaux was ahead of him and he had to keep going while trying at the same time to slow his own men down behind him. Ordish heard the shell come screaming at him much as Uncle had heard the shell that did for him. Except that this one was coming from behind him and here the ground was softer, the shell deeper before it detonated - but still no more than three or four feet away from him. He was still ducking to the ground when he felt metal tear into his side and was then only concerned to protect the wound from mud as he tumbled forward into the hole the shell had made. Under the ribs, through the ribs? He couldn't be sure precisely where he'd been hit. Only that the pain was intense and his hand as he struggled with his field dressing running wet and warm with blood. All he could do was lie on his side and hold the dressing inside the torn uniform and pressed against the wound.

Harry, Reggie and Frank had moved right from the edge of the wood to avoid that creeping barrage and the German machine-guns. They were on the reverse slope, the ground falling gradually away towards the distant Menin Road where through the rain they could see another raging, shell-exploding battle in front of former woodlands they'd known as Château and Railway. There were other pillboxes governing this slope and they had to move uphill again back onto the bog plateau, floundering from one shell-hole to another looking in vain for their line of advance. 'B' Company had disappeared from sight in that shell-pocked expanse of mud.

Wading from shell-hole to flooded shell-hole, Prideaux and Trussal knew the dangers of advancing too far. Neither man believed there was any chance of reaching even the second objective given the state of the ground and the machine-guns in front of them. And if they went too far there'd be precious little hope of communication with anyone behind them. They had their orders; withdrawal was for the moment out of the question. If they could establish some sort of line across the far end of this desolate plateau, they might be able to cover the next phase of attack by whichever unfortunate unit was waiting to follow them. But with every ten yards they made there were less and less men with them and in the sudden silence once the barrage lifted they could hear the terrible sound of bullets hitting heads and bodies. The men seemed to go down with nothing more than a grunt. How many of them were falling into the deep mud and water; how many of them drowning? In the end Prideaux waved the survivors to ground a hundred yards short of his target, all of them too exhausted to continue.

Sergeant-Major Trussal watched his Captain look round at the remnants of each platoon round the rims of separate shell craters, ten, fifteen yards apart. "Where are all my men?" whispered Prideaux. "Where are my brave boys?"

Harry now had seen them, and dragged the Lewis gun from one hole to another with Frank and Reggie on either side to then anchor once again what seemed to be the Company's right flank. They could only pick out a handful there from 4 Platoon, gathered with Bunny in the next but one shell-hole, even fewer from 3 with Webster now at their head. Prideaux and Trussal were four shell-holes away, Stevens beyond them. There was no sign of Ordish or either of the surviving

Sergeants - until the Sergeants' voices could be heard from behind. Banister and Percival were 'sweeping up', coaxing the lighter wounded and yelling at the plain terrified to move forward and join the others.

The German shells started again, not quite sure exactly where they were but wherever they were landing delivering enough sound and fury to keep their heads well down as they tried to dig themselves dry shelter into the walls of the craters. But every hole big or small filled instantly with water so instead they began to dig outwards to join the craters and form some semblance of a line.

"Good to see you, Sarn't," yelled Harry over a shell when Banister joined them in their hole. "Have you seen the other Lewis?" Harry was carefully cleaning their own gun, unwrapping the protective rags, building a ledge on which to rest it.

Banister was trying to reach for two wounded men he'd been helping and drag them into the crater.

The first of them, Curly Smith, had one arm out of action and as he rolled into the crater slipped down the steep side into the mud and water at the bottom. And began to sink. Frank slid down after him to grab his arms, only with a shout to find himself sucked down into the mud beside him.

"The rope, Reggie," Harry yelled - the thin rope they carried for the gun in one of the ammunition bags. Banister was hanging onto the second wounded man another German shell not that far away. Harry left the Lewis to Reggie and, digging his heels into the side, climbed down to Frank and Curly and tried to slip the rope in a sling under both their shoulders. Frank grabbed his arm in panic, feeling how quickly his legs were disappearing, Curly's clutching hands dragging him in.

"Run it round you, Frank. Run the fucking rope around you both."

Curly was already up to his waist, still hanging onto Frank: "How can it be so deep?" he yelled.

Harry managed to slot the rope under Curly's arms and break his grip on Frank. The rope was now knotted round them both and looped back in the middle. But they'd need a fucking crane to haul them out from there. No one in the crater could find a purchase with their feet.

Harry turned to yell up at Banister: "Need another rope, Sarn't! 2 Platoon!" Sergeant Percival would have a rope. Sergeant Percival probably had a fucking crane. And to Frank: "We'll get you out, Frankie. We have to wait till we can stand on top. Keep your mouth out the water and when it's dark we'll pull you clear."

"Jesus, Harry, I'll be dead by then!"

Banister crawled away through the mud channel they had dug to join the next two craters. Banister was thinking for the first time that this was going to be a difficult place to get out of alive and that suddenly he'd quite like to stay alive. Back home it was coming up for Bank Holiday weekend, the wife and bairns down by the sea with her sister in Sunderland. The odds of living or dying had never occurred to him before. War was war. It either happened or it didn't - as another two shells landed near enough to shower him with mud and the smell of cordite and steam. A sunny beach seemed very far away.

Ordish was also well in the line of fire and running out of blood and time. The stretcher-bearers knew where he was but each there and back to the aid post was taking them two hours or more, Ordish dreading the thought of that long, unsteady journey. Why hadn't someone sent more bearers? Who was dead and who was still alive? For sure there'd be a lot more dying under all these shells and bullets. Ordish tipped his hip-flask into the gaping hole of his wound, no longer conscious of the pain but knowing he somehow had to keep it clean. Where was his young soldier Harry? Get me back to the aid post, Ordish thought, and I'll be on my way to Heuveland Farm and hold his girlfriend's hand.

Chapter 20

'Walk don't run' Virgin Mary had scrawled in chalk by the two doors that led to the back yard and the field of tents. One nurse had already fallen badly enough in the mud outside to be out of commission with a damaged leg. The Cyclists had tried to lay duckboards for them as soon as light had come that morning but the uneven surface made them just as dangerous. As for the poor patients under canvas, their conditions were appalling, the ground-water running through many of the tents, the chill and wet from the relentless rain aggravating any condition the wounded might have.

Annie hated it out there. They all hated it. Especially that section of tents set aside for the dying. There just weren't enough nurses to make sure that no man died without comfort. One particular 'ward' they'd already named the inferno, a bell-tent with fifteen officers' beds all pointing to the centre, a guttering candle by each man's head, a central oil-lamp, rivulets of water running through and the endless death-rattle drumming of hard rain upon the canvas above them.

By comparison the wards inside the house were a paradise of warmth and light, though they were dying here as fast as the men were dying outside. Like them too many had been left too long in the rain and mud, uncritical wounds becoming fatal through loss of blood or shock or cold or infection.

The movement of casualties in and out had resumed with the morning, a hundred or so moved out by ambulance to the trains five minutes drive away, sixty or so awaiting burial, another 200 admitted in the yard.

Everyone's exhaustion was apparent with a growing sense of despair as they watched the soldiers' faces. The promised break-through had ground to a halt yet again in a murder of mud and machine-guns. "We are massacred without victory," one of the officers said.

And from him Annie learned that the Border Rifles had taken heavy casualties and were thought to be cut off somewhere within the enemy lines.

Chapter 21

Dusk and night were coming once again, Prideaux having to decide whether to hold their line of shell-holes or order a withdrawal. But a withdrawal where? To the pillboxes in the wood? All the way back to the old front line? Their orders were clear - to hold position until the next attack But when would that be? They were without supplies, without relief, without communication. Yet if they attempted a withdrawal under darkness the Germans would put up flares and tear them to pieces again with shell and machine-gun. Their only hope of retreat was to wait for the next wave of attack to push the German guns further from them. Prideaux sent Webster back as the most articulate swaddy likely to find his way back to Command. "Make sure they bloody well know where we are," Prideaux told him. "Tell them we don't want our own guns shelling us again."

Banister had returned to the 4 Platoon crater with the other rope, Frank and Curly Smith held now on both ends of separate ropes waist-deep in the mud. Harry was crouched, clinging to the slope, feeding Frank wet biscuit and bully beef from his iron rations. Curly was beyond feeding, semi-conscious, no one knowing the extent of his wounds under the mud. The other 4 Platoon survivors had dug out a flat shelf on the forward edge of the crater, Lars taking over the Lewis gun, one man in two lying on the lip to keep watch while the other tried to sleep. They were wet, they were hungry, they were exhausted, they were afraid.

As full darkness fell the deluge seemed to increase, enemy guns unsighted even when the flares went up like fire-balls in thick cloud. Harry and Reggie stood up with Bunny and Sergeant Banister on the edge of the shell-hole and hoped no random bullet would find them. Inch by inch they hauled both men clear of the mud and water: Curly had both legs smashed below the knee and wasn't going to last the night, Bunny giving him morphine against the pain; Frank shared a joke or two about falling in the pig shit and volunteered himself back on the Lewis gun to give Craig a rest. But those 10 hours of terror in that mud still lived with him and he spent most of the night digging himself a hole beyond the slope of the crater well away from the danger of sliding down again.

Two hundred yards behind them Ordish had been picked up at dusk, both hands gripped to the sides of the stretcher for the hour and a half it took the bearers to carry him, swaying and stumbling back to the aid post. He was still conscious enough to tell Colledge that one or maybe two days late he had fulfilled his own prediction, hit by shrapnel from their own creeping barrage and on his way, he told the MO firmly, to Heuveland Farm. Colledge signed his chit but doubted he'd arrive alive. Before he was stretchered away both officers swapped the names of those they knew to be dead or wounded from the Company - indeed from the Battalion. 'A' Company, in the second phase of attack half a mile to the north of them, had fared little better.

All night the rain increased and decreased in pulses but never stopped falling. Stevens crawled over to Prideaux's shell-hole, both of them now joining Bunny in a muttered agreement that there was nothing for the moment they could do except sit out the inevitable early morning barrage and hope Webster had reached Command to tell them exactly where they were. Stevens agreed to stay on the left with Sergeant Percival, Prideaux in the centre with Sergeant-Major Trussal, Bunny to remain here on the right with Sergeant Banister. But as he crawled back round the far side of the 4 Platoon crater, a German flare went up and Stevens found himself face to face with a totally disorientated, shell-shocked grass snake rearing to strike. Involuntarily Stevens recoiled, raising his own head. Almost instantly a sniper's bullet hit him sideways through the back of his skull and he slid off the edge of the crater towards the mud and water. Harry as the nearest to him scrambled down to drag the officer clear, the man whom most in 'B' Company would have called Harry's sworn enemy.

Stevens was staring at him blank and puzzled. Yet the 2nd Lieutenant still seemed quite lucid: "What happened?" he asked.

"Sniper, sir."

"I saw a snake. I saw a bloody snake."

Harry held him. He could feel Stevens' blood and brains thick over his hands.

"Am I hit bad?"

"Yes, sir."

"A blighty?"

"I'd say so, sir."

Stevens smiled but the expression in his eyes seemed to fade. He was far away for the next half hour and there was nothing Harry could do but stay with him and hold him cradled.

Then his eyes suddenly focused again: "What about that girl then, Lance-Corporal? Did you get to see her?"

Harry nodded at him.

"Bet you kissed her." A silence. "You want to know what's funny? I never kissed a girl in my whole life. Not really kissed."

Harry shifted his position as his leg cramped up. He still somehow couldn't bring himself to leave the man he'd always called 'bastard Stevens'. Maybe another twenty minutes passed until he saw the officer move one hand towards his pockets.

"Bible," he whispered. "Read something to me."

Harry found the small pocket Bible, slips of paper marking some pages. But it was far too dark to read.

Stevens whispered again with another gesture at his pocket: "I've a candle."

It took Harry five minutes to find and extract the stump of candle and matches without moving Stevens' head. It was Reggie watching them from above who clambered down and lit the candle for him. Harry slowly read the tiny print, a passage someone had marked with a pencil - his father or his mother? Stevens' eyes watched him through the feeble, flickering flame:

Whatsoever things are true, whatsoever things are honest, whatsoever things are just, whatsoever things are pure, whatsoever things are lovely, whatsoever things are of good report; if there be any virtue and if there be any praise, think on these things.

That seemed to calm Stevens enough to close his eyes and Harry blew out the candle.

Up on the rim of the crater the message had been passed along from Prideaux - no firing from any gun, no talking out loud, no more lights. Nothing that might give the German artillery observers any precise idea of where they were.
Lars and Reggie were on the Lewis gun, Frank too far forward in his excavated shelter to be of much use to them. He'd dug the hole down to three foot deep, a foot of water already drained into the bottom, but nothing as terrifying as that bottomless sucking mud inside the crater.
Bunny touched his foot from back inside the rim - "Alright?"
Frank stuck his thumb up, Bunny passing him his hip-flask. Another hour, Bunny reckoned, before first light would bring another barrage.
Prideaux now moved left with Trussal to take Ordish's 1 Platoon, moving Sergeant Percival to the middle with the remnants of 2 and 3. They had three Lewis guns more or less still functional, one with 1 Platoon, one centre with Percival and 4's 'anchor' gun on the right. "Enough to hold up a Battalion?" Trussal pulled a face at Prideaux.
And then young Webster came trudging back knee deep in the mud, too tired to care about the occasional spurt of machine-gun fire through the downpour. Eighteen craters he'd fallen into on the way. He handed over the written order from Command: " 'B' Company to support the third wave of attack at 07.00 through your position by firing left flank towards Bellewarde Farm while the attack swings right. When executed withdraw." Prideaux and Trussal passed the rest of the night trying to decide exactly where through the darkness and the deluge Bellewarde Farm once might have been.

Stevens was now beyond all talking, only a grim, gurgling, frothy breathing from his mouth that Harry had sometimes heard before, the sound of a head wound dying, as though the brain itself was draining back into the body.

Harry stared up at the sky for the first sign of daybreak. When he looked down again the breathing sound had stopped and 2nd Lieutenant Stevens was dead. Like so many wounded men, he'd died in that long cold hour just before the dawn. Harry washed the blood and brain with mud and water off his own sleeve and trousers, ripped the officer's red i.d. disc from around his neck, took the Bible, a hip-flask, wallet and letters from Steven's pockets and clawed a precarious way up the rain-running mud wall to hand them to Bunny back up on the rim of that fearful hole. A long, strange look Bunny gave him: "Good of you, Harry, to stay with him. Good of you to look after him."

What did he expect him to have done? Drown him in the water?

Bunny chucked the hip-flask back at him: "I'm sure, Lance-Corporal, 2nd Lieutenant Stevens would mean you to have a drink with him."

Harry looked back down into the crater: however well he'd tried to lodge the body, dead Stevens was slipping slowly with the running rain down towards the quickmud. By morning he'd be gone, yet another of the bodies who never would be found.

The morning bombardment opened with sporadic shelling, as though the German gun crews were waking up one by one or the one crew was pausing between each shell to light a cigarette. But they seemed this time to have a very clear idea of where the Borders were. Perhaps they'd thrown out some scouts last night. God knows there'd been enough to-ing and fro-ing and lighting of candles to signal their position for anyone who came near enough to see or hear through the deluge. The first shell landed behind Prideaux's group; the second, a minute or so later, plumb between Prideaux's crater and Percival; the third took out Banister's breakfast fire in the bottom of the shallow shell-hole next to Bunny's foxhole; the fourth hit the side of the crater directly in front of Frank, his carefully excavated refuge sliding down towards the mud and water and cascading into three half-submerged German soldiers, casualties from the previous morning's counter-attack. Frank, yelling, was threshing about between them, sinking once again into another flooded Flanders grave when the fifth shell landed with them all directly in that mud and water and lifted corpses and Frank high into the air, Frank's flailing body landing to straddle the lips of both craters, arms and legs still attached, kicking and punching at the mud. Harry retrieved Frank's rifle and pack and dragged him back towards the Lewis gun position, Frank wild-eyed and speechless but apparently unharmed.

Banister heard his own shell with maybe one second to move and had even snatched his pack and dixie with him. He was now patiently crouched again to build another fire, three dead men's water bottles scavanged from the shell-holes behind them. "It's not Jerry's shells I'm worried about, sir," he muttered to Bunny. "I'll wager our own guns don't have the first bloody idea where we are." A nightmare waiting to come true two minutes before 07.00.

They'd counted fifteen shells that breakfast strafe, a couple of guns or so laid on them while the main batteries were concentrating down towards Hooge on the Menin road or Frezenberg in the other direction - the major bombardments they'd been listening to all night. Their own creeping barrage was very different: maybe a hundred guns all aiming at a curtain line that seemed to actually bisect their position. They could almost identify two guns firing short, one in front of Prideaux, the other in front of Harry's Lewis gun. And both of them insistently consistent: eleven shells into the same five yard squares before the barrage started to creep forward. Webster, HQ with Prideaux, took shrapnel through one arm and both legs from three consecutive shells, eyes wide open while the Captain tied dressings to his wounds.

Frank had been within an arm's length of all eleven of their own, unhurt but brain-concussed. When Harry looked over to him, Frank's eyes had gone, not focused anymore and rambling in his mind even if his voice stayed silent. He gripped Harry's hand each time their eyes met - but Harry couldn't watch him all the time. They were firing left, as per orders, towards the supposed position of the farm, waiting for signs of the attack expected from behind them.

When the attack appeared it was Frank, facing the wrong way, who saw them first as they appeared through the curtain of rain - Highlanders in kilts, the soldiers the Germans called 'the ladies from hell', wading knee-deep in slow, deliberate steps through the mud like witches and scarecrows in the half-light, the music of a bagpipe growing through the blasting of shells. At which strange sight and sound Frank stood up and turned away. "I'm going home," he said to no one in particular and, discarding rifle and pack, plunged away from the shells into what he now imagined was the silence of the rain.

The Highlanders were concentrating: where they put their feet; how to avoid the next crater; officers following compass-bearings. They barely noticed the floundering Frank, barely even noticed the Royal Borders as they passed, though the Borders were watching them, to make sure the Scots really did swing right and away from the direction of their own firing.

"Shoot off everything," had come the word from Prideaux. "When we're out of bullets we will withdraw."

Sergeant Percival was looking back at the Highlanders passing behind them, the full fury of the German counter-barrage now pulverizing the mud plateau as far back as the shattered pillbox wood. When he saw Frank, Percival's first reaction was to yell him into cover for he seemed oblivious to the explosions all around him. Then it became clear to the Sergeant that Frank had neither pack nor rifle and that he was deserting his post. The shite young runt was running away!

Harry realized Frank had gone when he saw the discarded rifle and pack and hoped Frank had only gone to cover somewhere not too far behind. He could see Sergeant Banister behind them climbing towards them round the edge of the next shell-hole with a dixie of hot tea. Harry ducked for another shell. When he glanced round again at Banister a moment later he saw the Sergeant's helmet in the air and his hair flying in a piece like a wig, Banister himself dropping to one knee on the rim of the crater. Dropped the bloody tea and all, thought Harry. Get down before they hit you again! But Banister didn't move, locked by the mud into his attitude of prayer, the rain washing him clean of blood. A fragment of the shell had sliced off the top of his head. According to the Highlanders, Banister was still to be seen there praying two days later when the rain finally stopped. No one had liked to disturb him.

The survivors of 'B' Company withdrew in stunned silence. They were now beginning to lose the indestructible, three Sergeants down in just twelve hours. Harry was looking for the surviving Sergeant, hoping Percival hadn't found Frank without his rifle and pack. Reggie was carrying both, Harry telling him, if anyone asked, that they'd sent Frank to find more ammunition from the dead and wounded behind them.

A whole hour it took them to struggle in and out of craters back to the pillbox wood, taking turns to carry three of the wounded and Webster on their backs. They found German stretchers for the wounded and regrouped on the far side of their wood, the concrete bunkers now consolidated by a well dug-in Battalion of Scots Guards. Frank had disappeared, Sergeant Percival still ominously behind them, "to round up stragglers". In front of them, back towards 'home', they could see Engineers at work trying to lay tracks of duckboard across the former no man's land; they could also see the bodies of their own dead beyond the bank where they'd gone to ground that first morning. Two whole days ago.

Trussal led them stumbling through the flooded, pockmarked wasteland and onto the narrow causeway of floating duckboards to come face to face with another Company of kilted Highlanders on their way into the butchery. "Moving you back in platoons now, are they?" asked the Highland Captain.

" 'B' Company, 3rd Battalion Border Rifles, sir," barked Sergeant Major Trussal in reply. "What's left of us."

The Highland Captain pulled his men off the duckboards and nodded at his bagpipes: "Give them a tune, Piper!" Tune or no tune the fresh Highland troops looked with apprehension at the gaunt faces and staring eyes of the mud-caked men who were passing them and the wounded they were now stretchering. Prideaux at the rear exchanged salutes with the Highland Captain, neither man daring to look the other in the eye.

"Good luck, boys," came one muttered voice from the Rifles' ranks.

Chapter 22

Ordish was unconscious long before the ambulance delivered him to
Heuveland, his condition diagnosed as terminal by one of the doctors,
his destiny the twilight zone of the bell-tent - until Virgin Mary
recognised him through the mud and blood. "Can we have a go with
him, sir?" she pleaded. "He's Viv's cousin."
Ordish was carried under the lamps, never to know how close he'd
come to his death sentence. Virgin Mary helped cut the uniform off
him for a clearer and cleaner look at the wound. Both she and the
RAMC Surgeon felt round the jagged hole in his side.
"You wouldn't believe it, would you," said Mary firmly. "The
amount of healing the human body can do by itself out in the mud
and rain."
"He kept it clean." The Surgeon sniffed at the torn and half-closed
tissue. "Emptied his hip-flask into it, I'd say." He looked up at her.
"He's probably lost a kidney and most of his blood. We ought to cut
him open again. Take out the mess."
Virgin Mary shook her head: "Sew him up and let him recover first.
If he's cut open now, you're right, he'd never make it."
"He hasn't much of a chance either way." The Surgeon painted on
peroxide and sewed loose stitches he could open later. "Ground floor
room, Sister. Acute Surgical."
"Thank you, sir."

Vivienne ran into the medical officer on the stairs before Virgin Mary
could find her.
"Hope your cousin makes it, Nurse Vivienne."
"My cousin?"
"He's in A. S."
In her exhaustion it took Vivienne a few moments to realize that he

must mean Sam Ordish. Another half-hour passed before she could free herself long enough to cross the house downstairs and find Ordish in his bed. He looked very pale, almost translucent, shrunken with his loss of blood and fluid.

"He won't wake up till morning," Virgin Mary told her. "If he wakes at all."

"You recognised him?"

"He'd have been for the inferno if I hadn't."

Vivienne found Annie outside squelching in boots from tent to tent doing TPR's, temperature, pulse and respiration: "Your young man's officer is here." And as Annie looked round in expectation: "He's not conscious."

"Perhaps it means they're on their way out."

Annie had tried to push Harry to the edge of her own exhaustion, though each time she saw the blanket-covered stretchers arrive outside she knew that any one of them might be him.

"I think it's awful," Vivienne said, "the way he knew he would be coming here."

"Is he bad?"

Vivienne nodded.

Annie almost smiled: "Viv, I do believe you're in love with him!"

"That's nonsense!" Then Viv pulled a face: "Besides it's not allowed if he's my cousin."

Cousin or no cousin, Vivienne returned to Ordish when she went off duty that night and held his hand until the dawn. She hated it when soldiers died alone in that cold dark end of night.

The one time he opened his eyes and saw her there, he smiled in recognition: "My lovely cousin." That seemed to bring some colour to his face as Viv watched him by the light of his one candle. A little later he whispered: "Tell Annie, I know nothing about Harry. Last time I saw him he was still alive."

Chapter 23

Stumbling back into the old front line, Harry and Reggie had asked Bunny's permission to return and search for Frank but the young Lieutenant shook his head. His 60 man Platoon was already down to 19 and the shells still falling. A return to the wood and the pillboxes would be another 40 minutes of suicide through the mud. If Frank had been wounded he'd be picked up; if he was alright, he'd rejoin them soon enough.

Front line, reserve line, communication trenches, farms, villages, woodland, copse or castle - the few part-surviving features of their old landscape had been obliterated in the past two days by shellfire and deluge. Even a bee or butterfly couldn't navigate in this wilderness. Eventually they stumbled into a cutting, the line of an old railway judging by the shattered wood sleepers and bizarre skyward twists of steel like pipe-cleaners. What was left of 'B' Company finally halted, still within the radius of German shells, at the point where the Roulers railway had once crossed the Menin Road, 'A' and 'C' Companies already there, equally exhausted, equally depleted, smoke from kitchen fires making hungry men cry aloud for hot food.

There was an ammo wagon and armourers to inspect their weapons. The Lee Enfields had the mud wiped off, barrels and bolts oiled by a line of grizzled veterans who seemed to want to pat the silent soldiers on their heads for the awfulness they'd been through. 4 Platoon Lewis gun was as always immaculate, a nod of admiration from the armourer who handed Harry a new bolt assembly and gas regulator key, and swapped their empty ammo cans for loaded ones. Were they regrouping to return into the line? No one seemed to know.

For a grim long hour 'B' Company stood easy for roll-call as each unanswered name was queried - "Did anyone see what happened to him?" - a litany of deaths, known and unknown, the dead entered as 'dead', the unknown as 'wounded or missing': in all one officer 'wounded or missing', two officers 'dead', with three Sergeants, four Corporals, three Lance-Corporals and two score of swaddies.

When, at the very end, fourth Section 4 Platoon, Frank's name was called after Harry's, it was Sergeant Percival who answered: "Arrested for abandoning his weapon and leaving his post. Handed over to the Provost Marshal". In the blank silence that followed it was clear that no one could quite believe what they had heard.

"I sent him for ammunition," shouted Harry. And he repeated it in a lower voice to Bunny: "We needed more cans for the Lewis gun, sir. He couldn't carry his rifle and pack as well."

Sergeant Percival shouted back: "Silence in the ranks!"

"Column of two and march them out, Sergeant-Major" said Prideaux to Trussal. It seemed to Harry watching them that the Captain and Sergeant-Major were as astonished and incredulous as the rest of them.

Reggie was still carrying Frank's rifle and pack. He gripped Harry's arm: "Nothing'll happen to him," he muttered. "He's a good soldier. The officers won't let it happen."

"If the Provosts have him," said Harry, "the officers don't have bugger all to do with it."

Bunny, hearing him, was inclined to agree. Murmurings had spread about 'mutiny' in the French army earlier in the spring and how that had been summarily 'dealt with'. There was no reason to suppose that the British army, at the start of a new offensive, would not react in similar fashion with examples made *pour encourager les autres*. Bunny was already rehearsing in his mind a case for Frank's defence, which exercise numbed him as cold as the terror of the last two days passed in that hell of mud and machine-gun slaughter. He watched the remnants of his Platoon shuffle to attention, slope arms and left turn. They had endured magnificently: they had obeyed when obedience meant virtual suicide; they had improvised survival and defiance; they had held together with mutual trust and sacrifice; but he doubted whether a single one of them would ever understand or accept the court martial of one of their number who had momentarily lost his reason in that purgatory. Bunny caught Prideaux watching him. Let's just get on with it, the Captain's eyes were saying; this is not the time or place to contest what has been done. Bunny saw Reggie gripping Harry by one arm, making sure he wouldn't lose control. "Please God," Harry was saying inside his head. "Please let nothing happen to Frank." Where was he now? On his way to the Provost's cold cell under the town ramparts? Harry was conscious only of Reggie beside him. Within his dead-eyed exhaustion Percival's brief statement about Frank felt like a shell fragment, tumbling and echoing through his head.

Back down the Menin Road they now more walked than marched, mud-caked, blood-stained, bowed against the human and mechanical tide advancing towards them: fresh troops who tried not to look at them too closely but stared all the same from the corner of their eyes; Engineers and Signals with horse and carts; ammo limbers; lorries laden with duckboards; dispatch-riders on motor-bikes; and endless ambulances in both directions. Survivors were the least important item. Even in their column of two, 'B' Company took up too much room and merged into single-file through the mud at the side of the road, the last unit from the July 31st attack to finally withdraw.

At the ruins of the Menin Gate they passed the Town Major under his umbrella. He seemed to Bunny to be mentally reassessing the Ypres billets as he saw how few of the men were returning from battle.

By the time 'B' Company picked their way through the rubble to their cellar under the ramparts a runner had caught up with them to deliver Colledge's list from the First Aid post and fill the gaps in 'wounded or missing' - and thus from Colledge's scribble they heard of Ordish, Benson and Pimlott transferred to the Divisional Field Hospital at Heuveland Farm, Pimlott with his helmet still skewered to his skull.

Up and down the cellar the survivors of 'B' company had slumped over their packs and rifles like drunken men, most of them sleeping instantly wherever they lay down. And lying down brought at last to the Sergeant-Major's notice a piece of shrapnel in his own shoulder. Well-dulled with rum, he hadn't even noticed his wound. "Not exactly a blighty," he said. But down to the clearing station they sent him, filling his hip-flask from his own Sergeant-Major's jar.

"Uniforms and kit to be cleaned for parade in the morning," called an Adjutant's fruity voice as Trussal disappeared.

"Get your boots and breeches and battle-plans out of here!" Prideaux replied in a weary voice just loud enough to be heard the full length of the cellar.

The Adjutant had also left a telegram and a travel warrant: the telegram to inform Bunny that his father had dropped dead two days ago on his fishing bank along the Tweed; the warrant Bunny's compassionate leave to return home for his father's funeral.

Privilege and events, thought Prideaux, are conspiring against Frank Lowburn. There would now not be a single subaltern left in the Company to defend a court martial.

Beyond shock and sadness at his father's death, Bunny was thinking the same damn thing. As also Harry. He watched Bunny walk up the cellar towards him: "I'm sorry about your father, sir," said Harry.

"Thank you, Lance-Corporal. He's been a dying man for quite some years. But I had hoped to get to see him one more time."

"There'll be no one left for Frank, sir."

"No." Bunny handed him a scribbled pass. "Go and find Lieutenant Ordish. See if he's fit enough to speak for him." Bunny turned back again before he walked away: "I'm leaving a written statement as his officer. I think they'll have to read it out. That is IF they go ahead with this nonsense."

The moment he saw Harry move ten minutes later, Sergeant Percival was on his feet and after him, Prideaux having to call him back. "I've signed a pass for the Lance-Corporal, Sergeant. Let him go."

Harry walked the four or so miles out of town, staring at one foot in front of the other as though only his weary mind could drag them along through the ever pouring rain. The mud on him that had started to dry inside the cellar recovered its sheen and seemed to cement itself even more firmly to his skin and clothes. Without the pass in his pocket he'd certainly have been taken for a deserter.

He was onto the farm before he realized, so restricted was the visibility, walking into the yard of freshly delivered wounded most of whom, to another eye, mirrored precisely Harry's own mud-caked, bloodstained bewilderment. No one seemed to take much notice of him, assuming perhaps that he was walking wounded. He saw the tubs of water by the door into which the nurses and orderlies were dipping their boots before entering the house and he followed suit. He'd never imagined a hospital could ever be anything but clean but the mud here was everywhere.

Inside he became immediately more conspicuous and was asked by one of the orderlies what he required and where he was going.

"I'm looking for Lieutenant Ordish, Royal Border Rifles - I have a request from his unit."

The orderly referred to a sheet of paper from his pocket and led Harry into one of the downstairs rooms, twelve beds of unconscious forms, Ordish indicated by the window.

The Lieutenant's face was so pale Harry hardly recognised him at first. The blood seemed to have drained right out of him. It didn't seem right even to say his name but in the end Harry leaned down: "Lieutenant Ordish, sir?"

Ordish opened his eyes, smiled and took his hand: "Harry. Are you alive or are we BOTH dead?" The effort seemed too much. It was a while before his eyes opened again. "What's happened to the others?"

"It was rough, sir."

"Bunny?"

"He's alright."

"And the Captain?"

Harry nodded. "The only Sergeant left is Percival. He's had Frank put on a charge."

But Ordish closed his eyes again and made no response. Still holding his cold, damp hand Harry remained standing by Ordish's bed for another hour hoping the Lieutenant would repeat his brief moment of lucidity. It was there that Virgin Mary found him and, after a moment of deliberation, sent a nurse to call Annie.

Harry's desperation over Ordish was obvious: "He's needed - my friend needs him for a Court Martial."

"The Lieutenant has yet to be operated," Mary replied as kindly as she could. "He won't be fully conscious for many days, if at all."

Harry looked up and saw Annie hurrying into the room towards them. Even though he was standing there on his own two feet, she was convinced that to be here at all Harry must somehow be seriously wounded. There was plenty of blood on his uniform. "Harry?!"

Virgin Mary, with a warning look at Annie, turned away to the adjoining bed where a man was suddenly crying out.

"They've arrested Frank," Harry said to Annie. "The Lieutenant is the only one who can speak for him."

"Are you hurt?"

Harry shook his head. Annie could hardly believe the depths of empty exhaustion in his eyes and took his hand. At which moment Ordish briefly opened his own eyes and saw them standing there together, now no longer as young fawns but like spent ghosts from the different hells in which they had been living.

Virgin Mary turned back with a look at the watch in her top pocket: "Go off-duty," she told Annie. "Take him away and wash him and if he is not wounded, send him back from where he came."

The laundry was in the lantern-lit cellars below, tubs of water and endless lines of sheets hanging to dry. Harry followed Annie down the steps like a man sleepwalking. "How long since you last closed your eyes?" she asked.

"Not since I last saw you."

Annie had undressed enough soldiers in two years to understand the fixtures and the fittings - boots, buckles, belts and back-to-front buttons, the endless wind-on puttees, shoulder-flashes to remove and pockets to check so a man didn't lose anything when his damaged uniform was thrown away - a penknife and pocket-book. The mud had soaked grey and black through to Harry's skin, vest and long johns so stiff she had to cut them off. He stood there too exhausted for embarrassment, obeying as she took his hand and stepped him into a metal tub of water, her sponge exposing him, revealing from the grey-black dirt, features and limbs which she had on other men seen variously and grotesquely damaged and destroyed. As the dirt disappeared in wet running lines back and front, his tensed body seemed to shine like veined marble with the symmetry of a classical statue. Had she ever imagined him naked? Of course she had, though without knowing or even wanting to know how she would chose him to be. Now here he was under her hand and sponge, a naked exhaustion that watched her with surrender. She progressed him like the sheets from one tub to the next and filled the final one with what was left of heated water; then went to find in the cabinets at the far end of the cellars the soap and razors the nurses and VAD's used for shaving the men. By the time she returned he'd wrapped a sheet around himself and sat down on the floor with his back to the wall. She knelt beside him and started to lather his face.

"You shouldn'a be doing this for me," he said. "You're worse tired than I am."

She wiped lather away from his mouth leaving the lips red against the white soap. "When do you need your officer to talk for Frank?"

"I don't know. They say Court Martial happens very quickly."

"They can't do anything too awful to him. You said he's a good soldier."

"The best."

She started drawing the razor down across his cheeks. "See how we take care of our soldiers and make them well," she whispered, "- only to send them back to be killed or wounded again. It doesn't make sense, does it?" Annie could feel his muscles begin to relax, his eyes closing, until by the time she'd finished shaving him he was asleep. She felt easier when his eyes were closed. That black emptiness inside them, whether of exhaustion or endurance or suffering or actual pain, was unbearable to look at when you knew those eyes from a previous incarnation. He'd been there before, she knew, into and out of battle. But now it was different. Had it been worse? Had it been too long? Was it what had happened to Frank? But then she'd been seeing this expression in almost every soldier who had arrived in the last two days with whatever wound or hope of Blighty or survival. She thought now from Harry's eyes that these were the faces of men whose trust had been betrayed. She remembered the words of the Gentleman-Officer just one year ago in one of the letters he **had** sent to her: *They do not know, those who dispatch us, to where they send my boys nor what we are expected to endure. They have no idea.*

Annie looked at her watch, wondering how long Virgin Mary intended her to take off-duty. It was the first time she'd had the luxury of these wash-tubs available for her own personal use. She turned down the paraffin lamp and left a candle burning. At least from outside it would seem there was no one here. The Belgian girls who came to do the washing wouldn't be back until the morning. Annie locked the door and, stripping off her clothes, stepped into the tubs one by one herself. And in the last tub knew suddenly that Harry's eyes were open and watching her. She blew out the candle and knelt beside him. And felt his hands take her face as she bent to kiss his mouth.

Her own hands slid him along the wall to lie him down; and as slowly as she'd been with the sponge, touched his body that now seemed so instantly familiar. She covered him with kisses as he lay without moving, his muscles no longer tense and stiff. Only his penis hardened against her hand and he felt her kiss him there as well - as Annie felt him shiver when she held it against her face. His own hands and mouth moved down across her breasts, his lips and tongue kissing over her belly and into her groin, his body turning until they were upside down to one another. No one had ever loved her like that before. She even felt his mouth against her naked bottom but did not want to push him away. She'd never been, nor ever wanted to be so vulnerable.

Then his body turned slowly again until they were face to face once more and kissing on the mouth, her hand reaching to take him inside her. Where soon he cried aloud at his moment of release, his body in spasms that seemed they'd never stop. His weight was on his arms and she felt he was hovering over her like a bird of prey, not moving away until, eventually shrinking small, he slipped out of her. A few moments later she felt him move again and kiss her in that same place, licking her clean until she could feel with her fingers both their milk upon his face.

They'd lain there for a long time and silent when sounds from upstairs returned them to the world; and even then they dared not speak as though both feared that one wrong word would break the spell. After all, words in their letters had always been so carefully chosen. They spoke instead with their fingers and their eyes, bringing their faces close enough to see through the darkness, fingers tracing the lines of each other's eyes and cheek bones, pupils huge with emotion and the darkness, close enough for their lashes to be touching.

More noises from outside and upstairs intruded again, his voice reluctant: "I'll be needing a uniform," he whispered.

"I'll fetch a gun and put a bullet through your foot so you have to leave the war."

"Then they'd have me on Court Martial too."

"Not if it's me who shoots you."

His face was smiling: "You'd miss the foot and kill me."

She touched his foot in the darkness: "I'd press it there and pull the trigger."

"And I'd never walk straight again. You wouldn't want a cripple by your side."

"WILL you always walk by my side?"

"I can't see any other way."

"For ever and ever?"

"Well, you'll not be wanting me for ever and ever. One day you'll be returning home."

"Never without you." She laughed out loud still in a whisper: "Not now! Oh never! Really never!" Annie held out her hand to help him to his feet. They stood pressed together, even their breathing in unison. Annie pulled on her own clothes as he watched in the guttering candle-light, easy, swift movements and gestures he would never forget. She unlocked a door at the end of cellar and led him into the clothes store for him to chose from underwear and uniform. At least these ones were brand new, the first time in three years Harry would be free of lice - for a few hours. Annie gave him his shoulder-flashes with pocket-book and knife and watched him pull on the uniform. "Run away. I'll help you run away."

"You know I couldn't do that."

"Why? Because of your friends? Do what you can for Frank and then run away."

"You wouldn't want me anymore. You wouldn't trust me anymore. I wouldn't no longer be who I am. I'd have changed. What you see in my eyes and hear in my voice, you wouldn't know it anymore. You said you always knew from the beginning who I am - that's what you wrote to me. Like I feel I know who you are. That is who we are for one another. That is who we always will be."

A smaller door led from the storeroom up steps to the outside and neither wished to open it. Until they heard voices calling for Annie behind them.

Harry gripped her hands: "Nothing will ever be the same again."

Annie held his face in her two hands and kissed him: "You are inside me and part of me. I shall live for you now. You must stay alive for me."

He climbed the steps, looked back once and walked away.

The rain had stopped for the first time in four days, fitful streaks of light in the grey sky reflecting in the water. No one had seen him leave, only Annie now from her attic window watching him recede along the tree-lined dyke into the twilight as the Last Post was variously sounded from buglers in the ruined city ahead of him.

Chapter 24

"The accused, number 437856 Private Frank Lowburn, 1st Battalion Royal Border Rifles, a soldier of the regular forces, is charged with, when on active service, attempting to desert his Majesty's service in that he abandoned his rifle and walked to the rear while under enemy fire until apprehended by Sergeant Percival of the same Company and Battalion."

The words, read in a dead voice, leaked from room to room in the small sand-bagged school, just audible through and outside the building once the wind had moved the doors ajar. They were in a small village on the Poperinghe road, taken there by horse and cart in the early morning. Harry looked up at Reggie sitting opposite him. They'd been shut with Sergeant Percival into two small huts that had once been the outside toilets, their boots and equipment polished, hair slicked down, but not even knowing if they would be called as witnesses. The 'prisoner's friend' had talked briefly with Harry and Reggie the day before - a Lieutenant Dalton from 'A' Company, nominated by the Colonel who'd forbidden Prideaux to take part. 'Courts Martial are for subalterns,' he was alleged to have said. Needless to say this Lieutenant Dalton knew nothing about Frank and seemed unconcerned to find out very much. In fact, having returned from battle the same day as 'B' Company, he looked worse shell-shocked than Frank himself.

Harry had briefly and from a distance seen Frank arrive with his escort; but hadn't looked him in the eyes since he'd stumbled round the edge of that shell-hole five days ago. He should have grabbed for him then and there and hauled him down; yet part of him really had believed Frank to be on his way back to salvage ammunition from the dead and wounded.

The voices drifted once more from the main schoolroom: "Does the accused object to being tried by the President or any of the other officers appointed?"

Colledge had warned Harry that prisoners were often kept quiet with pills of one sort or another and Frank's voice, when it came, sounded flat, expressionless and slurred: "No, sir."

Why had Frank not said 'yes'? His subaltern 'friend' should have told him to object. The officers of the Court had arrived in motor cars from château country, a Colonel and two Majors looking spick and span and quite untouched by war. How could they begin to know what men had been through. Harry wondered if they'd already planned how far to drive for their lunch or dinner.

"You, Major Wardle, do swear that you will well and truly try the accused before the court according to the evidence and that you will duly administer justice according to the Army Act now in force without partiality, favour or affection - "   Fat chance of affection, thought Harry " - and you do further swear that you will not divulge the sentence of the court until it is duly confirmed and you do further swear that you will not on any account at any time whatsoever disclose or discover the vote or opinion of any particular member of this Court Martial unless thereunto required in due course of law - SO HELP YOU GOD!"

Those final words, delivered like a loud staccato chant, rattled the windows each time the oath was read for the members of the court. After which Harry and Reggie could hear low muttering as though, reading from their books, they weren't quite sure of the correct procedure. Perhaps it had been Lieutenant Dalton to suggest a mistake.

"For the benefit of the prisoner, the charge will be re-read."

"The accused, number 437856 Private Frank Lowburn, 1st Battalion Royal Border Rifles, a soldier of the regular forces, is charged with, when on active service, attempting to desert his Majesty's service in that he abandoned his rifle and walked to the rear while under enemy fire until apprehended by Sergeant Percival of the same Company and Battalion."

The President's voice intervened: "Private Frank Lowburn, are you guilty or not guilty of the charge against you which you have heard read?"

There was a long silence as though Frank was waiting to be prompted, Harry's brain yelling at him through the sandbags and bricks and mortar: NOT GUILTY!!

"Guilty," replied Frank's voice, without expression and only just audible. Harry yelled out loud: "NOT guilty, Frank!!"

And Sergeant Percival growled back at him from the adjoining cubicle: "Keep your silence, Lance-Corporal!!"

Harry stood up in the tiny hut looking like he'd break down the walls. "That fucking Subby told him to do it! Take the easy way. No bloody work for anyone. And hope the court has mercy!" Harry spat on the floor. "Now they'll all be off in time for lunch and smoke their damn cigars!"

He sat down staring at Reggie: "He's done for, Reggie! They've done for him!" Harry stared at the thin brick wall behind which Percival was listening to them. "They've all done for him! Bastard Sergeant and bastard Officers!"

Back in the schoolroom the President of the Court had asked Frank again: "You are pleading guilty?"

"Yes, sir."

The Colonel turned to Dalton: "You are satisfied the prisoner is conscious of his plea?"

"I believe so, sir."

"Before the Court considers punishment, does the prisoner wish to make any statement in mitigation of punishment?"

Frank spoke slowly, no doubt remembering words he had prepared with Dalton: "I had no idea, sir, what I was doing. Some shells landed close by and I remember nothing more. I remember nothing till I was locked up in the ramparts."

"Is that all you wish to say?"

"I volunteered at the start of the war and I've always done my duty, sir."

"Do you wish to call any witness as to character?"

Lieutenant Dalton stood up: "They're waiting outside, sir."

Harry was called out from the toilet and led into the schoolroom, Frank turning to look at him with that trusting but bewildered expression of young Frankie as a child. Very pale he was, standing at a corner of the room, Lieutenant Dalton sitting to one side of him. The Court was sat around a table in the centre of the room, the President looking up at Harry as he was handed the Bible: "The evidence you shall give before this court shall be the truth, the whole truth, and nothing but the truth. So help you God."

"So help me God."

The President peered at a sheet of paper: "His officer writes that the prisoner is a correct and courageous soldier, Lance-Corporal."

"He's brave, sir, and thinks never of himself."

"You have seen him in action before."

"Many times. He's on my Lewis gun, sir. The Battalion and the Division would tell you, sir, we've always won the prizes."

'Unfortunately this is not about winning prizes, Lance-Corporal."

"He's always been brave. I asked him to leave his gun that morning and fetch ammunition from the wounded." And turning to Frank: "You should have told them, Frank. I ordered you to go."

The Court President held up his hand: "We're not debating the facts of the incident. The prisoner himself has pleaded guilty."

"He isn't guilty! He was half-drowned in a shell-hole for 12 hours. Up to his bloody neck! Then shelled to buggery!"

"The witness must answer the question or otherwise stay silent."

The prosecuting officer had been out of the room to confer with Percival, his turn now to cross-examine Harry. "You have known the prisoner a long time?"

"Yes, sir."

"How long?"

Harry was silent.

"You were at school together?"

"Since five years old, sir."

Looks were exchanged between the members of the Court as though to say, 'his opinion then cannot be objective.'

"I am telling only the truth, sir. The prisoner was ordered to find ammunition and left his gun behind. I presume he then got himself lost."

Harry was nodded away and heard the mutter from the President as he walked out through the door. "The observations about the prisoner's movements on the field of battle must be ignored."

Belatedly Lieutenant Dalton attempted to intervene: "Perhaps, sir, the facts of the case have not been sufficiently established given the prisoner's state of mind. Perhaps, sir, the plea of guilty should be questioned?"

"Far too late...." - all this still heard by Harry as he returned to the hut, his place in front of the schoolroom table taken by Reggie who tried to smile encouragement at Frank. Reggie told them about the retreat from White City on the Somme a year ago - how Frank had stayed with one Lewis gun alone for four hours to cover the Battalion as they withdrew.   Somehow this story of defeat, retreat and withdrawal didn't go down too well with the brass poodlefakers sitting at the table.

"Are you suggesting that this explains why the prisoner retreated a second time?"

"I am saying, sir, he is a brave soldier who should be recognised for what he did."

And then it was over, Frank's guilty plea meaning that Sergeant Percival hadn't even been called as a prosecution witness. Frank was told to remain standing as the members of the Court retired to another room, Harry imagining he heard the clinking sound of a decanter and glasses. Harry kept his voice low, talking over the partition at Percival in the next cubicle:

"Satisfied, Sergeant?"

"He ran away, Lance-Jack - "

"Buried in the mud for 12 hours then fourteen shells right by his ear."

"He pleaded guilty."

"If anything happens to him, you're a dead man, Sergeant, so help me God!"

"And you, Lance-Jack, are on a charge.   I've a friend of yours outside."

As he heard the Court return, Harry still did not believe they could do anything more to Frank than lock him up and take his pay. The President spoke against the sound of distant guns:

"The sentence of the Court is that you should be held in a safe place until this sentence is confirmed and ratified by the Commander in Chief and that if confirmed, you should be taken out and shot at dawn. The Court makes no recommendation either for or against mercy."

Harry yelled out loud: "Fuckin' dressed-up murderers!!" - and was himself, five minutes later, arrested and sentenced for his various outbursts to four days Field Punishment Number One.

Harry had been marched into the sand-bagged yard when they led Frank out, Harry's last sight of Frank a small hunched figure with bowed head, suddenly aware of him there. Frank called out: "Don't tell them at home, Harry."

Don't tell them at home. How do we not tell them at home? What do they write in their War Office telegrams? 'Regret to inform you your husband/son/brother shot at dawn for desertion'? Harry would have to find out.

The reluctant Reggie and smiling Percival had already gone. The Provost Sergeant shouted Harry to attention and marched him into the street, "left-right-left-right-left-right" - where who should be waiting for him but his redcap carrot-headed friend from Pérignon with two of his mates and a good hard prod of truncheon into Harry's kidneys: "Got you now, Geordie," said the fat man.

They marched Harry back into town, hands behind his back and locked him into a separate part of the Battalion cellar, wrists still handcuffed to stop him smoking. Harry had the feeling his fat friend planned something else for him tomorrow - but couldn't even begin to care what might happen to himself. He sensed entering the cellar that 'A' and 'B' Companies already knew the worst about Frank; he sensed also that most of them, given the opportunity, would march with their guns and force his release. As for Sergeant Percival, no one was speaking to him from either Company, officers or NCO's.

At midnight Reggie came to Harry in the darkness holding a fag through the bars of the door for him: "What can we do? They won't let it happen, will they?"

"You tell me when you hear," said Harry. "If Frank's sentence is confirmed."

As the redcaps marched him out next day, Harry asked where they were keeping Frank.

"Nothing to do with us. He's Provost-Marshal's man."

Carrot-head told them to shut up: "Any prisoner on Field Punishment stays silent." First port of call it seemed was the redcaps' private cellar or one hidden part of it. Guessing their intention, Harry didn't bother to restrain contempt, looking round at the senior redcap with a sneer: "Bit near the enemy for you, isn't it, fat man? I see you blink each time you hear the guns."

Handcuffed, Harry could barely cover up against their batons; and, as they'd done to Frank in Pérignon, their blows were carefully directed to the body where no damage would be seen.

Ten minutes later back out into the sunlight, wiping away the blood he was spitting from his mouth, they tied Harry with straps and webbing, wrists and ankles spread-eagled cruciform to a wagon wheel, the supposed humiliation and deterrent. The soldiers passing in the square could see him as they marched towards the Menin Gate and turned their eyes away. No one enjoyed the spectacle of Field Punishment Number One.

Regulations specified no more than two hours at a time on the wheel; Carrot-top kept Harry there for nearly four, in a smell and choking air even worse than the worst of front line odour. The August sun following that endless rain was strong, not only drying the top layer of mud but cooking the refuse and human waste that had flooded for four days and nights through the ruined town. A putrid, pungent layer of fog hung six to eight feet above the ground, a decay in which scavengers rejoiced. Dripping with the heat, Harry's face and hands were black with giant bluebottles, undeterred by his attempts to shake them off, Ginger and his pals sat inside a ruined doorway taking pot-shots at the rats, laughing, smoking, drinking beer, singing their own murdered, obscene version of *The Blaydon Races*.

Every shout and cry Harry had ever uttered or wished to utter returned to him now in pain and anger - and in silence.

He shut his eyes and prayed for Frank, only the second time he'd talked to God since he'd been at school.

Chapter 25

Annie was living inside a private world with her body and her soul; her mind, sure to God, was no longer in control.

Had there been a lull - a reduction in the volume of wounded arriving in the yard or was that an imagined part of her distraction? Just as well for those wounded that Virgin Mary recognised her absence of attention and kept Annie away from the operating and treatment rooms. Annie would like to have stayed in the downstairs ward where Ordish continued to fade in and out and back into his life.

But Ordish had become Viv's property, her free time now spent in vigil by his bed. She'd almost come to believe that he really was her cousin.

Insofar as she had a choice, Annie preferred instead to stay outside in the field where she'd found in one of the 'special treatment' tents those other Border Rifle survivors, Benson and Pimlott. The Count of Montecristo Tent, the surgeons called it. There were many of the nurses and VAD's who, out of curiosity, peered inside but did not like to linger. Pimlott, helmet still hat-pinned to his head, had become something of a freak-show - with a guaranteed future in a circus, one doctor suggested. The orderlies built a superstructure for him onto a stretcher, his head protected with a wooden cage so nothing could touch the shard of metal that protruded through skull and helmet. He was reclined on the stretcher at forty five degrees, another wooden support to take his weight behind. The surgeons still had no idea how to remove the metal or indeed the helmet from his head. But Pimlott chattered happily away, explaining to the world how he'd saved Benson's life in no man's land - and since it was more or less the truth, Benson let him carry on, Benson himself also trapped in something of a box, a wood frame to protect his damaged pelvis.

Annie told them they'd had a visitor from their Company who had not had time to find them - not quite the truth, but she wanted them to talk about Harry. "Lance-Corporal Cardwell," she called him.

"Harry's still alive?!" Benson smiled. "I should think the Hun will win the war if he was ever killed."

"Do you know him well?"

"He took me into line my first time up. Had a fight with a Sergeant over a tin of photographs and letters." But in that moment Pimlott started coughing and Annie had to turn her attention back to him before that fragile head started knocking on its cage.

Annie assumed no one knew what had happened that late afternoon in the cellar. In reality no one did, though Viv and the other nurses exchanged their guesses. But Viv's direct questions to Annie lacked the subtlety to encourage confession: "What happened downstairs with Harry? Two hours you were down there. You washed him, Sister said."

"I washed him naked." Annie replied with a light smile so Viv would never know whether or not it was really true.

"Did he try to kiss you?"

Annie smiled again and remembered Viv's stern rebuke from what seemed long ago in Pérignon: "You cannot fall in love with someone's face - without knowing who they are."

"But I do know precisely who he is."

"You can draw his face on a sheet of paper, that's all."

"I could draw his soul in the sky or in wet mud."

"I don't suppose he even goes to church."

"I don't suppose I will ever go to church again. There's not much of God's mercy around here to believe in."

"God is on our side."

"I'm sure the Germans think the same."

Viv's frantic efforts to advise caution and 'correctness' had amused Annie at the time, based, as she knew they were, on Viv's class-structured world. Annie longed now to divulge to Viv her final secrets: to articulate the feelings inside her body; to describe the love-making that now haunted and sustained her; to explain the certainty that she would now never ever 'love' another man. But she knew no one else would ever understand.

"Tell me about your Lance-Corporal and his tin of letters," she whispered to Benson later that night and he told her, with some embellishment, what had happened in that estaminet. He'd heard the story in the Company about Harry's visit to Pérignon and already guessed this Annie was the nurse. Lucky Harry.

"His friend Frank's in trouble," she told him.

"Frank Lowburn?"

She nodded. "A Court Martial."

"I don't believe it. That 4 Section, they're good soldiers. They're the best of the best."

Chapter 26

Captain Prideaux used much the same language in a letter directed to the Commander in Chief channelled through the Colonel. But the Colonel refused to allow his written appeal for clemency to go any further, promising to telephone higher authority instead and use any influence he might have.

Three hours later he reported back to Prideaux: the Commander-in-Chief, firm within his stern Scottish upbringing, had decided at this stage of a new and major offensive that an example needed to be made and without delay. It was recommended that Private Frank Lowburn be executed 15 minutes before sunrise the following day.

"You must agree it does make sense," the Colonel said.

Prideaux put down the phone and looked out from the Officers' curtained-off alcove at his depleted Company, scattered down the length of the cellar through shafts of light where the dust swirled at every shell explosion from outside. He was quite unable to agree that it made any kind of sense at all to execute one of their best soldiers for a moment of madness while in a state of total exhaustion. Hadn't they lost enough men? Even now they were preparing to absorb replacements, lists of names sent down from Division redrawn into Platoons and Sections by the brooding Prideaux. He'd declined any offer of help from Percival in Trussal's absence and wasn't best pleased to see the pompous bloody Sergeant return as soon as notice of the C-in-C's decision had been officially posted.

"Request, sir, that Lance-Corporal Cardwell and Private Nairn be nominated for the execution squad."   Harry and Reggie.

"Get out of here, Percival!" And as Percival turned away: "As prosecuting witness You will not be attending."

"I'm the only Sergeant left in the Company, sir."

"Then I'll borrow a sodding Sergeant from somewhere else." Prideaux watched him strut angrily away. It had to be said that Sergeant Percival also was a bloody good soldier. But without an ounce of humanity or common sense between his ears.

Thanks to him Prideaux now had to pick twelve men from the Company who would be dressed and detailed as a firing squad - and wondered at the perverse mind who'd written into the regulations that a soldier condemned to death should be executed by his own kith and kin. **And** this time in front of them - for Prideaux had to draw up a second list (from both 'B' and 'A' Companies), the thirty NCO's and soldiers requested by Corps as an audience for this brutal spectacle.

Carrot and his pals had the pleasure of telling Harry themselves as they untied him from his second day of crucifixion on the wagon wheel: "They shoot your friend tomorrow morning" - then marched him to his further four hours of latrine fatigues. Twice Harry fell, weak at the knees from his three hours on the wheel or from what they'd told him. Both times he was kicked back up onto his feet.

Where were they holding Frank? How could he get to see him? Was Frank thinking, 'Harry'll get me out of this'? God forbid. 'There's nothing I can do, Frankie,' he whispered. "This time there's nothing I can do."

He emptied and cleaned and carried and emptied hour after hour until his throat gagged, stomach retching bile over his fiftieth bucket of shit.

They marched him back to the cellar without letting him wash, his hands and arms still covered in it, the rage and despair inside him checked only by the knowledge that anything further he did wrong would in no way help poor Frank.

Reggie brought paper and pen to his cell that evening, Harry writing one page to Frank's family and entrusting it to Reggie. He named them all in the letter, father, mother and two sisters, and wrote that Frank had been his closest friend since childhood; that he had died a good soldier, instantly and without suffering; and that all his many friends in the Company would never forget him.

Then unexpectedly, just before dark Captain Prideaux came to him, the Provost Sergeant with him to unlock the cell.

"I'll not see him die without a word from a friend," was all Prideaux said, leading Harry and Reggie from the cellar out into the twilight ruins of the town, the Provost Sergeant ahead of them. The Captain called in a lot of favours to have that door unlocked and the visit granted. He had the Sergeant stop by a water cart to give Harry a chance to wash.

They turned down steps into another cellar and what passed for the guardhouse. Diminutive Frank was the only prisoner in one of three huge cells, disbelieving when he saw them, his face splitting into an awkward, lopsided smile. The two guards with him unlocked the door but kept themselves between Frank and the others. Frank's imploring eyes were watching Harry in the lamplight.

"There's nothing I can do, Frankie. This time there's nothing I can do."

"I did wrong. I know I did wrong. I let you all down."

"You did nothing of the sort," said Reggie in anger. "You're the bravest man I ever known."

Frank looked beyond him at Prideaux in the darkness outside the cell.

"I say the same thing, soldier," said the Captain. "I shall write to your family and tell them you died with honour."

"And what will **they** tell them, sir, in that damn telegram?'

"That you were killed on active service. That's all they say these days. I shall make sure of it myself."

"Thank you, sir. I'm sorry, sir. I'm sorry to have let you down."

Prideaux had to turn away not to show the emotion on his face and hoped to God he'd have more self-control in the morning.

Harry moved forward towards his friend, pushing the guard to one side. He held Frank in his arms for as long as they let him and whispered in his ear: "Think of the snow on the hills, Frankie. Think of home."

Harry sat against the wall of his cell through every hour of the darkness, Lars, on guard outside, holding Woodbines for him through the bars. Prideaux was reading Lamartine behind his curtain, Percival the Bible; Reggie blew into his harmonica and no one shut him up; and 42 soldiers polished their boots and buckles. Reggie told Harry later, there wasn't a single man in 'B' or 'A' Company who could sleep that night.

*

'A' Company's Sergeant-Major Brown had the misfortune to lead the firing squad. Not unnaturally he'd had no previous experience but knew some of the men would be feeling ill and all of them nervous and reluctant. He summoned up the rum jar and fed them all a double tot before falling them in outside in the still dark square.

The other contingent, no less reluctant, was formed up by another 'A' Company Sergeant, Allison. The numbers detailed to attend had been sent down, counted and recounted, their appearance inspected. Each man seemed to have decided the least he could do for the condemned man was turn out smart and respectful. Allison counted three men with Bibles in their hands. Against orders from Division, Captain Prideaux joined them.

Neither squad could exactly march, the streets too full of rubble from another bout of shelling during the night. As the light began to grow, they played follow-my-leader out of town, along a rutted road to Esquelbecq and into the cobbled courtyard of what had once been a cattle farm. At the far end of the yard a single post had been erected, ominous, hideous and, it seemed to most of them, none too stable.

The firing squad were handed back their rifles one by one by an armourer, each Lee Enfield loaded with a single bullet in the breech, cocked and ready, safety-catch on, each soldier assured that one of the rifles had been loaded with a blank. Sergeant-Major Brown told them he would raise a handkerchief for them to take aim and release the safety catch; then drop the handkerchief for them to fire. "You will do the prisoner no favours by not firing straight. The position will be marked on his body."

Albeit flushed from their double tot of rum, all twelve men felt nothing but fear and dread. It seemed to them like murder.

The Provost Sergeant told Prideaux later that Frank had slept like a child for most of the night. Taken by motor van to the village he didn't have to walk far, the Provost Marshal and a Chaplain leading him into the cattle yard, the twilight still so dim and misty that Frank wasn't yet conscious of the 'spectators' drawn up at the far end; nor their collective breath like smoke in the chill air. He wanted himself to feel calm but once the Provost Sergeant had tied him to the pole, blindfolded him and pinned the white card to his chest, Frank started trembling and trembled throughout the short passage read by the Chaplain.

Even in the Battalion Frank had been a quiet boy and kept mostly to himself or with his few friends. Not many of those present knew him well but that didn't make the occasion any the less awful for everyone. He was still a comrade and had entered the arena marching in their own same uniform. Standing there in a slipping blindfold and visibly shaking he wasn't going to make it easy for anyone to forget.

The Provost Marshal nodded at the Sergeant-Major; who took the handkerchief from his pocket and raised it above his head. Everyone stopped breathing, their smoke in the air disappearing. For all of them the courtyard was completely still and silent.

Frank instead could clearly hear their big guns firing all around the town, a bombardment that had started the moment he'd stepped out of the van. He could feel the blindfold slipping down his face, but couldn't keep his body from shaking. And then his bladder opened and he thought with dismay, 'everyone's going to see I pissed myself'.

The bullets hit him suddenly, without warning, like Harry used to hit him as a kid, small fists and very hard, three, four, five of them. The thumps threw him one way and the other, everything suddenly very clear to him - not only the soldiers who'd fired and the men who watched, seen as though they were standing right close up to him; but also the snow on his own hills, as Harry had told him; the snow the day he'd got lost. He was hanging from his wrists and hurting; and then the pole fell over with him.

When the handkerchief dropped the rifles had fired in a straggle, more one after the other than together and not many of them on the target. The 'executioners' and 'spectators' saw Frank's blindfold slip off, his legs go limp and the post to which his wrists were tied topple with him to the ground. His head twisted and twitched as though he feared to suffocate against the gravel until the Provost Marshal stepped forward, revolver in his hand, and blew Frank's brains out with a bullet through his right temple.

That is what they all remembered - and the rising sun soon after, above the ground mist across the flat fields beyond the farm.

END OF PART THREE

PART FOUR

Chapter 27

For officers, NCO's and men, Frank's death changed everything for those who had been near him. While château madness would continue to betray the trust of soldiers on the mud slopes below Passchendaele, justice itself had been abandoned in that cold early morning cattle yard and their world could never be quite the same again. The doors that used to close in Frank's own mind now began to close for others: a greater divide between those who were your pals and those you hardly knew; and an even wider gulf between those who were out here and those at home who could never understand events and language that seemed now to guard a secret world.

That ragged volley of shots would also change the course of love and life and war for Annie and Harry and threaten the innocence they had discovered together.

*

Higher authority had made sure Harry was already strapped to his wagon wheel well before sunrise to avoid any histrionics from the 'mad Geordie', Reggie joining him out in the square, sitting at his feet and continuing to blow his tunes. Prodded by Prideaux and the Colonel, Division even tried to make sure the heavy guns were firing at dawn so no one outside that farm courtyard would, they hoped, hear the volley of shots echo over the Flemish countryside.

Harry saw the sunrise that execution morning as a line of deep yellow light across the jagged pinnacles of the old Cloth Hall - and knew that Reggie was also looking up at it, for it told them both that Frank must now be surely dead. Harry's mind and body were numb with a coldness even that sun could not warm when it had risen far enough to fall on him. A coldness, a rage and a guilt.

At least he'd been spared the carrot clown that morning. It was far too early for him to be on duty and the two redcaps assigned to guard him had the decency to remain silent when Reggie blew a quiet Last Post on his harmonica. They also kept to regulations, releasing Harry after his statutory two hours - and even spared him the latrine fatigue, sending him instead to a gang of number 2's clearing rubble from the streets where shells had landed the night before.

Reggie returned to the cellar for roll-call trying to avoid the shocked and silent faces of those unfortunates who'd been detailed to witness the execution. Reggie didn't yet wish to hear anything about it. Though he did gather that Captain Prideaux had remained in the execution yard on his own until the body was removed.

Thankfully 'B' Company was marched out of town later that morning to 'parade and exercise' with the newcomers who were beginning to arrive: three subalterns, three Sergeants and a dozen men, assigned to the Border Rifles from other decimated units as 8th Division tried to regroup as a fighting force.

Sergeant Percival had been distanced by the Captain, sent back to base for a course on Signals, the pigeons, semaphore and telephones that had failed them so conspicuously during their attack. Prideaux's request for Percival's permanent transfer had been refused. As the one remaining Sergeant from old 'B' Company he was considered 'essential for a continuity of Regimental practice'. Prideaux knew the decision to be fatally flawed. He could read that in his soldiers' eyes but was able to do nothing. He would ask himself what might have been different had Percival simply disappeared.

Frank's execution was announced that same day at every roll-call and parade in the British army up and down the line in what the Commander-in-Chief believed to be the ideal cautionary deterrent. But it drove men more to resentment than to fear. As far away as Rancourt on the Somme anger smouldered from muttering into shouting voices on parade, mostly Anzacs and the Canadians it must be said, for Dominion soldiers couldn't stand the British feudal disciplines to which they also were partly subjected. Most of them wondered why the poor British Tommy fought at all, yelled at and insulted by his Sergeant-Majors, patronised by his Officers, handed white feathers by his women if he ever dared remove his uniform while back home on leave.

It would be Canadians next morning who found Harry on his wheel, a group of them in clean uniforms looking for their billets to rejoin their unit. They spotted Harry's wagon wheel from across the square and changed direction towards him and Reggie on the ground with his harmonica.

"Who does he fucking think he is - Jesus Christ?!"

It was their Sergeant who asked the more direct questions: "Who's in charge of you? What you been tied up for, mate?"

Carrot appeared from his doorway pulling on his red cap: "Because he couldn't keep his fucking mouth shut." He shooed at them with his hands: "Nothing to do with you lot. You keep moving on. The war's still waiting for you."

But his red cap had little effect on this frontiersman Sergeant with his companion veterans of Vimy Ridge: "Don't worry, Lance-Corporal, we've already lived more of it than you will ever see." The Sergeant took out a knife and cut Harry's wrists and ankles free, two of his men joining Reggie to hold Harry and help him down onto the ground. The Sergeant turned to the Carrot again:

"You treat a man like that again, Ginger, we'll have to have you killed next time we see you. One way or another."

Big, brave Ginger with his cosh and pistol stood aside, spluttering with indignation. He could hardly put a dozen of them on a charge. Besides Harry was into his fourth hour on the wheel, not exactly rules & regs if anyone wanted to check up.

The Canadian Sergeant restored Harry's helmet to his head: "Back to your unit, matey."

Ginger held up his hand: "He's on latrine fatigues."

"I wouldn't say so, would you, lads?"

"You're on Field Punishment. Under lock and key, Geordie." The blustering, protesting Ginger watched Harry and Reggie walk away past him, shielded by the Canadians: "On another fucking charge you'll be when you get back," he shouted.

Harry and Reggie walked out of town in warm sunshine now the mist had cleared. The battle they had left five days ago was still in its infancy, gun batteries moving forward on the larger roads, fresh soldiers marching up towards the line, the to-and-fro shuttle of ambulances undiminished as casualties continued, dead and wounded by the thousands every day, the sound of shell and machine-gun perpetual from six miles away. For Harry and Reggie that battle now seemed distant and unimportant. Frank was dead and neither man dared to mention him between themselves. The previous day and night had passed in silence, today so far the same. Harry clearly knew where he was going on this walk in the sun and Reggie guessed and was prepared to follow.

*

Annie had been told about an execution when she'd asked about the volley of shots the previous morning. She hadn't discovered the circumstances nor the man's name until the evening when the Cyclists' Sergeant told her they'd buried a Frank Lowburn, shot by firing squad, in a cemetery outside the village a couple of miles away. She knew what Frank's death would mean to Harry; knew she had to see him; but didn't manage to slip away until next morning. She took a ride on one of the empty ambulances returning down the main road not knowing that in that same moment Harry and Reggie were walking up the track along the dyke towards the Heuveland Farm hospital. They would miss each other by five minutes and just two hundred yards.

Told by Viv at Heuveland where Annie had gone, Harry decided to wait as long as he could in the hope of her return but knew they'd need to be back in town themselves by sundown, Reggie for roll-call, Harry to infiltrate himself onto some detail of fatigues and establish an alibi should his fat ginger friend intend to pursue the vendetta. They visited Ordish, unconscious in his ward, "almost bloodless" Viv told them in hushed tones. He'd been operated on that morning, the surgeon deciding against the use of 'borrowed' blood offered by Viv herself. They'd read of the 'transfusions' being used elsewhere but the Heuveland surgeons claimed they were as dangerous as blood loss itself. Blood from another body might not be compatible; no one in Heuveland knew how to test blood; no one seemed to even know whether a woman's blood could be used inside a man. Annie was well aware that American surgeons, including her husband, had overcome those problems with sodium citrate to prevent clotting and serum to match the donor with the patient. They'd also proved in their hospital at Dannes-Camiers that there was a ready supply of soldiers in the rear who'd trade their blood for a flask of strong tea and an extra rum ration.

No, these Heuveland surgeons were the worst of an arrogant bunch sent out from their teaching hospitals in England and bringing with them the feudal customs that exacerbated the already paralysing social divisions from that abnormally caste-ridden English middle-class. Annie guessed most of them aspired to the upper end of that category with its hankering after the 'aristocratic'. Even her poor Gentleman-Officer had suffered from that handicap - but would never have understood it as handicap. After all, did he not care for his men? Only the orderlies and the anaesthetists had had any knowledge of the war but the advice from their experience was generally ignored, thus the many gas or 'breathing' cases who died from ether that should never have been administered.

We have two more Border Rifles," Viv told Harry. "Outside in one of the tents." And she told an orderly to take Harry and Reggie "to the Count of Monte Cristo".

The nurses' slang puzzled but didn't prepare either man for the sight of Pimlott inside his reclining wooden cage, both Pimlott and Benson laughing when they saw the expression on their faces as they walked in. "They're charging ten bob a time to see me," said Pimlott. "And when they've collected enough money they're building a special room for me back home."

"In the city museum," suggested Benson.

Harry stared in awful fascination. Why should Pimlott's skewered head and helmet be more grotesque than even more terrible wounds on a battlefield? Because of the clean bandages that surrounded it or the cage around his head? Or because his continued survival in that state seemed so improbable?

The face in the cage was still smiling: "Someone come to see me all the way from London. Taking pictures of the inside of my head."

"Found out at last there's nothing in there," muttered Benson. "Nothing that's not wiped off on a piece of 6 by 4."

"I saved his life," replied Pimlott. "Don't listen to him. He's stuck with me now."

"How's the Company?" asked Benson and Reggie named a few of their mates in 2 and 3 Platoons who were still alive. But told them also of the three dead Sergeants. It was a while before anyone mentioned him, but because the two wounded men knew already what had happened, Harry and Reggie had to talk about Frank for the first time since the execution.

"We heard about Frank," said Benson. "It's a fucking shame." He spat on the grass and dried mud beside his bed. "They say they're going to shoot another two since him. Making sure you're digging in - those of you that's left."

Harry was suddenly standing to attention as they spoke, as though he was still inside that Court Martial, delivering the evidence he'd now come to believe: "He wasn't thinking straight. I sent him to pick up ammo pouches. We were running out. But he didn't tell them."

"Someone talked him into pleading guilty," said Reggie. "So none of us could say anything that made any sense for him."

Benson looked at Harry: "You lived next to him at home."

"A mile away away across the hill and no one in between us, no. Knew him as a kid. Little short-arse getting lost looking for his Da's sheep." Harry looked away. "Signed on together when we could have stayed at home. None too pleased with me they'll be."

And from a short silence Benson said suddenly and with passion from his damaged pelvis: "This fucking war, it's going to do for all of us. We'll never live nor love again."

*

The ambulance-driver had left Annie with the Town-Major, as ever polite and unperturbed under his umbrella, choosing another one for her from the collection in his office. "You're very bold," he told her. "You shouldn't be within the range of shells. They throw three or four over every half an hour to keep us on our toes." He led her through the rubble to the Border Rifles 'B' Company cellar which they found empty; then showed her the wagon wheel where he knew her Lance-Corporal had been tied up that morning. "Field punishment," he said. "He's been up there four mornings now."

Annie stared at the wheel in disbelief, the thongs still hanging where the Canadians had cut Harry free: "Tied to that thing?"

"Yes," said the Major.

"That's like crucifixion."

"A necessary barbarity of war."

They checked on the fatigue parties, the redcap posts and every working gang in town, though the Major knew full well the Lance-Corporal had absconded. He always knew the movements of the men in his sectors but preferred to leave discipline to someone else.

Back in his office the batman brewed them both a coffee and Annie scribbled a note that the Major promised to have delivered to this Harry Cardwell. Politely he folded and sealed the page with a line of glue. An hour later on a crossroads outside town he stopped one of the ambulances bound for Heuveland Farm and waved the pretty American nurse goodbye, on her way back 'home'.

When Viv told her later that Harry had been there waiting for three hours, Annie ran upstairs in tears to punch her fists into her bed. She felt instinctively something awful might now happen.

Harry and Reggie returned into town but by another less obtrusive road, Reggie slipping back into the cellar as though he'd been sitting there all day long on medical, Harry attaching himself to his previous day's gang of number 2's, stacking bricks and stones to keep those ever-narrowing streets clear towards the Menin Gate - where the Town-Major handed him the note from Annie; and where the carrot

211

redcap eventually found him as the sun went down and Harry's period of punishment came finally to an end.

"Don't worry, I'll be seeing you again one day, Geordie."

"In your dreams, fat man. Every fucking night until the day you die."

*

I've looked for you everywhere knowing how you will be feeling and needing to be with you. There is no justice, Harry, and nothing I can say that will make you feel any less angry and grieved. My arms are around you until we can talk and love again. Your Annie.

No there is no justice except what we decide inside ourselves. I can't believe we missed each other when we both tried so hard. The Company is soon on its way somewhere and we'll no longer be able to meet. It begins to seem I have no feeling left except that need I had to see you. Take care of our Border Rifles left there with you. They are good people. H.

Harry's reply to Annie's note was still in his pocket when 'B' Company marched out of Ypres next day, south through Dikkebus and Kemmel. With every kilometre stone he counted, hope seemed to diminish of ever seeing Annie again. This war was going to drag them all down to that lowest common level of despair, destruction and death.

Some of the newcomers had tried to start some singing but Reggie's harmonica stayed inside his pocket. The 'B' Company veterans marched in sullen silence, grim inside themselves, none more so than Harry, staring at the road beneath his feet or at the pack of the man in front of him. There were moments that day when he could almost reach out and touch Frank marching with him; moments no doubt when Reggie on his other side felt the same. Did either of them wonder, did they even care who would take Frank's place and join them on the Lewis gun?

When he finally raised his head and took a look around, Harry saw ranks of men with more new faces than the old and heard unfamiliar voices he couldn't even understand, men he later discovered who'd come from Wales or Liverpool or London. And with them he marched into a vast tented camp on the French frontier behind Ploegsteert.

Only when their whole Section had squeezed into their small tent did Harry become aware he was now in charge of them. "Corp," called one of the new faces, "who's our Sergeant?"

Even the answer to that question Harry didn't know.

"Flowers," said Lars. "Sergeant Flowers."

Harry looked round at the faces stowing their kit. Four of Scottie's men had survived with Reggie, Dippy and Lars from the Lewis gun team. All the rest were new and Harry didn't even know their names. Until he remembered the chit a Sergeant had given him back in Ypres. He pulled the paper from his pocket and began to read the names out loud: "Edwards, Spear, Thackwell -" and one by one each man acknowledged holding up a hand, new faces edging into Harry's life, a new war, the new world to get used to - "Atkinson, Hook, Bell, Neeson, Parker, Walker, Wood, Garner, King, Hedley, Gummer - " and Scottie's survivors, "Bowman, Darker, Scrace and Blair."

Harry looked round the crowded tent. He doubted there was a single one as young as him, yet here he was in charge of them. And not in the old haphazard way, as it were between friends. There was no way of telling whether this lot knew what they'd be doing. Before, if he'd told someone to do something, it was always something he knew that they could do. Same for these new faces: they didn't know if Harry knew what HE was doing. They'd be watching and listening and judging him. When it's life and death you have to know who you can trust. He'd made a monkey's already, silent on the march and now not knowing who their Sergeant was. He had some work to do.

"Anyone been on a Lewis gun?" he asked. Two hands went up, Harry surprising even himself by naming them: "Hook and Hedley."

He needed another pair to make up a decent team with Reggie and Lars, preferably men who could think their way round problems. "Anyone worked on engines or motors?" And the hands that went up this time gave him more than his two. Harry picked the stronger looking, again matching faces with names: "Neeson and Walker". Harry turned to Lars: "Who had the cart?"

"2 Platoon."

"Take them with you, Lars. Go and find our gun and boxes." And as they shuffled towards the sunlight outside: "Lay out your bedding first or you'll find no room when you get back."

Good damn thing they WERE under strength in this village picnic of a tent. For an amalgamated Section they were still ten men short, given that Dippy would soon go absent again as an officer's batman - but four pair of gunners was more than any Platoon could boast. As for Sergeant Flowers, no doubt he'd soon enough make himself alive. 'Alive' was just the word in more ways than one, Flowers ducking into the tent five minutes later like a performer onto a music-hall stage; which, they eventually discovered, was precisely from where he'd come. "We've had complaints," said the smiling Sergeant. "Some of your loved ones back home, my dears, don't even know you're still alive." At which point Harry remembered his note to Annie still folded in a pocket. Sergeant Flowers handed out pre-printed postcards for the men to fill in and sign. Harry later carried them down, with his note, to the mail-bag hanging outside the Company tent.

Without Ordish's assistance and in Bunny's absence, it was one of the new officers who read Harry's reply to Annie - and found nothing of significance to censor or remember, beyond the fact of a Lance-Corporal writing to a nurse. The envelope was sealed and chucked into the pouch.

Until Bunny's return the Company tent was new faces all around and, like Harry, Prideaux also found it difficult to adjust. Not that these were rookies. Two of them, Oxley and Hubbard, 'City of London' and 'Queen's West Lancs', had been out there as long as he; the third subaltern, Hamilton, had volunteered himself forward from Corps, a junior château-wallah, for which no doubt he'd take some stick.

"Baggage," said Prideaux to them all that evening. It was an expression from Sudan days, those formative years of his apprenticeship as a subaltern: an expression used if not invented by his old Colonel. "I'll eventually find out what baggage you are carrying; but I need to tell you some of the Company baggage - part of which you already know. A Court Martial and a firing squad has not made life any easier for us." He planted the whisky bottle beside the lantern in the middle of the tent.

"The Border Rifles has had a tradition, some would say a bad reputation, of informality. Something to do with our regimental history of territorial defence or raiding parties to rustle Scottish sheep. We've always functioned better in small mixed groups. Not quite so hierarchical as other regiments. And in that context, knowledge of and respect for the men we command is fundamental."

Prideaux poured the whisky. "I know I'm teaching grandmother to suck eggs," he said, but nevertheless went on to explain how everyone had to function in a particular way, from the rifleman with his own gun and bullets, the Corporal or Lance-Jack in charge of him and a dozen or so others, then a Sergeant and a subaltern with sixty odd under them, to a Sergeant-Major and a Captain with 250. This is what the system was all about - and discipline not by fear but with respect its only cohesion. "If that respect is ever lost then all is lost."

And Prideaux knew that 'B' Company was as close as it had ever been to losing that cohesion.

Had he not been absent, Sergeant-Major Trussal would, in his own way and with rum not whisky, have performed much the same task with his new Sergeants. Instead, for the moment, they had to fend for themselves. Beyond a word with Prideaux and introduction to their officers, the Sergeants knew nothing of their new units. With Percival still absent on his course, they relied on the scattering of Corporals and Lance-Jacks still left over from the old 'B' Company. "Going to be bloody p-pushed to p-pull this lot together," said one of them - Sergeant Batterby of 3 Platoon.

Flowers waved a hand in the air: "My dears, I've inherited the best trained Platoon in the Division. Trouble is most of them are dead."

"Most of all of us were dead," said Sergeant Summers. "And who wasn't dead's still dead enough to die."

"4 P-Platoon?" laughed Batterby at Flowers. "Company anchor, they're calling you. B-Battalion b-bloody anchor, one of them said. Anyone'd think you'd got the fucking cavalry!"

"The cream of the cream, I have, my friend. Only trouble being, I can't understand a word they're saying to me, the old lot there."

"Geordies," said Summers. And spat through the flap outside their tent.

*

Harry knew what had to be done, yet did not know if he'd ever have the steel to do it, let alone how. He also knew he was withdrawing way inside his head much like Frank himself had done - and had to force his thinking to the outside.

"She has eleven major assemblies; sixty-two parts if you strip her right down. She weighs 26 pounds and fires 750 rounds of .303 per minute. Unfortunately your magazine drums hold only 47 or 97. You can work out for yourselves how many times you'd have to change the drum to maintain your 750." Harry was addressing his new Lewis gun squad, remembering the staccato instruction delivered at the course in Pérignon. The mechanics of instruction absorbed him. He didn't have to think. Even about Pérignon and Annie he managed not to think.

"Tool kit and spare parts; always carry them with you: clearing plug; bolt assembly; gas regulator key; gas chamber wrench; drum loading tool; barrel mouthpiece spanner wrench." Harry held them up one by one and demonstrated their function or use. "This is your Platoon's defensive weapon. You keep her clean. She doesn't like the mud. And by the time you and I are finished, you're going to be stripping and reassembling her blindfold inside thirty seconds." Harry knew he didn't quite sound like the Sergeant-Instructor at Pérignon but the effect seemed to be the same: Hook, Neeson, Walker and Hedley were watching him and the gun in rapt attention, as though their lives depended on it. Which unhappily no doubt they would.

Harry was somewhat carried away with himself that first day, Reggie having to remind him he'd been instructing his four 'victims' without a break for eight hours. The second day Harry had to devote more time to the non-Lewis gun members of his squad. Left to his own devices by Sergeant Flowers, Harry took the whole Section off under the rain towards the banks of distant woods and played grandmother's footsteps through rough pasture and undergrowth to develop their skills at silent moving for wire parties and patrols out in no man's land. He discovered that four of the newcomers had never ever been out in front. There'd be a lot of blooding to do the first time they went into line.

The second evening and night Harry had his Lewis gun teams sat around a candle, assembling and stripping in the half-light and the dark, watched for a while by Bunny who'd returned that afternoon from his father's funeral back home. Having been in England ten days or more, Bunny had some catching up to do - not only the new faces in his tents but the news of Frank's execution. Which had the same effect on him as it'd had on the men - a sense of disbelief and anger with, as an officer, an added sense of guilt. Could he now look Harry or Reggie in the eyes? What would he say to them? He could see Harry's face in that circle of candlelight, a mask of gloom all over him.

Like his mother's even darker mask of doom, watching Bunny at the funeral, convinced she would never see him alive again. She'd seemed to be burying them both that day, her husband and son, in a cold south London church far away from the river valley and border hills that had been the most important part of his father's life. The Clapham house afterwards was even colder, his sisters and the maids handing round cups of tea and cake when everyone there needed whisky. Whisky for Bunny had come later, in the dining-car out of King's Cross as he sped north on the sleeper to sign papers next morning for the Sheriff and free their Tweed-side home to pay his father's creditors. Three days he'd spent with the last of his father's malts walking those river banks for the last time, reading the casualty lists in the newspapers by candle-light at night, remembering his father's advice about drinking too much of the 'hooch': 'you'll be high in perception, son, but, contrary to fact and expectation, low in spirit'. The casualty lists were telling Bunny that of his 1914 cricket eleven at school, six were already dead and two were missing.

Bunny walked down the lines to Harry that same evening, the 3/4 Section newboys staring in surprise as they heard the young officer call their Lance-Jack 'Harry' and march him off into the twilight.

"It should not have happened," said Bunny, "and nothing can make it right. There isn't a single officer in the whole Battalion who believes Frank did anything to deserve such punishment. I have to say, it feels even worse to me than the death of my own father."

Harry said not a word; stared him in the eyes when he'd finished, nodded then turned away.   Bunny imagined his look implied unfinished business but had no idea what else he could say.

"This Frank Lowburn business," Bunny said to Prideaux later that evening, "it'll eat away at everyone."

Prideaux nodded but kept silent. If something had to be done, he still had little idea what it could be nor how it might be accomplished.

Next day Sergeant Percival rejoined them from his signals course, Prideaux keeping him as far as possible from direct contact with the men. He attached him to his HQ Section and gave him the task of sorting out the pigeons and the telephones - then petitioned Division once again to have him transferred from the Company. Once again refused, Prideaux for the moment kept Percival back at Divisional supplies and transport lines.

Chapter 28

Those few days of sunshine had only dried the Flanders crust. The water-table underneath remained a few millimetres below ground level and when the rain came hard again there was nowhere for it to go. At Heuveland the house stayed dry, the old buildings standing on the only lump of rock or sandstone for miles around. But in the yards and fields the rain could only follow contours or, in the absence of contour, accumulate. The 'inferno' and the field had become a lake, three permanent inches of dirty water in and around the tents that overflowed a bank into the burial ground to float recent bodies through loose earth back to the surface - a nightmare of the dead and dying in which Annie waded, fetching, carrying and so far as was possible, caring. She'd been wet and cold for days. All of them had been. Even the wounded in their beds, raised clear of the water on three levels of duckboards but soaked from the condensation that dripped onto them from the canvas above. In the Count of Monte Cristo tent they had to cover Pimlott's wooden cage with oilskin to keep dry his shard of steel. "You wouldn't want water on the brain," Annie told him with a smile.

As Viv had adopted Ordish, so Annie had now taken Benson and Pimlott under her wing, the two Border Rifles who made her feel that little more connected to Harry. Benson was the more articulate, Pimlott occasionally drifting into repeating circles as the intruding piece of steel began to take effect. Benson talked of his town and of his river and explained that the regiment was more from countryside than city, and how that made him something of an outsider among the herdsmen, the foresters, the shepherds and the miners. He told Annie about the wiring party in no man's land the night Raven was shot through the head and fell into his arms - and about how Harry dragged the young schoolboy officer off the wire and saved his life. Benson did not yet know of Schoolboy's death, trying to coax his men up the ladders for that second suicidal attack at Bellewarde Farm.

Ordish had returned to life, his jagged wound re-opened, cleaned and stitched up again, his bodily functions and organs normal, minus only one kidney. On or off duty, Viv hovered round him with her smile. Annie noticed she'd even taken to wearing colour on her cheeks and lips.

The flow of casualties remained as high as ever, more from bullet than shell they realized as mud deepened on the battlefield and absorbed the impact of high explosive. But for every wounded man brought back to them, it was said another two drowned in the mud.

Eventually, into Annie's cold exhaustion came Harry's brief words:

No there is no justice except what we decide inside ourselves. I can't believe we missed each other when we both tried so hard.. The Company is soon on its way somewhere and we'll no longer be able to meet. It begins to seem I have no feeling left except that need I had to see you. Take care of our Border Rifles left there with you. They are good people.   H.

His mind was somewhere else, far away from where he'd ever been before. Those four lines sounded so much like farewell that Annie buried her head and wept. And later, cold, wet, exhausted and despairing wrote her reply:

Wherever you are with your thoughts, please never shut me out. I know the temptation. It happened to me with Patrick when he was killed. I didn't even want to read the letters from his family. Which was bad for me and bad for them. Don't leave me now, Harry. For ever and ever, you said. I need 'for ever'.

Chapter 29

I walk another road and cannot know where it will lead me. If I was home, I'd find myself in a different valley where the country is unknown to me. These aren't good words for you to hear but then it feels that I wish to speak with no one anymore. I watch my men and teach them what I can, enough I hope to keep them alive. They are willing but most of them new to what will happen when we meet the war again. I tell them not to even think of being brave. Just to stay together and keep organised and not let each other down. Frank was brave and look how his life ended. Your words are always a comfort. I hope you will ignore my different mood and write again.

Harry posted his reply on the day they left the camp, Bunny reading it an hour later as the officers tried to clear the mail bag before departure. Bunny had never seen any of Harry's previous letters to Annie, only the odd page home to his family. He felt the words were cold but carefully chosen, more than anything else an apology to the girl. Bunny remembered her face glimpsed on the bus that day with Ordish near Heuveland and thought with sudden shame that he should have visited Ordish on his way back from home. He sealed Harry's letter as the whistles blew for parade - and walking out of the Company tent saw Sergeant Percival standing alone outside the Sergeants' tent. Bunny turned the other way, unwilling even to acknowledge his salute.

They were going up the line and Percival could no longer be absented, Prideaux talking now with each of the 2 Platoon Corporals to make sure any order Percival might give would be automatically repeated by them. It was almost assumed that the old hands would refuse to take orders from the Sergeant who'd had Frank Lowburn court-martialed. The Corporals themselves suggested a better solution: to make up 2 Platoon entirely with the new arrivals and sort away the 'B' Company veterans into the other three Platoons. The officers sat up half the evening in the Company tent swapping names around, Bunny insisting they leave 3/4 Section of his own Platoon out of the equation. Harry had mastered his new lists of men and Bunny didn't want their Lewis gun team or Harry's fragile equilibrium undermined.

It was next morning before Harry himself caught sight of Percival, the Sergeant barking and bellowing at his new swaddies to stack the duckboards in their tents and hang the straw palliasses on the line to dry. He saw and heard him again that afternoon, two Platoons in front of them on their ten mile march into the line. Percival had lost nothing of his strut and swagger, even less of his bark and bite. Harry counted six fatigues the Sergeant yelled at new swaddies whose feet were dragging, four cautions to each of his Corporals and a dozen curses questioning the love-lives of various soldiers' mothers. Newcomers though they were, he'd already mastered all their names and identified the weak and vulnerable. He seemed to have no realisation of what he'd done nor how he was regarded.

They were swapping with the Suffolks to plug a gap on the hinge of Messines and release fresh Battalions for the battle they'd left behind. At least here they were on higher ground. One by one that evening the three Border Rifles' Companies took over the reserve trenches of what was now assumed to be a quiet sector of the line. They had four days before they'd be moved forward into the front line.

The old routine should have taken over, assessing and housekeeping, with each Platoon sorting out their intended sector of front line trench. But this time it wasn't working. They'd lost too many NCO's and the new Sergeants hadn't yet had time to get to know their Corporals and their men. The old unspoken lines of communication no longer existed and there was little will to make the new lines work.   Everything was resented: trench repairs, wiring parties, carrying parties, ration parties and the rain that had now returned. Jobs were done to the minimum of requirements and no one except Sergeant Percival and his newcomers cared for the quality of what they were doing.

Not even Trussal's roaring voice managed to inspire pride or fear when he rejoined them. Prideaux told the Sergeant-Major that no one in either Company had laughed or even smiled for days. A brooding, sullen anger Trussal sensed as he walked the reserve trenches the evening of his return. Even the old Corporals and Lance-Jacks didn't look up to say hello and welcome him back. For them, anyone senior was as good as responsible for what had happened. Trussal knew that anger would continue to eat into them as long as Sergeant Percival's face and voice were anywhere present - and over their weekly 'review' and a pint of whisky in the dugout Trussal said as much to Prideaux and to Colledge. As the only way of getting rid of him, Prideaux agreed to put Percival's name forward for a commission - reluctantly because he didn't believe he'd make a good officer. A Sergeant-Major at the 'Bullring' was more his billet.

Reggie watched Harry the evening they took over the front line under a curtain of fine rain. Both of them had squeezed past Percival at the Company dugout, both of them had heard the Sergeant's growling mutter: "Pick your pigeon legs up and look smart" and "Name and number, Corporal, his fuckin' button's undone".

Harry quietly chose his spot at the end of their line, this particular trench giving most of them a man-size refuge under the fire-step like a miniature dugout. With methodical care Harry adjusted a pair of loose sandbags to keep the rain from draining in off the trench then laid out scraps of groundsheet to waterproof his hole - the plodding, careful method in his madness, thought Reggie, for Harry had been expressionless for days now, only occasional and restrained words of command to break his silence. With Lars the three of them had still been looking out for one another, saving rations or hot drinks, but Harry's jokes and banter had dried up. He wouldn't even hum along with *In The Evening By The Moonlight*.   Reggie blowing tunes seemed to trouble him.

Like all of them Harry had been damp and cold for a week now, the nagging chill against the skin, like the cold shiver of a fever that never quite goes away. Except for the minute or two after rum ration. Strictly against rules and regs, Harry had taken to saving some of his rum in a medicine bottle at the bottom of his pack. "For a rainy day," he muttered at Reggie the one time he caught him watching. Otherwise the methodical ruled Harry and his Section: kit, boots and feet kept dry, lookouts posted on a rota, the Lewis gun polished and cleaned each sunrise and sundown by the newcomers under Harry's gaze - Hedley, Neeson and Walker, for Hook had departed with Dippy to the Company dugout as officer's batman, Dippy as before with Bunny, Hook with Hamilton.

Harry kept half an ear open on the comings and goings throughout the Company as though he sensed Prideaux and Trussal's unease at their condition. He could tell from the state of the trench that collective housekeeping was hardly functioning, individuals or Sections keeping their own sleeping holes dry but no longer concerning themselves with repairs to sandbag walls or duckboards damaged by trench mortars. Except of course Sergeant Percival in his 2 Platoon, determined as ever that his soldiering be beyond criticism and that his unit set the example not only for the Company but the whole Battalion. And in Lieutenant Hubbard he had a compliant subaltern, experienced enough not to become too involved in the day-to-day running of his Platoon.

It was the late evening of day three in the front line when Harry slipped away unnoticed. He'd posted Lars out right on the Lewis gun, dispatched Reggie on a ration party and pencilled Neeson, Scrace and Bell in on watch. Everyone else was asleep. Along the Company front to their left Oxley was duty officer, Percival duty Sergeant. The night was moonless, the sky banked up with cloud, rain blowing across the front in squalls.

With two grenades in his belt Harry climbed up and over the double traverse in the centre of their Section line, out of sight from those on watch and in line with the marked gap in the wire used by forward snipers. The gap zig-zagged through four thickets of the wire, Harry's hands out in front of his face as step by step he inched forward, left, right and left again. He heard a sudden burst of distant laughter from the German line and imagined for a moment that they had spotted him. Once beyond the wire he plugged the barrel of his rifle and eased himself down into the mud, only a foot or so deep here. He rubbed the clay onto his forehead and around his eyes and felt himself invisible for the moment, animal-like and quite safe.

No-man's-land here was 150 yards of grim, dead swamp, the worst any of them had ever seen, a plateau churned up by tanks in the June attack, blown to buggery by artillery to form a deep 'lake' of mud now fortified on both sides by those thickets of wire. It was considered to be impassable even for a patrol let alone an attack - yet Sergeant Percival claimed to have plotted a route through the flooded debris for what he proposed to Trussal as an attack on a distant group of ruined buildings thought to be a German observation post. Trussal's reply had seemed to chase the idea away: "How many more men do you want to get killed?" But Harry was sure that Sergeant Percival wouldn't be giving up that easily.

Without the stars it was difficult to keep his sense of direction. Thirty yards or so out into no man's land, Harry didn't want to stray back into their own wire and risk a bullet from their own vigilant sentries; nor, as his hands groped for each crawled movement forward, did he want to slip off the edge and sink into that 'lake' of liquid mud. The wind kept carrying German voices to him, sometimes ahead of him, sometimes from the right. The Border Rifles, better disciplined or more tired, were keeping quiet. As so often out in no man's land, Harry began to feel the sentries' eyes up and down both trenches, German and their own, and convince himself that they could see him: had Jerry left him there as their game, to crawl around in the mud before they shot him?

Harry was looking for the second, middle, gap in the Company line, another zig-zag path through the wire where an eager Sergeant might be plotting a line of attack. He guessed he'd have to make about 200 slow yards through the mud and, ten minutes too late, he started counting his body-lengths forward. It was going to take him all bloody night.

From ten o'clock to three in the end. But the cloud was still heavy, the night dark and dawn a long while away. Moving closer to their own wire, Harry had actually smelt the smells that told him where he was - in front of the officers' dugout, their fug of tobacco and the batmen's earlier cooking like a thin vapour through the drain-pipe ventilator. He could almost hear them snoring.

Then: "Sergeant!" - Harry heard Oxley's thin London voice from inside the trench, duty officer addressing duty Sergeant Percival: "I'm walking the line east. You'll stay here."

"Yessir!"

Ten yards further on through the mud Harry found that second gap in the wire. It should have been unmarked from his side but the last wiring party had left one ribbon flying in the wind. Harry faced the gap to pick up his bearings; then crawled backwards yard by yard like a frog in the mud, further out into no man's land and found the defile where for a moment he could stand up. He took out one grenade and unplugged his rifle.

Harry's throwing arm had to judge it just right - forty yards or so along the line beyond 1 Platoon and thirty yards in front of their Irish neighbours, the grenade to explode before it hit the mud. As he'd hoped, the crump of grenade in no man's land brought the inevitable follow-up of a German machine-gun. An Irish Lewis gun wasn't far behind, then rifles and more grenades, all hell breaking loose from both trenches.

After seven hours in the darkness, Harry's eyes were well nighted as he sank down to watch what he hoped to be the parapet line of sandbags above the fire-step in front of him. And sure enough a head appeared, a lighter disc in the darkness, eventually a definite helmeted shape.

Whose shape? Harry still had to be sure. "Fucking Fenian fairies farting fireworks," came the unmistakeable growling mutter from the helmeted shape, followed by the movement of binoculars up to his eyes as though he was actually looking out at Harry. Harry slung his second grenade backwards over his shoulder, sighted the rifle again counting the seconds and squeezed his trigger in the moment before the grenade exploded.

Chapter 30

When Annie was later told the date and the time she knew exactly where she'd been. One month into the battle, it was the same dark September early morning blowing gusts of rain when they'd carried Pimlott and Benson away. Even Virgin Mary had come out to watch, making a rare appearance from the papers and chits and bumph that controlled the logistics of their supplies and recorded the names and destinations of the wounded men who'd been brought to Heuveland.

No one believed that Pimlott would now survive. They'd winced at even the thought of that hat-pinned skull in an ambulance bouncing along those ruts. Turbaned Indians were the stretcher-bearers that morning and must have grimaced the same for, after a few words exchanged between themselves, not one of them paused by the waiting ambulances but set out down the avenue of blasted trees to carefully carry Pimlott, skull padded in his head cage, the two miles to the train. Annie walked with them alongside the stretcher, Pimlott's hand in hers, his perpetual grin refusing to acknowledge the spasms of pain that were turning his face green.

Benson's waving hand passed them in an ambulance, Pimlott raising his free arm in reply. "They'll keep us together, won't they, Miss?"

"I expect so - " And she said as much to the orderlies on the train when Pimlott was carried on board, walking up and down the train herself until she found Benson. The orderlies promised to load the two of them on the ship together and labels were altered to make sure they ended up in the same London hospital.

Benson also took her hand before she turned away: "Hope you see Harry again soon, Miss Annabel. Tell him to stay alive."

She felt her heart pain at his words, as though through their departure, Benson and Pimlott, she was losing her last physical link with Harry. Then, smelling those smells of iron floors and carbolic, she felt also an irrational nostalgia for their own train and that previous way of life. Death had seemed more under control in those days. Outside on the wet ground Annie turned back to the distant lump of Heuveland with dread and despair.

No, not a morning she would forget.

Chapter 31

Percival's body had fallen back, doubled up into the storage sap between the double traverse, his arms out-flung and squeezed into that same narrow space. In the darkness no one passing would have seen him and it was Trussal looking for the duty Sergeant at first light who found Percival's rifle up on the parapet above the firestep, then the body down below. The bullet had smashed into Percival's skull at the point where the nose met the forehead and spun off through the rear of the eye-socket, the Sergeant's right eyeball bulging out from the pressure. Trussal doubted that Percival had been aware even for a split-second of what had happened.

The Sergeant-Major looked up and down the trench from the firestep: another fifteen minutes or so until stand-to. No need to call a stretcher quite yet. He levered off the dead man's helmet wedged into the sandbags, found the skull exit wound and eventually the spent bullet lodged inside the webbing at the back of the helmet. He flung it away over the wire into no man's land without even a glance. Either way, he didn't want to know. Either way the damn fool had deserved it - head above the parapet, his bloody binoculars still held in one hand. Perhaps there'd been a flare when the grenades went off and the shooting started; perhaps a lucky German sniper; or perhaps not.

Emotionless, like a lump of the cold mud smeared all over him, Harry crawled back into his Section line ten minutes before stand-to, an amazed Scrace up on the fire-step watching the Lance-Corporal emerge, a clay-covered slug crawling through the rain, a whispered password as he negotiated the zig-zag gap in the wire.

"Jerry patrol," Harry said to Scrace. "You must have heard them."

And Scrace after a doubtful pause: "Yes, Corp."

"Someone was chucking grenades."

Scrace nodded, watching as Harry eased himself upright in the cover of the trench and removed his helmet, the rain running veins through the mud on his face and over his shoulders down to the cloth of his battledress. Even under the mud he looked like a ghost.

"Stand down, Scrace. Call stand-to."

"Sir."

But Scrace didn't yet move, still watching as Harry squatted on the firestep to pull his rifle through, once, twice dry, the third time with oil on his four-by-two.

"Fire it, did you, Corp?"

"Bunged up with mud." And glancing up at him: "Stand down and stand-to, Scrace. Unless you want fatigues."

Scrace this time obeyed, walking down the line shaking the cape-covered bundles awake, a tap on the Sergeant's tarpaulin round the next traverse.

Sergeant Flowers, as always, snapped up like a jack-in-the-box: "Enjoy your day," he said to Scrace. But when, after brief ablutions, he turned the corner and saw the mud-encased Lance-Corporal scraping at his dirt, he was for once lost for words.

"Sergeant Percival's been shot," they heard Bunny say, out of sight around the next traverse, Flowers looking again at Harry, again without a word.

Reggie arrived with the Section share of breakfast from the ration party. He also stared at Harry. "Percival - " he began to say.

Harry nodded: "I heard." And that was the last time either of them ever mentioned the name again.

Then Bunny walked round the traverse with Trussal at his side, the Sergeant-Major looking mud-caked Harry up and down: "Fell over, did we?"

Harry stared him back in the eyes without reply.

"Not that you'd care one way or the other. Get your fucking clothes off, Corporal, and wash yourself under the rain. May as well use the bloody stuff to some good purpose."

And so for most of the morning Harry stood stripped off, each of last night's garments hung on a line of string under the rain while one by one Harry tried to squeeze the mud from them. And tried not to remember where last he had been naked.

When the rain stopped, Bunny had a punctured fire-bucket lit with coke down the sap where Harry had pilfered the hand-grenades yesterday evening - a fire in the ammo dump! At least it half-dried out his clothes and warmed his hands. Had Bunny guessed? The young Lieutenant also hadn't said a word. Sergeant-Major Trussal sure as hell knew the truth the moment he clapped eyes on him - but had said nothing. He didn't even seem surprised. They'd looked at each another with total unconcern, indifference even. Trussal was right: Harry didn't care, one way or the other. It didn't matter whether anything now happened to him or not. His only preoccupation had been to do the deed without involving anyone else and in that he hoped he'd been successful.

The conspiracy of silence spread to the Company dugout, hardly a word said by anyone about the circumstances of the Sergeant's death. "Sniper," Sergeant-Major Trussal had said at stand-to. And later Oxley thought it necessary to explain to Prideaux why the body hadn't been sooner found: "We were patrolling different parts of the line, sir."

"Wouldn't have made any difference if you HAD found him sooner. He was dead before he hit the ground."

Prideaux took out a sheet of letter-paper, the words already in his head. 'A courageous soldier,' he would write to the Sergeant's wife, 'who had been recommended for a commission - Died in action - Killed instantly without pain - His experience will be badly missed' - though nothing much else, thought Prideaux.

But then had he himself tried hard enough with Sergeant Percival? Could, should he have changed him, reined him in, modified his behaviour? Schoolboy had once complained about his Sergeant's harshness to the NCO's and men under him but Prideaux had done nothing, not even sent him on a course. Percival had been a field promotion from Corporal after their losses on the Somme, White City claiming two of their senior NCO's and Percival in the same battle conspicuous for his courage. Though his personal courage usually came at a price: thirteen of his Section killed or wounded at White City; half a dozen led or dispatched to their deaths during the following year before this present massacre in the mud.

True to habit, Captain Prideaux would end up blaming himself. As for the cause of Percival's death, the conspiracy of silence was never broken, Trussal never telling Prideaux what he had or had not seen in terms of the close-range nature of the wound or the clay-covered spectacle of Lance-Corporal Harry Cardwell that early morning.

Harry dressing back into his vest and long-johns was remembering where he'd first pulled them on in Heuveland's candle-lit cellar - and felt his body die in that moment. He'd now killed a man far outside the heat of battle, planned, premeditated, coldly executed. How could he be permitted to ever love again? Or to be more precise: how could or would anyone love him ever again? A few days later, back in the reserve line, he wrote:

There is for the moment no more life in me. I no longer know who I am. I have killed a man in my own Company. I have murdered. Where are you? I am lost. In my head and my body I am gone far away where I do not want to be.

He gave the open envelope to Bunny, both of them alone on watch that evening. "I'd rather no one read it, sir." Bunny looked at the name and address and sealed the envelope there and then in front of him.

Chapter 32

Annie read his three bleak lines as walking wounded and troops from the nearby artillery batteries gathered in the least flooded of the further Heuveland fields for a Sunday church parade. She stared blankly from the upstairs window at the distant ranks of men, officers on horseback, a band and the straggle of wounded from the hospital building and its tents picking their way through the puddles.

What was Harry saying? Did he really mean 'kill' and 'murder'? Was he using the words figuratively? His despair seemed so total.

Annie heard voices calling on the stairs and remembered suddenly a dying Fusilier in the 'inferno' bell-tent who'd begged to be taken to "sing the hymns". She had to hurry down and through the door outside, her thoughts abandoned, to collect a pair of orderlies with a stretcher. They waded their way through sludge and water across the nearer two fields, Annie conscious of the mud on her boots up the hem of her uniform as the ranks of soldiers parted to let the stretcher patients through to the front of the parade. The band was playing *Holy, Holy, Holy* as they set the stretcher across two puddles, boots under the handles keeping the canvas and the patient just clear of the water. Annie could hear a group of soldiers behind them singing their own version of the hymn: *Raining, Raining, Raining, Always Bloody well Raining.* The dying Fusilier smiled.

When the Chaplain read loudly from Exodus, intending to fuel the fighting spirit, Annie decided what Harry was saying to her in those bleak three lines. He would never have told her anything less important in those words. And he certainly needed some response from her. "Life for life," the Padre's voice yelled. "Eye for eye, tooth for tooth, hand for hand, foot for foot, burning for burning, wound for wound, stripe for stripe. AMEN," he yelled even louder. Then up off their knees he made them climb to sing *Onward Christian Soldiers* with the band. How lustily, how passionately, how gloriously they all sang out, most of them surely well aware that a few miles away German soldiers were also being told that God was on their side.

Annie looked down at her Fusilier, flat out on the stretcher, eyes ablaze, his thin voice doing not much more than breathe the words. She knelt with him in the water to hold his hand and watched him die before the hymn had even ended.

Sat upstairs in their tiny room that Sunday afternoon, Viv told Annie to show the letter to Ordish. "He'd never tell anyone. Besides, he calls Harry his brother. He'll never betray him."

Ordish, still pale and parchment in his bed, couldn't hold the letter and Annie whispered the words into his ear. Viv had told Ordish days ago about the court-martial and execution. Even in his half-absent state the Lieutenant, remembering the quiet Frank, shared 'B' Company's anger and recalled from Harry's visit, again a half-conscious memory, the name of Sergeant Percival. He took Annie's hand: "I'm proud of Harry if he killed him," he whispered. "So should you be." And a few moments later: "It would not have been an easy thing to do - and even less easy to think about doing."

As he watched Annie walk to the door, the Lieutenant wondered which of the Company officers would have read the letter; or indeed whether Harry had found another conspirator. If he had, then Ordish was sure it could only be Bunny. The new officers would hardly yet take risks with Prideaux's strict enforcement of censorship.

With much the same thought, Annie was aware that her reply might be seen by others:

I need to warn you that I could have read your letter wrong. If that is so, I know you will forgive me. But if I do understand then I can imagine who he was and why and say that I might have done the same as you. I am sure you do not have regrets – only the exhausted emotion of what was done. You should think of it as an act of courage. A necessary act of courage that only you could have carried out and does not alter anything between us.

The two of us we do not always obey the rules – the price (or the reward?) for having been out here so long. As I've said to you before, man will have changed by the time this war is over and the change will be in the way the survivors view that other world outside and how they choose to live in it. How will WE choose to live in it, Harry? You and I? For that is the only thought to keep my motor running – to be able to get up when they wake me, to be able to drag tiredness around on two legs that sometimes refuse to function, to be able to contemplate the awfulness of death ten times a day without total despair. We need to talk more than ever before. Is there no way we can meet? If you were an officer how much easier it would be and how unfair that is.

Your loving, always loving,

Annie

Ordish is improving and will now survive. Pimlott and Benson have gone – to Blighty that is – and sent a card to tell us that they survived the journey. They're both together in the same London hospital. The last thing Benson said to me was that he hoped I see you soon again.

Chapter 33

Harry was queueing for 'short arm inspection' when the mail was handed out, a grin from Bunny as he gave Harry Annie's letter and a packet from home.

Harry read the letter awaiting his turn to pull down his trousers and long-johns. Appropriate or inappropriate, he wondered. But he didn't want to leave reading it till later since they were on their way out of the line and into a long day's march. He couldn't make out whether her words felt like the rock to cling onto or brick walls building all around him. For the first time reading one of her letters, he did not form an instant reply in his head. There was no natural first line to say to her, no urgency of word or thought.

He watched Reggie in front of him peel down his trousers and underwear for the one-man VD patrol. It was the filthy state of those underclothes that embarrassed most of them more than the exposing of their larger or smaller private parts. How many times had any one of them done business on the latrine bucket only to find no paper in his pocket or water in his bottle? Harry shuffled into line, underwear still in reasonable condition from that morning in the rain. Colledge examined him with the aid of a ruler in one hand to lift the penis and a mirror in the other hand to reflect sunlight from the window on and around his genitals. Colledge also looked them each in the eye to judge whether anyone was near enough breaking point to deserve the day off sick and miss the march. He nodded Harry onwards - "Next!" - but for a moment watched the Lance-Corporal retrieve his pack, rifle and helmet and rejoin the column forming on the road outside. There was a nothingness in Cardell's face that Colledge had never seen before, a blankness in those eyes that were usually alert.

Reggie and Lars might have agreed with him. They'd been trying to figure out for days where Harry was with his head. Yet any mention of Frank or Percival was strictly taboo so investigation in that respect was somewhat limited. Harry still functioned as Section leader and Lewis gun Lance-Jack; functioned like a clock, most thought, as though he'd a list of jobs in front of him all day. He'd often move from one task to the next before completion of the first, leaving Lars to cross the 'i's and dot the 't's, as Sergeant Flowers liked to phrase it. Flowers had never seen the old Harry and wouldn't know the difference in his behaviour. Dear Banister, thought Reggie - he might have known how to jolly his favourite Corporal out of grey solitude, with an hand on his arm, a few jokes about Newcastle United, chat about the Northern League or prize running: Sergeant Banister sliced by shrapnel in cold black rain and clay on August Bank Holiday, while his unsuspecting family played and paddled on a sunlit beach back home (was the Sergeant still there where they'd left him, knelt praying in the mud?).

No one was quite sure about Sergeant Flowers. Even Harry in his withdrawn state had had occasion to ponder him - the first chubby man he'd ever known up on the line. Girth was something you only expected from a château wallah but then size of that sort was maybe part of Flowers' music hall act. His comic undertone could become irritating when he was playing the tough Platoon Sergeant but no one actually disliked him. Though equally no one could understand how Flowers had acquired his third stripe. 'Court jester', Prideaux called him. But then Flowers had needed humour, coming as he did from a Regiment cut to pieces on Gallipoli. Which was probably, thought Prideaux, where he'd been given his promotion in the field.

*

In his letter to Annie Harry found he could only write what was a diary. An account of events in the life of a soldier, Annie decided when she read it; but didn't blame him. Perhaps she was glad he **had** left the words of her letter alone for the moment, hoping that he'd re-read it over and over again and let them wash his brain. 'All I can tell you for the moment," she read, 'is what I see and hear and smell, as once you asked me to do." Annie even gave the letter to Viv for her to read out loud to Ordish.

There was singing for the first time in the column today - the first time that is since we left Ypres - and Reggie blowing the tunes on his harmonica. We move around still on the edge of that awful battle, always hearing the guns seeing the shells and flares by night and knowing where our comrades have to fight. And we wonder how far they have moved on from where we were trapped in those craters. In the back here you can tell by looking at men's faces who's already been in there and who is still to go. Us again soon, no doubt. There have been several sent back in a second time and we're almost up to strength.
We have replacements from other units (tell Ordish if he hasn't gone Blighty) so not all of the new ones are green. There's a Sergeant from the music hall - the Lieutenant can get together with him round the piano though I don't suppose they'd like the same music.
We've had bad billets - tents pitched in mud or dirty barns so we're all of us covered in lice again and not much hope of a bath and new clothes. You have to get wounded these days for them. We've been blooded twice this week, 'silent Susans' - high velocity shells on a reserve trench and four of 2 Platoon's new arrivals dead before they'd even started. They hadn't known which way to jump. Always mix up the old and the new, we used to say - but 2 Platoon is all new give or take a Corporal or two.
Food has been terrible - endless tins of bully beef and plum jam and all the other rations gone missing. Reggie and Lars have taken to cooking them together, fried in the lid of a canteen. A real treat if you've saved some rum to wash it down. Even the whale oil's

finished so trench foot has come back. The MO tells us to use bees wax in our boots though where the hell we find the bees wax he didn't tell us. All I get from home is shortbread and knitted socks that never last more than a week.

I'm writing this with the rain beating against the tin wall of a barn. And we're off again, night march through the downpour. North or south, I wonder....

*

Another night, another day, another march, another trench: post was taking more time to catch up with 'B' Company's zig-zag movements. Two weeks passed before a letter arrived from Annie again, Harry shocked to realize that he'd almost felt relieved to be left on his own inside his turbulence. Not that most days there was even time or energy to think.

They seemed to be permanently on the move, in and out of that tented camp, criss-crossing the border between France and Belgium up and down those pavé roads so murderous to march along, the large rounded stones twisting their boots and turning their ankles. The Battalion had become utility, pushed in here and there, plugging gaps, filling empty support or reserve trenches, no longer bothering to learn terrain that in a few days time would become last week's lodging. Division, Corps, Army, all were juggling units now without much thought to continuity, concerned only to keep a fresh supply of reasonably rested men to throw into the battle that was said, even in a normal week, to be killing 1500 men a day on those dreadful slopes above Ypres. And on the Divisional lists no doubt the Border Rifles were moving back towards the top and their return along the Menin Road.

'Stay away from the battle', Annie wrote to him. 'If it seems possible, the injuries, the general condition of the wounded, are getting worse.'

Scarcely a man comes in now whose wounds are not already infected from the mud and whatever lies within that mud. The buildings and the tents stink of gas bacillus, gangrene and septicaemia. Even the ether, iodoform or chloroform or whatever cannot hide the putrification or for that matter cure them. We have to keep washing the wounds and draining off the pus - so it's not uncommon for us to become infected ourselves. This morning Viv had to lance my wrist that was swollen with the stuff - my red and chapped and bandaged hands are not a pretty sight. Yesterday we also had the awful smell of burning flesh. The Germans are using liquid fire guns that spray the soldiers with burning petrol - a whole unit of Lancashires with their uniforms melted onto them. Some of them had breathed so much of the fumes and smoke they've been on oxygen all night. They have pain so excruciating that even the morphine will not give them peace. Sometimes we feel like respecting the wishes of those who ask to be shot and put out of their torment. Most of them are now in the 'inferno' expected to die.

At least an American doctor has arrived to visit from Camiers and brought equipment for doing transfusions - so the arrogant sons-of-bitches here have had to give way. Pity it didn't happen in time for Ordish.

Virgin Mary I have to tell you is ill in bed and refuses to be sent home, sitting up doing her paper work on a tray. She summoned me this morning and I wondered what now I had done wrong. But it was only to tell me that she was sorry I'd had no leave for so long but that it would not be possible until this battle is over one way or the other. She's told the Major that they'll *have to close down Heuveland once the frosts start since there's no way to keep the place warm. We'll all be glad to get away from here – even if one room in this house is sacred to me. I went down there the other evening to collect clean sheets and could not help but sit down and weep thinking of what life could and should be for both of us. Your flame still burns, Harry, and my body with it. But I am sure you are not in the mood to hear such thoughts. I do not imagine from your letter that you think very much of the future but merely concentrate on living through each day or night. All the same you are always with me and I with you.   Your Annie*

When I say the transfusions are too late for Ordish, I do not mean that anything has happened to him – only that they would have made his recovery quicker and easier.   I pray for you to stay away from the front line.

Unfortunately the château-wallahs had consulted the coloured flags on their maps and Division their lists. Battle-order filtered down the chain of command. "We're straightening the Messines line," the Colonel told Prideaux and the other three Border Rifle Captains. "Catching up with the push on Passchendaele. We need to knock Jerry's trench back a mile or two. Even more if possible. Whatever we can accomplish."

So back towards the battle 'B' Company marched and for once in the Salient found themselves well south of the Menin Road in country they hadn't known before. They marched through Neuve Eglise and Polka, skirted the tree-shattered Grand Bois and watched the sun set in a cold clear sky.

"Last supper," Reggie said when they found a mobile kitchen waiting for them on a shelled-out farm - 40 minutes respite before Bunny and Sergeant Flowers led them past the ruins of St Eloi in the moonlight, scrambling across what was left of the canal and up the slope towards Hill 60, nostrils already filling with that dread familiar Salient smell of sour death and sweet decay. Ten minutes later they were following-my-leader through an old battlefield of corpses that no one yet had managed to carry away or bury, some of them so decomposed their faces were half skulls, others with bodies so swollen they seemed they must burst from their uniforms. Harry's boot slipped on something hard and whereas previously he would carefully not have looked, this time he stopped and stared down into the eye-sockets of a man whose face Harry's boot had just torn from its skull. And as they walked and stumbled with the dead so the moon began to disappear, cloud gathering to deliver rain with a sudden hurricane of wind that seemed to express what nature thought of man's civilised endeavour. 4 Platoon pulled rain-capes round their packs and floundered on wet and cold until they reached their start-position where they found the other 'B' Company Platoons and Prideaux with his Stokes Mortar team, Bombers and Sergeant-Major Trussal. There they waited three hours, bunched together in a ditch up to their knees in liquid mud, dreading the order forward that thankfully never came. The attack ahead of them had disappeared, lost and perished in the wilderness of rain and mud - as it had that same night to the north, under Passchendaele at Zonnebeke and Poelcappelle.

Attack or no attack, Trussal issued the extra rum ration and the Border Rifles waded back into the dawn across that hillside of the dead into the cellars of shelled ruins in St Eloi - half a day of sleep and half the day spent trying to clean off mud from last night's abortive hike.

They were marched next evening cross-country towards Damstrasse and the White Château, ever further south and east and into a part of the front line that Flowers described as "almost neat and tidy". They were for the moment out of the Salient and away from that battle.

'We'll be back there before it's over,' Harry wrote. 'But for the moment we live in 'fools' paradise....'

.....The trench is only 3 months old and of modern and solid design. Perhaps we really are learning how to make this war last for ever. Wood stakes as thick as trees and double parapets of sandbags, dug-out shelter for everyone, forward saps in front of the wire so us gunners can cover repair parties, and the most beautifully clean stacks of stretchers I have ever seen. Did I ever tell you about our stretcher-bearers? God knows how they stay alive. We still have four regulars attached to us from before the last battle - and however bad that was for us, it was as bad or worse for them. They live their own lives, usually with the batmen near the Company dugout - the officers' one that is.
Even the weather has half changed for the moment - more cold and dry, what back home we'd have called the end of autumn and have been waiting for the first snow. But then that was high in the hills. Do you remember last winter? There were many mornings we woke up with two layers of clothes froze solid. We had five men go down with frostbite.
I do think of you when I allow myself to. It is not between us that I have changed but inside my own head and there is nothing I can do about it.

*

Somewhere out in no man's land a mistle thrush was trilling loudly in a solo and unseasonable dawn chorus that made Harry remember Frank back in both their springs and early summers, identifying then copying each bird-call as it joined the party. He'd even learned the nightingales they didn't have back home.

Reggie rolled over below him bundled inside his cape. They were out in a forward sap with the Lewis gun having covered a wire-party during the night. It was up to Harry when to return to the trench - before daylight? But Reggie was sleeping so deep it seemed a shame to wake him. There were streaks of colour in the sky over Harry's right shoulder and the unusual silhouette of bushes with a tree out in no man's land. And on and on the mistle thrush sang. It was the larks that Frank had loved at home, lying on his back in the heather and watching them circle higher and higher until they literally disappeared. Then at school one day a master had told them that the Romans on the Wall used to trap the larks and eat their tongues - so they both of them tried that for a while but had no idea what kind of bait to use to lure the larks into the net. When Frank's Da found them at it he cuffed the both of them all round the yard: "You don't eat songbirds!" he yelled. "Stone the crows," Frank had muttered in reply, but not within his father's hearing, "every bleedin bird has a bleedin song."

He would not stop, this thrush this morning - he must have found a discarded oxygen bottle. The ruined buildings beyond the hedge and trees in no man's land had been a German aid post before the June push, medical equipment scattered everywhere. Harry picked up a lump of mud and hurled it out towards the bushes. Beautiful birdsong did not belong in this wasteland. Sure enough the thrush stopped - for half a minute, only to start up again thirty yards further away. Where was he perched now? Somewhere on the ruined buildings? Snails, thought Harry. He's still finding slugs and snails to eat out there.

The thrush lived on that day in sole possession of no man's land, teasing with his endless song, silent only when machine and Lewis guns exchanged an occasional ritual of fire, to prove to high commands through their expense of ammunition that offensive spirit was on both sides still alive and well.

As was the mistle thrush who some time later that morning came hopping towards the sleeping Harry like a two-legged tank, giant in appearance and full of offensive spirit. The thrush seized Harry in his beak and dashed him repeatedly against a rock breaking not a shell but Harry's skull and pecking at his eyes from whose empty sockets

Harry woke in sudden terror. And heard far away in the silence the sound of the thrush knocking a snail's shell to pieces. Harry sat up and looked around.

Their section of the trench was midday quiet: Walker on watch with the Lewis gun through a sandbag parapet; Reggie and Neeson delousing their shirts over a candle; Hook and Hedley fast asleep; Lars smoking and reading his letter from home. He'd been reading the same letter now for weeks, wondering what had happened to his wife. Harry would have to mention that to Sergeant Flowers and perhaps to Bunny. See if they couldn't wangle him some leave.

Harry clambered onto the firestep next to Walker: "Hear the thrush breaking his snails?"

Walker laughed: "Is that what it is, Corp? I bin looking for a bloody Jerry sniper out there all fuckin' morning!"

That afternoon Bunny organised an urn of hot stew for his platoon, the Sections called down in groups of six to pick up their share by Flowers' dugout, Bunny walking on up the trench when Harry failed to appear with the other members of his Lewis gun team. Bunny found him sitting alone ignoring lunch, hunched over, writing on a pad, unaware of anyone around him.

"Alright, Harry?"

Harry stood up in alarm, looking for a moment lost, almost afraid. "Yes, sir." And Bunny turned away with a grin, convinced Harry was composing words of passion to the nurse. Lucky sod he was to have someone like that to send letters to - and receive them from.

Harry for once wasn't writing to Annie but jotting down what he remembered of the dream, trying to find his way back to a moment in that sub-conscious when he knew he had been clearly aware of Frank's presence, whether directly seen or not. In that way of dreams Harry had also been outside himself, observing how he'd succumbed so easily to the giant bird. Had Frank been standing behind in the distance somewhere? Or had Frank been in some strange way part of the mistle thrush.

"Frank Lowburn come back to sing for us," Harry had heard Darker mutter to Scrace, both of them listening to the thrush at stand-to that morning. "Wouldn't put it past him."

Nor would I, Harry was now thinking. And if it IS you, Frank, you're a right daft bugger to be singing out in no man's land.

At stand-to next dawn the air was cold enough for frost, a thick mist obscuring everything, Sergeant Flowers shaking them all awake, Harry still half inside another dream, this time him and Frank on their snow-covered hills at home looking for sheep and finding themselves trapped in forests of barbed-wire. Harry climbed to the firestep and looked round at Reggie who'd been on watch all night. Reggie grinned, putting a finger to his lips. In visibility like this they all had to keep silent and listen and stay stood-to until the damn fog lifted.

And then he started again, Frank out in no man's land, tweeting and trilling away as though it were a fine spring morning. Perhaps the bird was shell-shocked. "Shut your bloody song and get out of there," muttered Harry and flung a stone into the wall of mist.

The birdsong stopped for a moment. Then started up again - on, off, on, off as Harry hurled his missiles. Reggie and Lars were laughing at him, yet somehow it was no joke. When the bird started up the fifth time Harry, shaking as though with the cold, scrabbled up and over the parapet evading Reggie's efforts to stop him. Harry dropped into the sap out under the wire to the forward gun position; then rifle in hand walked out into no man's land through the mist, following the will-o'-the-wisp of that enchanted song that started up from a different direction each time he hurled something towards the sound, trying to chase him away. "You'll get yourself killed, Frank," he was whispering.

Harry hadn't noticed the thin sun rising through the mist, to clear the fog: it was like a curtain rising on a stage to suddenly expose Harry out in the middle of no man's land lost in his mad pursuit. It took him a while to realize how visible he was - until mocking German voices called at him and he looked up to see the line of German parapet in front of him.

The men of 'B' Company watched as Harry came racing back zig-zag towards his own line, Charlie Chaplin-like, rifle in one hand, the other hand holding helmet to his head, laughter and jeering from the Germans, grim silence from 'B' Company. Harry had all but reached the gun-pit parapet in apparent safety when a German sniper's rifle cracked and Harry sprawled.

Bursts of Lewis gun from Neeson covered Reggie and Lars as they climbed over to drag Harry to cover. Reggie cut open the front of Harry's uniform, the exit hole a jagged mess between his right breast and shoulder. Lars ripped out a field dressing, the cry echoing down the line for "Stretcher-bearers!"

Harry's eyes were staring at Reggie, hand clasping his.

"You're going to be alright," Reggie kept saying, wiping Harry's cold-sweat forehead. "You're going to be alright."

Bunny was standing at the dugout entrance as Harry was carried past, blood in a red froth around the dressing, Harry's eyes looking up at the young officer with bleak and blank despair - eyes that were already closing by the time the stretcher reached the Regimental Aid Post.

*

Next dawn in that 'B' Company trench the same thrush starts to sing again out in the wall of mist that still is no man's land. Bunny and Flowers stay silent as they watch Reggie crawl out along the shallow sap and disappear.

Reggie silently stalks the thrush's song, rolls a grenade under the shattered tree where the bird is perched and blows it into a cloud of tiny bones and feathers.

END OF PART FOUR

PART FIVE

Chapter 34

"It's a long journey," Colledge mouthed against his ear.

What journey, Harry wondered. Death? Is he talking about dying?

"You have to try and stay awake as long as you can. Keep breathing."

Breathing?

It is death. There was deep torn pain around his right breast, but more than pain it was the damage he felt inside, the impression, the knowledge of smashed bone and flesh and organs that could surely never heal. What organs were there there? His heart and lungs? Then death was indeed the destination.

Whatever the journey, Harry had anticipated its departure point: a monumental blow like a pickaxe between the shoulders, the sprawling fall as he'd tried to reach the gun-pit and the sap, the blood almost instantly in his mouth and out through his nose. He'd watched it pool and run on the earth in front of him; then heard Reggie's voice and felt Lars's huge hands raise him by the shoulders and haul him into the sap. The moment the mist had lifted in no man's land and he'd started his zig-zag run he knew the sniper would wait until he was almost home. He'd have done the same himself. It was more of a challenge; and in a sense it was more fair. He'd fallen where they could pick him up.

"Morphine," he heard one of the stretcher-bearers murmur and felt the letter 'M' daubed in blood with four finger movements across his forehead; then understood what Colledge had meant about staying awake as he slipped away down a long, warm tunnel towards bright light. Was this light something he had to stay away from? Should he be singing to keep himself awake? Like he sang with Peg into the full moon rising when the sheep went racing towards the light and their own two bodies tumbled in the heather with an adder hissing trapped somewhere under her coat. Nothing frightened Peggy and when she'd raised her haunch the angry snake had slithered invisibly away. Was that a dream?

It was the bloody ambulance that woke him up, jolting, thumping, swaying from rut to rut, the orderly at the side of the driver turned to hold the stretcher in place. For the medics it had been an easy night without casualties and Harry the only passenger - though he was aware from the noise what he'd now left behind. The shot that brought him crashing down broke what had been an unofficial truce, both sides sticking to the set-pattern periods of fire and otherwise living to let live, unit to unit for weeks on end. This was where both sides rested coming out of battle. No one wanted anything more than sleep; even the odd patrol or wire-party into no man's land was left alone if it did not come too near. But no longer so this morning when Harry's apparent death had unleashed the full and sudden fury of 'B' Company Border Rifles upon the enemy - Lewis guns, trench-mortar and the .303's rapid fire making a noise like a machine-gun Company. By the time Harry reached Colledge and the aid-post the artillery had joined in from both sides and were sounding like they'd carry on all day.

Divisional Field Hospital and Casualty Clearing Station passed him onwards, oxygen and tubes into his damaged lung and cavity from one, a change of dressing from the other; followed by his first thoughts of Annie when he saw the uniforms of nurses on the train, two women's pairs of hands turning him on the metal berth to drain the blood froth from his mouth. "Blighty," one of them smiled at him. "You'll be back home by tonight."

More of the 'M' sent him on another slide down another tunnel, dark this time and Harry wondering if he'd ever see the daylight again. Though when daylight did reappear the circumstances were terrifying, high above water and a ship, suspended by a crane with four other stretchers lashed to a wood platform that then lowered slowly into the ship's hold where another orderly was ready to drain more blood from his mouth. The smell and movement of the boat made him retch and threatened to choke him. There were pieces of his own flesh now with the blood in his mouth and the orderly clearly thought he was dying. "We're losing one here," Harry heard him say.

From the stretcher next to him a hand grasped his own and a voice encouraged: "Hang on, mate. Not far to go." Though when Harry gripped the hand back, the voice quickly changed tone: "Bugger it, you're not bloody dying. You damn near broke my fingers!"

They were the only moments in that journey he remembered and soon afterwards lost the passage of time, having no idea how long they remained on the ship, nor when night had arrived - or maybe departed also and arrived again. He no longer felt the need to know. Night and day were the same wherever he was, on a stretcher, in another ambulance, on a trolley, in a bed. But what a comfortable bed! He'd never known a bed like this before, sheets and blankets held above him on a frame to keep them clear of his wound and because he was forbidden to sit up beyond a certain angle, an old lady smelling of lavender who came in to feed him twice a day.

Where he was he had no idea. He could hear seagulls and the sea and at regular intervals thought he was listening to the Silent Susans and the crash of their detonations. So was he still in France? What had happened to that ship? He didn't have the energy to ask. He didn't even have the air to ask. If he opened his mouth it just stayed hung open; didn't even seem to be breathing. Perhaps he was breathing through the hole in his breast. The rest of his body seemed alright. He could reach as far down as his knees and feel everything intact. He could hold both hands in front of his face and count all the fingers. He could shit and pee from the usual places, though both required some assistance.

A nurse brought him a card after a day or two (or three or four - he had no idea): the pre-printed message to tell his family he was alright. The nurse sat by the bed filling in the address and let him scrawl his name; and, when he asked, produced another card, Harry dictating Annie's name and unit number off by heart. Unknown to Harry, the nurse added her own message written below, sister as it were to sister, for nurses themselves would never believe the messages printed on those cards - *L-C H.C. really is alright but it's going to take him time.* She added her own name (Ruth) in case this Annie wanted to write and ask her more detail.

So it was that Annie came to know that Harry was in Dover. All but dead when the ship arrived, he'd been taken to the Military Hospital above the town - surrounded by those seagulls and still, as the town had discovered to its cost, within the range of shells and bombs. But some of that Annie would already know.

Chapter 35

When she saw the handsome young officer ride into the yard, Annie had no idea who he was but watched him as he tied his horse to the rail and walked with a bouncing step into the house. Annie hadn't noticed on his tunic the coloured shoulder-flash of the Border Rifles; and in a sudden flurry of ambulances with arrivals from the battle she forgot all about him.

On its ground floor Heuveland was still a nightmare of mud and blood, Bunny staring at a heap of soiled uniforms that were being cut from wounded men as they arrived. An orderly pointed upstairs when Bunny asked the way and as he climbed Bunny watched the yard below where an RAMC Major moved from stretcher to stretcher among the new arrivals, his five to ten second assessment of each casualty clearly deciding their fates - those that would be operated, those left to die.

Ordish lying on his bed still looked like death himself, but managed a weak smile as Bunny walked in. "How many of us left?" Ordish asked.

"How are you?"

"Minus a kidney and everything still knitted together with string. Least that's what it feels like."

"No Blighty yet?"

"I asked them to keep me here. Not that they've tried to move me. Every time I get up and walk I bleed inside." He watched Bunny's face: "How many of us left?"

"We've been quiet for a while. Prideaux's still around. And Sergeant-Major Trussal."

"And the newboys?"

"Not bad. Not quite the same but not bad."

Ordish knew from Bunny's voice and face there was something else waiting to be said. "Had any leave?" he asked.

"For the wrong reason." Bunny found a chair and carried it beside the bed. "My father's funeral."

"I'm sorry."

Bunny smiled: "No more fishing, I'm afraid."

"I think Uncle's rod and line already taught me I'm no good at that."

Bunny lowered his voice: "Did you hear about Sergeant Percival?"

Ordish nodded and Bunny said no more about it.

Moments later Viv came in and had to be introduced to the visitor. She was a slight and graceful girl, open and smiling, with glances at Ordish of careful concern as though to decide whether the visitor would be good for her patient or not. Given the attentions he was receiving, Bunny wasn't surprised Ordish wished to stay on.

It was Viv who asked the question: "How's Harry Cardwell?" But as Bunny tried to phrase his reply, she was called away and never even heard his reply. Ordish knew immediately from Bunny's face that this was the something else that had to be said.

"Harry's been shot," said Bunny; and after another longer pause, watching Ordish: "Still alive when we last heard. Straight back to Blighty."

Ordish had flinched as though someone had hit him: "Shot where?"

Bunny indicated on himself where the wound had been. "In the back and out the front. One of his lungs, I guess. He was frothing blood." And after another pause: "He was in no man's land. God knows why. On his own. Trying to chase away a thrush that was singing. The sun came up and the fog lifted and there he was. It was stand-to. The whole Company could see him. That started something, I can tell you."

"Who went out for him?"

"The Lewis gunners. We let Reggie and Lars go back with the stretcher. Just in case Colledge wasn't there. Make sure someone else looked after him." Bunny remembered the scene downstairs just now, those moments of decision in the yard when one man chose for another the probabilities of life and death. It always paid to be recognised at the aid posts - as Ordish himself had been recognised by Virgin Mary on his arrival here at Heuveland.

"Was Colledge there?" asked Ordish.

Bunny nodded: "He said Harry was a fifty-fifty. All depends what hospital he's sent to."

"Harry can't die," said Ordish. "We'll all be dead if Harry dies." How do I tell Annie, he was thinking. How do I tell Annie when we don't even know how or where he is?

Ordish was spared the breaking of the news. On Bunny's way out leading the horse, Annie saw him again and this time recognised the green and purple flash. "Border Rifles," she said, turning with a smile. From seeing her on the bus Bunny immediately knew who she was and felt his heart shrink to nothing. "Do you know Lance-Corporal Cardwell?" she asked.

"I'm his Platoon Commander."

"Bunny," she smiled again. "Lieutenant Bunny."

"James. Second Lieutenant Andrews." He held out his hand. "You're Annie. Harry's Annie." Then realizing that could have sounded rude: "I'm afraid that's how we know you."

Bunny was twenty-one years old. Looking at this beautiful if somewhat older woman he had no idea how he should tell her or how she would react. He took her hand again: "Harry's been shot but we think he's going to be alright," he heard himself say - and watched her face drain of colour as though an energy, a pulse, had suddenly extinguished.

And that's what Annie felt - the lights were going out.

"He's going to be alright," Bunny repeated. "With any luck he's going to be alright." She didn't seem able to ask the questions so he went on, aware that she'd know only too well the implications of whatever he said. "The bullet hit him in the back - touched his lung."

"That's bad. That's bad."

"He certainly reached the boat. Word came back to our M.O. We're waiting to hear where they took him."

"How was he shot in the back?"

"Caught in the open - in no man's land - running back to the trench."

"Did **you** send him out?"

"He'd been out on his own. No one knows why. There was mist and it lifted with the sun."

"When did it happen?"

"Two days ago."

"He could be already dead!"

Bunny still held her hand, she looked so bleak and grey. He threaded his free hand through the horse's reins and offered her the hip-flask from his pocket. "I think you need a wee drop of this."

Her eyes looked at him for the first time since he'd told her. She unscrewed the silver top and tipped it back into her mouth, more a gulp than a wee dram. "I'm sorry to be so feeble," she said. "There's tens of thousands others in just as bad a way."

"We can't feel the same degree of concern for everyone."

"Do you feel for him?"

Bunny nodded. "So does Ordish. We've been in it a long time together - and most of the others dead."

"Have you told him? Ordish?"

Bunny nodded again.

"He used to help us with our letters." She was breathing very deep.

"Yes."

"I'm sure he must have broken all the rules and regulations."

Bunny released her hand. "All regulations need to be interpreted with common-sense."

"They weren't with Frank Lowburn."

"No." Bunny looked away. "That should never have happened. They've always been good soldiers, Harry's Section."

"He says you're a good officer."

"What little I understand about anything."

She rubbed her face not to show the tears in her eyes. "Will you let us know if you hear anything? I mean through Lieutenant Ordish." She seemed suddenly so lost Bunny would have liked to hold her hand again. Instead they shook hands in farewell and he turned away.

Annie watched him go, the bounce in his step now gone. He looked very young and miserable as he led the horse away.

Viv heard the news from Ordish and so far as she was able during her shift scoured the hospital for Annie - finding her eventually out in the bell-tents with the condemned, doubtless seeing in every wound and disfigurement whatever she imagined Harry's fate to be. She looked ten years older.

"With a wound like that you don't survive," Annie said.

"If he stayed alive as far as England, he'll be alright."

Their roles had reversed, Viv holding Annie in her arms up in their room that evening, lying down with her, stroking her to sleep.

Two beautiful women, Bunny had been thinking; and wondering very gloomily if he himself would ever have opportunity for romance. There were a couple of girls up north he really quite liked, younger than him, too young then. Bloody hell, he thought, I've been out here since my nineteenth birthday and those two girls 15 or 16 at the time. They were never around the times he'd had leave in Morningstone, both away at boarding school. But the girls' fathers had travelled down for his own father's funeral and both been in the dining-car on the train that evening after. Given the circumstances he hadn't thought to ask about their daughters, nor visited their homes during those melancholic days along the river.

More fool me, he told his horse as he rode cross-country back from Heuveland in the dusk, cape pulled round him, eyes screwed up against the rain, the tracery of black winter trees along the ridge against a lighter grey horizon, while behind him cloud piled up in vast fast funnels of dark smoke towards the west. Another few days 'B' Company would be back in battle and he didn't suppose they'd be spared the assault a second time. Nor the rain. He might never see another girl again.

Chapter 36

Had hours passed; or days; or even weeks? Harry was conscious only of floating with morphine and oxygen in and out of pain. The damage, the wound, the hole he felt inside seemed larger every time he woke, a hollowness expanding round that pain as though his body was wasting away inside. As for his breathing, he had no idea how or where that was happening, the mask over his nose and mouth checked by a doctor or a nurse, it seemed to him, every five minutes.
The girl who'd written the cards asked him to call her Ruth. He always knew when she attended him. Her hands were more careful than the others when they changed the dressings and he could always feel her face, her breath, near to the wound back and front as she sniffed for any evidence of putrefaction. Which eventually arrived the day after another nurse forgot to pour the disinfectant and somewhere deep inside his body a fragment of his dirty uniform released a waiting relic from the Flanders mud, perhaps one speck of the clay that had covered him that night of the shooting - Sergeant Percival returning to drag him slowly to his grave. No more than he deserved.
At least a letter from Annie told him that she knew where he was. There was no way he wanted her to suffer on his behalf and too long a silence from him would have convinced her he was dead.

Virgin Mary assures me that lungs cure well these days. They have learned lessons and new techniques. Make sure they clean your wound at least twice a day and drown it with whatever fluid they are using - I know that's painful for you. But the pain means sterilization. And they must ALWAYS replace bandages with new ones. You should take nothing for granted for they will be as tired and forgetful as we are - and God knows we make mistakes. Don't feel you're making a fuss if you tell them (which you must) of any different pain or sensation you experience. A lot of what they can know about you is only from whatever you tell them. Keep eating even if you don't feel like it and no cigarettes, Harry, until you're quite mended.

Enough of medical advice you do not want to hear! I can't bear the thought of you damaged and alone – no, I don't mean I cannot bear you damaged, I meant I can't bear you feeling yourself damaged. Especially after all the grimness of these last few weeks. Don't let your mind think too much. If it does, pretend great pain and get them to dose you with some morphine. It sends you on another journey (yes, I did try it once or twice after Loos). Lieutenant Ordish asks about you each time he sees me – I showed him your card. Viv's getting quite jealous of how much he cares. Your young Lieutenant Bunny (what IS his real name? He told me but I've forgotten) came to tell Ordish about you. Well came to tell us both, I suppose. He's also very much a good man and knows another one in you. Perhaps that's something the war will have taught us all – to recognise each other's qualities.

I hope you will not mind if I try to come and see you. Virgin Mary has the look in her eye that tells me she's plotting to find a way of sending me across the channel on some business. I can't think how she'll do that. But as I told you, she feels guilty about our lack of leave.

Think strong and be my friend for ever – A

Harry tried to write a brief reply but found no coordination between his eye and the pencil. He surrendered it to Ruth: "Just tell her I'm doing alright, even if I'm not - "

"But you are," Ruth protested loudly. "We're all proud of you. There's not many others who would not cry aloud with the things we're doing to you." She stopped as suddenly as she'd interjected: "I'm sorry. What else did you want written?"

"That I'm not troubled not to smoke because my mouth tastes so evil. And that I AM her friend for ever, with or without the journeys in my head."

"Gosh!" She looked away. "I wish my husband would write such words to me. All he talks about is lice and bad food and the cold. And who's been killed."

"It's not easy writing home when you don't think anyone knows what it's like out here. Out there."

"But I do know. I see the results of the whole awful business. Which of course I cannot write to him."

"Which regiment - ?"

"The Buffs."

"We've been next to them a few times. They're a good lot. You can write that to him."

She glanced at his name tag by the bed: "Border Rifles then."

"From the other end of the country."

"I can tell that from your voice." She watched him close his eyes for breath. "You mustn't talk no more." And turning away: "I hope you don't mind, but I wrote to her myself. Just to say how you really are. None of us ever believes the cards. They're for wives and mothers."

Harry watched her away, diminishing in her uniform towards the door. It was a long ward, beds and floor space packed, though most of the patients moved on after a day or two. Harry had never known such crying and shouting and screaming aloud during the night and wondered if he did the same himself.

A week later it was he who very nearly died one night, his own hands feeling a sudden warmth and wetness on his dressings. He tried to call out but found no voice and had in the end with his one good arm to throw a jug of water at the wall and attract attention. In the crowded state of the ward it was difficult for them to help him and impossible to carry him away. Once they'd stemmed the haemorrhage, it was Ruth herself who lay down on the bed beside him, sheets still soaked with his blood, and gave him of her own, her arm held by another nurse above him with a tube running from the inside of her elbow into his. "Like making love," he grinned. Ruth was 'not amused'.

Next day he was still grinning each time he looked at her. Harry never realized how near to death he'd come that night.

Chapter 37

Four mornings later, 70 miles away across the channel, 'B' Company went over the top north of the Menin Road beyond Windmill Hill and Zonnebeke, towards the slope and German pillboxes named as Tyne Cot. Was it named thus for the Northumbrians that died there in this dirty, God-forsaken October?

They thought they'd known bad weather, Reggie and the Lewis gunners, but no wind and rain had been as savage as this before. "It's the same for Jerry," Bunny told them with a grin, as bowed against it they single-filed along duckboard pathways through the swamp towards their start-point.

"But Jerry's sitting tight, sir," complained Dippy, heavy with his 'cow's udders'. "He's not trying to move. It's us poor buggers who have to run towards him."

Captain Prideaux, as always the first officer in position, walked down the shallow ditch of water from officer to officer. "Here we are again," he smiled at Bunny. But the older man's eyes were tired, his face drawn tight, no real humour in his voice. Oxley, Hubbard and Bunny had done it all before. But for ex-Staff-Officer Hamilton this was his first experience of real battle. Bunny watched him stare in horrified disbelief at the ground over which they were expected to attack, someone's line of arrows drawn boldly on a château map. "Jesus Christ!" Hamilton muttered. "Jesus bloody Christ!" Yet their sunrise rendezvous was much the same as it had been for everyone all that late summer and autumn - an uphill expanse of featureless mud and rain-filled craters with only barbed-wire entanglements a hundred yards in front of them to suggest where Jerry's machine-guns might be waiting for them, and the whole wide world already dancing with the debris of exploding shells.

There was no sun to rise that morning and needless to say their own bombardment hadn't touched the wire - not that they themselves came anywhere near to it. When the moment on the watch arrived, their own shells howled overhead in comforting support but once 'B' Company moved over the low parapet they found their boots dragging in the thick soft ground. As in a nightmare they were unable to run, scarcely able to walk and were felled and flattened into that wasteland of mud by bullet and shell before they'd made even thirty yards. Prideaux and Trussal, out in front alone, gestured the men down into cover. But what cover? Each man carried a pair of empty sandbags, every other man a trenching tool, the survivors flat on the ground trying to scoop the liquid mud into the bags and push up some sort of barricade to create a new position, a new front line, a shallow trench.

Lars in his first action as a Corporal crawled back the way they'd come to scavenge more sandbags and ammunition off the wounded and the dead and found the dismembered bodies of Spear, Atkinson and Bell, clearly caught by the same shell and Parker a little way off wounded with shrapnel-shattered lower legs: "Can't bloody move, Corporal. Otherwise I'd be with you." Gummer was still further back, a bullet through his head; King and Bowman both hit and badly broken, trying to keep their faces out of the mud that could drown them. Lars had already lost a third of his men. At least here the stretcher-bearers were near enough to have a go at evacuating the wounded, mostly dragging them back like sledges through the mud to the relative cover of the original attack trench.

The Lewis gun, as always, had found the extreme right flank, the Lance-Corporal waving to Reggie to make sure he was alright. Reggie waved back at Lars, holding up a hand of five fingers. So his five gunners were all complete: Dippy, Hook, Hedley and Neeson. Walker had been loaned to 3 Platoon, short on their own Lewis team.

As two months previously (as indeed at White City on the Somme the year before) 'B' Company found itself once again fragmented, the scattered survivors straggled across their designated patch of no man's land well short of their objective and uncertain how to continue. Unfortunately for the Company's chances of survival Prideaux's signallers had survived, their line intact. The message that came back from their situation report was predictable: "Pursue objective, zero nine thirty. Barrage to assist."

Sergeant-Major Trussal crawled his way from one sandbag position to another to make contact with his Platoon Sergeants. He found Batterby and Flowers had more or less consolidated their units with their Lewis guns deployed. But Sergeant Summers and Percival's replacement in 2 Platoon, Sergeant Wenham, both had disappeared and half their men with them, the remainder not knowing where they were. The ground sloped off to the left and Trussal imagined they had attached themselves to whoever their neighbours were in the attack. "Two Lewis guns and 40 men short," he reported back to Prideaux.

At the appointed hour and none too accurately the artillery again put down a brief carpet of shellfire ahead of them and in the silence that followed they stood up and walked onwards into the curtain of rain and cordite steam, without shouts or whistles that might be heard by Germans. They merely raised arms and waved each other forward into hopelessness, Lieutenant Hamilton, determined not to funk it, the first to follow Prideaux and the first to fall, caught by a machine gun burst that spun him round with three or four bullets before he fell out of its way. Sergeant-Major Trussal dropped on one knee beside him to turn his face out of the mud, finger feeling for a pulse. The Lieutenant was still alive and the stretcher-bearers not too far behind. Trussal stuck the officer's walking-stick in the ground as a marker and stumbled on, unsucking his boots from the mud, watching in front of him the bowed slow-walking forms of his soldiers, struggling, slogging through the curtain of wind and rain, soldiers he loved for their resilience however much he barked at them, soldiers he could mostly name without their faces, from the shape of their pack or the tilt of their helmet. They were his family and one by one he could see them fall, taking perhaps the bullets that were really meant for him. Stopping by Hamilton had made him now an unaccustomed rear-guard and he went on crouching by each fallen man he passed to turn their faces out of the mud: Atkins, Smith, Corporal Hill, Peacock, Sandy Elham, Lance-Corporal Ellis - he'd have to remember all their names if it ever came to roll-call. What a grim and ghastly place to die.

In the end, stopping once too often for the wounded, he found himself alone, the others having vanished into the wall of horizontal rain in front of him. He could tell from the sudden concentration of fire that the machine-guns had now sighted their targets and were no longer firing blind. He wished he was up at Prideaux's side to tell him to go to ground again. Of the same age and experience as Trussal, the Captain was a good Company Commander but too concerned with what his superiors might think of him.

Trussal had had enough of blind courage when it placed the lives of his own men at hopeless risk. He'd counted, since their arrival in 1915, 140 widows and even more fatherless children as sum total of 'B' Company losses. How odd the world was going to seem when this nightmare finally ended. Not that Trussal himself had a wife or children to worry about. Mrs Trussal had given up on him long ago, living for her woollens shop in Corbridge and the poorly sister who lived with her upstairs. She wrote to him once each week but had decided on virtual widowhood when he'd left for the Sudan twelve years ago. Since when she'd thought no more about 'army', beyond the organisation of women's groups knitting gloves and sensible cardigans for the troops once it became clear that the present conflict was doomed to last through a good few winters. Though Trussal had to admit she **had** been 'downriver' on the train to visit Sergeant Banister's family. Genuine sympathy was one thing she did do very well.

At the end of which musing Trussal had suddenly to throw himself flat under the express train sound of an incoming shell right on top of him. At least his instincts were still functioning in this bedlam. But once he'd dug himself out of the debris and a crater and once he'd checked his various limbs, Trussal found he'd again lost sight of the men in front of him. In which direction had they been moving? Across this featureless mud, into the blinding rain, under the canopy of shell and bullet, how on earth could he tell? He didn't even have a compass bearing and ten degrees wrong he'd be ending up in someone else's war. Who was it on their left? The Lancs? The Anzacs? No, the Anzacs were in reserve. Their turn next. Them and the Canadians, God help them.

Then, like playing blindman's bluff, he stumbled into Sergeant Summers, swearing his head off at the arrival of another shell; Sergeants Summers and Wenham with what was left of their missing 40 men - and a Lancashire Lewis gunner beyond yelling at the two confused Platoon Sergeants to bugger off back to their own damn piece of the war. At least, thought Trussal, the Lancs were progressing with a similar lack of success.

Sergeant Wenham had been a 'river and water' man at home, working on the Upper Tyne. Perhaps it was experience and instinct that found him the ditch, an indentation three foot deep running thick with liquid mud up which they now waded, a new ditch carved out by rainwater following the contours as it drained off the plateau. Further up its course Trussal, leading them, could see that it had actually scoured a channel underneath the German wire. It was like an open door that beckoned them and Trussal smiled. The act of war ran in his blood again. He wanted to attack.

Somewhere to the right, along the wire or further back, lay the rest of 'B' Company. Trussal sent two of the older Corporals crawling through the mud and calling in low voices, to make contact with them and report to Prideaux. Prideaux ordered the move left to join Trussal, leaving Bunny with the 4 Platoon Lewis gun to make the noise and diversion of an entire Company. "Decoy bloody sitting ducks," muttered Reggie.

Wading through the mud-flow under the wire, 'B' Company poured slowly through the gap like a mud-flow in reverse, spreading back out into a line up the slope towards the now visible German front line, a red flare sent up to warn Bunny and the Lewis gun section that their own men were now in front of them. Most of the machine guns firing seemed further away. With a last yelling, foot-dragging charge over the parapet, Trussal led the capture of a shallow enemy trench and the one machine-gun left there. The rest of the trench was empty, Jerry withdrawn to a stronger position thirty yards further up the slope. Prideaux, Trussal and Lieutenant Hubbard turned their backs on the two frightened German gunners with their hands up in the air. Hated machine-gunners didn't stand much chance of being taken safely prisoner.

Trussal felt like raising the regimental banner above the captured trench. Surely there'd be medals in it for someone - a tangible gain, a victory, however hollow. Instead they had to dig themselves back into the mud as the German artillery, predictably ranged and prepared, unleashed apocalypse upon them. A few moments later Trussal heard someone shouting at the two machine-gunners, forcing them up and out of the trench into the open where they were shot dead by their own compatriots.

Those more distant machine-guns had their revenge as Bunny and the 4 Platoon Lewis gunners moved to join the others, rising to run leftwards towards the Lancs position and the gully of flowing mud. Hook took a bullet in his thigh, a spurt three foot high of blood onto which Reggie threw himself tearing a field-dressing from his top pocket. Neeson helped him cut a length of puttee from Hook's lower leg to bind the dressing tight to the wound, and used the pull-through from his rifle for a tourniquet. The mud was spitting with the bullets which, apart from that first one, somehow missed all three of them. And then the cloud closed in again and the machine-gun was momentarily unsighted. They each took one arm and sledged Hook back through the mud and round the craters until they found the stretcher-bearers.

Two days later Reggie wrote to Harry:

'b' company captured a trench and all we could do was watch from the wrong side of the wire. Hooky caught one in the leg - not sure whether he made it or not - by the time we joined the others in the new position our orders were to cut gaps in the wire for the next advance. Wonderful! 15 bloody hours stuck out with the shelling and machine guns and no rations and our hands cut to pieces on the wire. I think another 12 of us got hit before we were recalled, 2 battalions of Anzacs taking over for the next attack. The Captain, Bunny and the S-M still on their feet but our Sergeant Flowers lost a bit of his music-hall chat after 24 hours out there. He said it was even worse than Gallipoli. I think we all feel as bad as last time, knowing this is just going to go on and on. As for your gun, the blurry thing jammed

ten times without your precious care. We're going to have to do your cleaning training all over again - says Lars (Lance-Corporal!). Oh yes - and on the way back, before rations, we were put on a burial detail. At least they gave us a double issue rum for that. We're back in the town in that old cellar of ours and the mad Major under his umbrella. I write this with the light of one quarter of a candle because I can't get to sleep. Talking to you usually does the trick! All the best - Reg   Tell us where you are if you're allowed. I must be due for leave sometime soon.

*

A letter from the front line was a new experience for Harry and quite unsettling. He wished he'd been there next to Reggie for the taking of that trench - and the whole damn slog of it all. As for not looking after his gun properly - perhaps he ought to write to Lars, or even Bunny.

After all, Bunny had written to him: just a few lines to say get well and come back soon, but nice from an officer. Annie certainly wasn't saying come back soon.

I beg you not to think of ever coming back out here. It is relentless, the killing and the wounding, this building and the tents as full as ever of men in terrible pain, maimed or dying. We seem to be saving even less of them now. Experience counts for nothing when the conditions each day are more and more appalling, the rate of infection worse than we've known it. Are they still bathing out your wound each day? Infection hides in the body and waits. It can wait a long time.

Annie hadn't told him she was coming to visit him because she didn't yet know herself. That, thanks to Virgin Mary, happened without warning, with hardly time to pack a bag.

269

Chapter 38

Annie stepped off the gangway to set foot on English soil for the very first time in her life. The ship from New York with Patrick had landed them at Le Havre in France; what leave she'd had after his death she'd always taken in Paris. Now, more than two years after her first arrival in Europe, she was walking down a quayside on the very tip of Great Britain looking up at white cliffs above the town and wondering where Harry's hospital might be.

The port and the train station with temporary buildings all along the pier were much the same as Pérignon or Etaples in France - a coming and going of soldiers on leave, the to-ing and fro-ing of supplies and of the stretchered and walking wounded - even a long column of newly arrived American soldiers in their scout hats exchanging shouted banter with a British leave draft.

But beyond the bustle of the port and railroad tracks the town was strangely un-peopled and subdued. And hostile, Annie felt as she pushed her way into a lunchtime pub ('Estaminet' she might have called it in France or Belgium, though she'd heard enough about 'pubs at home' to know exactly where she was). A row of older male faces turned to glare at her and the barman barely answered her query about the whereabouts of the hospital. "Every other damn building's become a hospital these days - but it's somewhere up the hill."

In the streets there was evidence of damage from bombing or shells and unfriendly faces that looked at her with resentment or suspicion when she asked directions in what she realized was to them a foreign voice. She began to wish she'd worn her uniform.

When she finally arrived, the hospital itself felt more familiar, but being something of a transit camp, the orderlies and nurses weren't used to the welcoming of visitors. Sprawled across buildings and huts there seemed no central authority that kept lists of the patients' names. In the end Annie asked for Ruth and had to wait another hour or more until she came off duty - a commonsense woman this Ruth who'd started, she told Annie, as a child nurse in a London hospital.

When Harry saw them walk into the ward, he thought he recognised Annie but then did not: not a grand lady like this to be visiting him, surely. It was the first time he'd seen her not in uniform, fresh in hat and scarf, brilliant red mouth and light blue blouse with that sudden smile to illuminate the whole room when she saw him. He hated to be lying down, motionless and pale, body broken, flesh wounded and smelling, he knew, of blood, medication and dirt, for they hadn't yet been able to wash him thoroughly. He didn't want her to see him like this. Today he couldn't even sit up; the wound had opened again, blood on his dressing, blood on the sheet.

She walked up to the bed, took his hands and kissed them both, wide eyes staring at her from every other bed up and down the ward. Ruth had warned her on the way upstairs: "There's not enough flesh there to start the healing from. So every now and then it just opens up again."

And it was just as well that Ruth added entering the ward: "End bed on the left." Harry was lying so flat and still and pale Annie would not have seen him. At least his eyes were strong, gazing through hers and deep into her head, the look that had always paralysed her thought. "You're going to be alright," she said and kissed both his hands again.

"I'm sorry I'm like this."

She bent down to whisper in his ear: "Your beauty is unchanged."

Ruth was smiling and began to turn away. "I'll tell the matron that you're a nurse. I expect she'll let you stay as long as you like."

"For as long as he wants me to stay," replied Annie.

Ruth turned back again to Annie: "Do you have somewhere to sleep?"

"I'll find somewhere."

"Come to us - nothing grand I'm afraid. It's only ten minutes away along the side of the hill." Ruth wrote the street name and number.

"She gave me her blood," said Harry as Ruth walked away. He pointed at his dressings: "Last time it opened up. The doctor told her to lay beside me. One tube out of her arm into mine. Saved my life, he said."

"She's very nice. I mean she understands what people feel."

"Her husband's out there. Wounded twice but never bad enough to stay away."

"You ARE bad enough to stay away."

He smiled: "I need new bits for my body." He took her hand. "Do you have news of the others?"

"Ordish - he's on the mend. And Bunny came to see him. Came to tell us about you. But I told you in the letter."

Harry reached for Reggie's letter on the table next to him. "Another show they had."

Annie nodded: "One of your new officers was knocked out. Ended up with us. Lieutenant Hamilton?"

Harry shook his head. He couldn't remember Hamilton. Most things after Frank's death he couldn't remember and of the officers it was only the survivors, Ordish, Bunny and Captain Prideaux, that he cared about. "They captured a trench," he said. "Without me!"

"You're never going back."

"Is that what the doctors say?"

"It's what I say. You're going to be alright and I want you to stay alive. You've done your share."

"So has Reggie. And Bunny. And Trussal. And Prideaux. And Lars. And Dippy. And Darker and Scrace. And Ruth's old man, come to that." He paused to breathe a while. " How's Viv. And Virgin Mary?"

"Viv dedicates herself to the welfare of your Lieutenant Ordish. Virgin Mary's buried in - 'buried in bumph' is what she says. The names of everyone who passes through. We didn't used to have any of that on the train. But you can't afford to miss anyone in the records - in case their family's trying to find them. Like in here, most of them in Heuveland get sent on. Does your family know where you are?"

"They know I'm alright. It's too far for them to come to see me. They couldn't do that, not with my brother at school and the farm to run. This time of year the snow could come."

"What happens then?"

"The sheep live out on the moors. Someone has to walk round and look at them every day when the weather's bad. Three or four hours of walking. Twice a day if it's snowing hard with wind. Make sure they don't get buried in the drifts."

"And if they do?"

"The dogs find them and we dig them out."

"And if you get buried?"

Harry smiled: "The neighbours dig us out." Harry remembered Frank and fell silent.

Annie fetched a chair from under the window, slipped off her coat and sat down by the bed. "Will you take me there one day? Let me see and smell where you grew up? Show me your hills?"

"It's very - well, it's not a comfortable place."

"Have I been comfortable these last two years?"

Harry took her hand. "I didn't mean it in that way, lass. Not about you. You could do anything and be anywhere. That's why you're so strong. I only meant up there, well, it'll be hard like it is forever. Nothing can change. It's too far away from the new things in the world. Too far away from everywhere."

"Perhaps that's where I'd like to be - far away from everywhere. So long I'm with you." She kissed his hand. "The two of us together, we could do anything we set our minds to. It doesn't have to be where you live or where I live. We make a new life. We're both strong, Harry."

"You never told me what it's like where YOU come from - where you lived with your husband."

"In a sail-loft on a harbour. Just one room. Very primitive. We gave it up when we came out here. What we had we put in store - a piano, a bookcase and a bed. We didn't have much."

"And before you married?"

"I lived with my family in the middle of town. Not very interesting. We had rooms above the shop." She didn't specify that they had sixteen rooms above the shop on all three stories. "The kitchen's in the attic so dishes have to be carried downstairs. Our food was always cold." She looked at him.

He was trying to picture it. "Go on."

"We used to have a garden at the back." Two and a half acres, she neglected to say. "But the shop grew bigger and the garden became a yard for the horses and delivery carts." She smiled. "They left two trees for us where we used to have a hammock and a swing." The sound of seagulls outside conjured up for her that garden on a stormy day.

Harry was imagining one of the larger shops in Alnwick or Morpeth. Around a market place perhaps. Children running up and down the stairs. "How many of you are there?"

"One brother, one sister."

"Is she as beautiful as you?"

"She IS beautiful. The talk of the town, you could say. Certainly the talk of the boys when we were at school. I used to have to carry messages to her."

"And who carried messages to you?"

"There never were any. I went to college and met Patrick and that was that."

"Where did he come from?"

"Also Boston." Annie remembered how she'd finally conquered her shyness that month she'd met him, dancing what they came to call the Shim-Sham-Annie whenever they could find a piano.

"So neither of you ever lived outside a town?"

"There is a place we sometimes go to in the country where my grandmother lives." Another sixteen rooms or so bought by her father for all of them, his mother the only full-time resident - with of course two maids, a cook, a groom, a stable-boy, three black gardeners and this time thirty acres of 'garden' including, for all Annie knew, racehorses and Irish Wolfhounds. Both had been her brother's ambitions. His only ambitions as she'd once told him. "I don't want to go back to any of it," she said to Harry.

Then the Matron, the Sister came bustling up the ward to give her permission to stay until dark, the inference also being that Annie would cope with the nursing of Harry. "I'll have the girls bring you water - " jugs of warm water and a basin with a sponge and towel. They wheeled a screen across one side of the bed.

"They haven't cleaned us before, not all over. The VAD's are afraid to move me and the nurses don't have time. I'm sorry, I'm proper dirty."

She smiled: "It'll not be the first time I've done this to you." Annie washed him back and front turning him on his side, sponge and towel under his standard issue pyjama top. The bottoms she had to slide off, knowing it embarassed him. She made her movements as clinical as she could and his penis stayed reasonably soft and still. They spoke in whispers.

"No damage down there at least," she said.

"Many have lost it all."

She nodded: "I've seen some of them."

"It's what most soldiers are most afraid of. That and their eyes."

"You're never going back. I'll not have 'that' or your eyes ever threatened again."

She washed his feet and carried the water away, down the ward to the nearest toilet, every other patient still watching her every move. As did Harry, not knowing quite what he felt. Would he have let his mother wash him as Annie just had done? Childhood illnesses had never left him feeling this helpless and since childhood nothing had ever been wrong with him. What would Annie think of him now? Would his weakness change her feelings towards him? He couldn't think of himself in any other way but strong; standing up, as it were, and facing anything and anyone. That was the way he had always lived - as Frank had known too well those times they used to fight as kids. Well, anyone up and down the valley. Harry remembered 'Squire' Planter in the big house beyond the village at what they called the top of the dale - in fact 10 miles below them downriver at the point at which the valley opened out. He'd once contested their grazing rights, a proper barney out on the moors and Planter with a shotgun. But Harry hadn't backed down and the old man knew he'd have to kill him to get him to move at all. That was the spring before the war and lambing about to start. Planter's men had come on horses next day and fired the heather to frighten off their flock. Harry and his Da spent all next night beating out the flames up and down the hillsides - though come the dawn Harry left one narrow valley burning when he sensed the wind would change and drive the fire back towards Planter's land. As indeed it had and burned two thousand acres or more. He smiled at the memory and wondered if Da had had any more trouble from that quarter. He'd never thought to ask when he went back on leave.

Annie returned, sitting down beside him once again, showing him articles in a newspaper that were claiming British victories in Flanders. "If they knew at home what victory was really like, the war would end tomorrow."

"Ordish used to say the war will end when the killing of a man becomes too expensive."

Annie smiled: "Lieutenant Ordish says when he gets out, he's going to join the revolution in Russia. But then he also said if the Russians give up on the Eastern front there'll be another German army against us in the west."

"And then the war really will never end - I expect your Americans could go on for ever. I mean, they haven't even started to lose men."

"I saw some of them down on the quayside, on their way out. 'It'll be over by Christmas now we're here,' they were shouting. 'We'll be chasing them back to Berlin.' I don't think they have any idea what they're walking into - not the ordinary soldier."

"Prideaux told us they're taking over a sector in the south to help the French. Leave us poor sods to bleed to death in Flanders and in Picardy."

Outside the dusk was falling and Harry closed his eyes. Another hour they'd be bringing round some food, change the bedpans then turn out the lights. It was a grim part of the day that made the night seem endless.

"Does Ruth have children?" Annie asked. She was already thinking about her billet.

"A ten year old boy, I think. Or maybe there's two. She talks when she's doing my dressing but I'm never really listening." It was then Harry realized this was Annie's first time in England, that she'd come to visit him and that he should feel in some way responsible for her. "You'll be alright," he said. And reaching for her hand: "I'm glad you came." His eyes closed again.

Annie stood up and reached for her coat: "I've made you tired." She kissed his cheek: "I'll see you in the morning."

This edge of town outside was even bleaker without street-lamps in the twilight, only a strange glow of reflected white from the patches of chalk cliff above the houses. Annie remembered that same glow in a darkened train, from white mud on the boots and uniforms of wounded men on the Somme. Where her Gentleman-Officer had himself been shot, whose memory now was sacred since his unsent letters had brought Harry into Annie's life - this younger man of few well-chosen words who'd conquered her entire world. And she his world? She doubted that. He was far too self-contained, entire unto himself - except when she'd undressed and cleaned him, as she'd just done, in front of thirty other men with both of them thinking only of that other time she'd washed from his body the blood and dirt of battle. But something had changed him more than the physical trauma of that bullet. There was a membrane, a gauze, a distraction in his eyes that in other wounded men Annie would have seen as the shadow of approaching death. It was more likely the shadow of another death that distanced him: 'There is for the moment no more life in me,' he'd written a few weeks ago: 'I no longer know who I am. I have killed..... I have murdered. Where are you? I am lost. In my head and my body I am gone far away where I do not want to be'. He still was lost and the two of them unable even to broach that subject, not in the company of thirty other men, perhaps not ever at all. Did Annie really need to know? Part of her, most of her, did not believe what he had said; did not want to believe. In ten years time, she thought, he'll tell me about it, long after the war, in that faraway distant place wherever they chose to live. Perhaps Italy or Mexico, the two countries she'd promised herself she'd be going to with Patrick.

Annie looked down the long street of identical houses all attached one to the other. 'Castle Villas' they were called. Castle Villas in Caesar Street. She'd felt exhausted physically for months and now felt the same in her head and heart. She almost wished she had not come to this grey and gloomy place which, except in physical detail, was so little different from the humdrum nightmare of the Flanders war.

Then cloud must have parted wherever the sun was setting, a sudden shaft of colours appearing across the hillside ahead of her to illuminate a castle on the very top looking like something from a storybook. My first real English castle, Annie thought with an unexpected smile. She wondered what it must look like to the French in Calais, perched comforting or menacing on their horizon.

The occasional headlights of an ambulance passed her, carrying the worst of the wounded up the hill from the ferries or back down again to the trains - another stage in that grim journey that had started back in battle with stretcher-bearers knee-deep through the mud. Annie assumed the ones in this hospital with Harry were those, like him, too ill to travel any further. She wondered how long before Harry was able to journey on - and where they would send him. Doubtless too far for her to travel. She'd never manage more than one or two days until they moved out of Heuveland. And then where would they go? Back to the hospital train? She'd be offered once again the option to return home - which she would not take. Would she? What was there to go back for? Her family; Patrick's family who would need to see her. That could be a visit, nothing more. A moving of her life away from there. They hadn't been allowed to take much with them to the war. She'd need her books; some of her clothes; a few letters and photographs; and whatever money had been accumulated for her. And if they wished it, once the war was over - if the war were ever over - then she'd ask Patrick's family to journey over so she could show them where she'd buried him in that village cemetery outside Lens from where she hoped they had not moved him. She hadn't wanted him treated like a soldier.

That shaft of sunlight had disappeared, the evening returned to grey. She stopped in front of number 116, used the brass knocker and turned to look at the other frontages on either side, stretching away into infinity. Some of the homes did not seem occupied, families who'd moved out to escape the bombing and the shells. "Feels like a ghost town," Ruth said as she opened the front door, "compared to what it was. The government'll take them over, they say, to house the sailors from the ferries."

Ruth took Annie's bag and led her inside, a room at the front of the house where a boy and a girl were reading, both standing up to politely shake her hand. "David and Elspeth," said Ruth.

"I'm Annie. How old are you, David?"

"Nearly eleven."

"I'm nine," said Elspeth.

And from the kitchen at the back an older woman cutting up vegetables looked up with a smile: "I'm Ruth's mother. You're very welcome here." Annie guessed it was the mother's house. "Have you always been in this house?" she asked the children.

"We were in London," said David. "My Dad's a messenger in the City."

"Couldn't make the two ends meet when the army took him," Ruth explained. "We had to move down here."

"Take the lady upstairs to her room, Ruth. We'll be eating in half-an-hour."

"And your father?" Annie asked as Ruth led her up the stairs.

"He was a bosun on the ferries. One of the first that was torpedoed. He went down with the ship."

"I'm sorry."

"Us coming down here makes it easier for my mother. I hope." Ruth opened one of the two doors on the landing. "I'm afraid the toilet's in the yard out the back." Someone had lit the coal fire in the tiny grate and the water in the jug was still pleasantly warm. Annie assumed from the two iron-frame beds that the children had lost their room to the visitor and over supper round the kitchen table invited Elspeth to return.

"I have to sleep with a light," said the girl.

Annie laughed: "That's not going to worry me. I've spent two years sleeping in the most awful places. A comfortable bed with a candle burning doesn't seem a hardship."

Ruth asked questions about Annie's life in France and the conditions of the hospitals. Annie didn't paint too detailed a picture of the real conditions. After all, Ruth had a husband still out there. But she did in the end tell them about Patrick.

"That's awful!" exclaimed Ruth's mother. "Doctors shouldn't be killed! And after coming all that way just to help."

"Where is America?" asked Elspeth later on in the candlelight from her bed.

"Five or six days away on a boat," said Annie.

"I'll tell them that at school tomorrow." And a minute or two later: "They won't believe me."

*

"This is your first time in England," Harry said to Annie next morning. "If you want to see things - go to London - you probably have friends."

"I came here to see you."

He hadn't exactly told her he wanted her to go; or that her attention, her nursing, troubled or embarrassed him. But it felt like it and she was hurt. A silly reaction she knew. She could surely make allowances for an exhausted mind and battered body. Twice in here he'd nearly died, according to Ruth. Coming back from that edge Annie knew that wounded men were often then afflicted by a fear they could not, by their very immobility, move away from. As though death stayed there with them by the bed to await another opportunity. She herself had seen men at Heuveland unable to sleep for the terror of that figure they imagined at their side; she'd seen men who even died from that manic denial of sleep - men who simply seemed to disappear within their own wide staring eyes until the brain and heart flared out like exhausted candles.

She had to change his dressing this morning and knew he'd hate her doing it: he'd hate her looking at that damage and hate her to see the pain in his face as she cleaned the wound. Trapped by my own profession, she thought; but then caught him watching her: "It's alright," he said. "If you don't mind, I don't mind. I'd far rather it was you." He drew her hand to the final layer of gauze. "Just peel it slowly - otherwise it feels my whole body's coming with it." She held one hand across his forehead and wanted to kiss him on the mouth and knew her eyes had tears; then felt his hand across her face to brush those tears away. This man knew everything, everything she felt and everything she feared.

"When a sheep gives birth I sometimes have to put my hand deep inside and turn the lamb. I'm not afraid of bodies. Even of my own. I'm only afraid of not knowing something about myself that someone else already knows."

She peeled the gauze, praying it would not tear a scab or pull the flesh. How many times had she dressed wounds in the last two years? How many thousand times? How many thousand soldiers even worse wounded than Harry? Yet now, for this moment, it seemed she was uncovering her very own wound. The dressing peeled without tearing flesh; there was no flesh to tear: she looked into a hole as large as a small saucer and watched his lungs fill and expel. She could also see where the torn tissue had been stitched together, close stitching, perhaps twenty of them. But no stitches yet for the exterior wound, not until the inner ones could be removed. Given half a chance the body will always repair itself but this seemed an enormous cavity to cover or to fill. "One little bullet did that?"

"Soft-nosed dum-dum," he replied. "Jerry snipers always use them." And after a silence: "So do most of ours."

She saw his fists clench and the knuckles turn white as she cleaned inside with disinfectant. 'If it hurts they're OK,' she remembered Patrick saying. 'It means the tissue's still alive.'

OK or not, she felt weak when she had finished, sitting on the chair by the bed, emotionally drained. It was he who had to take her hand with a grin. "Good thing I'm not in your hospital every day." He drew her head down against him.

"Does it embarrass you to have me here in front of all the others?"

"One of them said last night seeing you sitting beside me he reckoned I'd died and gone to heaven."

She looked up: "Promise me you'll never die."

"Sometime somewhere we all have to die."

"Then promise me you won't die before I die."

She had for a moment the look of a young girl in the school playground and Harry smiled.

"It's not funny. Loving someone isn't funny. That's what I've decided." And for no reason at all Annie started to cry, cursing herself for so doing, hiding her face against him again. Harry could feel the shaking of her shoulders and eventually the wet tears through his sheet. He'd seen a few men cry in the trenches, men whose friends had been wounded or killed, men who'd had bad news in a letter from home, men who'd simply had enough. But women and girls? He remembered his mother crying when her father died; remembered how Mary in Rothbury had wept when he told her he was going out with Peggy (but then Mary was already walking out with the blacksmith's son, Mick - Michael Alton, later 'A' Company Border Rifles, killed on the first day of the Somme: Harry always thought he should have written her a letter). Women crying was more difficult to cope with than a man: they were either inconsolable or it was your fault. He could guess with Annie that part of her emotion came from sheer exhaustion: that moment when you're no longer on the army clock, no longer part of the organisation; that moment you finally unclench and let go. The last time he'd been back on leave he'd done the same his first evening home - sat there at the table with bloody silly tears running down his face: he'd never seen his brother look more puzzled - or probably his mother. But then he'd deliberately turned away from her.

'Fucking tired,' he'd told his Da outside in the moonlight later. 'Fucking exhausted' (Father had been trying to distract him with the moonrise and Harry had snapped at him: 'You want to hear that white cold savage bastard really talk?')

The crack of a midnight sniper's bullet, he'd meant by 'talk'. But now Harry held Annie's head against him his fingers through her hair. God knows she'd been through quite enough.

Annie instead was thinking, now he'll believe his wound is really bad; that I'm crying for him. And all I want him to believe is that he's going to be alright, to have the strength to recover, the will to carry on. But she knew he had that strength. He wasn't going to give up living, whatever nightmares chased round his head.

They stayed like that for then what seemed like hours, his hand stroking her head, both of them silent, the sunlight in ever longer dusty shafts from the windows across the room, the seagulls crying in the sky outside, and another soldier breathing gulping, rasping gasps two beds away as he slowly died, Ruth sitting by his side until he'd gone. Everyone heard the silence when he finally gave up trying to breathe: one man's moment of death remembered by twenty nine other men and two women, none of whom ever would forget.

Annie watched Ruth across the kitchen table that evening eating her food, drinking her water, scolding her children for their hunger. How many deaths had Ruth witnessed; how much terrible dying had both of them witnessed? Padres, Priests and Chaplains avoided such moments, concerning themselves instead with the living. They had no real answers about so much gratuitous, careless death and the words of their prayers, while comforting the dying or dispatching the already dead, angered Annie with their threadbare philosophy. They shouldn't be here. They shouldn't be part of it. They had nothing to say.

The two of them had walked home together this evening, Ruth aware of Annie's earlier tears. "When the stitches come out of the inside, then they'll be able to close him up," she told her - a bit unnecessary to explain that to another nurse, but enough to restore Annie back to the normal world.

Ruth's scolding about hunger reminded Annie about the promise she'd made Viv to bring back fresh fruit if she could find any. They were starved of it at Heuveland and no local market in Ypres or Poperinghe as there'd been at Pérignon. What little fruit there was came out of tins, most of it sickly sweet with syrup.

"There's a man comes in the morning by the Priory station," Ruth's mother told her. "A horse and cart with apples and pears from the orchards."

And so it was next morning that Annie's last six hours in Dover were handicapped by 30 pounds of fruit in two canvas bags, walked back up the hill to the hospital and down again to the docks when it was time to go.

She managed to say goodbye without emotion, to the children and Ruth's mother in the early morning, to Ruth and Harry at the hospital at lunchtime.

"You know I never say goodbye," she said to Harry. "I'll just be on my way as though I'm going to see you soon again. Write me a few lines whenever you can - or get Ruth to write them for you."

Harry hadn't slept that night and was more than ever exhausted. She waited till his eyes were closed, kissed him on the cheek and held his hand. When he opened his eyes again, she'd gone.

Chapter 39

Passchendaele had finally been taken, ninety-nine days after the battle had started, the Canadians, the Anzacs and the Royal Naval Division fighting their way onto the ridge and into the piles of broken brick, all that was left of the village. The soldiers were at last able to gaze down a slope in front of them instead of the perpetual hill at which they'd been looking since 1914 and up which they'd been fighting since August. And instead of grey brown mud, they could see beyond them green fields and undamaged trees stretching out towards Bruges and Ghent. All this was told 'B' Company by Captain Prideaux who'd been sent up there to reconnoitre trenches intended for the Border Rifles once the attack force was relieved. "Jerry's trying to shell the ridge off the map. It'll not be a cushy place to hold."

After a brief spell in a rest area and a week breaking in new replacements, they were, courtesy of the Town-Major under his umbrella, back in the Ypres cellars that had, for all the bad memories there, become a home from home, their billet in the Salient. The five mile advance achieved at Passchendaele hadn't sufficiently distanced the German guns, express train shells and silent-Susans disturbing every night's sleep, dangerous enough to keep them hurrying through the streets of rubble whenever they were outside. Reggie built himself and Lars a canvas-shelter in one corner of the draughty cellar and set about sewing a fleece lining into his battledress and greatcoat. The rain had turned to dry winds and frost, a bitter cold by night and not much better in the daytime, trudging the duckboards along the Menin Road with equipment and supplies to stockpile for their new posting - wood posts and wattle for the trenches they'd be digging, bundles of sacking and chicken-wire for the dugouts, wood boxes full of grenades and flares, rolls of barbed-wire for the 'parties' out in no man's land.

Some of that Reggie had to tell them back home - about it being cold. The snow had come on the hills at Elsdon and they all thought he was down south, soft in the sun. He hadn't written too much about the cold the previous two winters, not to fret Eileen. She thought cold and wet the two worst enemies of man. There'd been a picture of little Lisa in their last letter - a photographer organised by the colliery club so every family could send their pictures to the men away at war. Lisa smiled shyly out of the picture at him, standing by the stage in the hall where she was going to be a shepherdess and an angel in the Christmas nativity. Surely to God he'd get some leave soon.

*

It was already bleak midwinter at the Flemish farmhouse hospital when Bunny visited for the last time on the afternoon before their move into the line. He looked around at the nurses and orderlies packing equipment into chests and took off his cap politely as Annie crossed the yard towards him. Bareheaded he seemed to her still young enough to be at school.

"I have no news of Harry," he said quickly. "Good or bad."

"He's on the mend," she said. "Sewn up like a sack. I've been to see him." She watched him gaze around at the lorries and carts being loaded. "They're closing us down here. There's no heating for the winter. So they'll give us five days' leave and send us back to where we came from." She turned away. "Lieutenant Ordish has the room with the piano," she called back at him.

"Is Harry still in Dover?"

"They've moved him on - but he hasn't yet written to tell me where."

Bunny watched her stride away and wondered if he sensed a coolness in her voice. The field of tents had gone, the wounded moved to the base hospitals or the lucky ones back home. Just a handful remained in the wards inside the house, Ordish now the sole occupant of the smaller downstairs room that had been the surgeons' mess. A fire burned in the grate, a battered piano stood to one side of the window, Ordish smiling a welcome at Bunny from his faded dressing-gown, a rueful smile in return from Bunny when Ordish asked him where they were.

"Back on the Menin Road." Bunny told him about Prideaux's recce and the impending move up onto the ridge, dreaded by them all. "Stay well away," was Bunny's advice to Ordish, opening the whisky he had brought.

Ordish was watching Annie through the window in the yard. "I'll be gone from here tomorrow," he told Bunny. "I've two weeks leave before the medical board. A few days by the sea. A few days in Paris." He gave an almost defiant nod at Annie outside: "She's coming with me to the seaside. For company." He glanced at Bunny: "Viv doesn't know. I wouldn't want her to feel neglected. Besides, Viv's going back home for her five days of leave." And at Bunny's look and raising his glass: "Oh nothing improper with Annie, I don't suppose. I only kiss her hand - and her cheek. Everything else belongs to him. Our young soldier - and I don't believe he even knows it. Love, Rabbit, is very strange."

"She seems different - Annie. Since she went to see him."

"She's discovering that love is also difficult - and possesses many moods."

Bunny smiled: "You're a wise old thing, Sam. Years of experience, is it?"

"Very limited experience."

"No one waiting for you back home?"

Ordish shook his head: "Not that I know of."

"Why are you up for a medical board?"

"Return to duty. Get back into the war."

"You hate the war."

"We all hate the war."

"But **you** could go home."

"And make it all the harder to return?"

"Don't return. They'll offer you something else. A staff job."

"Until this is over there **is** nothing else. Could you walk away from the men out here and read their dead names in the papers each day?

Until it ends we are part of a different world that no one else can understand. It would be very difficult to live with those no one else's."

Bunny filled their glasses, watching in silence as Ordish lit his pipe and stared out at the red evening sky reflected with the pollarded willows in the dyke outside. Ordish turned with his melancholy smile: "Don't let the war kill you Bunny. One of us has to get out of it alive."

Back outside Bunny could find neither Viv nor Annie to say goodbye, imagining he'd never ever see either girl again. He walked back towards the town along the dyke 'high in perception, low in spirit', the sound of Ordish playing the battered piano fading away behind him.

When Viv said goodbye next morning with tears in her eyes, Ordish managed his breeziest of smiles and, kissing her cheek and both her hands, promised he'd write to her and that one day they would meet again. Of Annie he said nothing. He'd tell Annie to tell Viv later that they'd met by accident on leave.

Annie wasn't quite sure how Ordish's invitation had happened, nor why she should be spending her five days with him and not return to Harry. Not that she yet knew where Harry had been sent. There'd been one letter, part from him and part from Ruth describing in vivid detail how they'd removed his inside stitches and closed the outside wound with fifty more. Once they were removed, he was down for a long convalescence and due to move any day. But there was still a distance in his words and Annie sure he would not welcome another visit from her quite so soon again.

Then Viv announced she was going home for her five days and next morning Ordish asked Annie if she'd care to join him in a small fishing village he knew somewhere south of Abbéville. He'd sent a telegram: the hotel had two free rooms; the food and wine were recommended; and the sea would do them both the world of good.

Which she did not doubt. But how to tell Viv that she was going off to share her leave with her room-mate's beloved 'cousin'? Luckily

Viv had already been asleep when Annie came to bed the night before and Viv herself helped evade confrontation in the morning with a waved and shouted swift farewell to join the lorry that was driving the homeward bound nurses to the railhead. After all, she and Annie would be back together again at the end of the week. Annie would tell her about Ordish when they returned - to wherever it was they were returning. They'd been told they were to rejoin their train but according to Virgin Mary none of the transport wallahs knew where the train had ended up. Some were even claiming it had been sent to Italy with the five divisions on their way there to stiffen the front against the Austrians. It would matter less if they were sent, thought Annie, now that Harry was no longer in the war. She wondered where he was and how he was and, in the recent absence of conversations with him in her head, desperately tried to picture him.

*

Annie would have discovered Harry buried in a dishevelled English garden, banks of dark green rhododendron screening lawns from garden sheds and service yard, from beyond which came the sound of wood being cut, the rhythm long and slow, two men on a two-handed saw. As she drew nearer she'd have recognised Harry, thin and pale; and she'd come to realize that the man across the saw from him was blind and in need of Harry's careful attention and guidance as they placed the teeth of the blade on the log for the next cut. Beyond them through the shrubbery she would see other convalescent soldiers, armless, legless, others sightless, walking or being wheeled around lawns and along paths in the overgrown garden.

Harry had arrived ten days ago, delivered like a parcel with a label round his neck, five hours on a train trundling through towns he'd never heard of: Ashford, Tonbridge, Redhill, Guildford; another hour in an ambulance through beech woods to this large red-brick house.

Had the house been private with its partitioned downstairs rooms? It felt more like a workhouse or a school. The upstairs rooms were even smaller, no more than three or four beds in each with one chair to a bed and a table round which they ate drab, cold food. The floorboards were bare, paint peeled on the walls, the bathrooms froze and hot water was only available in rota once a week. Definitely 'other ranks only'.

Harry used the saw two-handed but favouring the left, hunched over to minimise the pull on muscles around his wound. The visiting doctor who'd specified this as his daily exercise clearly knew very little about anatomy but doubtless believed that pain was good for healing. Just as well Harry's partner couldn't see the spasm that sometimes crossed Harry's face when right arm and shoulder moved too far.

Blind Alec had been in their room when Harry first arrived, the orderly dumping Harry's kit on the bed nearest the door. The other occupant was an amputee, Jack, cheerful in his way, just about mobile on his crutches but not much good for helping Alec. It was Harry who took on the task of feeding the blind man at each meal, loading and lighting his pipe, shaving him each morning then leading him downstairs and through the garden for their daily chore. Alec, from a London regiment, had damaged his eyes in the gas attack at Ypres in 1915 and after two years of partial sight was now completely blind and waiting a vacancy in one of the homes where they could retrain him to do something useful with the considerable remainder of his young life. As a 'non-return-to-combat' case, Alec came in for little attention from doctors and even less sympathy from middle-aged orderlies who seemed to blame the wounded for the dirt and monotony of their jobs.

Only the women visitors from local villages cared very much about anyone here. They came in as unpaid volunteers to walk and wheel the inmates across the shady white frost lawns or read to them indoors and bring them cakes and magazines. They arrived variously by motor-car or horse and trap, which vehicles became the wounded soldiers' fantasies of escape. For they were still under military discipline and as such, wounded or not, treated with little respect. Getting them back into the war seemed to be the priority here, the visiting doctors concerned only to scrutinise for malingerers.

In such a gloom, Harry now regretted his distancing from Annie in those short days in Dover. He wondered whether she'd been maybe jealous of Ruth's attentions; or whether he believed she had acquired another emotional attachment.

*

Annie wondered much the same as she walked with Ordish across a vast expanse of wet low-tide sand round the bay beyond their fishing village. It was their second day there, the first spent by Annie sleeping fifteen hours until woken by the hotel maid afraid she'd fallen ill. Exhaustion was slow to wear off - though not for Ordish whose energy seemed revitalized by the sight and sound and smell of sea. In a sense he'd been resting three months now in the confines of Heuveland. Here under huge skies and wide horizons he felt a sudden liberation of the mind and body and communicated his *joie-de-vivre* to Annie. She imagined him an outdoors man, a country person - quite mistakenly since Ordish's knowledge of the countryside before the war had been confined to those Sunday bicycle rides that had also become the only source for him, through his young shop-girl, of another even richer experience. An experience he would not deny contemplating with Annie.

He wondered if she would; wondered if he could. Who would be betraying whom? Was it an unfair advantage over Harry that held him back; or the fear of rejection? He remembered the Gentleman-officer's letters, that sense of honour with its attendant guilt prevailing. Ordish was ready enough to admit that his own sense of honour was far less absolute, more empirical - and that it had not prevented him from hurting both his fiancée and his shop-girl.

Such preoccupations did not yet occur to Annie, except the feeling she had somehow been less than open with Viv. Instead she repeated the question Bunny had asked: "Why did you not go home?"

"The two worlds are too far apart," Ordish replied. "How can you talk to a mother or a father or a lover about experiences so far from their knowledge they only stare at you and think you are painting some grotesque picture just to shock them?"

"**Do** you have a lover?"

"I had a lover - and hope she has the good sense not to wait for a man who will never come back." He added after a short silence: "Though I fear, if I tell the truth, I never had any intention of marrying her."

Annie glanced at him but did not pursue her question. There'd be other occasions less personal to challenge the melancholy fatalism that always seemed to cloak him.

He was looking sideways at her: "**You** have a lover who surprised us all and would have surprised your Gentleman-officer even more. The shepherd boy who dares to love you and the rest of us can only stand and watch." A pause. "And wish him well." Then after a silence. "And let me say, if you both survive the war together, you will find somewhere in the world where your differences of background and education will no longer matter."

"If he learns to live with what he's done."

"The killing of the Sergeant?" Ordish was silent a long time, watching as they walked the sunset colour thick as blood across the sea and sand. "What your Harry Cardwell did, if **he** had not done it, would certainly have been accomplished by someone else - in a less intelligent and less humane manner." Annie stopped and stared at him, Ordish taking her hand. "Harry's become older and wiser than all of us. And probably wishes he was still a boy."

They turned to look behind them at their mile of footprints across the sand, rapidly disappearing as the tide came in; and, still hand in hand, walked back through the sand-dunes to the village.

That evening they ate fish together and drank Montrachet from a bottle in a bucket of cold water. Annie watched Ordish's melancholy vanish with the wine. "It is so good," he said, inhaling it before each sip. "I knew nothing about wine until we came out here - there's one positive side of this war! It was Raven and Prideaux who taught me - they took me through the lists when we went out to eat, trying a different red and a different white each time until I found the ones I like." They both looked round at the rare sound of a motor-car outside and the two uniformed men who entered, a Captain and a Major, both nodding across the room at them. "Royal Welch," said Ordish. "They were in the October show."

"I remember. We had three tents full of them out in the field."

Ordish smiled: "Which is how I knew."

"I bet they're not here on leave. Officers' privileges."

"I can't accept that!"

"If we were nearer the war this place would be posted with officers-only notices," Annie said. "Harry'd not be allowed in here, yet you and he have an entirely equal chance of being killed. I find that difficult to accept."

Later, when the Captain and the Major, with another nod, departed in their vehicle, Ordish played the piano in the hotel bar and Annie danced with a gallant French fisherman so old he'd surely fought with Napoleon. It was nearly midnight when Ordish escorted Annie to her room, walking in to smell its perfume and gaze at a moonlit sea from her window.

"Do you want me to ask you to stay the night looking at that moon?" she asked.

"Oh yes," he replied without turning round. "I would have wanted that. The moonlight and your warmth. But I shall not stay because if we had been sure we wanted it, you would not have had to ask." Ordish kissed her hand goodnight.

Each day became, comfortingly for Ordish, restfully for Annie, the same: a walk, a lunch, another walk and a gently intimate dinner that left both of them safely in their separate bedrooms for the night. Ordish told Annie about his fiancée; Annie told Ordish about Patrick and their shortlived marriage; Ordish confessed his carnal love for the pretty shopgirl on her bicycle; Annie described her meetings with the lovelorn Gentleman Officer - and admitted her own carnal thoughts about him. And both of them inevitably talked about Harry, Annie's first glimpses of him in Pérignon, Ordish's first combat with him on the Somme when, at White City, Ordish and Bunny had been the last to leave the rearguard of the Lewis gun and admire the courage of their eventual retreat.

"Why did you help him with our letters?" Annie asked.

"I was there at the railhead when he bought the tin. I don't know. Maybe I also fell in love with your photograph."

"Did you read my letters to him?"

"Only one." They were sitting in the sun down by the harbour sheltered from the wind. "You are both very unafraid to reveal your feelings for each other."

"I knew - I know - that I love him more than I will ever love anyone. It sounds terrible, but even more than Patrick."

Ordish took her hand and nodded: "You move through life and love just one or two people. I mean really love. Apart from parents and brothers and sisters and all of that. And the people you so suddenly love can be anyone. Rich or poor." He glanced at her: "Man or woman."

"You also love my soldier?"

"I'd put my arms around him now if he was here. I don't believe I ever knew anyone who knew himself so well or made me feel so safe. I think if Harry was killed we really would lose the war. If I believed anymore in a God, I would pray to him for Harry every minute of the day."

*

A dirty trolley of congealed food wheeled with a thump through the door, pushed by one of the more disagreeable orderlies: "Eat up and stop skiving. The war's still waiting for you all."

Winter has moved on in the dishevelled Victorian garden outside, Harry's face more than ever a mask as he stuffs blind Alec's pipe and lights it for him. Alec has never mentioned family; there are no letters by his bedside; no mail that ever arrives for him. He's as completely alone in the world as anyone Harry had ever known. So Harry reads his own letters to him, from his mother, from Reggie and eventually one from Annie that he read to Alec but slowly in case it became too personal to read out loud.

I am writing this on a train travelling round the side of a lake in Switzerland, blue water and snow mountains beyond on one side, steep terraced vineyards on the other. We're out of uniform - civilian girls! - to be allowed through here, for it's the shortest way and not cluttered with military transport (Switzerland is not in the war). So maybe you have guessed we're on our way to Italy where they've sent our beloved train! Virgin Mary sits across the compartment from me, a bottle of wine and a glass in her hand - to the horror of the Swiss ticket collector who sometimes comes to peer through the corridor window at us as though we were strange animals in the zoo. She's taught me that, our Mary - never to travel without a clean glass and a corkscrew! We've already been going two days - from Base Camp to Paris, from Paris to the frontier where we had to walk half a mile between two trains carrying our kit. We've all been writing letters and all been arguing whether to post them here in Switzerland where Virgin Mary says the system works well - or wait for the military post in Italy which Viv says we should do if the addresses we're writing to are a military destination. Viv's been contradicting everything I say. She's cross with me because the few days of leave we had when Heuveland closed I went with Sam Ordish to look after him. He was sent to convalesce by the sea and was not strong enough to be alone.

At which point Harry stopped reading. He felt as though the flat of a spade had hit him on the side of his head.

"She sounds very nice," Alec said. "You're lucky to have a friend like that."

"She's American." Harry went on talking to stop his mind running so fast. "Came over as a nurse - her husband as a doctor. He was killed. Their ambulance was shelled."

"Where?" The question that every soldier always asked to see if he had also been there.

"Loos."

"1915?"

Harry nodded; then remembered Alec couldn't see the nod. "Yes. She was in the same ambulance - thrown out while he was burned inside."

"Bloody Jerry shelling ambulances."

"I don't suppose from where they were they could see what they were shelling." How many days of leave had she had, he was thinking. How long had she and the Lieutenant been alone together?

"I expect she's beautiful, is she? The nurses who looked after me, I couldn't even see them. Did she look after you somewhere?"

"We met."

"Where?"

"In Pérignon."

Alec smiled: "I know Pérignon. We had a short leave two miles north. Got very drunk in town one night."

Hadn't she had enough leave to have come over to England? Even if she hadn't received his own letter, Ruth would have told her where he'd been sent. No wonder she'd taken so long to write to him.

Alec was smiling again, sightless eyes turning towards the light from the window as the sun came out outside: "Did she write any more?"

"No. No, not really." Harry could no longer share the letter, not knowing how it would end. He'd have to read the rest of it later when he was alone. There were two more sheets of writing. Maybe later on she'll be saying goodbye and it's all over.

"Got to pump ship," said Alec swinging himself off the bed - one of the few things he really could do on his own. Harry watched him feel his way along the wall to the door and disappear down the corridor.

Letter resumed while we wait in a station called Brig for our turn to go through a tunnel. On the other side we'll be in Italy. The snow on the mountains is all around us and the train now very cold (they've detached the engine). I think they're letting us get out to have something to eat before we go on. Someone in the corridor says the Swiss will do anything to take money from us – like holding up the train so we have to eat here instead of Italy where they say it's cheaper. But the someone was a Frenchman who doesn't like the Swiss! That was enough though to decide Virgin Mary she's not going to post letters here! So I'll finish the letter in Italy.

Was she also writing another letter to Ordish? Harry could picture Annie talking the words of her letter, the expressions in that lovely face, her eyes, her smile. They became a squeezing of pain in his heart as bad as anything he suffered from his wound. He could even hear her laughing voice:

Italy! Oh yes, Italy! Everything I ever imagined. Chaos and confusion on the train station platform, voices shouting, young boys and girls trying to sell food, old women carrying ducks and hens under their arms or in baskets (live ones I mean). We're clearly back in a country at war – uniforms everywhere, and controls. They stopped the train as soon as we left the tunnel and police climbed on board to check everyone's papers. They were looking for German or Austrian spies someone said. Apparently it's easy for them to cross Switzerland and enter Italy. The tunnel lasted forever (someone said it is the longest in the world). Then the train lights went out and left everything in darkness.

Virgin Mary was holding the door tight shut so no men could get in! There'd been plenty of them in the corridor walking up and down and staring in at us. They got a fright when we came out the other end and we'd all turned into a compartment full of Sisters! Yes - we changed in the dark, putting on our uniforms again for Italy.

This town is called Domodossola, all lit up in evening lights, smart carriages on the street outside and a bar selling wonderful coffee and cakes. Unfortunately (fortunately?) the Italian Movement Officer on the station knows nothing about us. We sit and wait for 'wires' to be sent. Sam had already told me about Italy - he said he loved it. Everything certainly smells different already: That coffee, those cakes (butter pastry), frying onions from a restaurant, really pungent cigar smoke and once you get away from all of that, the suggestion of pine trees somewhere nearby.

Sam Ordish again. Perhaps he was on the bloody train with her. Harry skimmed the rest of the letter: the nurses sleeping a night on another very slow train; waking up in an army depot somewhere near Verona; finding their old train on a siding, filthy and defiled: *It had been used for carrying corpses away from battle. Pigs for not cleaning it, whoever they were.*

Harry folded the letter away deciding he would not look at it again. There was little mention of Dover nor of memories nor any feelings at all - but plenty about Sam Ordish and his 'melancholy musings'. Harry pushed it into his kitbag and pulled on his coat.

"Come on, Alec, let's go and cut some wood."

Chapter 40

For a few weeks she explained his silence through the difficulties of communication - military forwarding addresses on the Italian front were said to be less specific than elsewhere, though some were claiming they received answers to their letters quicker than they did in Flanders or Picardy. Beyond those few weeks his silence began to possess Annie, wrapped similarly in her own shroud of silence. There was little outside activity to distract any of them from the routine of work on the ambulance train, nothing to alleviate the claustrophobia of those metal-floored carriages once the novelty of their living quarters had worn off, two wagons-lit and a dining car attached to the rear of the ambulance cars. Annie was still sharing with Viv, one berth with two bunks, Annie on the top. But since the train was working two 12-12 shifts and Annie and Viv working separate ones, they hardly ever saw each other, the coolness between them continuing without either overt hostility or any attempt to return to their former intimacy. While Viv neither noticed nor cared, Virgin Mary, to whom the mailbag was always brought, was well aware that Harry hadn't written to Annie since their arrival in Italy more than a month ago - surely the cause of Annie's own silent withdrawal.

Mary was working a 6-6 shift to cover everyone, more often than not the 6-6 becoming a 6-12. She hadn't quite realized how fatiguing the system had turned out to be for everyone else. The 12 hours off were as unpopular as the 12 hours on. Once you'd had your sleep there was nothing else to do but read or write or sprawl at the dining-car tables - and risk being called upon to help out along the train. Eventually some of the other girls came to Annie and asked her to intercede and suggest three shifts of 8 hours each.

So it was that Annie found herself one cold and clear December afternoon walking arm in arm with Virgin Mary under the heavy stone arcades in the centre of Bologna, Annie's task to intercede, Mary's to discover the reason for Annie's mood and Harry's silence. Had the love between them died? And if so why?

The two women stopped to buy hot chestnuts in a funnel of newspaper from a brazier and watch a ragged shepherd from the mountains play his small bagpipes, a child at his side collecting money.

"Gianni says they come from further south," said Mary (Gianni being one of the Italian doctors on the train). "We saw another on the station. He thinks that's where they sleep. They bring their sheep and goats down off the mountains when the snow arrives and leave them in the villages with their wives. Then walk to the cities to make money from their music around Christmas. Seems they've always done it."

The talk of shepherds and snow made Annie turn suddenly away not to show emotion. It almost felt for a moment as though Harry was standing there with them or watching them across the street. Was he reading the letters she was sending him? She knew he was alright: she'd written to Ruth asking her to find out and Ruth had written to the convalescent home who'd eventually replied to say his health 'continues to improve'. What had happened to him? Was it that visit to Dover - which had been sometimes awkward? Was it something she'd said or written? She'd tried and tried to remember exactly what she had been writing. She'd actually been trying not to write too much about emotions, sensing from Dover that Harry was still in turmoil about the killing of the Sergeant. The melancholy of the bagpipe tune gave her a lump in the throat and prickled at her eyes. Perhaps that's what she needed, a damn good cry. Then, with a glance, Mary passed her a chestnut she had peeled, took her arm and they walked on.

Their train had been put into the workshops for 24 hours or more having some of the wheels repaired or replaced after weeks of punishment on damaged tracks near the front line north of Venice. The wounded and the dead (yes, still the dead - the end carriage was reserved for them) were then ferried back west to Vicenza and Verona or south to Padova, Rovigo, Ferrara or Bologna, as often as not with Italian surgeons on board; and difficulties for the nurses to communicate either with the wounded or the senior medics. But at least there was a willingness to cooperate once everyone on both sides had learnt the dozen or so words that were essential in both languages.

It was the Italian alpine troops that Annie liked the best with their stoic dignity, their mostly mute sufferance of wounds and their endearing affection if not craving for the most ferocious spirit Annie had ever tasted. This 'grappa' was apparently served to them in daily tots much like rum with the British troops. Eventually the Italian women who ran the dining-car took to keeping a supply hidden away behind the washing-up sinks.

There were plenty of Alpini under the arcades this afternoon, their single-feathered triangular hat conspicuous among the other uniforms and other feathered hats that thronged the bars and food shops. Without exception every soldier out of the line complained of hunger; but without exception here in Italy the nurses never saw a soldier the worse for drink however many bottles of wine and tots of grappa seemed to be being consumed.

"I'm starving," said Virgin Mary. "It's teatime."

"Tea is awful here."

"So coffee it is - with or without your grappa." They'd both noted that early morning habit of some of the doctors to tip a slug of grappa into their hot black coffees at breakfast. Virgin Mary had decided not to object to those secret bottles underneath the sink. Inside or outside the body, the stuff was an excellent disinfectant, and enough of it within the brain also functioned as a suitable anaesthetic.

Mary looked around at Annie. There was still a brimming in her eyes - but neither of them addressed their two tasks until seated in a hotel lounge with coffee and cakes in front of them.

"So what's happened to you?" asked Mary bluntly. Annie looked up at her in surprise. "You're not the Annie I once knew. Don't you like Italy?"

"I love Italy! It's the kindest, most exciting place I've ever been!"

"Then when the war is over you should come here with your Harry."

"Not mine anymore, I think."

"Did he say goodbye?"

Annie shook her head. "He just doesn't write."

"Most men never write in my experience. But then unlike you I'm not a beautiful young maiden inspiring poetry."

Annie laughed suddenly, her peal filling the room, turning the head of every man present. "You're trying to provoke me, Mary!"

"Well at least you've smiled. For the last three weeks the only people you've smiled at are wounded men who, on a merely professional level, needed your comfort."

"And now I need yours?"

"I don't know. You tell me."

Annie paused a moment. "The girls need your help."

"What's wrong with them now. Italian food?"

"We love the food."

"So?"

"The shifts are too long - too long to work and too long to rest - with nothing much else you can do."

"Why is it every time they wish to complain, yours is their only voice?"

"Because they think you listen to me."

Mary laughed: "Do I?"

"I thought - maybe - three shifts of 8 hours, one on, one off - the same two groups alternating, so no one ends up always sleeping in the day."

"Far too mathematical for me, Annie. You'll have to buy me a grappa before I could understand how that would work." Annie could see mischief in Mary's eyes: "Viv asked me if she might stay in the hotel by the station. Do I gather that you and she are carefully avoiding one another? Lieutenant Ordish, is it?"

Annie felt herself blush.

"Oh I know you didn't leave Heuveland together but girls gossip, I'm afraid, and in that dining-car it's sometimes difficult not to overhear."

It was entirely innocent!"

"Between the two of you, perhaps. But not to the outside world. People always like to imagine the worst - or the most exciting. That's why our young ladies pretend to protest so much about the way Italian men look at them."

"How **do** they look?"

"Most of them we've passed in the street today have quite shamelessly undressed you with their eyes." Mary laughed again. "I'm really rather jealous. I mean, they're not going to undress someone who looks like Queen Victoria."

"Mary - !"

"And as for Ordish, if your Harry knows you were together, maybe that's the reason for his silence."

Annie's thoughts stopped dead with a crash - much as the train had done against the buffers last night in Padova (most of the nurses on duty falling down as a result). Had she told Harry? She **had** told him. Deliberately - not as a confession but to show that it was an entirely natural episode. Would he have construed something else? She felt a kind of panic at the thought, already composing in her mind the next letter she would write him.

"We can all be a bit possessive," Mary was saying. "Viv of Ordish, Harry of you; even me of my poor lost brothers. Another of our human frailties."

Annie couldn't remember the precise words she'd written to Harry about Ordish and the seaside: she knew she hadn't been exactly specific on how many days of leave she'd had; and she had rather made it sound as if she'd been sent there to nurse him. Of that she could be guilty. But Harry wouldn't know and surely hadn't imagined anything else. But then in his present mood, withdrawn and vulnerable, perhaps he had. So how on earth could she correct it? Annie held up her hand and, to the hotel waiter's total astonishment, ordered two large grappas.

"Good girl," said Mary and rubbed her hands. "Now I think it's high time we shocked and surprised another smart restaurant full of pompous gentlemen. At my expense tonight. The later we get back to that very cold train, the better it will be for our health."

Chapter 41

Annie's letter, carefully composed, written and rewritten a dozen times through the three days the train remained in Bologna, finally reached Harry on Christmas Eve - only to be folded away into his kitbag and join her other four unopened letters. For someone longing for the sound of her voice, longing to know what she had to say, it was a strange thing to do. If she'd really said goodbye she would hardly still be writing to him. Yet Harry couldn't physically open the letters for fear of the words he might find inside - though he knew full well that one day he would have to force himself to read them.

'Christmas' seemed to be obligatory with visits from local priests and parsons and activities encouraged by the volunteer women visitors to help create festivity. Candles and cotton-wool snow decorated a dry pine Christmas tree in the entrance hall; groups of wounded men were cutting, colouring and pasting paper decorations indoors; while Harry and Alec were making wreaths in the garden from holly and rhododendron foliage - to give the house, thought Harry, an even more dismal air. But at least that activity was proving to Alec that he could still work well with his hands. Harry now discovered Alec had been a tailor's assistant before the war, part of a family business in Croydon, to which family he was only a distant cousin. His own parents both were dead, victims of a collision between two trams while he'd still been at school. The family had given him work but not taken him in; he lived in lodgings for ten years before joining up on the first day of the war, for the first time in his life to find himself companions - all of them now dead.

On Christmas Day itself, a Tuesday, the inmates were more or less left on their own, most of the local staff spending the day with their families. Food had been left to heat up; some bottles of beer and brandy donated by a local store and stacked along a table in the hall on a help-yourself basis; and an attempt was made at communal jollity by dragging their tables into the corridor or onto the landing so that they could all eat more or less together. Afterwards they sang carols in the downstairs 'rest room', with their amputee room-mate playing the piano.

It had been, thought Harry, a very gloomy day; though Alec, who could only hear the proceedings, declared it to have been a most enjoyable occasion - whose final drama was played out in the evening when a piece of cotton-wool 'snow' dislodged and fell onto a candle, the Christmas tree exploding into flame and everyone believing for a moment that a shell had landed.

As if in sympathy and as a result of fire-fighting exertions, Harry's wound opened and bled that night and, given most of the staff were still with their families, he had to cope on his own with disinfectant and dressings, trying to sterilize everything he touched to avoid infection.

*

If he'd known what else elsewhere had happened, Harry would have thought it an even gloomier day. For on that December 25th Bunny's charmed-life-luck seemed to have run out, on a sector of the front so quiet 'B' Company had half expected to be playing football with Jerry in no man's land.

Bunny had spent most of the last ten days trying to organise the festive season back home for his mother and sisters on this the first Christmas for them since his father's death. He'd planned each day for them from Christmas Eve to New Year's Day in meticulous detail, described in letters not only to each sister but also to the cook and the maids and to two London cousins, one on his mother's side, one his father's, both of whom were asked to help fill those dread days with social activity. His instructions were followed to the letter: cold salmon in aspic for Christmas Eve; matins at the local church on Christmas morning and lunch afterwards pre-booked at a Park Lane hotel; lunch with one of the cousins on Boxing Day; dinner with the second cousin on the Thursday.

Instead, on that third day of Christmas and about to depart for their second cousin's house, Bunny's sisters heard the crunch of a bicycle up their short gravel drive and rapid heavy knocking at the front door - the telegraph boy with a touch of his cap as he handed the maid a telegram from the War Office. How many times had they heard of it happening to someone else; and even seen it up and down their street? No one cried out: Mother, as she'd said at father's funeral, already knew it was inevitable; both sisters seemed paralysed as they passed the slip of paper from hand to hand:

Regret to inform you 2nd Lieutenant J. Andrews killed in action France December 25th 1917.

Reggie had seen it happen from the moment Bunny grinned his "Happy Christmas" at them, Sergeant Flowers behind him with the rum jar. The minnie, rotating in mid-air, seemed to be Jerry's Christmas stocking. The bastards had been singing Silent Night in their trenches the evening before. Perhaps they were now winging over a canister full of German sausage. Reggie yelled a warning but Bunny, ten yards beyond him, ducked the wrong way round the traverse, into instead of away from the falling mortar. He was lying in a massive puddle of blood by the time anyone reached him, stretcher-bearers not quite believing God or Jerry could be so spiteful on a Christmas Day.

Reggie wrote to Harry: 'The Lieutenant was actually singing Partridge in a Pear Tree when I yelled at him. Perhaps I shouldn'a have yelled so loud and he'd not have moved the wrong way. Trouble is we all had the rum in us. Quite a lot of it by then.'

Colledge later blamed himself for whatever mistake had been made. Bunny, unconscious, had a scalp wound and damage to his hands and arms but did not appear to have suffered badly to the head or internally. Perhaps a cracked rib or two.

He was into the ambulance and on his way back to Blighty within ten minutes. No problem, thought Colledge. The boy deserves a rest. It being a quiet day, Colledge departed an hour later for his Christmas lunch in 'A' Company dugout, leaving an orderly to complete the paper work for Division. Captain Prideaux was on leave in his father-law's Sussex lanes and the newer 'B' Company officers did not think to check on details or follow Bunny's progress.

When Prideaux read Bunny's name in the casualty lists on the front page of Thursday's Times, it became the first time his wife and two sons had ever seen him cry, his soundless tears quite alarming them, however quickly he turned away to hide distress. Captain Prideaux mourned for 24 hours walking on the downs, keeping well away from the rest of the family. Until, coming back from one such walk next early morning, he read the front page insert that answered his prayers and insured that never in his entire life would he ever read a newspaper again:

2nd Lieutenant J. Andrews mistakenly reported dead in yesterday's column, is only wounded and recovering in the Dover Military Hospital.

Prideaux opened a bottle of champagne at nine o'clock in the morning and later played football with his two sons on the lawn. God was in his heaven once again.

Bunny turned out to be one of Ruth's patients, held over in Dover for the lack of ambulance trains on Boxing Day. By New Year's Eve he'd be in London and two weeks later sent to one of the Oxford colleges for convalescence.

*

Harry's establishment did not supply The Times; didn't supply any newspaper for that matter, apart from whatever the orderlies or voluntary ladies passed onto them. Harry heard about Bunny in Reggie's next letter, Reggie unable to give news of their wounded officer beyond the reports they'd had back from Colledge's dressing station, including the rumour that mistaken paperwork had led to the premature announcement of Bunny's death.

Everything had fragmented - starting with Frank and Percival, then Harry's own wounding that should have been a death, the business with Ordish and Annie, and now Bunny. And nearly as bad, Reggie's other recent news, the death of Pimlott in the London hospital, unable to survive the attempt of surgeons to remove the shard of steel inside his brain. Had they buried him with his helmet still hat-pinned to his head? And what of Benson? How did he now feel to have lost his strange companion? The only good news in Reggie's letter were the returns to 'B' Company of Craig and Webster recovered from their wounds. Harry felt he should be back out there with them. Instead his wound kept seeping blood, Harry confined to his bed, blind Alec's turn now to look after him which manfully he tried to do.

Pitiful they were in that cold January, huddled in their room, Alec unshaven or blooded from attempts to shave himself, Harry staring at a grey sky outside wondering if the skies in Italy were blue for Annie. But still he wouldn't read her letters nor write his own.

Chapter 42

The Italian sky instead was black and cold, Annie and Viv walking together through narrow streets and alongside canals in a hoar-frost frozen Venice early morning, hearing and smelling the city as it woke - a boatman's occasional call at blind canal junctions, the slap of displaced water against stone walls, the smell of baking bread and from somewhere overhead someone's coffee. Neither of them had ever felt so cold, damp-cold, arm in arm and hugged to one another even if friendship had not yet been entirely repaired. "Do you think a bar will open soon?" Viv's voice was a whisper as though she feared to wake the city. Their footsteps were bad enough, echoing sometimes in front of them, sometimes behind, like their shadows moving in the gaslight. Both of them were convinced they were being followed. "Hot coffee and milk and a bun, that's all I ask," came another whisper.

The train had arrived at four o'clock in the morning, waiting for a transfer of wounded later in the day. They'd clambered off in the darkness and walked into a deserted city, leaving the other girls asleep, no one else quite that desperate to see *La Serenissima*.

Annie was finding or losing the way, over stepped, humpback bridges, down dark, dead-end alleys, alongside large canals and small, always following the first pale light in the sky, determined, as she'd been told to do, to stand on the eastern edge of the island and watch the sun rise out of the lagoon. She didn't tell Viv it had been Sam Ordish who'd given her that advice. It was after all Sam's shadow who still stood between them, as she now guessed he also stood between Harry and herself.

Ordish had finally written to Viv who couldn't help sharing his news with Annie, the first time in two months that the two girls had really spoken.

In the end, against my wishes, they have now sent me home, not considering me yet fit for combat. So I sit in the barracks filling in lists of stores and soldiers (in that order - for the War Office stores are considered more important than the men). I chose to also live in barracks, being unable to find any point of contact with civilian life - which for the most part seems to carry on as though the war out there did not exist.

Out there, out where? You must tell me where you are since I can only address this to your unit number and hope the military post functions in its usual efficient way. Annie told me there was a rumour of you being sent to Italy. You will know by now that I met with Annie during her few days of leave. I hope your own leave went well at home.

Heuveland already seems so long ago but vivid in my memories of how you nursed me so carefully and encouraged me. I hope we can meet soon again. Give greetings to Annie - and remember your 'cousin' to Virgin Mary!

My Best and most affectionate Wishes - Sam.'

ps. You'll have to give the bad news to Annie that Pimlott (of the hat-pinned helmet) died during his operation. His papers arrived today from London.

"Pimlott?" Viv asked as she stopped reading.

"The Count of Monte Cristo." How long death had waited for him, thought Annie, and how unfair.

"Why did Sam say 'Best Wishes' and not write 'love'?"

"I think men are afraid to use that word," Annie had replied. "My husband never said it once - at least not to my face. Though I'm sure from what Sam said about you when we were together that he does feel a great deal for you." Annie was still thinking about Pimlott and Benson in their Count of Monte Cristo tent. How would Benson have taken the death of his friend?

After a long silence (they'd been sitting in the train on their bunks, Annie above, Viv below), Annie had reached down to stroke her hair and try to indicate to Viv how innocent the seaside stay with Sam

Ordish had been. "I know Heuveland was awful in many ways. But being able to watch Lieutenant Ordish recover in that way and be something to do with it - we never have that on the train. We clean them and we dress them and we suffer their pain and often their death but after a few hours they're away. Those who recover do so somewhere else. And we never see it happen. And that's what real nursing is about - helping people to recover in their bodies and their minds."

"And that's why you went away with him?" Sam Ordish, Viv meant.

"There wasn't time to go to England and find Harry. I didn't even know where they'd sent him. We had four days, Viv. Five at a push. I just needed to be somewhere where I didn't have to think. And, yes, when he asked me, I suppose I thought Ordish might need some assistance. Which of course he didn't. He might have done but didn't."

Had Viv forgiven her? Annie wasn't sure. But now a week later, coming to Venice they'd decided to go out together on this early morning adventure. And after watching the sun rise through the mist across the water and seeing hearse boats rowing in a long black line towards the cemetery island, they began to hold hands again. An hour later they hugged and kissed in the darkness inside a deserted San Marco, all friendship and feeling restored.

"How **is** Harry?" Viv asked.

"He doesn't write. I mean he's on the mend. I know that from another nurse in England. I write to him but he doesn't write back."

"Shall we light a candle for him?"

And light a candle they did, in the Chapel of St Peter. Annie now knew she'd be permitted to write to Ordish herself and ask him to intercede with Harry.

Later, outside in the piazza, a steam launch landed boisterous sailors from a ship, uniforms who waved and whistled at the two nurses sitting at a café table.

It was nine o'clock, walking along the Riva degli Schiavoni warmed by the sun and well fuelled with coffee and brioches, when they saw a strange long line of gondolas leave a narrow canal by the 'Arsenal' and realized it was time to hurry back to the train, less easy now the narrow alleyways were crowded with citizens on their way to work or uniforms on leave. The gondolas, fifty or sixty of them, were carrying stretchers, two to each boat - a grotesque flotilla of the nearly dead, poled from the Naval Hospital up the Grand Canal. To most of the passing Venetians it must have seemed like a rehearsal for Carnival.

At the station the stretchers were off-loaded and carried up the steps onto the platform where Annie and Viv, breathless, had rejoined the others, ready to load the wounded into the train.

Chapter 43

Venice seemed impossibly far away when Ordish finally read Annie's letter. The envelope had journeyed the whole Western Front, army franks to prove it, before ending up at the Border Rifles' barrack in Alnwick nearly one month later.

Venice really was your early morning dream and I thought of you and thanked you for your good advice. A few hours are not enough in such a place.
Your letter to Viv cheered her immensely. She had been silent for weeks but has now forgiven me for having spent those days with you at the seaside. I fear Harry feels the same way she did. Since telling him I was looking after you for those few days he has not written, however many times I write to him. If you see him or speak to him or write yourself, will you for my sake set his mind at rest about the two of us and tell him we are only friends (a grateful friend who thanks you for those five days of rest and tranquillity – but how I am now paying for them).

Ordish looked out across town roofs at distant trees in the castle park. In his self-absorbed state he hadn't even asked himself where Harry was - nor any of the other wounded (except Bunny to whom he'd written warm congratulations upon his Christmas resurrection). The only soldiers Ordish was directly told about were the ones who'd died, for it was he who wrote the standard letter of condolence on behalf of the commanding officer - in case the subaltern in the field had been unable to write himself. There wasn't much excuse with Harry, no difficulty in tracing a wounded man: a Sergeant downstairs updated the regimental list every day, trying to plot the likely availability of the recovering wounded and place a mark against their names to prevent them being assigned to other units by the War Office clearing house. No: Ordish would have to admit that he hadn't asked himself about Harry because he felt a guilt towards him - a guilt now doubled with Annie's letter.

He sent his orderly downstairs for the list of 'B' Company wounded, ticked some chosen names, then walked along the uneven wood-floored corridor to knock at Brigadier Linton's door, careful to straighten his tie and smooth his wild thin curls. Linton was senior officer at the barracks, a good old-fashioned army martinet, loud of voice and manner - but also man of humanity who regularly shared his carefully collected selection of Clarets and other cultivated pleasures with the few junior officers he respected and took under his wing. Ordish hoped he was still counted among them. Last time they'd 'sipped the jug' Ordish had, in his cups, unwisely voiced support for the revolution in Russia, adding significant apoplectic hue to the Brigadier's already ruddy complexion. Linton was of a vintage that, to his obvious distress, precluded by many years any active participation in the war, a frustration taken out on his long-suffering horse who had to endure the charge of the heavy brigade each early morning in the castle park (way back in the previous century the Brigadier had served in one of the Indian cavalry regiments).

Ordish was still waiting outside the door. You knock loudly and you definitely wait. Rumour had it that an RSM had marched in one day, unsummoned by the "Come!" to find the Brigadier being serviced by a chambermaid crouched low beneath his desk.

"COME!!"

Confidence was the key when you walked in; Linton could smell (and punish) weakness or indecision at a thousand paces. Ordish entered head thrust forward, straight-backed below the neck, legs snappy in their march.

"My Bolshevik Lieutenant, no less!"

"Sir!" A salute and what Ordish hoped was a respectful but disarming smile. 'Bolshevik' didn't sound too hopeful.

"I have, sir, the names of some sound 'B' Company men I thought I ought to visit. Those up-coming to their medicals."

But no. Not for the moment. Ordish had first to endure a lecture and a reminiscence. In the 1880's the Brigadier had had an encounter with 'Russians' well north on the North-West Frontier at the Mintáka Pass: "Russians are not born to revolution; Russians are feudal. Their men are serfs who would not even breathe a word of insubordination. This so-called revolution will collapse." And on and on and on....

Ordish's attention wandered round the room whose floor and walls bore witness to many a distant and heroic campaign: a tiger rug with snarling head and teeth; a stuffed cobra facing a stuffed mongoose; an elephant's foot for cigar ash and waste paper. Ordish was surprised there were not a few preserved native heads ('spear-carriers' the Colonel liked to call them) to join the tusks, the wart-hog and the hippopotamus hung ungainly upon the walls. Yes, floor for India; walls for Africa. Yet for all his old-fashioned ideas, the Brigadier remained a decent man concerned about the welfare of his officers and soldiers. It was to this concern and to Regimental pride that Ordish now appealed as Linton paused for breath.

"Sir, I wouldn't want these men to think we had forgotten them."

"FORGOTTEN?!"

"These are the long-term wounded - three months or more in hospital or convalescence. And I fear, sir, three months or more of silence from the Regiment."

"SILENCE?!"

"A lack of communication. We only send them notification of their pay, sir, as and where appropriate."

A loud clearing of the throat as the Brigadier's eyes tried unsuccessfully to drill into Ordish's brain. Brigadier Linton was the only man in the Regiment who knew that Ordish possessed a Military Cross, awarded when subaltern in an artillery regiment at the end of 1915 ('heroic display of courage in an ammunition dump when the Officer ignored a potential explosion to rescue five of his men rendered unconscious by fumes while under enemy fire'). They were short of MC's that month, Ordish had decided. It was a decoration he chose not to wear nor have acknowledged in any way. After all, he'd come to the conclusion that artillery was far too noisy and dangerous; he'd funked out to the infantry two months later, following his Newcastle school-pal, Jack Fullager, into the Border Rifles - 2nd Lieutenant Fullager of 2 Platoon who'd been killed at White City and whose dead body Ordish never saw. For Ordish, Jack was still alive.

"I thought a visit from an officer, sir, would stiffen their resolve to return."

Linton looked down Ordish's list. "How long will this take you?" His voice had returned to normal.

"A week, sir."

"You'd better go away and do it then." Another enormous clearing of the throat and silence. Ordish almost expected him to hawk again and expectorate into the elephant's foot. "We'll open a bottle of wine the evening before your departure and you can tell me how you think this war should be fought." A few days previously the Germans had attacked on the Somme in thick fog; the British line had broken and was falling back; some said the road to Paris was now open.

A week later, mildly hung-over with good Claret and too much Port, his brain still echoing from Linton's bark, Ordish packed a bag and departed on the train. He saw two wounded from his own Platoon in Leeds, both unlikely to ever fight again; another two the next day in Leicester, neither of them very keen at the idea of coming back into the war, though both accepted the travel warrants he gave them, north to Alnwick for when they were discharged.

On the third day he found three more, one in Luton, two in Watford, before making London in time for theatre and a late meal with a distant cousin. Any 'family' was something of a trial for him, his brother's death at Gallipoli the one topic his mother had made sure everyone would always talk about when two or three were gathered together.

It was a relief to reach Bunny next morning, convalescing in an Oxford college - Bunny who had a university place at Oxford and wondered if he'd ever survive to take it up. He was bandaged but mobile and they walked the towpath up the Thames to Godstow through a spring-like afternoon, chased by a bull in a field by the ruins of the nunnery, feted by children and their mothers through the tiny village street in Wytham, puffing strenuously up into the ancient wood under its mysterious canopy, the ground a mass of bluebell leaf. Both men made a promise to go back there for the flowering, if both of them were still in England - "two weeks time," Bunny said. "We'll bring Harry with us. Have a democratic picnic."

"I'm hoping to see him tomorrow. There's a train from Reading that should get me somewhere near him. God knows what his place will be like. The two swaddies in Leicester were in something like a workhouse. One law for officers, another for the other ranks."
"Socialist Sam!" laughed Bunny and Ordish told him of the various arguments he'd been having with Brigadier Linton.
"Did you know," said Bunny, "he was Prideaux's Captain out in the Sudan? Prideaux wrote about him in a letter - said he'd always tried to be as good an officer as Linton - and care for his men and subalterns in the same way." Bunny had had a recent letter from Prideaux and couldn't quite believe the old man's affectionate tone. Old man? Poor Prideaux wasn't that many years past forty. Forty five perhaps. But then anyone in this war seemed old past thirty. Bunny glanced at his companion: Ordish was definitely not 'old'!

They dined that evening at the Radcliffe Hotel, looking round at normal life continuing normally for the well-dressed and the wealthy. Even Bunny expressed an almost socialist twinge as he wondered aloud just what these comfortable ladies and gentlemen could be contributing to the war; though, as Ordish reminded them both, they wouldn't find many couples here who hadn't lost sons or nephews somewhere, sometime during the last three and a half years.
Bunny and Ordish shook hands at the college lodge as the porter waited watch in hand to lock the gate on the stroke of eleven o'clock: "See you back on the line," Bunny said; and Ordish nodded. They'd both read the headlines on the evening papers in the hotel reception:

another German breakthrough had been confirmed, only Flanders holding on; otherwise the Western Front had broken from the Somme as far north as Arras, all that hard-won territory conceded to make a mockery of their long-ago dead at White City. But then, as Ordish again pointed out, it has less to do with ground won or lost than with lives: "Who first bleeds near to death will lose the war. And with America on our side, we have a few million men more to sacrifice than they can ever find."

Twelve hours later Ordish was walking through beech woods on the south side of a hill where the bluebells were already in almost full flower and stretched through the trees as far as a limited horizon, the sun and wind creating waves of light green leaf above his head against a storm-grey sky, a dancing dark blue carpet on the floor of the wood, so profuse he could not help but tread stems and flowers into the mud and ask forgiveness of St Francis. There's nothing in the world as blue as bluebells, Ordish thought; and tried to remember whether they were flowers or birds to whom St Francis once had preached. A farmer's wife had indicated this narrow path through the wood - 'a mile shorter', she'd said - and with rain blowing up from the west that had seemed a good idea.

His destination made itself obvious beyond the wood with ha-ha and a fence, three stories of red brick that had probably been an isolation hospital, inmates wandering in various conditions of decrepitude through the grounds. For 'inmates' they were, another 'workhouse' institution with, it seemed, little care and even less attention.

The Sergeant in Alnwick had telegraphed Ordish at the Radcliffe that same early morning to tell him that 'B' Company Benson was a new arrival in this same 'workhouse' and it was Benson Ordish first encountered, walking with a frame along the gravel driveway. Benson's damaged hip had healed rather better and quicker than he might have hoped. Another month or two and he'd be dragging his repaired body back into the war. The word was out already: every regiment required to send every available man to France, for back in France, not Flanders, was where the war was now being waged, Paris threatened once again, the Germans driving deep into Picardy which only three weeks ago they'd thought to be secure. 'An open war is what we need', Brigadier Linton had barked. An open war was what they now had - and, thought Ordish, none of us with any knowledge how to fight such battles. Out of our trenches we will be novices again, learning other skills from hour to hour.

The look on Benson's face when he saw Ordish was comedy and disbelief. "Sir," he said and felt he ought to straighten up and salute but Ordish merely shook his hand and took him by one arm to help him walk back towards the house and escape the impending rain.

"Have you seen Harry?" Ordish asked.

"Harry Cardwell? Harry's here?!"

A ground-floor patient for his immobility, Benson hadn't been upstairs and so poor was coordination and communication inside the 'workhouse' that Benson, unbelievably after three whole days, still had not been told that Lance-Corporal Harry Cardwell of his same unit was an inmate in this same building.

Though his whole week had been engineered for this one meeting with Harry Cardwell, Ordish lingered downstairs with Benson, apprehensive about Harry's state of health and state of mind. The storm shower outside came and went in a flurry of hail against the windows, Benson describing the final days of Pimlott, his friend's eventual inability to speak, his death when the surgeons finally withdrew the shard of metal through his head. His mother and father had travelled south to see him, the mother since losing her reason, unable to banish from her mind the image of him in his wooden frame, helmet nailed to his head with that steel splinter.

Eventually an orderly gave Ordish the number of Harry's room and the Lieutenant slowly climbed the stairs trying to put together in his head the words he thought he might need with the Corporal.

Harry was prone once more, and had been prone for nearly a week, another reason why Benson hadn't had occasion to see him. Haemorrhage had given Harry's skin the colour of the grey wet porridge that lay untouched on his bedside table. He seemed to be past caring. He watched Ordish walk in the door without a flicker of surprise or even visible sign of recognition.

"Hello Harry."

A nod, no more and Harry's face a mask, the other two men in the room glancing at them, feeling a tension. Ordish looked round with a nod, shook hands with each in turn, having to guide the blind man's arm towards his own. Then the amputee pulled himself up from his chair holding his crutch and led blind Alec from the room, slowly down the stairs and out into the garden, Ordish watching them first from the door then from the window.

Harry had turned his eyes away, avoiding the sudden blue sky and sunshine outside, fixing on the ceiling in a dark and dusty corner. Ordish didn't like the look of him at all.

"You're having a bad time."

"Bloody thing keeps bleeding, sir."

"So did mine. It just takes time." A pause. "Benson's here." This time Harry did glance at him. "He's downstairs. Arrived three days ago and had no idea you're here."

"Is he alright?"

Ordish nodded. "Pimlott's dead." Harry looked away again. "They sent me down from barracks. Make sure everyone's being looked after."

"In this hell-hole?"

"Yes. I'm sorry it's so grim." Ordish tried to engage Harry's eyes again. "I saw Bunny. He's almost fit. Had you heard about him?"

"Reggie wrote, sir."

"Are you reading all your letters?"

Harry stayed silent. So that's what this is all about, he thought. They've been writing to each other.

"Annie says she hasn't heard from you."

"Nothing much to say, is there, sir."

"Don't bloody 'sir' me, Harry. We're two men talking. Annie wrote me one letter - asking me to find out about you." Another longer silence. "She and I had some leave together. It was only a short time - I can't remember, three, four days by the time she was free of Heuveland - she had no idea where to find you and I needed nursing and Viv wasn't around."

"Viv **did** come back to England?"

"She knew where she was going. She knew she could do it in time."

"I don't blame anyone in any way - if that's what you mean."

"Annie blames herself. For not coming to see you here. She said she'd written you that. She's afraid you're not reading her letters."

"You can tell her I'm alright, sir."

"Well, it doesn't bloody well look like it." Silence again. "For God's sake, you're a fighter, Harry."

"Only when I'm on my feet."

Ordish sat down on the edge of Alec's bed, took a deep breath and tried again: "Annie looked after me, that's all. Spent most of the time talking about you. You're the only important part of her life, Harry. She feels lost if you won't write." The flat, dead calm of Harry's expression began to irritate Ordish. "DO you read her letters? I mean, I can't believe you would not reply if you were reading them. You don't give up on people, Harry. That's not your way."

An orderly walked in with a tray. Someone somewhere downstairs had been told there was an officer around - a belated attempt at making a good impression, a gesture of hospitality, one teacup and, by the omission of a second, a gratuitous insult to the inmate. Not that Harry seemed to mind nor even notice. Ordish took a newspaper from his pocket: "Have you read the news today?"

Harry shook his head.

"The Germans have broken our line again, north of the Somme."

"So much for White City, then. All our people killed for nothing. And everywhere else. And everyone else."

Ordish turned his chair slightly away from Harry, not to have to look at that flat dead expression. "What happened to Frank was an injustice and a crime. Whatever happened to Sergeant Percival was something that had to happen - whoever did it, however it was done. You cannot hold the thought of them inside you for ever more." Harry did not reply. Ordish did not expect him to. "It doesn't affect the way that I think about you - nor how Annie feels about you." Damn it, thought Ordish; why did I link our two names like that? He muddled on: "When we were together those few days, she talked about it. We both believe it is more about your courage than a crime." Grey silence in the room and Ordish imagined Harry's eyes fixed upon that dirty corner of the ceiling. The Lieutenant stood up and walked to the window to watch the lame leading the blind - Jack, the amputee hopping on his crutch across the lawn, free hand on blind Alec's arm. "There's many soldiers in this place with a lot worse wounds than you or I. They're getting on with their lives without much help from anyone else. I'd have expected you to be thinking more clearly than you are. Not losing your brain inside yourself."

Ordish turned back to the bedside table and Harry's belongings neatly stacked to one side. "Kit inspection, Lance-Corporal." Ordish upended the kitbag onto Alec's unmade bed, a dozen carefully addressed envelopes falling out among the clothes, each one of them still sealed shut. Ordish took a penknife from his pocket, extracted the blade and carefully, deliberately, slit each envelope open, dropping them onto Harry's bed: "Now read the bloody things, Cardwell. Like you said long ago about the gentleman-officer's letters, there's someone's life in there. You should respect it." Ordish turned and walked out of the room.

Harry was thinking, it's always the people you liked the best who could make you feel the worst. Like the headmaster and his wife back at school when he'd been fifteen years old and they'd caught him reading with a candle late one night. They hadn't hit him or even shouted but made Harry feel so guilty he physically couldn't come into school next morning - till Frank came and dragged him down the stairs. Everything they'd said in their quiet voices had been correct: where the boys were sleeping there were endless stacks of books and papers; they'd all have burned alive if he'd gone to sleep and knocked the candle over. And likewise now, Ordish had left him feeling like a piece of spat-out cud, someone without human feelings, someone no longer a friend and no longer at the level of consideration he once had been. And, as with the headmaster and his wife, Harry wanted Ordish to consider him. He wanted him to come back now and reassure him; smile that melancholy smile, sit on the bed, take his hand, anything to make him feel a part of his world again. He remembered the headmaster walking him aside next morning in the playground to reassure him no one would be told: "I'll not discourage anyone from reading," he'd said. "But if you have to read so late at night then come down to the kitchen and use the lamp."

He'd kept his word. There was no letter to take home on Friday night and Harry had made sure he brought a knotted cloth of large brown eggs to school next Monday morning. "Stay-overs," the other children would yell on Monday mornings as Harry and the others clambered off the cart with their rolled-up sheets and pillow-cases, five boys and three girls gathered by the haulier along the road - those (like his brother now) who lived too far up the valley to make the journey every day and had to sleep Monday to Friday in the attic of the headmaster's house. They paid a penny for bed and a breakfast, though if ever anyone arrived without the penny, the headmaster's wife never said a word.

Only eight years ago that was, thought Harry, and here's me feeling ninety. One year later old Maurice had died and he'd had to leave the school and start working on the farm, Maurice who'd been their shepherd and coughed himself to death a week after he'd been trapped in the snow for half a day.

For the life of him Harry couldn't remember what book he had been reading that night with the candle. He'd read just about everything from the shelves in the Head's sitting room. Something about France or Italy, it had been: The Black and Scarlet or the Scarlet and the Black. Yes Italy, he thought; and gathered Annie's letters off the bed into a pile, laying them carefully on the bedside table. Bugger the haemorrhage, he decided. He wasn't letting a bloody officer put him down. He'd get dressed and join Alec and the amputee down in the garden.

The letters stayed on his table another week, no longer out of sight but not yet read - until blind Alec talked to him one morning over the saw. "The last letter she said she'd been staying with someone. Was that the last time she wrote?"

"I haven't opened the other letters."

"Does that mean you're not writing to her?"

None of your business, Harry thought, though he didn't say as much.

Alec wasn't going to be put off by silence. Another two logs later he went on: "If I had even just one letter from anyone, I'd be reading it all the time. Well - I'd be asking you to read it to me."

"Yes - every bloody day. Just as well you haven't got one then."

Alec laughed as Harry humped another trunk onto the horse: "I expect she's wondering how you are."

"I'd get you to write and tell her, if you had eyes to hold a fucking pen."

Alec smiled again. He was feeling the new trunk, diameter and texture already better than Harry at sizing. "Two minutes, this one," he said, one hand on the top of the saw as Harry positioned the blade. A two minute cut he meant.

"Two by four," said Harry and Alec grinned. Four two minute cuts is what Harry meant, not the pull-through cloth for a rifle. Alec sized the thickness, Harry sized the length. But '2x4' was also a sort of password between them: no trench talk today.

"Old blind bastard," muttered Harry.

"Young blind bastard, you mean. It wouldn't matter so much if I was old." And away they sawed, Harry's wound hurting like the furies, his eyes avoiding the downward glance to see if it was bleeding again. Biggest bloody laundry bill in the whole building, the head orderly had complained.

It was easier talking to someone who couldn't see your eyes, would not read your expression - though Alec had become quite expert at reading the tone of Harry's voice and was learning now how to chivvy him; how to snap him out of mood: "How many letters DO you have?" he asked.

"Alright, you bugger, I'll read them to you. One each day until you tell me what to write her back." And then, thank God, Benson joined them on his walking frame and changed the conversation.

Ordish had walked away from that 'workhouse' convinced that if Harry remained there much longer he'd not survive. He didn't seem to have the mental strength to endure either infection or another haemorrhage.

He returned north with a handwritten copy of Harry's medical notes.

His mother's neighbour in Newcastle was a surgeon at the hospital. He'd somehow get Harry transferred north where the Regiment could hold a watching brief - and wrote as much to Annie without telling her quite how bad their young soldier was.

He hasn't read the letters - maybe now he will, though I think everything is going to take him time. I blame myself, in terms of both of you, for my selfish invitation to you and those five days by the sea - however wonderful they were for me.

I am staying two nights with my mother in Newcastle to talk with the Surgeon next door, the city much alive around me, and apart from occasional uniforms, not much evidence of war. I don't know why that angers me so much. What do I expect the poor civilian to do? Wear sackcloth and eat ashes?

As for home, every room is still my brother's shrine so even where the war is carefully acknowledged, it's not exactly the most reassuring place for me.

Chapter 44

The train had been parked for a week, the tracks cut behind them on a blown-up bridge, their location now a level crossing on the outskirts of a village, their function for the moment an overflow for a Casualty Clearing Station, their specialization the severing of damaged limbs and the storage and care of the amputees until communications were restored.

On most days the heat and smell were unbearable, some carriages sheltered by the shade of trees, others out in the open sunshine screened by inadequate sheets of canvas. And whether under the trees or beyond them, everything ended up covered with the sticky residue that fell from their leaves; covered also with flies, Virgin Mary walking up and down the train fan in one hand to keep them off the wounded and a swatter in the other to kill them. Eventually they had to detach the 'mortuary' coach where they were storing the severed limbs, nurses and surgeons gathering on two ropes like tug-of-war teams to haul it and its stench as far from the rest of the train as was possible. On average they were cutting two legs and an arm a day, casualties from the mountains where shells and mortars exploding against rock created cloudbursts of steel and stone splinters and long shards of flint. Hit in the head or body a man would almost always die; hit in a limb, the arm or leg would seem unrecognisable, flesh and bone in lacerated slivers so painful and so grotesque that some of the wounded died of shock before they could even be moved.

"The mountains are cruel to those who love them," said their senior Italian, himself an alpinist and Alpino - and exquisite surgeon, who used the sharpest saws and knives and always tried to leave as much of a stump as possible for the artificial limb. Their treatment carriage had been turned into an operating theatre, table and lamps borrowed from a nearby hospital, together with old torn sheets in which to collect the debris.

"A bloody meat factory we've become," Virgin Mary said one evening over dinner. "And no damn butcher to take our produce."

No disposal system was what she meant. So the nurses went out next day and started themselves to dig a pit in their long dresses with shovels and spades, a well-calculated gesture for within the hour the Italian surgeon organised a Company of passing infantry to complete the task. Under darkness that same night the surgeon and nurses carried twenty arms and fourteen legs wrapped in their blooded sheets and dropped them inside with a generous sprinkling of quicklime. After which Viv was sick for most of the night, Annie and Virgin Mary very high on grappa - before they returned to their patients in the morning.

How they kept those men alive no one really knew - as much with their own willpower or prayer as with medical care. Every old man and woman in that level-crossing village came forward once a week to give their blood - and every Company or Platoon that marched by them on the road were similarly drained. The Italian surgeon, Virgin Mary and the girls worked on, notwithstanding the heat and the smell, the flies, the occasional gangrene that demanded another trimming of a stump, or the sheer discomfort of those narrow, fold-down iron bunks. Some of these wounded, from a supply corps, had come from a distant Mediterranean island, speaking a language even the surgeon couldn't always understand, though Annie and the other girls understood enough to know that if they were ever to set foot on this Sardinia, they could stay there for ever more with the promises of hospitality pressed upon them by grateful men whose wives or mothers would always bless them. So spake the surgeon who even though he couldn't understand, knew enough about them and their island to understand that this 'hospitality' would bear no relation to their wealth or means. These were people who would kill their last sheep or goat to feed a stranger who'd been accepted as a friend.

At which talk of shepherds Annie slipped away. Her own Harry would behave the same. If he still was 'hers'. Ordish's letter about

Harry had arrived, on horseback around the smashed-up bridge, and in a quarter of the time Annie's letter had taken to reach him. He explained and apologised for the delay, sending her the envelope with those dozen franks from up and down 'what once had been the Western Front'. She imagined him, like Virgin Mary, with maps laid out on tables, trying to plot from newspaper reports what was really going on.

The true story must be worse than we are being told. Pérignon is taken and only Amiens now defended as a non plus ultra. In one way it makes a nonsense of all those battles we have fought and all those men who died. And yet the winning or the losing of the war, I'm sure, has more to do with the numbers of men lost than the territory gained. And the Germans ARE losing men. Even as voluntary prisoners coming forward of their own accord because they now believe we have more food than they. Maybe if we manage to push them back within a month or two, before they dig themselves in, the end really would be in sight. For 1920? What old men we all will be!
'B' Company escaped retreat, stuck as always on the hinge, back on the Menin road again where the British Empire will never surrender Ypres. Poor mutilated city. Will they ever rebuild her? She will be like an old friend now with all her nooks and crannies, her bad memories and the relief, sometimes, of finding oneself back inside her walls.
Yes, I am trying to return. It is the only life possible while the war continues. Harry doesn't say as much (says hardly anything at all), but I fear, if he heals his wound he will feel the same. As will you. Until the last shot is fired, I don't believe any one of us three (and many thousands more) will ever be able to disengage.

I've heard from Lieutenant Ordish - Annie wrote to Harry - *He says he will have you moved from where you are and where they're not curing you sufficiently well. I shall come and find you wherever it may be, whenever I am able to and reassure you as I reassure myself that no feeling between us will have changed. You are hurt by what you imagined and which was not true - just as I am hurt by not hearing from you, by knowing nothing more about your life, as though you were determined that I should no longer belong. Sometimes this brings me the nearest I have been to giving up and going home.*

She wrote those words just four days before a letter from her mother told Annie her father had been ill, first in hospital, now back home in bed. And for the first time in these three years of absence Annie felt an almost unbearable surge of emotion for her suddenly so distant father, yet somehow distant as he'd always been: the father she remembered once a week telling stories late at night; the father she remembered holding her hand each Sunday walking through the park or running on the beach; the father striding round the store in his high collar and tails, assistants, even customers bowing to him; and the father who shouted, roared at her sister the evening he found her lying in the stable with one of her admirers. Perhaps that roaring had been so sudden, so severe, so frightening, they'd all been distanced from him, sister, brother and herself, leaving home one by one within the next two years, her sister to marry that admirer and move to New York, her brother to live with his grandmother in their country home, Annie with Patrick in their sail-loft by the harbour - and then off so foolishly to find the war.

"I have to see him," she told Virgin Mary.

Next morning she woke to smell coal smoke and hear their engine making steam. The bridge and tracks had been repaired, the carriages of their train gathered and re-coupled, their movement-order taking them west to leave their amputees at hospitals in Vicenza, Verona and Milan. In each city they decided to accompany the wounded in the ambulances and, saying goodbye, hand them over personally to whoever it may be, doctor or sister. After a week shut together in the train, the wounded had become 'family' and couldn't be discarded and passed on in quite the usual way.

Messages had been sent, through Virgin Mary or the Italian surgeon

Annie supposed, for once the train had parked near the middle of Milan they were visited by someone who called himself the American Consul, an Italian from New York who seemed to spend his time sourcing merchandise to send to Brooklyn and finding markets for various manufactured articles from small factories in New York. All this Annie discovered in the few short days she stayed with him and his family while waiting the passage he had found her on a ship due in Genoa from Naples and on its way to New York. The Consul's town house was in one of the narrow streets within sight of the cathedral and inside the system of canals that circled the centre of the city. Apart from the delight of walking those streets, visiting cathedral, castle and art gallery, Annie also found herself in 'family life' for the first time since leaving home, young children at school, a nanny looking after them at home, a cook to ask Annie what she liked to eat and maids to clean and iron her clothes. She'd walked into the house that first afternoon in her nurse's dress and cape, a figure of instant fascination for the children - and indeed for their mother and the Consul himself, Annie then having to describe some of her adventures and in particular, withholding certain details, the shell explosion that had overturned their ambulance and killed her husband. They seemed awestruck, all of them, that she was able to recount that incident and that she should have stayed on with the war. Next morning Annie returned to the cloistered hospital to visit her Sardinian patients, the Consul's wife accompanying her, determined to contribute something to the war herself (Annie later knew from the children's letters that the Consul's wife continued those visits and eventually became expert in the rehabilitation of limbless men and the fitting of artificial limbs).

In the afternoon and the following morning the Consul's wife took Annie to her own dressmaker for a revision of her outdated civilian wardrobe - the fiery young dressmaker, Serena Bacchetta, anything but serene, full of passionate ideas, not how women were 'expected' to dress, but how they 'should' dress. She set to work with great enthusiasm on Annie's slender frame and next morning took her shopping, reminding her she should bring something home for her sister and her mother (silk and lace). Annie wrote again to Harry, determined now that he should know each detail of her life and have no more cause to doubt her.

I AM going home not by choice but because my mother writes to me that my father is ill. And I fear of course, since it will take me two weeks to arrive, that he will die before I can see him. I have just returned through crowded narrow streets from collecting the Consul's children at their school and buying them a forbidden ice-cream at a bar. This city is such a strange mixture of the ancient and the modern, even the hospital where we left our soldiers a medieval building of quite breathtaking beauty, yet around the corner elegant shops of unforgivable luxury and new fashion. So I dream of showing you this place one day and visiting this family that has so kindly taken me into their home (you will see from this letter-paper how grand they are - grand in both senses of the word).
Saying goodbye to Viv and Mary (and the other girls) was difficult. They are on their way back to the front (a more improvised place than France or Flanders but every bit as awful). There is talk that the train will soon be returned to France - apparently it was a train financed by subscription and the subscribers are wondering where their carriages have got to! I think we nurses are merely considered as part of the furniture. Where the train goes there go we. At least back on the north front I would be nearer you - IF I ever come back from America, I can hear you say. Well I will return. Even the idea of absence from the war, whether here or

up north, is something unreal – however much we hate everything that happens.   Perhaps that is the greatest mystery of all – for I know you feel the same, that while your friends are still out there you feel you should be with them. No, not even that; you feel you want to be with them and not miss anything they experience or suffer.

Tomorrow I leave on the train for Genoa to join the ship – which then stops only once, at Barcelona, before reaching New York. But that means a whole week or more on the sea and me absolutely certain to be sick! On my way back I shall find a ship to land me in England and come and look for you.

Read me, read me, read me. You do not have to write until you feel the need – and naturally until you know that I am back.

Chapter 45

"Taking a lot of damn trouble over this Lance-Corporal, aren't we?"
"Over all of them, sir. The Lance-Corporal happens to be the one who needs most care."
"These places then, these secondary hospitals - not much bloody good?"
"Not the ones I saw."
"Always take care of your wounded, we were taught. I mean, the swaddies will always know, whether you do or you do not. And if you don't, well the buggers won't fight if they think they're going to be neglected. My father learnt that in the Crimea." The Brigadier refilled their glasses. "Come to that I learnt the same in India, whatever colour skin they were." Ordish watched him carefully cut the end of his cigar. "In fact the better you treated the darker ones - well, they'd practically commit suicide for you." Linton cocked an eye at Ordish as though expecting him to smile or look away.
"That's very reassuring, sir. Not the suicide, I mean, but the fact that we can still understand those feelings."
Prior to the lighting of the cigar, there now came a deep clearing of the throat, Ordish as ever on such occasions in this room, watching the elephant's foot. But Linton swallowed it back down. They were sitting over one small oil-lamp, shadows leaping up and down the wall with the movement of the flame. The Brigadier rented a house with a maid down the street where they usually did their night-time drinking. Tonight they'd stayed in barracks, ignoring the occasional creaking along the uneven corridor outside as others returned to their beds.
"I'm recommending you for Captain, Ordish. Prideaux's on his way to Colonel and I'm not having an outsider poach any one of my

Battalions. Prideaux should have happened long ago. But no one in command much likes the Border Rifles. They think we're still marauders."

"We're bloody good fighters, sir."

"Precisely! As I take it your Lance-Corporal is?"

"The best, sir."

"Up him to Corporal and we'll try and make a Sergeant out of him."

"Thank you, sir."

"And you do whatever you think you have to do."

And thus was it done, over welsh rarebit with a bottle of Château Lafitte and a lamplit scribble of names on a sheet of paper.

The surgeon neighbour of his mother had been absurdly pleased to be able to do Ordish a favour. He turned out to have known Colledge from medical school and clearly suffered a certain amount of 'war guilt' stuck safely here on the north bank of the Tyne. This Cardwell would be given a bed and his treatment personally supervised whenever they could bring him north.

Ordish had always wanted to see those naked grass and heather hills from where Harry came. They were something of a legend in the city, in the smoke. Even more of a legend for the Regiment. Was that not where those original border raiders hid, in the then still wooded valleys, ready to attack or to defend.

Given carte blanche by the Brigadier, Ordish took two soldiers with him, new recruits in training, both from farms. They picked up a pony and trap where the railway ended, believing it would be an hour or so up the valley road. Two hours later, nearly three, they were finally approaching the farmhouse, "about as near to Scotland as you can be without actually stepping over," Ordish told the two soldiers.

Ordish should have anticipated the Cardwells' mixed emotions to see uniforms arrive, the belief at a distance that it must be Harry returning home, the fear as unfamiliar faces drew near that Harry might be dead. It was Harry's younger brother who came from the house to meet them, despatched by his mother to hear the worst: Albert, strong-eyed handsome as his brother, Ordish thought, watching him wave back at his mother to signify all was well.

Once father had returned down from the fell, Ordish left the swaddies to help on the farm with the mother and the brother (it was still Easter holiday and lambing not yet started) and took the father with him back into Alnwick where, it being late evening, he found Mr Cardwell a room for the night in barracks. He'd be taken to Alnmouth station first thing in the morning.

And so it was, one soft full-spring afternoon on the saw with Alec, that Harry watched a familiar figure approach through the flowers of the shrubbery, an older man in his ill-fitting Sunday suit, the sleeves and trousers an inch or so too short, a look of apprehension on his face, the same expression Harry remembered from every morning in childhood when that same face peered out of the upstairs window to read the weather.

"Hello Da!"

"Son."

They shook hands, Harry's cautioning left hand on father's wrist to lessen his iron grip on Harry's weak right hand.

"Come to take you home. Well - as far as Newcastle. They've fixed you a place in the hospital there."

"Who?"

"Your Lieutenant Ordish."

"And home?"

"Your officer brought two men to help while I'm gone."

"Lambing?"

"Another week or so away. No scottish rams this year." Father smiled and looked him up and down: "Your mother'll be glad to see you - all in one piece."

Alec was also smiling as he listened to them, sightless eyes turned towards the sun, but the smile a little frozen on his face. It seemed he was about to lose his pal.

"This is Alec, Da. He can't see you too well." Alec held his hand out, Harry's father taking it. "He comes from London. I told him, he'll have to come and stay with us one day; get the fresh air."

"I'll miss the letters," Alec said in a lower voice. At one letter a day they'd caught right up to date and had had to start once more at the beginning. There wasn't much they didn't now know about the geography, tastes and smells of Northern Italy and Annie's itinerant ambulance train.

"I'll write and tell you about her - " and Harry could see his father wondering who 'her' might be.

Harry held Alec by both shoulders: "You look after yourself, you blind bastard."

"If you get back out there, kill some Jerry for me."

Harry looked back at Alec, abandoned by the saw-horse as he and his father walked away: Alec's hand was running slowly along the top of the saw, his head motionless, turned again toward the sun. He seemed utterly forlorn.

On his way back inside to pick up his kit, Harry found Benson in his ground-floor room. "If you can make the stairs, see if you can't get yourself into my room. Look after blind Alec. No one else'll do it."

Harry hadn't meant it as an order but Benson knuckled his forehead: "Yes, Corp."

Up in his own room Harry shook hands with the amputee: "I'll come and see you, Jack, if it's ever over."

"Good luck, Harry." Nearly five months they'd known one another in that room.

Benson called after Harry through the open door downstairs as they walked away: "See you back on the line, Lance-Corporal."

"I hope to God not," Harry's father murmured. He had a motor-taxi waiting outside, hired with money given him by Ordish. Even their train ticket was first class - army money, the Lieutenant had assured him. The doctors reading Harry's medical notes insisted his was an accompanied journey. There would even be a cab for them later that night in Newcastle and a bed paid for Harry's father before he returned home next day.

Harry became a minor celebrity at the hospital in Newcastle, no one ever having seen a wound that continued to open so spontaneously: "In much the same way," said the surgeon neighbour of Ordish's mother, "as the statue of a Catholic saint performing miracles." There weren't many miracles the hospital could perform for Harry, beyond perpetual care 24 hours out of 24. Each attempt either wound made to open would be quickly spotted and coagulant applied, until both entry and exit wounds gave up trying, saving, Harry thought, their efforts for another more vulnerable time.

Brother Albert and his mother visited one day, having to beg the matron for entry after their long journey down the valley and on two ill-connecting trains. Outside hours they were allowed upstairs, mother bursting into tears when she saw her eldest son lying so prone and still - and refusing to believe Harry when he told them he hadn't been feeling so well for months. But she patted her face quickly dry again, hoping no one else in the ward had noticed her distress. Ma wasn't one to lose her dignity, especially when dressed in her severe Sunday suit. She brushed now at her collar and straightened the line of buttons down her front, Harry remembering those same gestures when she used to cover the dress with apron and one of father's old shirts, coming back from chapel to cook the meat. She liked to stay dressed for Sunday lunch. After all, she and her parents had been in service at Wallington Hall the other side of Simonside; they knew about the grander formalities of life. Not for the first time Harry wondered how she must have felt the first night she spent up the valley at the farm. Did she ever realize how far away from everyone she'd be? Father had met her at a fair in Rothbury, Da with his half-a-thousand head of sheep and ten times as many acres to call his own. He must have seemed a very eligible suitor.

"Have you seen the news?" brother Albert asked, the progress of the German breakthrough, he meant. Harry nodded. "Do you think the war will wait for me?"

"I wouldn't want it to. Nor would you want to if you knew what it was like."

"I wouldn't mind. It's what a man must do."

"Shut your mouth, Bertie," mother said. "It's bad enough having one of you gone for a soldier and coming back hurt."

They gave Harry what news there was from up and down the dale, births and deaths, the figures from their lambing, the sharing of the shearing with all the young men gone to war, and a new gravel track built across the hills by the army.

Harry was sorry when they had so soon to go, mother's eye always on the clock. They'd a train to catch for Morpeth where they'd stay the night with cousin Will; then the second train on to Rothbury in the morning and a four hour walk home if a carrier didn't pass. Harry watched mother's dark suit out the door at the end of the ward and remembered Annie's hat and scarf, brilliant red mouth and light blue blouse as she'd walked into the ward at Dover.

Chapter 46

Annie at that moment felt like a wrung-out half-drowned bird who'd flown the Atlantic alone with her own two wings, dehydrated, shaking on her legs, and now disorientated by everything around her. Those six days on board the ship had been purgatory, shut for most of the time into her cabin, visions of icebergs and torpedoes haunting the intervals between sickness. The cab ride to Grand Central across New York felt like sitting in a picture-house watching movies through each window, glimpses of faces and bodies whose lives she no longer understood, as indeed the landscape through the window of the train and the people walking up and down the car.

Now in Boston she had to take a grip, try once more to control events around her before facing the family. She placed her bags in a cab, giving the driver their address and a handsome tip (would she have done that in Italy without fearing never to see her bags again?). Checking her appearance in the ladies room, she imposed self-confidence upon herself and set off walking down main street ram-rod straight to repossess her old home-town. She hadn't expected to meet anyone she knew, nor for anyone to recognise her - yet became aware of heads turning as she passed, men and women, but mostly women. Annie began to glance at them as she walked - to eventually realize how slighter and shorter in cut than their's was the dress for which Serena Baghetta had had her girls stay up all night cutting and sewing in Milan. Her ankles and calves were highly visible and the line and shape of her thighs, perhaps even her bottom, quite unhidden. How typical of New England, she thought: in New York no one had looked twice. She could have been dressed half-naked in rags and no one there would have shown the least surprise; but here, Bostonians, still small-town in attitude, turned and stared in shock or envy. She wished she had worn the uniform in the way she, Viv and the girls had adapted it to their comfort and practicalities, with high hem and loose-fitting bust and waist. That would have made the good New England ladies stare even harder, wondering what uniform it was and raising eyebrows at the scandal of a woman's body showing something of its natural shape.

Such minor irritations vanished as she turned up the slope of Plymouth and the Square and could see at the end of the street on the far side her father's shop, a skip of heartbeat as she came near enough to read his name proudly on the sign; and began to fear what she would find at home, unable to imagine her indomitable father as an invalid.

Now one or two seemed genuinely to recognise her in the street, a woman smiling, a young man and one not so young raising their hats to her, Annie acknowledging these only half-familiar faces with an inclination of the head. She made for the private entrance down the side-street adjoining the shop, the stone steps and stone porch of a respectable family house added by her father just before she'd left for France. The maids, forewarned by the arrival of her baggage in the cab, were watching out for her, front door opening before she'd even reached the top of the steps - two maids she did not know curtseying as she entered, watching her open-mouthed as she took their hands one by one and looked them in the eye: "I'm Annabel." And to the oldest one: "How is my father?"

"Not allowed in the shop, Miss Annabel. He has to rest for two whole months."

"Annabel!" she heard him call from one floor up. Which room was he in? She'd almost forgotten the geography of the house, the new entrance having changed the layout of the staircase.

The older maid preceded her up the stairs and opened a door, Annie seeing armchair and desk before remembering it was her father's study. He was standing by the window - from where, she guessed, he had been watching her whole last half-mile from the Square. He now was turned towards her, away from the window, holding out his arms. In that moment, not before, Annie realized she had not seen him since Patrick had been killed.

"You left here as a young bride; you come back as a widow."

And for the first time since he'd died Annie wept openly for her husband: after she'd embraced and kissed her father, she knelt down on the floor and cried out her eyes, her father holding her head against him. The anquish of that sudden weeping quite alarmed him, a silent howl as she had never done from when she'd been a child.

Where had she been since then? In a far country, yes; in even further countries of her mind, yes. Her father must be wondering who she had become; still fruit of his loins, yes; still illogical, hardheaded, obstinate progeny of his Irish mind and soul, yes. But citizen of Boston or New England, no. Citizen of Europe maybe, or citizen of the world? They were describing the war in Boston newspapers as the 'War of the World' and she had been a part of it; was still a part of it.

Perhaps Annie felt she'd lost herself inside it, leaving no way out. Trapped: once trapped in Boston, now trapped in Picardy, Flanders or Italy; once trapped with Patrick, now trapped with Harry? Harry will have to come here one day, she was thinking; walk into this study and shake hands with her father. What would mother and father make of her silent shepherd? What would he make of them? And her brother and sister? Annie could imagine her brother Daniel now, inside the hutch of father's office, overseeing the shop with his mother in father's enforced absence, the pneumatic tubes spitting out invoices and payments from every department, a frantic counting of money and entering of books. Was her brother using an abacus to calculate his future fortune? How unfair she was to mock him with his race-horse and Irish wolfhounds. Even Daniel would acknowledge the world was made of more than dogs and horses - as indeed he did, coming through from the shop with mother as soon as they heard Annie had arrived. He was wary, almost apprehensive as he kissed her, wondering, like father, who his sister had become. Already, from the letters she had written, he knew she was well beyond his own experience or perceptions. He remembered the soft-smiled, handsome Patrick and couldn't imagine how his sister had coped with her husband's violent death right beside her. And not as an accident, not being hit by a cab or a tram; but as a deliberate and voluntary exposing of both themselves to danger and death, bringing medical aid to soldiers in a war that at the time hadn't even been American.

Mother of course cried the moment she saw Annie, realizing immediately how much she'd changed, the ageing in her eyes, that accumulation of many unknown circumstances somewhere faraway, love and death and dreadfulness that she sometimes had alluded to in her letters, mother's tears silent like her daughter's always were.

They should have talked for hours, catching up on three years of family life. They did talk - but only to Annie's questions: about Granny and Aunty Ethel, Uncle Kearon, Cousin James (gone to the war on the draft); about sister Beverley in New York and her new baby (they were coming up on Sunday); about those of the old shop staff Annie remembered; about school friends shared with Daniel. But the moment they tried to ask her about the war, the conversation died - and all her fault. Her eyes would turn away not to show emotion, her answers monosyllabic, her thoughts as full of Harry as of Patrick, or of any of the thousand wounded soldiers she had tried to care for. What could her poor family even begin to understand? Why should she inflict any of those memories on them? The war was something separate that did not really touch their lives.

At least she knew after that first day that she would be going back as soon as was decently possible. Had she ever doubted it? Though mother sensed it as soon as Annie herself. Out of hearing of her father, she began the blackmail of obligation: 'You've done your share of good works.' 'I need you here - your father needs you here'. 'Do you want to kill your father?' 'How can you be so selfish?' And on and on, drip by drip, only Daniel winking to keep her aware of available sanity.

Dear Daniel who for all his faults and doubt, took her aside the second night home and told her: "Take no notice. I know you have to go back. I don't know why you have to. But I see it in your eyes. They are not really here with us. I have to say I wish I had something that big to call me." She kissed him for that and he hugged for the first time since they'd been at school.

He then asked her which friends she wanted to visit.

"I'll visit no one," she told him, "except Patrick's family. If anyone else wants to come here to the house - well, I can choose whether to see them or not." She looked at him. "It's not me being difficult. It's just I don't know what to say to anyone anymore."

"Even me."

"I don't know, Dan. I'm just glad they haven't sent you out there."

"Like James."

"Is he really out there?"

"Not yet. They're still training. In Canada, someone said."

"The Canadians are big in France - and Flanders. The shock troops, they're called. Them and the Anzacs."

"Anzacs?"

"The soldiers from Australia and New Zealand."

"And us?"

"We don't really count, not yet."

Daniel had to take the atlas down to understand Flanders and Picardy - and for Annie to show him all the cities in Italy where their train had been. Where were they now, she wondered: steaming up and down the railway lines near Venice, or on their way back into France?

Patrick's family received her with great emotion, if not quite their usual warmth. They were still puzzled, would always remain puzzled, why a young married couple had volunteered for a war so far away, so unconnected with the real world around them. It was only natural that they should in part blame her - and wonder why she was still out there. She knew as she walked in that if they cried, she would also cry. But they did not. She guessed their grieving had already been done and had long ago exhausted them. She shook their hands, none of them offering a kiss and, mother, father, sister, sat down as for a formal tea. She'd brought sketches for them of Patrick's grave, that painted wooden cross in the village cemetery outside Loos. She'd also brought them his instrument case; postcards of the last places she and Patrick had been together; and some of the letters they had sent him.

Later, before she left, Patrick's surgeon father wanted, on his own outside in the grassed yard, to be told exactly how his son had died. Annie spared him the smell of Patrick's burning flesh and hoped they'd never dig up his coffin and discover how mutilated their son and brother had really been at the moment of his death.

Annie left the Donovans believing she would never see them again, a feeling of finality in their farewells. Patrick's sister, Helen, walked her up the street back to the tram: "It's been kind of hard for us to take in, I'm afraid. And it doesn't seem to change. You know, things still come for him in the post - or you meet people who haven't heard. And it all comes back. Which doesn't mean to say it isn't worse for you."

"Maybe it's easier being out there still - having to get on with it all. In the end there's no time to think about anything. Except the last wounded soldier you were looking at."

"I really do admire you," Patrick's sister said after a long silence and as the tram approached. "And so does my father - and so also would my mother if she took the time to think." Helen hugged her and kissed her on the cheek, which sudden moment of affection did make Annie cry. She had to climb on board the tram with a hankerchief to her eyes, wondering why sometimes, as had happened on her first meeting with her father, the smallest, most simple expression of emotion could break down that protective wall.

Granny tried to do the same on Sunday when Daniel drove them up to see her in the country. She took Annabel simply by the hand and drew her into the tiny private room behind the kitchen where she spent her evenings. Granny had a framed studio photograph on her desk of Annie and Patrick in their wedding clothes which she picked up and kissed and made Annie feel like another silent howl - which Granny wanted and Annie certainly did not. The day was far too young and for that matter far too cold, no heating in the house, a sharp north wind blowing down the Connecticut and a great deal more to struggle through, not least the arrival of her sister.

Beverley, baby and husband Jake drove up from New York in their motor-car, late, chilled and exhausted, Beverley irritable as ever when life was anything less than perfect. She was offended that Annie hadn't seen them in New York on her arrival and made her now promise to stay over on her way back. Beverley had already decided Annie **was** going back. Annie guessed Beverley quite liked to own a sister on the 'Western Front'. She could imagine the party

Beverley would throw on East 37th the night before her re-departure for Europe. Bev had missed their original farewell, thinking it was something of a temporary lark. But now Annie as a widowed war nurse was an asset. She might even earn some kind of Federal or Civic medal, Bev had suggested at the tail-end of a letter. Oh what a cat, what a bitch you are, thought Annie of herself as all this passed through her head. Bev is my sister: we always fought - but we protect one another and if anyone threatened either one of us the other would take up fists, knife, even gun to defend her.

As indeed Daniel. What a young gentleman he'd turned out to be, and with sensitivity and wisdom. Some awareness of the human condition he'd acquired in these last three years; from where or whom, Annie wondered. Lucky dogs and horses, she supposed. Oh what a cat, what a bitch. How Virgin Mary would be castigating her for unkind thoughts about her siblings; or even Viv, who deeply loved her own sister. But perhaps even Viv and Mary sometimes behaved badly when they went home, familiarity not breeding contempt but intolerance.

Beverley calmed down, admiring Annie's Milan dress, Annie genuinely able to admire her niece. The day then seemed to improve, north wind turning round to south, as Granny said it would. They ate lunch on the veranda, Daniel opening two bottles of wine in deference to Annie's European habits, though whisky was still served to their father and coffee to the others. Annie had admitted to her brother how wine and even grappa had become something of a habit in Italy, a way of finding oblivion and sleep. But not today with the sun now shining and the butterflies and buttercups in the meadow where Dan kept his horse. They walked down to the river and picked cherries from the neighbour's tree and chased one another, Bev included, as they hadn't done for years. Jake seemed amazed to see his wife behave with such lack of decorum which only made Annie and Dan even more outrageous. In the end, with Dan's help, Bev stripped off Annie's suit, claiming it as a forfeit to be taken back to her dressmaker in New York, Annie returning to the house laughing in her slip to find an old frock and blouse that still fitted her.

Annie did see some girlfriends in the days that followed, the ones whose news she had followed in various letters - best friend Sara, married to a lawyer, who'd written 'appalled' on Patrick's death; or Elizabeth married to a chemist, Deborah married to a doctor, Sandy married to a broker (whatever a 'broker' was - there were certainly no girlfriends married to a shepherd!). Like the family and the Donovans, they shied away from talk about the war. They seemed to recognise the impossibility of ever comprehending how it was; even seemed to realize she had lived in a part of the universe where not even man, let alone woman, had ever been before. That much they were beginning to understand from the newspapers.

It's going to take time to get you out of here, Daniel had warned her. He'd meant with mother, though Annie had fully intended to spend a week or two with her father. He still was weak from whatever had happened to his heart, his doctor only advising rest. Bev was trying to have him brought down to New York, Jake saying he knew someone in the Central Hospital. But father wasn't going to move from home where he could feel himself still connected with the shop. It had been the most significant part of his life and he wasn't about to close his eyes to it. Nor did he really trust Dan to keep supply up to date. That was all experience - anticipating seasonal demand, making sure suppliers were geared up in advance. Retail was tricky, transport never reliable, storage space limited. All this came out to Annie during that second week at home, more as explanation than complaint, in some ways an *apologia pro vita sua*, a settling of accounts with Annie's childhood when he'd never ever had enough time for his younger daughter, Bev the eldest having had her time already claimed, Daniel, the only son, only needing to ask for attention to be given.

Father and youngest daughter had been allowed to walk together in the park that first week, one of the shop drivers taking them there in a delivery van - until mother discovered and objected to their form of transport. Father refused to pay for a cab or car so instead that second week they sat out in the yard, father making Annie describe Paris, Venice and Milan. It was the following Thursday before he mentioned the war again, Annie having to describe its geography as she'd done for Daniel, father taking down the atlas once again, and this time marking with a pen the towns in Flanders and Picardy where Annie's train had been.

"How," he asked, "is it organised?" And eventually: "How bad are the wounded when they come on board?" How do you do it, he meant. How can you come home so calm and only cry that once? And, of course, how can you bear to go back again? All that left unsaid. As Dan had warned, it would take time.

Chapter 47

Harry also had come home, a long, slow five hour walk up the valley to acclimatize himself, thanking but refusing the various lifts offered him by passing carts. His Da saw him from high on the fell while herding sheep with the dogs into a hemmel. Once the sheep were penned father cut down the hillside to join him, the dogs racing ahead when they scented Harry, two border collies trying to leap into his arms, two figures then walking up the narrow valley track towards the isolated farm, the dogs bounding all around them, Harry in his uniform, his father carrying his kitbag. "Bloody fool walking this far, after all the care they've given you in hospital."

"Had to try myself out. See what I'm fit for."

Mother was waiting, watching from a window of the farm, wondering how many folk will have seen Harry pass along the valley. Albert instead was running down the grass bank through the wind-stunted trees to meet them, putting up a dozen baby rabbits as he came, leaping like the dogs into his brother's arms.

This time Harry didn't dissolve into tears over the tea table. There seemed nothing left to cry about, certainly not with what he had to do. He knew as soon as tea was over he'd need to cross the hill and visit Frank's folk and still didn't know what he could tell them about Frank's death.

It was Saturday evening yet they'd all stayed in, the Lowburns, knowing he was coming home. He was glad he hadn't left it for chapel on the Sunday with too many people around and everyone trying to hear what had happened. After all, up the dale a war death was still a novelty, Frank only the fourth of five soldiers killed. Though five out of twenty men of age was quite enough and had already crippled several farms.

Frank's sister Kate was there, green eyes red from weeping again at the memory of her brother's death and staring almost pleading into Harry's. She'd hugged him hard as he'd walked in the door. "Frank was the bravest man I ever knew," he told her and the others. "His officers said the same - I hope they wrote to you."

Frank's father nodded.

Harry looked him in the face: "I'm sorry I took him with me, Mr Lowburn - being he was younger than me."

"He'd have had to go sooner or later. I'm not too old yet for the acres we graze. He'd not have been reserved. Besides, if he wanted to go -"

"He was the bravest man in the Company, Mrs Lowburn." Harry meant the remark for Kate too. Ten foot Kate, as tough and shy and fast as a red mountain deer. She'd only kissed him the one time in his life, yet Harry still remembered the sensation, Kate bending down and his mouth feeling like it was being licked and swallowed by a boisterous dog. He still remembered the glow that had given him. Who knows, if he hadn't met Annie he might be thinking now of marrying Kate and joining their two lands.

She led him out when it was time to go and walked him up the track. Her father had unstopped the whisky and they'd all had too much to drink. She kissed him again, bending down from her greater height, licking around and into his mouth: "I know you miss him as much as we," she said. "And I know he was happy being able to be with you."

Perhaps Kate's kiss was the best cure Harry could have had for the confusion he'd been feeling about Annie. What would she have said if she'd seen them kiss? And yet it was as innocent as sister kissing brother - as Annie had said her stay with Ordish had been.

That night in their room Harry took out the opened letters, Albert watching from his bed: "Da says you have a girl."

"I never told him nothing."

His brother grinned. "How was Kate?"

"She was crying."

"I didn't mean about Frank - I meant about you."

"How should she be?"

"She's not that much older than you and every boy this side of

Rothbury wanting to court her. They say she's going to marry Bill or Mick Planter."

"Those bastards?!"

"They're going to toss a coin for her. Bet you wouldn't mind. Going with her, I mean."

"Go to sleep."

"Did she kiss you - Kate?"

"Watching from the hill, were you?"

Albert nodded at the letters. "Who IS the girl?"

"Go to bloody sleep." Harry pushed the letters into his pocket and returned downstairs, lighting a candle on the kitchen table. He knew he'd only half-listened to the letters when reading them to Alec. If he was going to write to her he needed to know exactly what Annie had been trying to say.

I believe I know what you have been thinking and why you might be angry with me - but really everything was so entirely innocent that I never thought it could be misunderstood. I am talking of those few days spent with Ordish after Heuveland when I should have tried harder to find out where you were and come to see you.

You once talked to me about losing your sense of reality. If you do not write to me I will lose mine for you are my only reality. I want to give you life again; I want you to give me life.

If the moment ever came, how could he ever bring her here up into the hills? Yet even if he told her not to, she'd still come on her own. She was that kind of woman, strong and self-willed, like Kate or Peggy. Albert had told him about Peggy, married somewhere in the softer cow-country down the valley. As for Kate, he'd have to make sure she didn't feel encouraged by him; Frank's sister was always going to be special but only ever as a friend.

An east wind brought the sound of the chapel bell up the valley next morning, father, mother and brother, dressed for Sunday. But to his mother's pain and bewilderment Harry refused to come with them, telling her he could no longer listen to prayers and hymns about a merciful God, though inside himself he was maybe more concerned about his own guilt and God's reaction to someone who had in cold blood killed another man.

That afternoon, after an almost silent lunch, Harry took down the shotgun to go hunting rabbits in the wood, memories of Sundays long ago as he and Albert left their father asleep in a chair inside the open back door, out of the wind but still in sunshine. Walking down the broken wall alongside the wood suddenly felt like walking down a trench, the snap of a broken branch in the wind a rifle shot that made Harry duck and his brother turn and laugh at him.

They positioned themselves downwind and silent to even the crows in the wood but when Harry saw the young rabbits come out to play he couldn't bring himself to pull the trigger. Albert watched his brother in astonishment and took the gun from him: "That's tomorrow's tea." A while later, with two rabbits dead, he asked: "How many Germans have you killed?"

"I don't know. They're never close enough to see." Except in their counter-attack at Bellewarde wood, Harry thought to himself. But then it was far too dark to make them out. We were just jabbing with the bayonet or lashing out with a knife. Kill or be killed.

"What do they look like?"

"I never ever seen a German in the face," Harry replied. "And I hope you never do."

"Johnny Snell in Thropton, he volunteered and he was only 15. Just told them the wrong birthday."

"You'll not do such a daft thing and break your mother's heart. I'll come and break your arse myself if you ever try."

"She's asked the preacher to come and talk to you."

"You tell her that won't do either of us any good." And after another fifty silent paces up onto the moor: "There's no God out there with the guns, Bertie. No God and no glory."

Harry had a letter from Reggie in his pack to re-read that evening and bring back that bleak reality:

We gave up Passiondale up there on the hill like turning our backs and walking away from it - across all last year's no man's lands over the bodies of all our friends. And as soon as we dug in again Blair copped it from a minnie in the trench. We couldn't find enough of him to fill a sandbag. Don't even try to come back. They say your wound is bad enough to keep you there at home. Don't play the hero, Harry, or the war will do for all of us.

Harry opened the back door and looked and listened to the night outside, an owl calling in the wood, a curlew and wind in the grass; sheep racing across the hillside above the farm from a fox, or towards the full moon that rose in front of them - to make him remember Peggy in the heather.

He returned back inside to write to Annie:

I'd like to bring you here one day and show you these hills where I once belonged, but no longer do. Where will any of us belong if the war is ever over? It is easy to become distant from everything as I have been since Dover. The next place they sent me I shared a room with a soldier who'd lost his sight with the gas and another who'd lost his leg. I should have learnt from them how much more they will suffer from their wounds than I. Instead I was only concerned with myself.

Whatever I thought I no longer think and it only matters because it came between us. I should have been stronger and not acted selfish. Coming home and having to talk with Frank's family has given me back my sense of things again. How weak a man's mind can become with just one simple bullet through his body.

*

A week later Harry attended the medical in Newcastle that he hoped would return him to the front; instead, pressing too hard with a probe, the elderly examining doctor managed to open Harry's entry wound under his right shoulder drawing not only blood but what he considered to be pus: "C3. Unfit for active service - return to barracks".

So back to Alnwick Harry went for the first time since he'd been out in France, entering the line of temporary buildings within the castle walls and, after reporting to the Duty Sergeant, coming almost immediately face to face with Ordish. They both felt they would rather have shaken hands or even embraced rather than salute; but salute they did.

"I'd say it's your good luck," said Ordish reading the Medical chit, "but I dare say you think of it as bad." Ordish looked beyond him at the Sergeant: "Do we have a comfortable bed for the Corporal, Sergeant?"

"Sir, yessir."

"Corporal?" Harry asked.

"We have another stripe for you, Cardwell. Walk with me into town and we'll celebrate over a pot of tea. Then I'll take you to see the Brigadier."

"I never applied for promotion, sir."

"You should have had a pair of medals at White City and Bellevarde. A second stripe's the least we can do. If the Brigadier has his way there'll be a third for you before this war is over." And as Ordish led the way back out of the castle: "We do basic training here and weapons over in Otterburn. Otherwise it's all bumph and filling forms. You won't want that." Ordish went on as though avoiding silence: "You'll be due another leave while you're here - unless there's a flap on, you'll be able to choose when you take it. Be straight with the Brigadier about what you want. He already knows about you."

"Knows what, sir?"

"That you're one of our best."

They sat down in the window of a tearoom at the only table not occupied by country ladies in for market day, Ordish watching

Harry's blue-eyed gaze checking there was no one in the shop he should be greeting. There wasn't the awareness here of military protocol that might have raised eyebrows at the sight of an officer and non-com sitting down together. Ordish poured the tea: "Am I forgiven - for interfering in your private affairs?"

"Nothing to forgive, sir."

"I think there probably was - in terms of minding my own business."

"I wrote a letter, you can tell her - I mean in case it doesn't get to her, not knowing where she is."

"I don't write to her, Harry, and she doesn't write to me - only the once about you because she had to know."

Harry asked about 'B' Company and Ordish drew a pencil map on one of the files he was carrying to show him how the salient had shrunk and hinged, 'B' Company now no more than a mile from the Menin Gate, and long overdue for rest.

Ordish paid the bill and they walked across the Market Place through the arch, the Battalion HQ office facing them across the sloping street. 'A' Company's Allison, now a 'C3' Sergeant-Major, was on the downstairs desk, a nod and smile for Harry whom he hadn't seen since Ypres. Upstairs Ordish gestured Harry to wait in the creaking wood corridor while he knocked to check the C.O.'s room. As often as not this time of day the Brigadier would be head down fast asleep on his papers. Not today. The "COME!" was instantaneous.

"Corporal Cardwell, sir," said Ordish's face at the door and Harry marched in to salute.

"Anything to say, Corporal?"

"I want to pass my medical, sir, and get back in the war."

"Good man!" A clearing of the throat. "I'd be out there myself but they say I'm too damn old."

"Sir."

"What is your expertise?" Linton asked.

"Lewis-gun, sir."

The Brigadier turned to Ordish: "Then we'll use him on instruction, Lieutenant."

Less than a week later Harry found himself back in the border hills not that far from home on the Carter Bar side of Otterburn with a bunch of raw recruits teaching them the language of the trenches, the difference between parapet and parados, as they dug long holes in the Northumbrian turf, learnt the Lewis gun and practiced their shooting on a range, trying to avoid the sheep that insisted on grazing the short heather round the targets.

Annie's letter had caught up with Harry the day before he'd left Alnwick, having journeyed from the convalescence home to Newcastle Hospital and on to the barracks. He read her words each evening as soon as he was alone in his small Nissen.

I AM going home not by choice but because my mother writes to me that my father is ill. And I fear of course, since it will take me two weeks to arrive, that he will die before I can see him......

By now, he thought, she'll be on her way back:

.....On my way back I shall find a ship to land me in England and come and look for you.

Harry felt the tug at his insides each time he read and re-read those words, with the anticipation of seeing her again. Would she return? How would she find him?

*

Risking more misunderstanding Annie sent a wire to Ordish as soon as she fixed the date of her departure and anticipated arrival. At least she knew from his letter where Ordish was; and Ordish would know how to contact Harry. In ten days time a Cunard was leaving New York in a convoy for Liverpool with first class berths still free, Dan himself offering the extra money needed. "I should be dissuading you from going back," he told her. "But either way I know you'll go and father told me to make sure you're comfortable."

Reclaiming her borrowed clothes from Bev (and enduring the inevitable party she threw for her) Annie boarded ship on the 10th of June, a contingent of US soldiers filing up the other gangway. Dan had also come to say goodbye, the sight of those troops leaving no doubt in his mind that his sister was returning not only to the war but also into danger. He felt an anguish and a guilt and would return to Boston that evening with the intention of persuading his father to let him volunteer.

*

Ordish received her wire on the very day Annie sailed, requesting that he leave word for her in Liverpool how to reach Harry. Her time was limited, a telegram from Virgin Mary already giving her a reporting date in London for a travel warrant to rejoin the ambulance train, now on its way back into France. How, wondered Ordish, to bring the two lovers together and give them time and circumstance? For the moment, out on his training, there was no way of releasing Harry for more than 24 hours without antagonizing the Brigadier who'd already bent the rules enough on behalf of their young Corporal. Annie would have to travel from Liverpool by train, a puzzle to be solved by one of their RTO's. If she could be brought to the station at Alnmouth and Harry meet her there, Ordish would find them somewhere to stay for the night. He could hardly expect Harry to sort out the complexities of hotel rooms. Ordish remembered from his own weekend cycle rides into the country how difficult it could be to circumvent the determination of hoteliers that 'adultery' should not take place within their establishments.

So Harry found himself mysteriously recalled, riding a motor lorry back to Alnwick after ten days on the moor. He reported to Ordish in barracks and was given Annie's telegram from New York, Ordish explaining why it had been sent to him and why Annie couldn't know where to address it direct to Harry. He also explained how the RTO had sent a travel warrant to await her arrival in Liverpool (another breach of regulations that would have to be explained to the Brigadier if he ever found out). Harry read the telegram again and knew that, had it come to him, he wouldn't have known what to do about it, except try and meet the boat in Liverpool for which he wouldn't have been given leave, not in the middle of a training course. "This 24 hours you have off," said Ordish, "we'll put down to a medical - requested by the surgeon in Newcastle who was looking after you. I can get a letter from him."

"Sir."

Ordish handed Harry a slip of paper and a receipt. "This is the time of her train according to the RTO. The hotel's up the road from Alnmouth station - two rooms in both your names already paid for. You can pay me back another time. It had to be arranged in a hurry - only 24 hours for you and 36 for her and she has to get down to London by tomorrow afternoon. There's a motor lorry taking a leave draft to the train - you ride with them as though you're going to Newcastle."

Harry stared at him. Would the Lieutenant be joining them? "I never stayed in a hotel," he said to Ordish.

"When you walk in the door there's a desk. You ring the bell and give them the receipt and they give you the keys for the rooms upstairs. I told them Annie was your cousin from America and this your only chance to meet and talk - because you're both on your way back to the front. Which is only half true - but I'm sure God will forgive us all for one small lie."

"You don't want to see her yourself?"

"She wants to see you not me." Ordish smiled at him. "God's sake, Harry, I watched you buy those letters and her pictures 12 months or more ago. I watched you write to her and the letters she sent back. I've heard you talk about her and heard Annie talk about you. I know you mean more to one another than any other two people I have ever known. Except perhaps Uncle with his wife. I just want you to be able to meet again - before - well, before whatever happens to us all."

Harry stared at him a moment in silence. "Are you trying to get back with the Company, sir?"

Ordish nodded. "Another month before the bloody doctors will clear me. I take 'B' Company. Prideaux gets the Battalion."

"About time, sir. Maybe now we might begin to win the war."

Ordish laughed. "You always say the most unexpected things. I want to see you alive at the end of it all, Harry. And that IS an order."

"I want to see YOU alive, sir."

'A' Company Allison walked in with an armful of papers and a look of surprise at Harry's last remark.

"Corporal Cardwell has a medical in Newcastle, Sergeant-Major. Will you make sure he's on the transport with the leave draft."

"Sir."

And Harry, saluting Ordish, could only, in front of the Sergeant-Major, say: "Thank you, sir."

They were on the castle side of the barracks, Harry walking into the NCO's hut, empty at this time of the day and smelling of leather boots and sweat. He stared at himself in the mirror to one side of the door, not, as was its function, to adjust his tie and cap, but to stare instead at a pale thin face he hardly recognised. For ten days now he'd been shaving without a mirror on the moor and had had no reason to look at his reflection with any interest. But now, only a few hours distant from her, he didn't seem to be the man that Annie once had known. In Dover at least he'd been an invalid in bed. Standing his five foot eleven inches as a walking man, he seemed to himself a ghost of the person he had previously been. He rubbed hard at his face to bring something less than white to his skin, colour that as quickly disappeared. He licked fingers to press across his eyes; ran both hands through his flat dead hair; and wondered how she would even know him.

Annie, alone in her compartment north from York, was also examining herself, in the tiny mirror from her handbag. She was looking almost too healthy from all that sitting in the sun with her father and undiminished by the Atlantic crossing that had for once been calm. There'd even been some sitting out on deck and eating in the dining room, only the presence of those soldiers on the lower decks and the 'torpedo' drills reminding her that this was no holiday voyage.

They'd berthed at Liverpool early that morning, the Railway Transport Officer on the train station writing out her itinerary and helping her purchase tickets: "I recommend first class, ma'am" - advice she would come deeply to regret.

She was as nervous as Harry about their meeting. Would there be enough time to overcome the awkwardness between them, given what had happened. Who knows his state of mind: Harry had been home to his roots with his family and friends and perhaps that former girlfriend who might have more to offer him than this American nurse from so far away.

At Newcastle she boarded the Edinburgh train, a ladies first class carriage at the front and unconnected with the other carriages by corridor. The guard passed by on the platform before departure to check the compartments through the windows but not opening the door to ask either for her ticket or her destination.

Harry had been to Alnmouth once before, on one of the annual seaside trips organised by the chapel. He remembered the getting up in the middle of the night to be down in Alwinton in time to join the others on the Planters' huge hay cart; then the long, slow plod over the hills for the first train at Glanton. The day they'd gone to Alnmouth it had rained from beginning to end in a cold northwest wind, everyone soaked through to the skin by the time they returned home in the dark. Tonight seemed much the same, though with sultry stillness instead of that cold wind. There was lightning from down near Ashington or Blyth, a rumble of electric storm that may or may not move north and seemed to reflect Harry's apprehensions. He was unsure of everything: should he knock at the hotel door or just walk in? He did both, tapping on the glass and pushing open the door. He explained to the landlady that his 'cousin' was not arriving until 10 o'clock that evening and she gave him both the bedroom keys, Harry then choosing what he considered the best room for Annie. Both were bedrooms more comfortable and furnished than he had ever seen before. Would they spend the night together? Would they make love? He felt too apprehensive to even consider it. So much had happened since Heuveland, perhaps too much, his head still shadowed by Frank and Sergeant Percival. Would she ask him about it? What would he say if she did? He could hardly behave as though nothing had happened: apart from Annie having guessed from what he'd written, the fact was there, an imprint on his soul that she could surely read.

When he returned downstairs, the landlady told him, being too late for a meal, that she would prepare a plate of sandwiches for them both and leave it in the dining room with two bottles of beer. He thanked her and returned to the station, a good half hour too early for the train. He was standing in the waiting room when he heard the approaching engine whistle and stepped outside onto what was the down platform. In his confused state of mind he hadn't even worked out from which direction she'd be arriving, north or south.

Neither was Annie sure on which side the platform would be, standing at the window of the compartment and seeing him alone on the opposite platform as soon as the train entered the station, but travelling surely far too fast. The train did lose speed and steamed through as though pretending it would stop, moving in the end so slow that their eyes met for what seemed a full half minute. Instead, enveloping him in smoke and steam, the train clanked on past the station, relentless piston by piston, its lights disappearing into the night, Harry left incredulous and shouting, Annie distraught.

"She should have told the guard at Newcastle," the porter on the station said to Harry. "Last train's a troop special - only stops to set down at request - except at Berwick." The RTO had failed to read the footnotes in the timetable.

"Can she get back from Berwick?"

"Not till the milk train. 'Bout four o'clock in the morning from there."

Harry shook his head in disbelief and turned to look back up the tracks expecting those lights to reappear or Annie to come walking out of the darkness.

Enclosed in her compartment, Annie had no one to ask what had happened until they did finally stop in Berwick where she was also told about the milk train. The station-master there left the waiting-room open for her and lit the small coal fire.

By the time Harry thought of a similar solution in Alnmouth, the porter had locked up and gone home. Harry looked back up along the road at the lights of the hotel. They'd be expected now and the landlady hardly likely to leave the hotel entrance open all night long. She was waiting for him, guessing what had happened when she saw him arrive alone. He told her about the milk train in the middle of the night. "I'll give you the downstairs key," she said, "if you'll lock the door behind you when you come in and leave the key on the desk." Harry ate his sandwiches and took the other beer and second plate of sandwiches up to the room he had chosen for Annie. Would there be even time to come up here? Which train would she have to catch in the morning to reach London? He didn't dare to lie down on the bed or even sit in the armchair, afraid he'd fall asleep. Eventually he returned to the station, through the gate left open for the milk churns, onto the platform where he curled up on a bench to wait. The storm still rumbled somewhere far away but seemed to have moved out to sea. All the same he pulled his cape around him in case the rain decided to return.

Annie had dozed the three hours before the milk train arrived, two passenger carriages on the back of a line of wagons, both carriages peopled with a scattering of untidy sleeping soldiers returning from leave. Which is much what Harry looked like when she saw him in the light of dawn, rolled up in his Border's cape, stretched out on the station bench, oblivious to the train as it pulled to a halt, oblivious even to the noisy milk churns as they were dragged from their wagon. Annie knelt beside the bench and touched his face almost in the fear he might be dead he looked so still and pale. His eyes opened briefly, not knowing for a moment where he was, imagining Annie to be a dream; until he heard her speak: "Harry. I'm sorry, Harry, about the train," she was saying in her quiet, level voice. "They didn't tell me I had to ask them to stop."

He opened his eyes again, staring at her, in confusion about what he had been dreaming - the mistle thrush and Frank and a sniper's shot that hit him this time in the head, which must have been in the very moment she touched his face. He sat up and took her hands: "I fell asleep. I'm sorry." They were searching in each other's eyes for signs and signals, indications of mood and emotion.

"So little time and we've already lost most of it," she said.

"We have a room. We have rooms, that is - we both have a room in the hotel." He raised Annie to her feet as he stood up and they embraced, Annie into the collar of his cape, Harry's face into her hair and breathing her fresh sweetness. Then he remembered from where she had been travelling: "How is your father?" he asked.

"He'll probably outlive both of us." She laughed: "I think it was my mother's way to try and bring me home."

"She didn't expect you to come back here then?"

Annie shook her head. "And neither did you." She held his face in both her hands, a touch, a gesture that was only hers.

"That's not so," he protested. "I was always sure you would return."

"And sure that you would see me?"

"There's something for you to eat at the hotel - just sandwiches. And a bottle of beer." He led her out through the gate where two dairymen were loading the milk churns onto a cart, up the deserted street to unlock as quietly as possible the hotel door. An oil-lamp had been left to illuminate the stairs, Harry opening the room he'd chosen for Annie. Annie drew him inside with her. Dawn through the curtains was all the light they needed, Annie removing her hat and coat. Glancing round at Harry, she then continued, taking off her dress and unbuttoning her blouse. She knew from her short months with Patrick there were times when, if you hesitated with more ladylike behaviour, the moment would pass.

Harry half turned away: "Don't you want to eat something? The plate of sandwiches was on the table in front of him with the bottle of beer and a glass. Annie slipped between him and the table, reaching to undo the two buttons of his cape: "Lie down with me. Take off your clothes and lie down with me. We have no time to be polite." Backs turned to one another, they continued to undress, Annie the first to lie down on the bed.

He looked round at her: "I feel myself to be a different man - "

Annie held out a hand to him: "You are not."

" - I even see myself a different man."

Naked himself he lay down on his side facing her, his left hand arm curled around her head and hair, his right hand holding her body on the hip. She traced his face with her lips and fingers, realizing she hadn't sketched him once since Dover. Had landscapes in Italy been more important than her memory of him? As they watched each other, both were wondering, are we still the same? She could feel the dressing on his back and touched the indentation around his right breast where the flesh and skin at last had healed. "Does it hurt still?" she whispered.

Harry shook his head. "Tell me how you are - what you have been doing."

"I'm on the moors instructing. I mean teaching the guns and the trenches to new recruits. Being out in the open, I've been alright. And only a few miles from home. It's my country."

"And at home?"

"I don't get to see them."

"But how are they?"

"My brother's waiting for his turn in the war, hoping it will stay for him."

"Meaning your turn's over?"

"They're not going to let me out of uniform for a few hundred sheep on the borders."

"But you'll continue to instruct?"

"Seems like it."

"If you ever go back to the front, I'll never talk to you again."

Harry was silent. He wasn't going to argue, not now, not with so little time.

"When I come here again we'll make sure of the trains and make it longer and you can take me home with you. It's strange to be so near to where you were born and not be going there."

"And your home? Was this the first time you'd been back since your husband was killed?"

She nodded. "If you can believe it, I hadn't realized that, not really thought about it, not until I saw my father. And everyone else."

"You saw his family?"

Annie nodded again. "And you saw Frank's?"

"I tried to make them proud of him. I'm proud of him."

"And he'd be proud of you. Like I am proud of you. And the Lieutenant - who says if you were ever killed we would lose the war."

Harry's face broke into what would have been a laugh if they had not been whispering.

"Have you forgiven me?"

"For what?"

"About him. About Sam Ordish?"

"He said there's nothing to forgive."

"I should have come to you instead."

"You didn't know where to find me."

"Someone would have told me."

"It was a bad place to be, where I was. You would have been unhappy to see me there."

"Better than not seeing you at all."

"He's always tried to help us - the Lieutenant. I don't know why. He even booked these rooms for us."

They heard the pendulum clock downstairs strike another quarter, both of them aware of minutes ticking relentlessly away. "I want to love you," she said, her body pressing against him. "I want you to love me."

His initial movements were sudden, almost violent in his haste, their mouths coming together, the hand on her hip moving over her thighs to make her shiver. Annie reminded herself, not for the first time that evening and night, that she was in the danger days of her month, the second week, she used to calculate, being her fertile moment: 'Very imprecise,' Patrick had always told her with a smile - but never protested at the precaution they accidentally discovered and which she would now try to practice with Harry. As she had longed for since Heuveland and so often dreamed of, he turned down on her with his kisses and his tongue; and Annie held him between her lips - a long moment of stillness until he checked, pulled back and withdrew. But this time her mouth followed to take him inside, her lips and fingers moving that soft skin until she felt his whole body suddenly stiffen with his spurting spill of warmth, once, twice, again and again and again.

"Oh pet," she heard him breathe, his whole body beginning to relax slowly away from her.

"It had to be this way," she said. "This time it had to be like that."

"You'll not like the taste," he eventually whispered.

*

The porter stared at first then turned away in embarrassment. The soldier in his cape and the woman in her long coat were clung to one another as though against a gale or raging torrent, the train already entering the platform.

Harry could feel everything of her body pressed against him as she could feel his. "Don't say goodbye - " she was saying. "Don't say goodbye."

Chapter 48

She heard some of the stations called from the platforms outside,
Durham, Darlington and Doncaster, but head back against the
cushion and eyes closed against any conversation, Annie saw nothing
of the length of England she travelled through that day. She was still
with him, his eyes devouring her, his bitter-sweet taste still in her
mouth, his breathed whisper in her head: 'Oh pet!' How still they
had lain in the half hour left to them, how hastily they'd had to dress
and hurry to the station, how desperately they had held one another
and avoided saying that 'goodbye'. She felt her whole body had
absorbed him; she even realized, suddenly opening her eyes wide in
surprise at the carriage ceiling, that she wanted his child inside her
and that next time, any time in the future, she'd never again think of
precaution.
Did she doubt there would be a next time? He was safe in England
and she'd take good care of herself. But how much longer could the
war go on? She hadn't seen any young men on the stations or on the
trains who were not in uniform. Sometime someone must decide the
killing should not go on for ever, though doubtless they would not
decide soon enough. Harry might be safe in England for the moment
but Annie knew full well he'd always feel a need to return to the war
while Reggie was still out there, while any of his companions were
still out there; just as she was returning now; just as Ordish will
return. She'd told him again, as they'd hurried back to the station,
"I'll never speak or write to you again if you go back. Your body is
damaged. There are many ways you can make them keep you back in
England." But she knew unless there was infection still inside his
wound Harry might pass his medical within a month or two. She
almost hoped that the Germans could win the whole damn war by

then. They were deep into France and Annie remembered her Gentleman-Officer explaining how the French would always make peace terms rather than have the Hun ever occupy Paris again.

They hadn't spoken of the events of war that morning, only of themselves. He'd told her how it felt to go back home; told her of his family; and of Frank's. As she then told him of her visit to Patrick's house, the father, mother and sister, the photographs of Patrick on every shelf and table; and of the guilt she felt. The same guilt Harry felt about having taken Frank to war. Patrick's sister had made her cry; Frank's sister, kissing him that night, had made Harry cry - 'and showed me how the appearance of things is not always the truth'. Sam Ordish and herself, he meant. She was grateful that he'd said it and remembered that, in the very moment he'd spoken the words, the clock downstairs had rung another quarter - and remembered also how he'd jumped stark beautiful naked out of bed as though the mattress was on fire, her train only twelve minutes away.

She must have laughed out loud. The elderly gentleman in the corner of the compartment lowered his newspaper and was staring at her. She hoped she hadn't also been talking out aloud, the childhood fear she'd always had that her most dreadful thoughts could be heard not only by God but by anyone else within earshot.

At the last stop before London two ladies entered the compartment to sit opposite Annie, glancing sideways at first, then quite openly examining her appearance in minute detail, skirt, jacket, blouse, shoes, gloves, hair and hat. Suddenly longing for the dignity and anonymity of 'uniform', Annie stood up and took down her bag, an officer watching her from the corridor sliding open the door for her. She changed in the narrow toilet at the end of the corridor, her 'uniform' a little creased, Signora Bacchetta's dress and blouse folded carefully away for who knows when - for the end of the war? The officer standing in the corridor was so surprised to see the elegant lady he'd been admiring return as a nurse that he actually saluted as he opened the door for her again, squeezing thin to let her pass. The two ladies and the elderly gentleman watched open-mouthed as Annie re-entered the compartment, stowed her bag and sat down again in her new identity. She imagined they were wondering how an ordinary nurse could afford a first class ticket. She surely belonged with the servants and the soldiers down in third.

Annie watched through the window as the metropolis began. London seemed immense, even more so than New York, the endless miles of houses and factories, roads, tunnels and bridges before the train arrived; then the confusing maze of streets around the station that seemed to have no pattern, lines of tall red buses to remind her of their near-miss shellburst in Flanders and, everywhere, crowded sidewalks where people seemed to plunge rather than walk, heads bent in their hurry.

She took a cab to the station at Euston where her larger bag had been sent on from the boat; and a second cab to take her to an address called Devonshire House where she picked up the travel papers left for her: departure for the coast from a train station written as Charing Cross, her final destination a town somewhere in France called St Dizier.

She embarked late that evening not far from Dover on the darkened pier at Folkestone, a small group of nurses among a multitude of soldiers, Annie looking under the light of hand-held flares for the tell-tale cap badge or cape of a Border Rifleman. Unknown to her a couple of them had passed through off the same ferry an hour ago in the opposite direction: Reggie himself and Ed Darker, two 'B' Company Borderers homeward bound on leave.

*

Harry had spent the day as dazed as Annie, riding the branch line back to Alnwick, walking through the town to barracks, waiting there for the next transport to the camp on the moors.

After Annie's departure he'd returned to the hotel, eaten the sandwiches and drunk the beer not to offend the landlady; he'd even opened the bed in his own room and lain on it to make it look as though they hadn't shared a room. Lieutenant Ordish would be proud of him. The landlady had had a glimpse of Annie when they'd left that morning, not, Harry thought, quite believing that they were cousins. But since an officer had booked the rooms, she would surely not believe that anything was untoward. When Harry paid for the sandwiches and beer, she even expressed the hope he would return one day. He supposed she felt maternal towards the young man in his uniform. Perhaps she had a son herself serving in the war. Harry dare not ask. A similar question on a train going back on leave a year ago had provoked a flood of tears and despair.

Annie's loving lived with him all day and now all night, eyes open in his Nissen hut. How her mouth pursued him for that 'precaution'. Peggy had loved him that way once, perhaps for the very same reason - and told him after with her laugh that he tasted of salt water and the sea.

Ordish absented himself deliberately that day, not wishing Harry to feel he needed to account for the night before, nor enter any argument about payment for the hotel - which Ordish had no intention of letting Harry reimburse.

Coming back later that evening he found Bunny in the orderly room, bags on the floor, discussing his billet with the Sergeant-Major, both officers then required to walk along the street for a claret or a port with the Brigadier. Bunny in his medical had also been C3'd, his return to the Battalion delayed for a month. The doctors were going soft. The Brigadier decided Bunny should take charge of the training on the moor and build up a decent cadre of new recruits to plug the holes in 'A' and 'B' Companies. They'd been operating recently at six to ten men short in every Platoon.

*

It was Harry's second day back on the moor, his spirit flat, the training listless, a dozen recruits picking up his mood and complaining of hunger and thirst. They were two miles from camp in a wooded valley below the moor where twin lines of trenches had been dug, 'ours' and 'theirs', and the recruits initiated into the rituals of no man's land. Then Harry heard a few lines of Tipperary blown and sucked and saw two familiar uniformed silhouettes appear on the skyline walking down towards them, subaltern and swaddy, Bunny and Reggie with his mouth-piece. The two companions embraced, Harry chiding Reggie for 'wasting' a day of his precious leave.

"No one home," he was told.

Bunny's transport had stopped in the middle of Elsdon that morning, the last chance for a discreet drink in a pub and - "blow me, there was Reggie" - Reggie still in uniform told by his parents that his wife and daughter, away staying with her own parents, were not due home until tomorrow.

Training was suspended for the day, the recruits sent back to their tents, a night ops planned instead that evening. Harry, Reggie and Bunny lay back smoking in the bracken, revisiting and updating news about 'B' Company survivors, the demarcation between officer and men forgotten.

As often they were almost within shouting distance of home. That evening, when Reggie and Bunny elected to come with them on the night ops route-march, Harry in charge of the compass contrived to get them 'lost'. They walked off the moor into the Cardwell farmyard and kitchen where Da pulled out the bottles of beer he'd been saving for birthdays and Christmas, he and Albert sitting up with the soldiers until midnight listening to Bunny and Reggie and occasionally Harry telling somewhat exaggerated tales of Ypres and the Somme to the new recruits and listening to Reggie's mouth-organ - until well after midnight, when Bunny tapped his watch and they said goodnight.

Harry marched them back up the hill onto the border, Windy Gyle to Woden Law their line of march and Kielder by the morning. Reggie dropped out as they crossed the Carter Bar road, turning downhill, three hours walking home unless someone passed to give him a lift.

Bunny spent the rest of that long dark night trying to imagine what it would be like cut off on these hills and in those valleys for weeks at a time by the winter snow - or for that matter burnt by the summer wind and sun until the water in the wells and springs ran dry and each drop had to be carried in from goodness knows how many miles away. What a way to spend a childhood. No wonder Harry was tempered so hard, honed so sharp.

In low cloud next morning Harry really did manage to lose them with his map and compass, stumbling finally onto the Edinburgh railway line, all of them spending a couple of hours fast asleep on the platform at Rickarton Junction waiting for the branch train down the valley to what they hoped would be their transport at Kielder village.

Later the same day Reggie's Eileen and little Lisa returned on an empty coal cart, opening the kitchen door to find Reggie head down on the table fast asleep, the screams of "Reggie!" and "Daddy!" heard all round the village. For the next few hours Reggie caught up with gossip from Tow Law and the not so good news that their old home (with most of their furniture) had been burned in a fire, hence the reason for Eileen's visit. The elderly miner who'd taken over their house had had a fall with a shovel of burning coal he was carrying in from next door for his grate. Only a line of women and children and water-buckets down the street had saved the house from complete destruction.

It was at Tow Law Reggie had been working when he'd signed up for the war, having moved from open-cast at Elsdon to his father-in-law's colliery after he married Eileen - Eileen whom he'd met when they'd been kids at a choir festival at Durham Cathedral and written letters ever since. 'Hilltop Desolation,' he'd once called her village, surrounded as it was by bleak stonewalled fields and wind-stunted hawthorn. But it was a warm enough place once you got within the walls - and as ever the miners stuck together through thick and thin in their colliery clubs.

Afraid at first of going underground, Reggie had been well looked after by his father-in-law, always on the same shift, always next to him at the face. Five years he had there before that summer of 1914, Lisa about to start school when he went away in uniform, Lisa who now had hardly recognised him. The colliery moved them out of their house once Reggie signed on and Reggie's own parents' home in Elsdon had had the extra room, Eileen's parents only one up and one down. So back to Elsdon they'd had to come - and leave most of their furniture for the moment in the Tow Law house. In the fire they'd now lost their only armchair, kitchen table, sideboard and mirror. Apprehensive of his sorrow or anger, Eileen was relieved when

Reggie shrugged their loss aside. Eileen felt she had to tell him that when the war was over, he must feel free to choose whether they returned to Tow Law or stayed in Elsdon.

As always leave was far too short, wife and daughter just getting used to him again when it was time to dress up once again and return to the war. Reggie was thankful he'd seen Harry, looking a touch more cheerful than his letters. It was clear he'd not be staying home and Reggie could only hope his perishing wound would open again and keep him C3 for the duration.

Which in the end it did, out on the moor two weeks later, the recruits having to carry the Corporal back to camp. The Newcastle surgeon ordered Harry two weeks resting by the sea, Ordish once again the fairy godfather who found and fixed accomodation for him.

'I'm with a fisherman's family' - Harry wrote to Annie - *their sons away in the navy, their bedroom let out. I imagine they wonder who I am and why I'm not in uniform. They feed me at breakfast and at tea and in the day I walk along the sea to a nearby castle, a ruined castle, a wild place when the sea is rough and somewhere to think about good and bad memories. Somewhere to take you if we are ever here together again. The fishing boats go out every day even in the worst of seas and come back with nets full of herring - which is all I get to eat, them and the kippers they smoke all around the harbour. Not that I mind. Fish is something we never had at home and I'm happy to eat it here even at breakfast (when the hens don't lay).*

They certainly did wonder about him and mutter, the old fisherman, his wife and their neighbours, the ladies in the tea-shop, the working women under their scarves in the smoke-houses, even the children at school. Until the evening Harry stood up from his tea feeling a rush of warm sweat down the back of his shirt and heard the fisherman's wife exclaim aloud: "Bless me, young man, what have you done?!" He was soaked in blood from his shoulder down to his waist and yet had felt nothing but that warmth. The fisherman's wife and daughter-in-law took over as efficient as the Newcastle surgeon though a hundred times more painful, ultimately a thousand times more effective.

"You should have told us you were wounded and we'd have cared for you better," the younger one scolded as she cleared away the tea, stripped him to the waist and laid him face down on the table, sending her father-in-law to fetch the 'medicine chest' from their boat in the harbour - the 'chest' a wood box lined with waterproof and containing lint, a roll of bandage, a steel knitting needle, three small bottles and pieces of what looked like dry bracken or seaweed. "Our men can be cut real bad and be half a day out to sea," she said. "Doesn't matter how it hurts or what a mark it leaves, you have to be clean and dry inside."

He felt her pour from one of the bottles into the entry wound, Harry smelling the pungency of what he took to be a very strong whisky. The old fisherman stuffed a folded leather belt between Harry's teeth and held him down while his daughter-in-law lit a taper from the fire to the whisky, keeping a wet cloth round the wound to confine the burning. The pain was brief but deep inside him as he clenched his teeth around the leather then watched the older woman take from the 'chest' a long frond of dry seaweed and the knitting needle, held into the kitchen-grate until it glowed red-hot. The older woman used the hot needle to feed the seaweed into the wound, deep into the cavity until it all but disappeared. "Sea Tangle," she told him, "to drain you dry." She dropped her voice to a whisper in his ear: "Even gets rid of a girl's baby when she doesn't want it."

Each day they made him walk, north to the castle or south to the Black Hole and Cullernose Point; and each evening eased the frond a quarter inch out, the next night back inside again; and each teatime fed him with 'specials' from their nets, the little codlings and baby haddock poached down to the sticky jelly of the flesh and bones mashed with parsley, salt and pepper. "Fish," the old lady told him. "Fish until you live or die with the sea."

One evening, laid on his bed upstairs, the entire family gathered round, the village doctor this time with them. They withdrew the seaweed frond, dry as a bone they told him, and the doctor stitched the bullet hole closed: "for once and all", he said. Harry was to remain immobile for a week while the flesh sealed, one half-turn on his side the only permitted movement to enable him to pee into a bottle, the old lady telling him sternly: "Your number two's will have to wait."

Every morning, noon and evening each woman and girl of the family took turns to feed him, and made him tell them his stories of the hills, the winters and the summer sheep-fairs, the wrestling and the running, the shearing and the selling, the snow, the rain, the wind - the elements they could understand. They even moved the bed and propped him up on pillows so he could see the harbour, the old man waving one raised arm from the deck to Harry's window whenever they cast off, Harry counting the boats out at high tide - and counting them back against the quay upon the next, even at night when he would count their lamps as, swaying with the swell, they entered the harbour walls.

By the time his week was up and he was allowed to move again, the 'number two's', at first an hourly urge to be repressed, had become a dull and painful impossibility, solidified into that grim, heavy ache Harry remembered from the trenches and for which Colledge always issued devastating syrups. The village doctor returned with his own cure, another syrup, advising Harry to stay down in the yard within swift reach of the toilet. Harry was thankful to be alone when the moment finally arrived, the accompanying noise or smell or both enough to frighten the line of gulls on the roof and send them flapping and crying, swooping away back down to the sea. All of which he wrote in rude detail to Annie the day before he had to pack his bag and leave.

Departure really was quite difficult, tears all round as the two women kissed him and the old fisherman shook his hand. "Come back," they said. "Stay alive and come back to see us when the war is over."

Chapter 49

'I'm back on the train in a very different place' - Harry would read on his return to barracks - *after two days of travel further east than I had been in France before and the whole system different because for the moment we are under the French army, not being able to take the train back into Picardy. The girls had already been here two weeks by the time I arrived and are still trying to get used to it. Having complained about Italy while we were there, they now miss it - or miss the Italians who for all their confusion were easier to deal with.*

The German advance had squeezed the Channel side of the Western Front. Supply wagons, troop transports, ambulance trains were all crammed onto the rail tracks in the corridor between Amiens and the sea. There was no room for Virgin Mary's train on their return from Italy. Eventually, switched north from Dijon, they'd taken the place of French transport that had been lost during the German offensive, working the line between Langres and St Dizier along the soft green valley of the Marne, carrying the wounded out, the fresh soldiers in, French and sometimes American. In places it could have been England or New England, river banks, rolling pasture and low wooded hills.

Annie found the mood on the train sharper among the girls, pleased though they were to see their 'spokeswoman' return. In the more relaxed conditions of their Italian life most of them had had flirtations and friendships and now were missing the company of men. Here in France they had no home town, no fixed abode and only very occasional male staff on the train.

Still waiting for something to arrive from Harry, Annie wrote in her second letter:

Virgin Mary's quite a bear these days, impatient with us all, intolerant of French bureaucracy. Unless our line moves forward again, I fear we are stuck here on our to and fro journey up and down this river, our only diversion the occasional arrival of American troops or wounded – when Mary yells "YANKEES!" to me down the train as though they needed an interpreter! Yesterday there were two dozen, badly smashed but well taken care of, and onto the train with them came an American surgeon and two medics. Oh what a fluttering there was among the girls – even Virgin Mary herself! Me, I just kept quiet, not wanting to have to explain from where I came, not wanting to have to tell them about Patrick. But someone told them all the same, Viv I guess. The surgeon said 'I can't imagine anyone having been out here so long to still possess a human face and smile. We weren't told how awful this was going to be.' Well, he WAS in something of a state of shock as were his poor wounded. From what they said it was the same damn story – an attack running into no man's land (well at least they've learnt they DO have to run) and all the wounded flayed with machine-guns, shells and liquid fire. The wounds, the damage, they are always the same and have been since the beginning (except the fire which is new this year – but then before we had the gas). All these extraordinary sophistications to the art of killing and maiming. Who dreams them up, who invents them? And by the way, in case you were considering coming back out here again, maiming is now considered to be the ideal objective. The dead are dead and left behind needing nothing more; the maimed instead require attention, medical supplies, people to look after them. And their presence on the streets, at home with their families, in expensive institutions, undermines civilian morale. That is the new wisdom.

She hadn't heard from Harry since their brief meeting; did not know how it had left him; and needed reassurance that for him it had brought them back inside each other's lives. Harry's three letters came to Annie all at once, written from home, from Otterburn and from the fisherman's house in Craster. All had been routed through a French sorting office in Lyons, each of them gathering dust in Chaumont while a clerk tried to track the nurses' unit number, unaware their train was passing by his office twice each day.

Annie resisted the temptation to open the most recent first. His first letter, the one from home, she knew had been written before their meeting, yet still might be the most significant - the laying of the ghosts:

Whatever I thought I no longer think and it only matters because it came between us. I should have been stronger and not acted selfish. Coming home and having to talk with Frank's family has given me back my sense of things again. How weak a man's mind can become with just one simple bullet through his body.

She decided she would read each one in chronological order and write to his words before opening the next. That way she would miss nothing of his thoughts, the progression of his feelings and how, if at all, their short meeting might have changed him.

I am back on the moors not far from home, sleeping in a Nissen hut by night, all alone with the guns and ammunition locked up beside me. The recruits have to sleep in tents - taking them down each morning and putting them up each evening. They consider that very unnecessary and hate it! Most of them now are clerks from offices or shops and quite unused to the country and any physical labour - digging trenches, carrying rolls of barbed-wire and pickets and the Lewis gun magazines. I try not to enjoy torturing them and tell myself I am teaching them how to survive when they get out there.

Or perhaps, thought Annie, teaching them to be fighting alongside him and saving his own life. Harry didn't mention a return to the war but it seemed implicit in every line. It was an even more sensitive issue since she'd now received a letter from her brother Daniel to tell her he'd be ignoring father's prohibition and signing on the dotted line as a volunteer as soon as their senior cousin could take his place at the shop. *Watching you climb on board that boat, I could not believe your courage - and now need to prove my own. Life has been far too comfortable for me.*

'Silly foolish boy', Annie wrote back, cursing the German U-boats for having brought America, belatedly into the war. *I hope they spend months training you and that you'll arrive too late to prove yourself a hero. Though, alright, I admire you for having done it.*

The idea of both her young men endangered in France or Flanders would be too awful. How long will they keep Harry C3? And does he realize if he comes out here again he will lose me?

'You gave me life again' - he wrote about their brief time together - *did I give you life? You made two hours last like two days and loved me in a way that was maybe all my pleasure and none of yours - though you must have felt your power over me.*

But it was my pleasure I do assure you and much much more than just the pleasure of your pleasure. That moment is still with me and I imagine will have to last a long time.

There were more Americans today puzzled at everything, not even knowing how they'd come to be wounded. Don't worry – they do not make me think of home. Home was just to say hello and come away again. Home is over.

Virgin Mary reluctantly had said the same. She'd managed a week back in England when the train returned to France. At home her parents were still mourning their dead sons and with her arrival a mutual sense of loss only intensified, aggravating their despair. Mary had come away feeling distanced, helpless towards them and unhelped by them, raw nerve-ends that would have to wait for the end of the war and probably a lot longer than that. One surviving brother had been invalided home, the other sent with his unit to the Italian front, his path almost crossing with Mary only a few hours apart.

As before, Annie was the only person with whom Mary felt able to share her thoughts - and this time Annie, part in need, part in the spirit of friendship, told Mary of her brief rendezvous with Harry. Virgin Mary, bless her, was "pleased as punch" with a very generous hug and almost tears in her eyes: "Good on you both if you can make new life grow from all these years of death. You work hard at it and nothing will stand in your way," she added. "Neither background nor culture." And a few minutes later, after an appraisal of new wounded carried onto the train: "Take no notice of anyone who tells you any different." Viv she probably meant; Viv whom Annie had already told, the younger English girl shocked that she and Harry had actually shared a hotel bedroom together. "For exactly one hour and a half!" laughed Annie.

It seems each time we are together the problems are no longer there. Do you feel sometimes we float, you and I, in an unreal world? Which world is real? The world with you or the world without you? I cannot even remember what thoughts I had before I met you

- not just thoughts about women and love but thoughts about anything. Perhaps I didn't really think until you opened up my mind. And then my body.

It was you who opened me - first with your eyes, then with your words and finally with your mouth and body to make me know that I could never ever love another man. Not even with Patrick did I ever feel that so clearly. So you have, if you like, imprisoned me, this lucky bird inside your cage who'll never fly again if not with you.

'I look at the world through your eyes now,' he had written, 'always looking for the words that will describe it to you'. And Annie realized she was doing exactly the same, unconsciously transcribing everything that happened, everything she did into words in her mind. Which was maybe why she was sketching now hardly at all. The last sketch she'd made, late one night on a French train station, had been her memory of Harry lying on that hotel bed - and before that her father sitting in the yard at home, sun-hat on his head, newspaper in his hands.

Annie was still reading Harry's third letter, wincing at the burning whisky, marvelling at the seaweed and laughing at the rude details of his number two's when the fourth one arrived, a wad of mail left on the end table in the dining-car, Harry's envelope held up and waved at her by one of the girls. And of course this fourth one, a long letter, brought the news she had been dreading.

I have returned to barracks, Bunny and Ordish already left for France with the recruits I was training. I found a letter from you and can now imagine you with your Yankees on the train riding up and down the river. I hope they never take you near the front again. There was also a letter from Reggie - so I know them all to be in a rest area for a while, though the new recruits will have a week in the Bullring if they're unlucky. And Ordish and Bunny with them.

There was a parcel for me from Ordish - do you remember me telling you about Uncle's fishing rod? Well now I have it to return to his wife. Somehow - I must have told him - Ordish remembered Uncle had asked me to visit his family and this is his way to make sure I do. I dread the thought and wonder what on earth I can say to them. That fills my mind I'm afraid so I shall finish this letter when it's all over tomorrow night (even the Brigadier knows I am to go and has given me a letter to take with me).

Sunday night.

Back in an empty barracks and feeling like I've lived through Uncle's death again. I don't think you ever do know how you feel, unless you have to think about it or talk about it - which is why none of us do much talk about these things. The Sergeant-Major had me on inspection before I left so you'd have been surprised how my boots and buckles were shining. It was the end of church by the time I arrived in the village (by train - which did stop!) so there were plenty of people around to ask the way - then a maid to answer the door who looked twice as old as Uncle's wife. She was with her children in what we call a living-room, not the front room but not the kitchen. She looked so surprised when she saw my uniform - and maybe afraid. She's a tall, strong woman yet even with all those children around her she seemed frail - but was somehow still their home and family. I had to say to her, I was with the Lieutenant when he was killed. She would not cry in front of them but took me into another room to ask about her husband's death. What could I say about that dirty night in that wet trench, the pieces of smashed duckboard stuck into the parapet smoking like blown-out candles in a cake, his blood that ran like water into the mud, and dear old Uncle feeling his hands everywhere looking for his pipe? Then I saw the damn pipe on the shelf above the fireplace which made my heart jump and a shiver down my back. Even on a chilly day which it was, an east wind up the Tyne valley, the fire wasn't lit. It was a very cold room with his picture and his pocket-book on a table, all his school books still on a desk with his master's gown - just like my old headmaster. Why the hell, I wonder, did Uncle volunteer? He'd have done much more good going on with his teaching. But all those things I could not say. I just told her he'd been talking normally and asking me to visit - and that he then sort of fell asleep.

She made me stay for lunch - which didn't please the old maid - and I tried to play with the children. I don't think I was very good with them until they took me in the garden and we played chasing each other. Which is what they'd done with him last time he was home on leave. I couldn't tell what it meant to them that he wasn't coming back. I couldn't even tell if they really understood. The two young boys wanted of course to go into the army. Hopefully there won't be a bloody army anymore when they grow up. The girl is going to be a schoolteacher and the baby one isn't talking yet. The mother has had to take up teaching herself as I believe they're short of money. Wonderful how we look after the families of our dead soldiers. And if it's like that for an officer, God knows how they treat the rest. I do believe the envelope the Brigadier gave me contained some money for her. She folded it very carefully away into a tin.

She thanked me a lot for coming - and of course I gave her the fishing rod which will now wait for the boys - who asked me to come back. Maybe one day I will go back and say hello. I feel bad about them and

pray I will not have to do that for anyone else.
Sorry to be so gloomy. Actually the sun was shining all day long even with the wind. I need you more than ever when I am sad and down.   Your Harry

I have not yet told you and am sure you do not want to know but the medical board passed me fit and sometime, though no one knows when, they might send me to the front again. It'll be a long time yet for they give me leave at home again before I go.

You'll lose me, Harry, if you come back to France or Flanders – she wrote back – *I can't go through all that again. I promise, you will lose me.*

On Virgin Mary's maps the war was returning into more familiar country, the Germans in retreat, "having over-stretched their piece of string", one French medical officer said as he checked his quota of wounded off the train at Joinville. "They'll be back in Berlin by Christmas." His optimism seemed almost obscene given the state and number of his casualties, ferried down from a particularly grim trench raid somewhere to the north of Rheims. The route of the ambulance train had been extended now to Châlons and beyond, crossing the vineyards of Champagne on rail lines that had only just been laid or re-laid, the nurses having to walk alongside the train at times to warn the driver if the lines of steel twisted out of shape or broke under the weight of their heavy carriages. They were within the sound of guns again, both large and small, proximity to the front line reminding them of Heuveland in the way they were once more dealing with untreated casualties and having to decide which of them were dying. The treatment coach was reinstated as a theatre, two French surgeons posted on board, war-tired, not to say exhausted, but always able to raise a smile for anyone less resilient than them, Captain Boeldieu and the younger Jean-Pierre Rosenthal (also presumably a Captain though he never used his rank). They were often to be found on empty return journeys at a table in the dining-car, Jean-Pierre having cooked them a meal complete with vintage wine from the food-parcels he regularly received and from the bags of tins and hams and bottles that hung from hooks in his berth.

For the first time there were also German wounded loaded on board, segregated in locked coaches and under armed guard, not that any of them were in fit condition to run away. 'Hulking damn Saxons' Virgin Mary called them, though did not spare anyone's energy and attentions in the caring for them. But critical or not they usually took second place in the priority list for operations. Annie would have described them more as under-nourished than hulking, nearer to starvation than she'd seen anyone in the war so far. Cigarettes were all they seemed to need. Feeding them too much merely made them ill.

Viv had decided she was in love with the younger of the two French surgeons, Jean-Pierre, a slight and aristocratic thirty year old with a German name, originally from Alsace. Groomed and elegant insofar as was possible in such surroundings and with a well-trimmed moustache, he had careful smiling eyes that, true to his profession, would always take time to assess any situation. Assessing Viv could not have been difficult, her eyes following him every time he passed, her schoolgirl French always trying to make chatter in the dining-car. She'd even taken to wearing colour on her lips and cheeks again. Tiring of Ordish's wandering attentions she had clearly changed allegiance. Annie wondered if she'd yet tried to knock at the Surgeon's door in the sleeping-car. Both Surgeons had the privacy of single berths.

"His family own a distillery," Viv announced one morning as they were scrubbing down the carriages - so perhaps she HAD knocked at that door. "In the German part of France," she chattered on, her eyes not quite meeting Annie's, which usually meant she had been a naughty girl but was not prepared to share the secret. "They hope to have their business back after the war" - the distilling of plums and cherries into spirit, it seemed.

Virgin Mary decided there was a mystery about this Jean-Pierre, a vulnerability, a detachment: perhaps the fact that most of his student and adult life had been spent in Paris and far from his family - which came out late one night when Viv in the dining-car asked innocently from where his luxury food parcels arrived. From home, he told them; from where they always had arrived all through his Paris life. Viv laughed at that idea: wouldn't it have been easier just to send him money? "Besides, your home is now inside Germany."

"I have cousins in Dijon."

When next day Virgin Mary asked Annie whether Viv needed protection against her French suitor, Annie suggested it was Jean-Pierre who needed the protection. And not only it would seem from girls. She'd been following him as they off-loaded wounded and heard a pejorative "Juif!" hissed by a passing French officer who seemed to know him. Annie caught the look in Jean-Pierre's eye: he was almost apologetic with his shrug. Not until sometime later was Annie able to look the word up in the latest addition to their library, the French-English dictionary that had taken the place of Italian on the shelf in the dining-car. *Juif - Jew*   Perhaps, she thought, that accounted for a certain cool formality between the two French Surgeons, Captain Boeldieu   addressing Jean-Pierre as 'Rosenthal' but insisting always on his 'Captain' whenever Jean-Pierre addressed him. Not that the 'Captain' objected to the meals cooked for him by the younger man; nor the wine served with it and cigars offered after.

Annie had never understood the 'thing' about Jews: she'd never been able to identify them at school or university nor ever worried about who was or who was not. She hoped Viv also didn't understand, whatever it was one was meant to understand.

But all too soon for Viv the interlude was over, Jean-Pierre with his valises and bags of food and wine kissing each of them goodbye, Captain Boeldieu more correct with his salute. The train was moving out of their sector, both surgeons transfered to a posting in Bar-le-Duc. Further west the allied front line had begun to move forward, the railway lines freeing up around Amiens and consequently beyond. Their ambulance train had now been routed along relaid lines, roundabout to the junction at Compiègne. Then two days later they were shunted slowly north, again on rebuilt tracks, returning finally to Pérignon as the heat of a late Indian summer ended in a storm.

We hardly recognise the town, so badly has it been shelled, and so thoroughly looted by the Germans in retreat. New railway lines have been pushed through the ruins, mountains of rubble and rubbish to either side. Though we found our schoolhouse and old quarters we were sent back to sleep on the train. The town is still full of booby-traps. Many are injured and maimed and several are dead from picking up innocent looking objects – even bottles of wine and food. The soldiers hate it and as a consequence the German prisoners are not treated well. Many of them are used as 'sweepers' to test for booby-traps in every house, in every cellar, even in the remains of people's gardens.

The French front line ahead of us is almost up to St Quentin; the British line further north beyond Bapaume (I read this from Virgin Mary's maps which she updates every day). I think that means we have recovered most or all of the old Somme battlefields. In Ypres the German line still holds tight around the city and has not moved. We seem to be back into almost the same situation before the German advance. If it wasn't for the bad condition of German prisoners I would say (Virgin Mary says!) we'll now dig in for another four years of glorious combat in the trenches. But the faces of those Germans suggest they no longer believe that they can win.

I am myself of the opinion (which I dare not speak aloud) that I no longer care who wins so long as the whole damn business of killing and wounding ends. I do not even know what the difference between winning or losing would mean for the ordinary person.

Once again landscapes for the train had changed, even the countryside more of a wasteland now the Germans had passed through, first in advance, recently in retreat. Farms and villages, previously untouched, had been destroyed, bridges blown, fields cleared of crops and animals. Casualties did not diminish; if anything they had increased, the British and Empire troops now on the attack once more, their ambulance train back onto Divisional level, ferrying the wounded back from the temporary field hospitals. Their journeys to and fro were longer now, sometimes taking all day and night, through Pérignon where the hospital had been destroyed, and on first to Abbéville to drop the lightly wounded or those who should not travel, then Boulogne, welcomed with smiling faces by the soldiers however bad they were, since it meant they were on their way back home, back to Blighty and out of the war.

Harry instead was moving in the opposite direction, a letter no longer franked from England arriving to break Annie's heart and soul.

I spent a week at home - a good time really for I was able to help my father repair a broken barn and some of the stone walls under the moor. He's going to bring beef heifers into the lower fields and another milk cow. He's even bought more geese and hens at market. Says we must be self-sufficient in case the war gets worse.

I am writing to you from the quayside at Boulogne in such a confusion of men and machines that I am sure we'll still be here at Christmas. My orders send me to the Bullring so I am still maybe two more weeks away from 'B' Company. Do not be angry. There is nothing I can do.

It seemed to Virgin Mary that Annie's tears were of rage, determined and unforgiving: "He's back in the war. I shall neither read his letters nor write to him again."

Chapter 50

Almost as she said those words, Harry, clambering from a train, found himself back where the two of them had in a sense begun, on that long grey moonlit road at the railhead and the wayside Inn, the Estaminet, the 'Spanish Farm' where he'd bought the tin of letters and her photographs. Harry could hear the same loud laughter and voices of a leave draft waiting for their train: if he walked in, would he see the same burly Seaforth Sergeant and poor dead Schoolboy with Ordish at the piano? A pair of redcaps watched him from the station building. Perhaps his fat friend Ginger was still around looking for revenge. Harry, as before in a well-worn uniform with rifle and pack, turned on his heel and walked his slow steady pace down the empty road, back towards the distant flashes and rumble of guns on the horizon - though that horizon of war now seemed much further away.

An hour and a half later Harry recognised the farm where the old Divvy transport lines had been; but the cooks' and blacksmiths' fires no longer warmed the night. There were still horses stabled, one of them being brushed down by a black man in the moonlight. There was an Army Service Corps depot, a guarded artillery store and a dozen itinerant soldiers sleeping or dozing round a spent brazier among whom, of all people, Harry recognised Benson who'd been with him on that other night more than a year and a half ago. Harry walked off the road into the yard towards him, Benson not seeing him until he was standing right over him.

"Hey Corp!!" Very lost in his gloom, the startled Benson had been staring at the ground. He pulled his gangly body to its feet and shook Harry by the hand. And finally smiled.

"That's better. Keep smiling, Benson."

"Kept us alive, you did, Corporal, with your letters. You should be writing comic books."

"How is our blind bugger?"

"I took him home to London on my way back north. I don't think they really wanted to know about him, his uncle and his aunt. But I'd been teaching him on the sewing machine in the laundry downstairs. Once he'd showed them what he could do - well, cheap labour isn't he."

"And our one-legged friend?"

"Jack's still there. Going mad, I think."

"Not much of a place, is it."

Benson shook his head. "Anyone'd think the war was our fault, the way they treated us." He looked at Harry: "You alright?"

Harry nodded.

"Two stripes then?"

"Hang around long enough, Benson, they'll make you Colonel."

"Were you in the Bullring, Corp?"

"Six bloody days."

"Didn't see you there. Mind you, wouldn't have been looking anyway. Kept my eyes shut half the time and just got on with it." Benson was on his way back for the first time since his wounding, apprehensive and, as with many of the returning wounded, fatalistic. Having survived the first time, he did not believe himself likely to survive again.

"Then the same must go for me," said Harry when Benson had explained his gloom. "And I'd rather not have to think that way." Harry jollied him with an arm across his shoulder as they carried on down the road together: "Come on, chum. You keep me alive, I'll keep you alive."

Half an hour further on they came to the ruined hamlet which had once been for them that 'limit of the known world'. But the entrance to the old communication trench was now blocked off, a signaller laughing out at them from his candlelit shelter: "the war's moved on, pal." His mate called after Harry: "not that we won a battle, mind you. Jerry just up'd and left of his own accord one night when everyone was sleeping."

In the dawn they turned north towards Zonebeke, crossing the old battlefields where the villages no longer existed, where nothing anymore existed, the road itself built up on duckboards and sandbags over a familiar wasteland of dried mud, stagnant water and shattered trees.

Then out of the quiet, out of nowhere, came the sudden screaming express-train roar of a long range shell tearing into the ground not far away, Harry pushed Benson down and dropped himself to one knee as though making an obeisance, tipping his helmet towards the shellburst to protect his face and head, a movement so graceful, so dignified that Benson didn't know where to look when Harry caught his eye and smiled. He loved the man.

Two hours later they were beyond the old battlefield, walking under trees in the sunshine, marveling that the war had reached untouched countryside. They followed their noses to the smoke of breakfast fires at what now passed for Divisional Transport lines - horses and carts, steam and motor lorries, even a pair of tanks. The first of a few familiar faces smiled at their return, Colledge from his dressing station tent always glad to see his one-time patients returning fit and well. Harry told him about the seaweed cure.

"Laminaria Digitata, I think it's called," said Colledge, "or Digitala or something of that sort." Harry glanced inside, relieved to see his tent was empty. "Haven't had a customer all week. I'm not complaining." Colledge asked Benson about Pimlott and his hat-pinned head.

"They put us in the same ward, sir, when we got to London. I think he must have asked. They kept taking pictures inside his head -"

"These X ray things - ?"

Benson nodded. "But they still didn't know what to do. I'd started walking by the time they decided to cut him open. Anyway, sir, he sort of knew he wasn't coming back that day. Said 'cheero' and shook my hand."

Colledge led them to the kitchen cart then directed them onwards once they'd had their bread and bacon. The Company was in reserve a mile further on, shaving, washing, eating breakfast round the edge of a harvested field, Prideaux, now Colonel, coming from his farmhouse HQ to shake Harry by the hand, Reggie and Sergeant Lars dancing a jig with him as he arrived at 'B' Company, Sergeant-Major Trussal grinning at them, shouting at them, gruffer than before, the tobacco and the rum beginning to reach his voice. Bunny waved his cap and walking-stick from further away, Captain Ordish clambering out of the Company bivouac to see what all the fuss was about. Harry and Ordish came face to face with more between them, spoken and unspoken, than even father and son or brothers could ever have. Ordish smiled the rarest of his open smiles.

It turned out to be an easy time to settle in, the Border Rifles staying in reserve for another two weeks, only moving forward once in that time, three miles into another farmhouse with its surrounding fields. Harry was back with his Lewis-gun Section, half-remembered faces he could even name though apart from Reggie and Dip he'd only known them for little more than a month, that grim 6 weeks that followed Frank's execution: Hook, Hedley, Neeson and Walker and among the rest of 3/4 Darker, Scrace, Wood and Garner. Lowrie was back as Section1 Corporal and Webster for 2, Lars now their Sergeant and Bunny still their Sub. Even Craig was only round the corner, Sergeant for 2 Platoon - enough of the old crowd to make it seem familiar, and all of them with another year's experience of survival.

Try not to be angry with me. I have to tell you there is no danger where we are. Walking backwards the enemy finds it more difficult to range his guns and we're well out of reach of the machine-guns. We're just careful where we put our feet and what we pick up - for booby-traps. And careful what we drink since we're told that Jerry is poisoning the wells as he retreats. It's a very different war without the trenches. We still find ourselves staying near to ditches in case we need cover. Old habits. Reggie says to say hello. Did I tell you he came to see me on the moors when he was on leave. He has a wife and a young girl so it was good of him to give up a day for me (he's hoping there'll be another child expected after that leave!)

Ordish is well and now a Captain - our Company CO. I really have to say he's been the best of friends and I regret again whatever I thought ill of you both.

Harry was not to know that, like him before, Annie would not be even opening his envelope, let alone reading his words. Eventually the lack of a letter from her would tell him what he'd already begun to suspect - though he kept writing to her in the belief, correct as it turned out, that she'd still be looking out for his envelopes to know he was alive.

*

If she was being truthful, as one night she was with Viv and Mary, Annie would have to admit her anxious anticipation of his envelopes was even greater now that she wasn't even opening them, each arrival conjuring up his eyes and his smile, alive and well.
"So for God's sake why not read him?" Virgin Mary asked.
"I cannot bear to know where he is or what he's doing and then have to imagine his danger all day long." She added after a silence: "I swear to God I'll either kill him or never leave his side again."

*

'B' Company were taking their turn up front, one of the spearheads moving forward through fields and woods with the sudden unease of men who'd spent three years living below the parapets of trenches. Advance and open country to them meant swift, unheard death from shell or bullet, even though at times it might appear to a spectator that they were playing an innocent game of leap-frog, Platoon by Platoon, Section by Section from one position to the next, their black and white figures jerking forward in short runs like movies in a picture house while above and all around them in the intervals of sunshine hung the blazing colours of autumn woodland. They seemed to be trespassing with their violence and were about to be punished.
It was a cold October Sunday afternoon. They'd even had a church

parade before moving up for their ration of attack, an advance across a shallow wooded valley to take up position on the opposite ridge. 1 and 2 Platoons enjoyed a cake-walk with Ordish at the narrower top end of the valley, making their objective before 3 and 4 were even halfway down the hill.

CSM Trussal was shouting them forward with his huge voice and Boer War bravado, leading his half of the HQ Section towards the riverbank and a narrow wooden bridge. Harry could see it happen before it even started: bloody Sergeant-Major didn't want to get his feet wet. Any damn fool would have kept well away from the surely marked target of the bridge and waded the four yards through the water. But no, Trussal was going to cross by the bridge and was already halfway across when a machine gun opened up and tossed him like a rag doll from the planks, his rage trumpeting blasphemy and obscenity so loud they could surely hear it back in London, his fists punching the water and the rocks around him as life streamed away from him red into the river. Benson and Lars pulled him out from under water, already dead and gone with the anger still in his mouth and eyes.

From then on it was murder once again, both Platoons that had been bunched behind Trussal towards the bridge now enfiladed and spreading out along the river bank. Retreating back up the slope, Harry placed the Lewis-gun behind a tree and tried to pinpoint their tormentor while the other Sections waded through the water and onto the forward slope. The machine-gun, it had to be said, was a suicide job. 1 and 2 Platoons were already on the skyline to the left and only now realizing what was happening to their right. There was no way the Jerry team was ever going to survive. It was just a question of how many Borderers they could take with them. Lars was the next one down but hit only by a ricocheting stone. Then Sergeant Summers with his rhyming slang and one of his Corporals, their bodies riddled in half like Trussal. And finally Harry's Section 3 runner, Neeson, at which moment Harry's Lewis-gun bullets found a way through the brushwood cover and the machine-gun suddenly stopped. Another of the 3 Platoon Corporals ran forward to throw a grenade and it was over - a long fifty seconds that had killed five or maybe six of them. Harry ran sliding down the hillside to Neeson, crumpled but still kneeling. "Stretcher-bearers!" Reggie yelled. God knows how far behind they were. Harry rolled Neeson onto his back, pulling out his field-dressing. The bullet had hit him in the side, through his liver and his gut.

Bunny and Lieutenant Hubbard were shouting the rest of their Platoons onwards across the river and up the hill towards the ridge. "Lewis-gun," Harry heard someone call and he and Reggie had to move on. Half-an-hour later they'd made their objective but behind them and below them Neeson died there by the riverside before the sun went down. A bad, bad day.

From then on, as evenings grew shorter, progress slowed, Division and Corps concerned to keep the line of advance as straight as possible, not to create vulnerable salients. That much at least they'd learnt in these four years of war. And while they stumbled slowly on, rumoured mutterings of peace arrived with every ration party. Not that anyone believed them. Each year they'd been out here, it was always going to have been 'over by Christmas'.

"Where are we?" Harry asked in the darkness of one early evening, lying on the embankment of a sunken country track, peering over the natural 'parapet' into an equally natural no man's land of unharvested maize.

"Still on the Western Front," came the reply. And to confirm the diagnosis a shell blew a hole in the middle of the corn in front of them.

"Ours or theirs?"

"They'll both kill you if you don't keep your fuckin' head down."

The orders came echoing up the track to one side of them: "Roll out wire and dig yourselves in!"

"Slit trench, Harry," said Reggie.

Harry closed his eyes: "Dear God, are we to begin all over again?"

"Bet only bloody 4 Platoon's digging in," grumbled Scrace, knowing that he and Reggie as the ex-miners would be given the hardest excavation, a flint-stone bank as it turned out, on the top of a slope where the sunken track made a right-angle, 4 Platoon the anchor on that slope while whoever was on their right flank caught up with them. 2 and 3 Platoon were in the wood to their left, 1 Platoon and Company HQ around a farm two fields behind them in support.

The ground in front of them sloped away so the rolling out of wire became just that, the smallest man in the Section, Darker, crawling out into the field towing a bundle of stakes, the others humping barbed wire rolls over the 'parapet' down into the maize leaving Darker to secure them twenty yards in front. In the end, taking turns, they dug all night, a right-angle slit-trench in the flint-stone bank at the top of the slope for the Lewis-gun, then small two man bays every ten paces into the front bank of the sunken track until they joined up with Section 2 and Benson's laughing face in the darkness. For all the noise they were making, Jerry for the moment had not placed them, his occasional shells falling too long or short to worry them. No doubt, Harry said to Reggie, the spotter planes flying over in the dawn would mark their line and life become less comfortable. Perhaps, they both were thinking, we'll dig our bays a little deeper in the morning.

Instead stand-to and the daylight brought Bunny and Lars up the slope towards them, the Sergeant grinning at Harry and Reggie, chucking them a bucket: "You Lewis-gun heroes were always good at digging. Platoon latrine, Corporal, at the bottom of the hill. And make it nice and cosy!"

Bunny had crawled into the slit-trench beside the Lewis-gun, quartering the ground in front with his periscope binoculars, marking up his map, labeling the wheat in front of them as '5 Acre Field'. "Mind those trees for snipers, Harry," Bunny muttered as they left, Harry watching him crouched and stumbling, bent more double than usual down the sunken track. As rumour continued to spread about an armistice, dread caution had entered all their souls. 'Either got your number on or not' no longer worked when everyone was wondering how many more days they still needed to survive. No one wanted to get killed at the very arse-end of the war.

"Bags first!"

"Bloody upwind I'm going then! There isn't a stink in the British army worse than yours" - Harry and Reggie playing the fool as they dug out a short sap for the bucket in the forward bank of the track at the foot of the slope, hanging a sack curtain over the entrance. Harry grinned as Reggie told him: "Bugger off and let me shit in peace!"

Reggie pulled the sacking closed, lowered his trousers, took out his mouth-organ and squatted over the bucket. The morning was so still even the Germans could hear him - and made a raucous mocking of the tune he was playing, *Auld Lang Syne*. 'We're here because we're here because we're here because we're here....'

Then Reggie remembered a tune German prisoners had taught him the cold pre-Christmas of 1916, a whole lorryload of them singing, everyone of them with tears in his eyes. Sure enough, as he started now to play that tune, the German line sixty yards away fell completely silent until, with the return of the first line of the melody, one strong, clear German voice began to sing:

Es ist ein Ros enstprungen
aus einer Wurzel zart
Wie uns die Alten sungen
von jesse Kam die Art

On both sides of no man's land everyone listened in silence to the harmonica and the voice, Bunny as he walked bent double up the track, Sergeant Lars who remembered the song from that 1916 Christmas, even Ordish who ducked out of his HQ farm building at the foot of the slope to be able to hear it better, half-remembering the words.

Harry was humming quietly with the tune, sat under the bank upwind from Reggie, waiting his turn on the bucket. He was wondering at the German words of that song and idly watching Bunny, Lars and Ordish, all within his range of vision. Together they became one minute of picture, time and tune that would keep rotating in his head.

The song ended and with his personal business also complete, Reggie stood up, turning to lay the mouth-organ on the forward lip of the sap while he cleaned himself. Having listened to his music, their small 5 acre world must also then have heard the precise single crack of sniper's rifle, Reggie, trousers round his puttees, falling back, blood spurting from his adam's apple. Harry stared rigid and unable to move as Reggie collapsed through the sacking, out across the track. Bunny ran to throw himself on top of Reggie and staunch the flow of blood, yelling for "stretcher-bearers!"

My arse is dirty, Reggie was thinking. "I'm still fuckin' dirty!" he tried to say. He could feel someone pulling up his pants and trousers - Scrace and Darker while Lars helped Bunny clamp a dressing on the throat. The four of them holding his arms and legs ran him down the track towards the farm building and the stretcher-bearers.

Harry still hadn't moved, staring at the torn sacking, the upturned bucket and the mouth-organ in the dirt. Ordish had watched Reggie pass on the stretcher and now walked up the track towards Harry. He stopped in front of him and Harry rocked forward, arms around Ordish's legs, head buried between his knees.

Bunny and Lars were running still with Reggie, across the field towards 1 Platoon and Company HQ, the stretcher-bearers coming to meet them. A shell, another Jerry thank-you for the music, crumped into the trees beyond them, throwing them all to the ground. The stretcher-bearers arrived, applying another dressing to the spreading stain around Reggie's throat and tying him to the stretcher. But they made slow progress under three more shells alongside a copse at the edge of the next field. Divvy lines and Colledge were still 150 yards away. They laid the stretcher down to tighten the dressing round Reggie's throat - only to realize he was already dead. They could hear other distant cries for "Stretcher-bearers!" where the shells had landed in the trees. Rolling Reggie off the stretcher, they then saw the exit wound that had effectively bled him instantly to death. They cut the i.d. disc from around his blown-out throat and covered his staring face with his helmet.

Later Bunny walked back from the line to stick Reggie's rifle, bayonet down into the ground, marking his body.

They buried Reggie where he lay at the end of that same afternoon (with two others from 2 Platoon killed from the shelling in the wood). This time there was no Reggie to blow the Last Post on his harmonica but Ordish had sent back to Prideaux and Prideaux to Division for a bugler. Bunny watched the young man arrive and tried to imagine the life of this boy-soldier, keeping his bugle, boots and buckles polished to wander the countryside each day from burial to burial.

Harry hadn't moved from the morning, except to walk now to the field. He seemed to have frozen into cold stone, staring at Reggie's body rolled up in a greatcoat, lowered with the others into the hole. Should I drop the mouth-organ in there with him, he wondered; or save it for his wife and daughter? Never had the Last Post felt so bleak, Harry still standing like the block of granite by the graveside as two Chinese labourers filled it in and marked the triple burial with a board of names and numbers.

Ordish took Harry back to his farmhouse HQ the two of them sitting down with Bunny to compose a letter, or rather three separate letters, one from each of them to Eileen and little Lisa. Harry couldn't recall the address in Elsdon. "Doesn't matter," said Bunny, remembering the village. "Everyone'll know their name."

Bunny didn't trust the look in Harry's eyes and said as much to Ordish. The Corporal's frozen state reminded him of Harry after Frank's execution when he'd been closed up like a limpet for weeks. Ordish followed Harry out into the evening.

"Wish it had been me, sir. Swear to God I wish it had been me. Reggie and Frank. Me instead of both of them."

"Well, you can't get killed twice, Harry." Ordish took him in his arms and held him deliberately to provoke, to trigger release. "Let go, old son. Don't hold it in. Does all of us good to shed some tears." Harry remembered how he'd held Frank the night before his execution and how Prideaux had led him to the cell - and finally was able to weep. Ordish continued to hold him, Harry's shoulders shaking in the darkness.

"They got the sniper," Ordish said. "Little bugger in a tree. Lars got him with the Lewis-gun."

Next day Harry wrote four lines to Annie. But his letter about Reggie's death remained unopened on the train with all the others - and was, when she finally opened them, the letter that caused Annie most guilt and most distress.

*

They moved three, four, five fields and woods further on and into another sunken road for another improvised trench in front of another no man's land of unharvested wheat. Ordish found a more forward farmhouse for his home, leaving the old farm building to Prideaux's Battalion HQ.

Harry had kept to his silent self, scribbling sheets of paper that everyone assumed were letters to his girl. Harry wasn't really sure what they were - mostly memories of the three of them together, the good times and the bad, from the moment he and Frank had signed on and met Reggie next day in the barracks. When I get killed, he thought, someone will find these pages and discover how we lived the war, the three of us together. As for Annie, he began to fear he'd written her the final letter if she would not help him now with her wisdom and her warmth. Following a word from Bunny, Sergeant Lars decided to leave Harry alone, making sure he had a double tot of rum each day and letting Lance-Corporal Thackwell do the bossing for 3/4 Section.

These were quiet, misty days of falling leaves and first light frost as darkness came, the air not moving, holding smoke from their braziers, cigarettes and pipes in a low, thin haze - and making Ordish remember Guy Fawkes bonfires up and down the back gardens at home.

It was at stand-to a few evenings after Guy Fawkes when an officer on horseback rode slowly up the sunken road in the dusk, dismounting by Ordish's farmhouse - Colonel Prideaux.

"Peace talk?" asked Ordish.

"So they say." Prideaux was reluctant with the orders he'd brought, accepting Ordish's whisky before going on. "Division have ordered raiding parties." He placed the written orders down on the table. "The offensive spirit is to be maintained up to the very last minute of the war."

Ordish stared at him.

"One raiding party every night."

"I'll not send men out to be killed the very day before an armistice."

"No one yet is certain about an armistice." The reluctant Prideaux finished his whisky and turned to go. "It's a Divisional order for every Company in the line, Sam. I'm sorry."

When the Colonel had departed, Ordish looked up at Bunny and laughed.

"Do you want me to put a gang together?" Bunny asked.

Ordish shook his head and poured another whisky. "I shall go out alone, Bunny, and make noises of offensive spirit and attempt not to kill any Germans." And when Bunny tried to remonstrate - "Stand down the stand-to and take the ration party back to transport lines, Lieutenant."

Captain Ordish slowly dressed himself for combat in the candlelight - his Sam Browne and pistol and a greatcoat and knapsack whose pockets he filled with grenades.

He had a word with Scrace and Darker on the Lewis-gun then walked up the sunken lane as far as the hunched and staring Harry and handed him the knapsack while he climbed over the bank into the wheatfield.

"Where are you going, sir?"

"There and back to see how far it is." Ordish gave him his melancholy smile: "You don't have to 'sir' me, Harry. Not now." He reached to take the knapsack and Harry watched him stride away waist-deep through the wheat, 20, 50, then 70 yards out into no man's land. Harry stood up to climb the bank after him; but found Scrace and Darker suddenly on either arm:

"Captain said no one was to follow him, Corp."

"What the fuck's he doing out there?"

"Taking a look. Just taking a look, he said."

Out of sight of them now, Ordish stood still in a blackness so silent he could hear the scuttle of a field or harvest mouse around his feet and the murmur of voices from the German line somewhere in front of him. He wondered if they also knew the war was about to end and that they'll all be going home. Home to whom, home to what? Did any of them on either side really know how the world would be when the guns finally stopped firing? Did any of them really know why they'd been fighting the war in the first place?

From maybe 4 miles away he saw a flash and heard the falling of a shell. Then a short rat-a-tat of distant machine-gun, one of ours. And finally a pair of mortars, two of theirs - someone obeying orders and maintaining an offensive spirit. Is that why he was out here? And to make sure no one else was killed? Or was it to remember his dead brother at Gallipoli? Or even to test himself, as he always felt obliged to do, in one last act of foolish bravado? Or merely to be alone in this final moment of the war?

A mile or so to the east another machine-gun opened up, this time provoking the dropping of a flare. Perhaps it was time he joined in. Mustn't give higher command any excuse to further malign the much-maligned Borderers. Ordish took grenades from the knapsack with alternate hands, pulling their pins with his teeth, crouching and hurling them first to one side then the other as though scattering seed - their explosions, Ordish thought, like fireworks celebrating peace.

The Germans, 100 yards away or more, were not sure quite what was happening. Was it their own side throwing grenades? Eventually, to be safe, they responded with a roar of flame-thrower from their most forward position, a spurting dragon's tongue of liquid fire spat out into no-man's-land, reaching towards Ordish, the wheat burning suddenly in a semicircle around him. Ordish dropped his knapsack and started to run. By fire he did not want to die.

He was briefly visible to Harry in front of the flames, until another dragon's tongue turned the Captain into a torch, his arms windmilling wildly around his head. Harry felt himself dragged down as he scrambled to climb the bank, Darker and Scrace pinning him by his arms and legs on the ground. There was a machine-gun firing now and the flames billowing towards them with a sudden gust of wind, another half-hour of smoke and fire until the wheat burned itself out, another half-hour holding Harry pinned to the ground: "Captain's orders, Corp." By which time, when they raised their heads again above the bank, Captain Ordish had disappeared.

The machine gun frightened everyone, Bunny, in Ordish's absence, passing Company orders for everyone to sit tight. It was Benson, arriving from 3 Platoon with an Indian stretcher-bearer, who accompanied Harry, the three men crawling into the wheat field to find Ordish's charred body. There was little of him left, his uniform melted onto his skin, his flesh melted onto his bones; no pocket-book, no pipe, no photographs from his blouse. Even his face had vanished from his head, burned away.   When they defied the machine-gunner and stood up to return, the stretcher had no weight as they carried him back. Ordish seemed already to have vanished, as determined to skip his burial as he'd so often skipped parades.

*

Two hours later, ten miles away, distant, mostly scruffy figures in woodland converge slowly through early morning twilight to gather round immaculate Staff Officers on horseback. An official preamble is read out - then the words: "Hostilities will cease at 11 o'clock this morning. God save the King!"

*

"A gallant man and gentleman," murmured Colledge after their Lord's Prayer, both he and Bunny already turning to stare at a brightly coloured horseman approaching in a loose jingle of bridle and spurs across the field. Captain Ordish had been laid in a temporary grave scratched into the edge of a gravel track by Harry and Benson on their return. Harry didn't want what little was left of his friend lost in the earth of a field.

"Back to your positions," Bunny now told them, the men dispersing slowly from that faint scar in the earth, Bunny and the Sergeant towards the brightly coloured horseman arriving at the farmhouse.

They left Ordish's body in the open shallow grave, faceless eye-sockets to the heaven he did not believe, his officer's cap hung on Harry's bayonet stuck into the ground. Harry walked away as blank and uncomprehending as he'd been at Reggie's burial.

In the farmhouse the message was relayed to them by the Staff-Officer - "hostilities will cease at 11 o'clock this morning. God save the King!".

Bunny, grim and tired, uncorked the whisky bottle: "Is this what they were waiting for? The eleventh hour of the eleventh day of the eleventh month?" He tossed the bottle to Sergeant Lars. "Whose bloody joke was that?! And almost in a shout: "Stand them to, Sergeant."

Lars took the bottle out into the 'trench' calling up the sunken road: "Stand to! Your last stand-to. Another four hours it'll all be over."

Lars moved up the sunken lane, a slurp of whisky for every man awake. He reached Harry at the anchor end and sat down beside him. "Back home for us at last."

"This is home," replied Harry. "There is no other place to go. They should leave us out here for ever. In the dark, to watch over it all."

"Germans have surrendered," said Lars.

Harry turned to look at him: "I don't even know who the Germans are."

And when Lars returned back down the lane, Harry, shaking with suppressed emotion, climbed over the bank into the burned wheatfield that was their final no man's land, walking through the half-light to find the mark in the ashes where Ordish's charred body had lain, Ordish's horse-hair switch five yards away where he must have flung it, visible now in the daylight: his identification. Harry picked it up. That much at least was his.

Harry turned his head to the north, walking on towards the German lines, until suddenly below him in a fox-hole the far side of the wheatfield, he came face to face with an equally tired, equally dirty, equally alarmed, bespectacled German soldier blinking through his metal frames. The two men gazed at one another.

The German whispered: "Was machst Du hier, Tommy?"

Harry stared a long half minute. Was this the man who'd torched Ordish?

"Camerad," said the German and reached up to shake his hand. Harry turned to walk away, unaware that in another fox-hole across the ditch another German soldier was slowly raising a rifle to draw Harry into his sights, criss-cross between the shoulder-blades.

Chapter 51

Everyone remarked on the silence, the absence of that dull artillery rumble that had been an almost continuous background to their lives for so long. And ever since the guns had stopped she seemed to have been contemplating wreckage as peace now brought the reckoning - of ruined farms, villages and towns, none worse than their own Pérignon; of fields and hillsides covered with makeshift wooden crosses and body sacks; of roadsides and rail yards heaped with the debris of war, shells and shell-cases, field-guns and mortars in their rows, broken vehicles and tanks, equipment old and new, here a pile of uniforms, there a pile of boots.

And in every waking moment with a dull ache in her body, Annie thought only, obsessively, of Harry, not knowing whether he was alive or dead. If he was alive surely he would have written. Or was it once again his turn to punish her? She'd now read his last unopened letters and despised her own stubbornness. Even more so when they heard from a field hospital that the Border Rifles had been one of the Regiments to take casualties during those last days of war.

Their train continued to journey through November, north, south, east and west from Pérignon, dispatched hither and thither, even into Flanders, to help the clearing out of forward hospitals. And for once the red cross trains were given priority. The wounded had precedence, though for many it would be too late. "What misery to die when the fighting is finally over," said Viv in tears one evening as one of her young charges died in his metal bunk on their way to Abbéville.

Annie sat on Viv's bed that night and held her hand, the berth too narrow for them to lie down together. "I imagine it's always a misery to die".

"I'm sorry. I didn't mean it in that way - "

"Don't worry. We've all lost someone in this war - every woman on this train."

"Some more than others. I mean, your Patrick and Virgin Mary's brothers."

"And your betrothed. Your Colin Hunter-Brown? We've all lost someone, Viv."

They were all of them numb. There was too much memory to filter out before the world could begin to seem anything like it had been before. Of course it never would. They'd have to invent a new reality with whatever they could salvage from their past.

Now, on Viv's berth, the two of them reminded themselves how quickly the euphoria of victory had vanished with the six bottles of champagne they'd drunk on the evening after armistice (dispatched in a wood box to them by Jean-Pierre - how on earth had he enabled it to arrive so quickly? Viv, finally laughing, declared it her duty to find out).

Annie kissed her goodnight but lay with her eyes wide open on her own bunk, Harry's face as always coming to her in the darkness. 'Where are you,' she whispered. 'Where in God's name are you?'

Virgin Mary had guessed Annie's thoughts, watching her wander the train each day as she wandered the wards of hospitals by night, checking the face of every wounded man. Dressed now as a senior nurse and carrying what looked like lists in her hand, she could get in anywhere. Mary was afraid Annie might soon start opening the body sacks. She spoke to her when they were back in Pérignon: "You'll never find him like this," she said. "If he is alive he will come to you. We're where we always were. This is where his search would start."

*

The dismantling of war was infinitely more complex than its inception or activation - and now included responsibility for their enemy. Expecting to be home in days, men were warned they could be out in France, Flanders or Germany for weeks longer, if not months. No longer under rules of combat, whatever High Command might say, the ordinary swaddy had had enough, the murmuring of discontent spreading as fast as the Spanish Influenza.

Such discontent within the Border Rifles - a threat of 'mutiny' so far as Linton was concerned (**'Crack the whip - Courts Martial!'**) - brought the portly Brigadier out to France and Flanders for the first time since the early mobile skirmishes of 1914. He loudly huffed and puffed with Prideaux, but once he'd walked, appalled, across the battlefields that trench warfare had created, he began to mollify his ideas. This was not war as he had ever known it. Many of the trenches still remained uncleared, skulls, bones and uniformed skeletons visible, everything below ground level flooded from recent rain. He wondered how anyone could have survived let alone fought in these conditions.

Prideaux, as much for his own reasons as for Linton, took the Brigadier on what they came to call the pilgrimage. The Brigadier pulled rank for a driver and a car and down the congested cobblestone roads they were driven, retracing some of 'A' and 'B' Companies' endless marches. They stood to attention with the RSM at both White City on the Somme and Bellewarde Farm under Passchendaele and read the list of dead out loud, name by name from Regimental records. And those were only half the men that they had lost.

They watched gangs of Chinese and African labourers shivering in the cold as they tidied away the apparatus of war; and witnessed everywhere the scourge of that influenza now creating its own huge casualty list of dead among both soldiers and civilians. They watched the redistributing of earlier deaths, the recovery of haphazard burials, among them Ordish, Uncle and Reggie, and the slow, painstaking creation for them of a proper place of rest, formal British war cemeteries beginning to take shape, scattering themselves round Flanders and Picardy like visiting cards.

They were also present for a ceremonial 'going down of the sun' at the Menin Gate, not yet knowing that Belgian buglers would return each evening of every day of every week of every month of every year for ever more and halt the busy evening traffic in the middle of what would become a rebuilt Ypres - to blow the British Last Post at that very Gate through which so many soldiers of the Empire had marched out to their death.

Linton forgot his resolution about 'Courts Martial' and instead with Prideaux drew up a timetable of demobilization on the basis 'first to join, first to return home'. Which meant that whoever was left of the K-Ones, the first Kitchener volunteers, were to be given their demob ticket as soon as cleared with High Command. The demob programme was to be announced to the men by each Platoon commander.

And finally, the Brigadier asked for the names of those who'd died in the very last weeks and days of war: those whose deaths their families would find even harder to accept. They were the families he would personally visit. Linton had begun to understand from his short visit, and by looking his soldiers in their eyes, that the world really would never be the same again - and he believed, fervently now, that this had been the war to end all wars. No one could ever seek such madness again.

Chapter 52

The ambulance train made its final journey through a snowstorm, steaming into the railhead at Pérignon one early morning to off-load Virgin Mary and her nurses at the low station platform before shunting slowly away. The blue and gold Wagon Lits from Italy were also detached and left at the platform, Virgin Mary and Annie wondering what would happen to the sleeping and dining cars that had been their home for nearly a year (the ambulance carriages were destined for Köln to help reorganise the Germans' own military casualties).

And thus did Virgin Mary's nursing corps disband, farewells on the station platform as Annie, Viv, Mary and the other nurses separate with their baggage to their various destinations: Viv towards Bar-le-Duc in search of Jean-Pierre; Virgin Mary back to Milan in Italy where her one surviving brother was recovering from wounds in that lovely medieval hospital; most of the others on the train for Boulogne and home; and two of the more adventurous girls crossing the tracks for a lift to Paris with a French Officer.

On her own travel warrant Annie had written Abbéville as her destination, being the most likely place to check full British casualty lists. Failing that she would return to Northumberland and hope to find the Battalion in Alnwick, for surely they would know where Harry was. But remembering what Mary had said - 'We're where we always were. This is where his search would start' - she decided for the moment to wait here in Pérignon. She and Mary hugged each other long and hard and promised to meet again.

Annie was left standing there on the empty platform. Rain in the early morning had melted the snow, leaving the rail tracks in a lake of still water that reflected from beyond the tracks a line of soldiers on the road as far as the eye could see, marching in single file. Annie imagined Harry in the middle of that endless army.

As Harry was imagining Annie. Demob in his pocket he'd come to Pérignon under the snow with a forlorn hope - only to find the school rooms empty and be told that Annie's nursing unit had been disbanded. Harry had used the school to bed down last night, picking the very room that Annie and Viv had shared - with that street-corner below from where he'd watched.

He dreamt, as he was dreaming every night, of that moment in the wheat field when he'd turned away; that moment in no man's land when surely he had been destined to die but had not, thus the repeating nightmare. He remembered the shout from behind him - "Schiese nicht! Lasse in leben!" - and, not understanding the words, remembered turning to see the bespectacled German soldier scrabbling over tufts of grass and mole-hills, through brushwood pickets raised as camouflage, across a ditch and a wire fence to knock the rifle out of his companion's hands. "Es ist alles fertig!" It's all over. It is finished.

But in the nightmare of course the other German shoots. Harry couldn't understand later why he had made no move to take cover or defend himself. Is that what happened to Ordish?

Ordish had left his shadow over all of them, his missing presence with them through a month of garrison on the German border with nothing to do except check the papers of German soldiers, ex-prisoners and wounded, as they straggled back home across the frontier.

Bunny was Captain in charge of 'B' Company, Lars promoted to Sergeant-Major, Harry, under protest, given his third stripe. Until, with the Brigadier pressing hard from home, High Command sent the first demob papers - for CSM Lars, Sergeants Craig, Cardwell and Webster, Corporals Dippy, Carter and Lowrie, and Captain 'Bunny' Andrews, the only K One's left in 'B' Company. Together they hitched rides and walked back the usual way, transport still in chaos, Harry saying his farewells to them all at the Spanish Farm, diverting there on his cross-country way to Pérignon. Bunny had wished him luck with a smile.

*

Harry woke with the cold in the school room that next morning, walking the town in search of hot coffee among the ruins. Shelled out of their bars and cafés the locals had set up food stalls by the old rail yards, hot coffee and hot bread. Harry saw in the distance the ambulance train on its final run and, still from a distance as it pulled away through a column of soldiers marching on the road, he'd also seen the group of nurses left behind with their bags on the low platform – and he knew that she was there.

That column of endless marching soldiers was still reflected in the water, Annie alone on the platform watching them pass. Then in a gap between Platoons, Companies or Battalions she saw Harry standing on the bank beyond the road, his upside-down image in the water, staring at her. She closed her eyes in denial - but this time there was no train to fail to stop; there were no bugles to summon him away. She opened her eyes and waited for another gap between Platoons. He was still there reflected in the water and when she looked directly up at him he gave her that half-smile of his no one else had seen since Passchendaele.

He stepped between two Companies breaking their reflection in the water to walk towards her. As every passing soldier turned his head to watch and call and whistle, Harry took Annie in his arms. For them the end of the war was over and, whatever it would bring them, their life together had begun.

* * *

Love Of An Unknown Soldier is the first volume in the Harry Cardwell Series.
A Long Road Home, *When War Came Again* and *First Snow of Winter* will be published in 2012.

Cover: Christmas 1916: an Australian Observation Post near Fleurbaix, on the Somme front - painting by William Barnes Wollen (1857-1936)

Printed in Great Britain
by Amazon.co.uk, Ltd.,
Marston Gate.